The Late Work of Sam Shepard

Also published by Bloomsbury Methuen Drama

The Late Work of Sam Shepard

Shannon Blake Skelton

Bloomsbury Methuen Drama
An imprint of Bloomsbury Publishing Plc

B L O O M S B U R Y
LONDON · OXFORD · NEW YORK · NEW DELHI · SYDNEY

Bloomsbury Methuen Drama

An imprint of Bloomsbury Publishing Plc

Imprint previously known as Methuen Drama

50 Bedford Square	1385 Broadway
London	New York
WC1B 3DP	NY 10018
UK	USA

www.bloomsbury.com

**BLOOMSBURY, METHUEN DRAMA and the Diana logo
are trademarks of Bloomsbury Publishing Plc**

First published 2016
This paperback edition first published 2017

British Library Cataloguing-in-Publication Data
A catalogue record for this book is available from the British Library.

ISBN: HB: 978-1-4742-3472-6
PB: 978-1-350-03560-7
ePDF: 978-1-4742-3474-0
eBook: 978-1-4742-3473-3

Library of Congress Cataloging-in-Publication Data
A catalog record for this book is available from the Library of Congress.

Cover design: Louise Dugdale and Eleanor Rose
Cover image © Corbis

Typeset by Deanta Global Publishing Services, Chennai, India
Printed and bound in Great Britain

To find out more about our authors and books visit www.bloomsbury.com. Here
you will find extracts, author interviews, details of forthcoming events and the
option to sign up for our newsletters.

Contents

Acknowledgments

I would first like to thank Gretchen Hedrick. Through late nights she has always remained confident in my abilities as a scholar, teacher, and artist. Kieran and Keaton have consistently helped me to be a better person and father.

I would also like to thank my mentor and friend Mike Vanden Heuvel. He has been a guiding and supportive force through the process of researching and composing this project. Without his unparalleled insight, this project would have never reached fruition.

Scholars Aparna Dharwadker, Kristin Hunt, Michael Peterson and Craig Werner offered substantial feedback and suggestions throughout this process. Without them, this manuscript would not have made it out of the proposal stage.

Randy Gordon, Leigh Elion, Steve Lambert, Stephen Lucas, Sarah Meinen Jedd, Ryan Tvedt, Leslie Wade, Bill Whitney, and Bethany Wood all assisted both directly and indirectly in this process. I will be forever grateful for their help and support. Mark Dudgeon and Emily Hockley at Bloomsbury Methuen Drama and Project Manager Grishma Fredric have provided peerless direction through the evolution of this manuscript.

My family has been enthusiastic and supportive of this project. Danny and Diane Skelton, Don and Artyce Hedrick, and Nita Jones have provided me with time and insight as well as support during this process.

I would also like to thank The University of Wisconsin-Madison's Department of Theatre and Drama, Department of Communication Arts and Integrated Liberal Studies, and Kansas State University's School of Music, Theatre and Dance for their support of my teaching and research.

In addition, the Browne Popular Culture Library at Bowling Green State University, Shepherd University's Contemporary American Theatre

Festival, and Emily Mann at ICM provided unpublished Shepard manuscripts that were valuable to this project.

The following individuals have shaped my life, worldview, and pedagogy: Robert Wyche, Kae Koger, John Tibbetts, David Gross, Barbara Clayton, Mark Medoff, Steve Grossman, and Diane Jones Skelton. Perhaps this book can serve as a minor token of my appreciation for how they have contributed to my education. Unfortunately, three of my mentors are no longer with us. Without Jan Jones and professors George Wedge and Robert Findlay, I would have never discovered my passion for drama and literature. Their voices, insight, and friendly words are always with me.

I am privileged enough to have a career that is challenging and gratifying. I am able to teach with – and learn from – amazing students. I thank them for proving to me daily that education, literature, and the arts are noble pursuits.

Though this project could never have been completed without the assistance of others, I assume sole responsibility for any oversights or mistakes present within its pages.

Preface

My personal history as a teacher, scholar, playwright, and writer, and the work of Sam Shepard have been intertwined for the past two decades. As with many of my generation (those born between 1970 and 1980), my first encounter with Shepard came via the cinema, namely his turn in 1983's *The Right Stuff*. His portrayal of pilot Chuck Yeager crystallized traits that would forever be associated with Shepard and his persona. In the performance, Shepard rarely smiles, displaying a stoicism that seemingly reaches back to the frontier ethos of the nineteenth century. As an aging Post-Second World War jet-pilot, Shepard simultaneously embodied the future (the impending space race) as well as the past (the romanticized heroism of the cowboy). His performance as Yeager is imbued with a sense of hope often tied to pushing the limits of exploration; in turn, that hope is tempered by a haunted reverence for an age—an age of naïve simplicity—eclipsing before his eyes. In essence, Shepard as Yeager stands on the precipice of American history, teetering between the future and the past.

From 1983 onward, Shepard's work seemingly stalked me (or I stalked it) through the cinemas, theaters, and bookstores of my adolescent stomping grounds of East Texas. As the preeminent playwright of the American stage and a Hollywood leading man, Shepard held a ubiquitous presence in American culture in the 1980s. This presence even reached into the small towns and proverbial "flyover regions" of the United States. That said, Shepard's family plays seemed to differentiate themselves from other work of the 1980s. These family plays ignited the stage with ferocity, madness, volatility, and crude eroticism as well as moments of tenderness. For many Americans, Shepard's family cycle seemed simultaneously familiar (in its subject) and unfamiliar (in its operatic brutality). Though the work often fractured taboos and shocked audiences, these same audience members could appreciate the hope, beauty, and humor often hidden amid the grotesque violence and primal savagery.

Attending a high school theater festival in the early 1990s, I recall my fellow students atwitter after witnessing a haunting, vicious play that worked like a bizarre backwoods reinterpretation of *Romeo and Juliet*. Students spoke of the violence, the sexuality, and the profanity of the work and the resultant queasiness that swept through the audience. Yet, the imagery and dialogue haunted the teenage audience. The play was the subject of conversations for the entire next year among us drama students. Of course, this was a production of Shepard's *A Lie of the Mind*. Its impact on my fellow students forever altered my belief in the emotional potentiality of live theater.

Also while in high school, I assisted in a minor way with a local college production of *True West*. When my teacher explained the premise, I was dumbfounded, yet intrigued. My assignment was to locate sound effects that could serve as the coyote yelps and howls that are heard throughout the play, signifying the encroaching wildness that sets upon Austin and Lee. The images from that production of *True West* still linger in my mind: toasters ejaculating bread, letter and number keys flying into the audience as a golf iron obliterates a typewriter, two grown men attempting to kill one another. For an adolescent thrilled by musical theater, punk rock music, comic books, horror movies, the Beats, true crime, and Tennessee Williams, Sam Shepard pointed toward a mode of writing and theater that was hypnotic, frightening, and thoroughly engaging.

That summer, I ran across Shepard's *Seven Plays*. The collection features the author on the cover, staring at the reader with an expression that could be best described as a mixture of hate and contempt. The volume accompanied me to college (where I saw *Fool for Love* in a dorm basement) and it remained in my possession as I tried to write my own variations on Shepard's early plays. Whenever I found myself unproductive, paralyzed by writer's block, I would crack open a volume of Shepard for a reminder of the potentiality of theater: a giant lobster-man storming the stage in *Cowboy Mouth*; a character jumping through the upstage wall only to leave an "outline" of his body ala *Looney Tunes* in *La Turista*; a massive mechanical snake slithering through the desert in *Operation Sidewinder*; the strange, unknowable rituals conducted by damaged men in *Buried Child* and *A Lie of the Mind*.

As a secondary teacher, Shepard was always a playwright that I could foist upon my male students who resisted almost all things theater. I remember sending home *The Tooth of Crime* with a student. He returned the next day spellbound by the black leather, spike-studded throne and fascinated by how the relationship between Hoss and Crow paralleled the East Coast/West Coast rivalries of hip-hop culture at the time. Another student, this time an aspiring rock musician, took home *True West* and returned the next day with a stack of no less than four volumes of Shepard from the local bookstore.

Shepard's work not only engages me as a scholar and teacher, but also reminds me—again and again—of the power of uniting the literary with the performative, the tender with the savage, the grotesque with the sublime. That said, Shepard and his work represent a unique presence in American theater. This is partially a result of the writer's willingness to engage in a multitude of subjects and forms to further investigate dilemmas that are superficially American, but are in actuality tied to larger existential questions regarding identity, genealogy, and responsibility. Though Shepard's cultural moment peaked more than two decades ago, Shepard remains a presence in American theater— and like Beckett and Williams in their autumnal years—continues to press the potentialities and possibilities of theater.

Introduction

During the 1960s and 1970s, Sam Shepard emerged as one of the most distinguished dramatists in American alternative theater. Born on November 5, 1943, Samuel Shepard Rogers III was a prototypical "military brat" of the mid-twentieth century, hauled to various Air Force bases around the globe until age twelve, when his father and family settled in Duarte, California. Bypassing a potential career in veterinary science, Shepard joined the touring repertory Bishop's Company and in 1962 traveled east as a performer. Deciding to stay in New York City instead of returning to California, the young actor shed the "Rogers" portion of his name and recreated himself as a writer. He eventually carved out an identity as a rock 'n' roll cowboy-playwright whose experimental works became staples of the Off-Off-Broadway movement. From his initial play *Cowboys* (1964) to his collaboration with Joseph Chaikin *Savage/ Love* (1979), Shepard had no fewer than thirty-seven scripts produced in a fifteen year period. These were presented at an array of theaters, from the decidedly diminutive Theatre Genesis and Caffé Cino to the more esteemed cultural cathedrals of the Royal Court and Lincoln Center. These plays garnered Shepard numerous awards, multiple grants, and considerable acclaim as a distinctive voice in American theater. In all, between 1964 and 1979, Shepard earned seven Obie awards, two Rockefeller Foundation grants, two Guggenheim grants as well as fellowships, and awards from both Yale and Brandeis. In 1979, Shepard was awarded the Pulitzer Prize for *Buried Child*. With international recognition and prestige, Shepard's renown as a dramatist increased by the close of the 1970s, but this only hinted at the popular and critical acclaim that would accrue in the subsequent decade.

It was during the 1980s that Shepard's popular and critical success reached its apex. Shepard's "cultural moment," in which he achieved popular and critical success as an actor and playwright and transformed into a celebrity, spans from 1979's *Buried Child* to 1985's *Lie of the Mind*. From a combination of Shepard's heightened profile as a film actor and his creation of more accessible plays in a "realist" vein, Shepard's persona evolved from an alternative theater fixture to that of a mainstream, celebrity dramatist. In some respects, this transformation of Shepard from an alternative theater outlaw to a famous, popular dramatist parallels the taming, domestication, integration, and assimilation of various strains of the counterculture into mainstream American culture. The 1980s witnessed the premieres of the plays *True West* (1980), *Fool for Love* (1983), and *A Lie of the Mind* (1985), works that would become hailed as emblematic of Shepard's vision of the American family. These plays would eventually be considered Shepard's most lasting contributions to American drama and are entries in what I refer to as the family cycle. It was also during this decade that Shepard explored other forms of expression beyond the stage. He published a work of autobiographical tales and ramblings (1982's *Motel Chronicles*), received an Academy Award nomination for his performance in *The Right Stuff* (1983), debuted as a film director, and witnessed *Paris, Texas* (which was adapted from Shepard's writings) earn the Palm d'Or at the 1984 Cannes Film Festival. It was also during this decade that Shepard was admitted into the American Academy of Arts and Letters (1986), cementing his legacy as a writer recognized as significantly contributing to the canon of American literature.

In 1985, Shepard willingly took an absence from the theatrical world to pursue further opportunities in film. The result was his directorial debut *Far North* (1988), which humorously chronicles the Chekhovian aspects of a rural family in Minnesota. Though few recognized it at the time, *Far North*'s parody of patriarchal assumptions and privilege served as the beginning of a new cycle of work. Following this hiatus from theater, Shepard returned to the stage with *States of Shock* in 1991. The one-act play, written in the shadow of the Reagan/Bush conservatism of the 1980s and Gulf War I, trafficked in Beckettian imagery and seemingly inexplicable action and dialogue. The work resembled neither his earlier, more experimental plays nor his recent family cycle which had moved Shepard's dominant aesthetic toward a variation on realism. With both *Far North* and *States of Shock*, Shepard signaled a transition into a phase in which he would experiment in form, subject, and media for the next two decades.

This later phase of Shepard's work, which is the focus of this project, involves a variety of media (including short prose, plays, performances, and screenplays) and radically ebbs and shifts through a panoply of concerns and styles. This phase, beginning in 1988 and continuing to the present (2015), which I have termed Shepard's Late Style, is distinctive for its *mélange* of media and forms, employed to further explore themes and concepts located in earlier cycles. The phase's heterogeneous and eclectic quality stands apart from Shepard's previous work, for this Late Style mediates and re-mediates, transgressing boundaries of genre and form, yet consistently reflects upon Shepard's established corpus (a term that will be explicated later in this chapter). In essence, the Late Style features the shifting of the Shepard persona, the exploring of new forms, subjects, media, and aesthetics, and the returning to familiar dilemmas and crises, only to posit solutions regarding such dilemmas.

The focus of this project is what I refer to as the Late Style. There is, of course, a tradition of viewing an artist's output in a chronological, evolutionary mode of progression. This view reached its cultural zenith in the nineteenth century, yet there has recently been a reinvigoration in the subfield of studies of *spatsil*, or late style. Two volumes that inform this subfield—as well as this project—are *Late Thoughts: Reflections on Artists and Composers at Work* (2006), a collection of essays edited by Karen Painter and Thomas Crow, and Edward Said's posthumous volume *On Late Style* (2006).

Yet the Shepard corpus, which consists of the author and his persona as well as his writings, films, and performances, creates a highly intertwined, intertextual web that stretches across various media. In such a system of transmedial textualities, it is difficult to view the literary output of Shepard without considering the various other components of the persona that constantly inform the work. I do agree with Painter that the concept of a general "late style" that can be ascribed to artists is problematic, for it can lead to sweeping generalizations and reductionism. Specifically, for Painter, "The idea of lateness seemed a faulty construct—or, more precisely, the traits that were supposed to define a late style seemed spurious" (2006: 5).

The notion of a late style serves as a method to examine the specific elements that characterize a distinct style for Shepard in this latter period of his life and career. Traditionally, *spatstil* tied the produced artwork to the life of the artist. It was believed by many proponents of an artistic evolutionary style that the late period was characterized by the artist reflecting upon the self and the production of art. This is supposedly informed by the mental and physical decay brought on by the natural psychological and biological processes of the human body. This totalizing and essentializing theory of a late style or lateness is precisely that which Painter presses against and what I hope to resist in this project. Shepard's Late Style is unique in its heterogeneity and does not neatly fall into the dynamics ascribed by *spatsil* scholars of the nineteenth century.

Toward the conclusion of his life, Edward Said wrote extensively about the late style of composers and writers. Fundamental to Said's understanding and consideration of lateness is Theodore Adorno's "Spatsil Beethovens" (1937). Adorno postulates that Beethoven's late style is unique for it resists traditional assumptions regarding the later works of an artist. For Said, the late style is the "moment when the artist who is fully in command of his [sic] medium nevertheless abandons communication with the established social order of which he [sic] is a part and achieves a contradictory, alienated relationship with it. His late works constitute a form of exile" (2007: 8). This "exile" is characterized "not as harmony and resolution, but as intransigence, difficulty and unresolved contradiction" (Said 2007: 8). For Shepard, lateness has served as a sort of self-imposed "exile" that began with his hiatus from theater following *A Lie of the Mind* (1985) and has been characterized by his inability to ascend to the critical, artistic, and popular heights he attained during his cultural moment. Lateness, for Shepard, seems to be a move toward resolving and revisiting some lingering dilemmas, yet also a willingness to explore other aesthetics and media.

Said illustrates the dynamics of lateness for some artists through Ibsen,

> whose final works, especially *When the Dead Awaken*, tear apart the career and the artist's craft and reopen the question of meaning, success, and progress that the artist's late period is supposed to move beyond. Far from resolution, then, Ibsen's last plays suggest an angry and disturbed artist for whom the medium of drama provides an occasion to stir up more anxiety, tamper irrevocably with the possibility of closure, and leave the audience more perplexed and unsettled than before. (2007: 7)

Though Shepard's late period cannot necessarily be viewed as tempestuous as Ibsen's late works, Shepard's Late Style has resisted the clichéd notions that an aged artist in their autumnal period will offer gentle reflection. Indeed, Shepard's late work has—on occasion—left the "audience more perplexed and unsettled than before" (Said 2007: 7), yet it is more varied and eclectic and thus resists any particular assignation of mood (such as "angry and disturbed" for Ibsen).

The Late Style of Shepard involves a maturing of the Shepard persona, as well as an exploration of different media, subjects, and aesthetics and a willingness to pose solutions to dilemmas previously considered yet never resolved. This Late Style returns to familiar subjects and finds Shepard interrogating his own celebrity persona and position in American culture, reexamining notions of authenticity, ruminating on trauma and memory, interrogating imperialism, working in the mode of a political dramatist and reengaging with that most controversial of themes associated with his work: gender.

To analyze Shepard's Late Style, it is necessary to introduce a number of theoretical approaches and terminology that will be used throughout this project. The term "corpus" indicates not only the Shepard persona, but also his body as a celebrity, as well as his numerous writings and endeavors. Shepard's corpus is indeed a "body of work," but unlike many other writers, Shepard's "body of work" quite literally involves his "body" for Shepard is a performer of a "persona" as well as an actor in film, and on rare occasions, the theater. This manuscript analyzes Shepard's Late Style corpus and argues that through various media, genres, and forms, Shepard is revisiting familiar tropes and seeking to propose solutions to dilemmas that have haunted his writings. To proceed, as noted previously, I recognize Shepard's corpus as being uniquely transmedial and as such, this project will examine the dynamics of intertextuality within that corpus.

As noted, this late period is marked by Shepard moving beyond theatrical endeavors and exploring different media. Shepard had previously worked in music and published prose collections such as *Hawk Moon* (1973) and *Motel Chronicles* (1982), but this Late Style has Shepard pushing into other media, writing stories, plays, and screenplays, and working as a theater and film director as well as a motion-picture actor and stage performer. Across these various media, Shepard retains certain aspects of his preferred subjects and themes, as well as core elements of his persona. Indeed, the intertexuality of late Shepard is transmedial. According to media theorists Marsha Kinder and Henry Jenkins, the term "transmedia" can be understood to be a mode of storytelling that transcends one medium and develops on various platforms. This is usually exemplified by such properties as the *Star Trek* franchise in which the universe and narratives move back and forth across different media, be it fan fiction, comic books, video games, films, television programs, or novels. For this project, I am interpreting the term "transmedia" in a slightly different manner. Shepard's corpus creates an intertextual web that moves through various media, but both the intertextuality and transmediality are constantly reasserting the understood aspects of the Shepard corpus. Indeed, as Leslie Wade has noted, "[Shepard's] vision and his accomplishments cannot be contained by a single medium" (1997: 226) and through its various iterations across media, the Shepard corpus, be it Shepard's performances, personas or writings, is again and again reasserted and re-performed.

As mentioned, this late period of Shepard is also intertextual. As noted, with the term corpus, I consider "Sam Shepard" to be a combination of the writer, his persona, his various performances, and his writings. To consider this corpus, it is necessary to recognize that Shepard's work—regardless of whether it is a formal piece of writing or the performance of a persona—is highly intertextual. Indeed, if the corpus of Shepard is the text, it is intertextual, for as Linda Hutcheon writes, "No text is without intertexts" (Dunne 1992: 11). Intertextuality, in its most rudimentary sense, is according to Thais Morgan "structural relations among two or more texts" (Dunne 1992: 8). All of Shepard's corpus—from his persona to his writings—stand as texts that are intricately intertwined with one another. To fully comprehend Shepard's "project" of his late career, it is necessary to consider all manifestations of the corpus. This book will locate the relational points between these works when pertinent, but it will further argue that this late era of Shepard is a distinctive period as it shifts the Shepard persona, experiments with different subjects, genres, and aesthetics, and attempts to locate solutions to conflicts from earlier works.

The most obvious consumers and decipherers of the intertextuality of the Shepard corpus are those Shepard aficionados that make up the Shepard "textual community." Stanley Fish has used the term "interpretive communities" to define those "who share interpretive strategies not for reading (in the conventional sense) but writing texts, for constituting their properties and assigning their intentions" (1982: 171). The Shepard cult is not expected to "write" or "create," but can be conventionally viewed as the consumers of all aspects of Shepard. As a result, it is not their interpretations that construct the community, but rather their appreciation of the various *texts* (writings and performances, for example) of the Shepard corpus. The textual community that revolves around Shepard interprets each work within the context of that corpus. Scholars and journalists have been aware of these fans of Shepard for years, as they earned the contempt of Jill Dolan (as explored in Chapter 6) and were even identified by Steven

Putzel as "Shepard groupies" (1987: 174), further revealing Shepard as a "rock star" of American theater.

This creation of a cult is, of course, not without precedent, for it can be a result of the dynamics surrounding a celebrity or superstar, and if that celebrity is visible across various platforms and media, the cult has the potential for growth. As scholar Christine Geraghty notes, the "relationship between the audience and the star is deemed to be best figured by the fan whose knowledge comes from a wide variety of sources" (2007: 99). And with Shepard's corpus, the sources range from television and film to published plays and short stories. Each cultural product is haunted by the presence of the Shepard persona. Members of the Shepard textual community are often aware of the intertextual lacings of these different endeavors. Being a member of this textual community brings an increased understanding of each work by placing it within the continuum of Shepard's corpus. Indeed, Shepard's work serves readers and audiences outside of the textual community, yet those within the textual community are granted an enhanced experience through their ability to place each subsequent work within the corpus of Shepard.

The Late Style also allows Shepard to pose resolutions to dilemmas. Characters in these late Shepard works often demonstrate through action—essentially, performance—the ability to resolve issues and concerns previously explored in earlier Shepard works. As noted, these works often ended without any formal resolution. As Mike Vanden Heuvel notes, Shepard's "plays end on a note of despair and entrapment" (1981: 212). The Late Style of Shepard aligns with and goes beyond Florence Falk's assertion that in Shepard's plays characters attempt "to perform their way out of, or around, disaster" (1981: 182). As Falk explains, "Performance resurrects. Performance kills. Performance resurrects because it rests on memory yet commands expeditions to the new" (1981: 182). Shepard's late works resurrect not only characters within plays (such as the metaphorical reanimation of the title character in *The Late Henry Moss*), but also familiar, Shepardian character types and scenarios reminiscent of his past work. Through these resurrections, Shepard has his characters engage with these recognizable past Shepardian tropes and *perform* their way toward resolutions. Unlike works from his previous periods, Shepard demonstrates through his characters certain methods and actions that must be performed to reach a resolution regarding the conflict within the play.

Regarding resolutions, Shepard himself, as well as his critics, often complain about the author's inability to reach a satisfying conclusion. Shepard has commented that he finds ending a work particularly challenging and that his plays essentially just "stop" and do not provide a conclusion. In 1984, Shepard commented that "a resolution isn't an ending; it's a strangulation" (Bottoms 1998: 3). This results in his work often ending with haunting ambiguity. The Late Style differentiates itself in many ways, and one noteworthy aspect is Shepard's willingness to provide resolutions to dilemmas posed in his previous works. In much of Shepard's work, imagery, scenarios, and characters are presented with a situational crisis, yet no resolution to the conflict is ever reached within the work. Indeed, the plays preceding the Late Style often include inexplicable endings that revel in their own unwillingness to bring closure to the scenarios. For example, in the Late Style, Shepard resurrects the issue of sibling rivalry initially breached in *True West* with *The Late Henry Moss*. Unlike *True West*, which does not offer a solution to the conflict, actually concluding with the brothers in the process of killing one another, *The Late Henry Moss* demonstrates how characters can performatively confront their shared past of trauma and reconcile their conflict. Quite simply, *The Late Henry Moss* postulates *how* one can solve the personal conflict at the heart of *True West*. To fully engage and comprehend the dynamics of Shepard's Late Style, it is essential to recognize that these late writings offer resolutions to the dilemmas posed in earlier works.

This investigation of Shepard's work is unique in that there exists no scholarly project that thoroughly analyzes this series of works and this phase of Shepard's career. Beyond filling a void in scholarship, this project will also prove that even though Shepard has passed his cultural—and perhaps even artistic—moment, this later phase of work, spanning from writings to film performances, stands as a complex system of reengagements and renegotiations with past concerns, while also plunging into territories previously unmapped. As Shepard's vision in this Late Style exceeds a sole medium, it is integral in considering him as an artist to account for his written work both on and off the stage. Scholars have often obeyed disciplinary restraints regarding Shepard's writings and have rarely written across the media of theater, literature, and film. As a result, this project utilizes a transmedial approach to Shepard's work. With explorations in writing for film and the page, Shepard not only reconsiders long-lingering issues present in his drama, but also confronts new concerns that are tied to the medium of their production. With these reconsiderations in combination with different media, Shepard's aesthetic transforms from one closely aligned with a variation on realism to an aesthetic that weaves, ebbs, and stutters through a variety of styles. As his media and concerns alter, so does Shepard's aesthetic.

An added complexity to approaching Shepard is that he is a prolific motion-picture actor. These endeavors are informed by his identity as an author of works concerned with the American West, family, masculinity, and mythology. In turn, Shepard's writing is informed—particularly in the Late Style—by his status as a celebrity with cultural cache. The public persona of Sam Shepard, which displays a mixture of cowboy stoicism, auto-didactic intelligence, and a skeptical respect for the masculine codes of the American West, is a distinct creation of Samuel Shepard Rogers. In fact, one could argue that one of Shepard's most notable creations is that of the Shepard persona, essentially a man seemingly cleaved from both his appropriate time (the nineteenth century) and landscape (the American West). These discussions of self, identity, persona, and authenticity, as conveyed by the persona of "Sam Shepard," will not be exhaustive in this project, but Shepard's iconic status as a celebrity writer/actor persistently looms over all discussions of his work, in whatever form that work may take. As a result, Shepard's writings and performances—be it as a character in a film or as the Shepard persona itself—can be collectively termed his corpus.

The praise that accompanied Shepard during his cultural moment was all pervasive. Because of the acclaim earned by his plays, as well as his success as a film actor and emergence as a celebrity, Shepard garnered not only the attention of theater critics and scholars, but also was celebrated in popular magazines such as *Esquire*, *Rolling Stone*, *Newsweek*, and *People*.

Many scholars themselves also recognized the cultural force of Shepard. For example, scholar Leslie Wade begins his volume *Sam Shepard and the American Theatre* with the following passage:

> No playwright in the recent history of American theatre has garnered more attention and acclaim than Sam Shepard. From his early experiments in the Off-Off Broadway avant-garde to his widely renowned family plays, he has fascinated audiences with effulgent, often hypnotic drama of American anxiety and ambition. With a career that has spanned three decades, Shepard has achieved rank and stature accorded such figures as Eugene O'Neill, Tennessee Williams, and Arthur Miller. The leading dramatist of his generation, Sam Shepard has become the latest Great American Playwright. (1997: 1)

Scholar William Demastes has also praised Shepard, noting that "throughout his nearly three decades of playwriting, Sam Shepard has expanded the frontiers of American drama with an energy and inventiveness to rival even Eugene O'Neill" (Bennett 1993: 168). Bonnie Marranca termed Shepard the "quintessential American playwright" (Smith 1998: 36).

In addition to scholars, Shepard also accumulated praise from critics and journalists for his writings and his performances during his cultural moment. Martin Esslin claimed that "Sam Shepard is contemporary American theatre" (Wade 1997: 1) while Jack Kroll's hagiographic profile romanticized Shepard as "America's cowboy laureate" who has been "the great red, white, and blue hope of U.S. drama since he was barely out of his teens" (1997: 4). Journalist Pete Hamill termed him a

"New American Hero" (1983) and even the *doyenne* of American film criticism Pauline Kael weighed in, noting in his debut film performance (*Days of Heaven*) "the irregularly handsome, slightly snaggletoothed Shepard . . . makes a strong impression; he seems authentically an American of an earlier era" (2004: 24).

The critical reception of Shepard's plays from the past twenty years has been mixed. Though scholars continue to respect Shepard's work from his earlier periods, there is comparatively little material concerning his more recent work. With the appearance of other playwrights inheriting the mantle of "Great American Playwright" and the mixed reception to his later work, Shepard's reputation in this Late Style remains contested among scholars. Gone are the hyperbolic celebrations from the 1980s. As with many playwrights in their autumnal years, Shepard's late work has been greeted unenthusiastically. Like Tennessee Williams' later work, Shepard's writings from late in his career have elicited critical derision—and at best—ambivalence. Though Williams' late work has recently been exhumed for reevaluation and belated appreciation, Shepard's Late Style continues to have diminishing impact upon contemporary theater. That said, this period finds Shepard—as it was with the aging Beckett and the long-in-the-tooth Williams—willing to experiment with concepts and forms.

This project centers upon the following questions: What is Shepard's Late Style? How does it serve the Shepard corpus? In what ways can we understand Shepard's late work as it no longer garners critical adulation? How does an artist navigate the various media at their disposal? What relation does the persona of Shepard have to his written and performed work? How does a maturing artist reexamine familiar issues and themes, yet also explore new subjects, aesthetics, and experimentations? How does the Late Style of Shepard seek to demonstrate resolutions to dilemmas previously posed in earlier cycles of work? An examination of the Late Style of Shepard reveals substantial answers to these questions, and when pushed further, the relevance of the Late Style to Shepard's entire corpus emerges. Shepard's work can be organized into phases (as detailed in Chapter 1), yet to fully understand the entire corpus, scholars must consider the work from the Late Style of Shepard.

This project investigates the Late Style of Shepard through six chapters. The introduction explains the subject, the approach to the work, the goals of this project, and questions posed by such an examination. Chapter 1, entitled "'How Many Lives . . . Within This One?'[1]: The Performances of Sam Shepard," considers the Shepard persona as it is performed across media. As an actor and celebrity-artist, Shepard's persona has gained great circulation over the past three decades. In the Late Style, this persona alters and shifts once again. The second chapter "'What's Beyond Authentic?'[2]: Authenticity and Artistry in *Don't Come Knocking* and *Kicking a Dead Horse*" discusses Shepard's self-reflexive analysis of authenticity and the role of the artist in American culture. Though Shepard's work had previously interrogated the concept of authenticity, the Late Style's consideration of authenticity is distinctly informed by Shepard's status as a celebrity. Chapter 3—"'One of Us Has Forgotten'[3]: Memory and Trauma in *Simpatico, The Late Henry Moss*, and *When the World was Green*"—centers upon Shepard's concern for personal history, and traumatic memory and its relation to a perceived truth. For Shepard, the interplay between memory and truth results in a struggle for determining a comprehension of the past that consistently informs the present. "'I Miss the Cold War So Much'[4]: Interrogating Militarism and Conservative Narratives in *States of Shock* and *The God of Hell*," the title of the fourth chapter, examines the politics of Shepard's works during Gulf War I and the so-called "War on Terror." As previously stated, the Late Style of Shepard is marked by a decidedly blatant engagement with contemporary politics. As a result, this chapter analyzes the plays *States of Shock* and *The God of Hell* within the cultural climate that produced each work. This reading of the plays will exact how and why these plays comment upon conservative politics and militarism. Chapter 5, "'Surrounded by My Primitive Captors'[5]: Hybridity and Hegemony in *Silent Tongue* and *Eyes for Consuela*," examines Shepard's consideration of identity and borders in relation to conflicts between indigenous and invasive cultures. The final chapter of this book, "'Where's All the Men?'⁶: Men, Women, and Homosociality" analyzes how Shepard reconsiders and reengages with the issues of gender in the Late Style.

As previously noted, this project investigates an important component of the writer's corpus that has been neglected. That said, there is no shortage of scholarship on Shepard's work that predates the Late Style. Indeed, Shepard and his work have been the subjects of voluminous scholarly texts and articles. From 1979 (with *Buried Child* and Shepard's earning of the Pulitzer Prize) to 1985 (with *A Lie of the Mind*), Shepard experienced a "cultural moment."

During this "cultural moment" Shepard earned both popular and critical attention as a writer and Hollywood actor. As a direct result, a "Shepard industry" of sorts developed in academia. This Shepard industry produced a deluge of papers, texts, monographs, companions, and dissertations centered upon his work. With Shepard's theatrical hiatus following *A Lie of the Mind*, his less than successful experimentation with film directing (1988's *Far North*) and the tepid reception of his plays from 1991 to the present, the once vibrant Shepard industry of scholarship slowed exponentially. Between 1985 and 1995, there were a total of thirty-three dissertations and theses produced on Shepard and his work. During that same time, there was a staggering eighty-one scholarly articles on Shepard's work published. The ten-year span between 1985 and 1995 could certainly be termed the height of the Shepard industry. In contrast, between 2000 and 2010, there were only nine dissertations and theses and fifteen academic articles published on Shepard's works. Almost exclusively, these projects focus upon his plays from 1964 to 1985.

The turn away from Shepard in theater studies can be attributed to a certain "Shepard fatigue" that occurred among scholars and artists in the late 1980s and early 1990s. This turn away from Shepard was enacted both by scholars as well as theater artists. This was exemplified by Jill Dolan's insightful, but scathing review of *A Lie of the Mind* in the *Hudson Review*, Joseph Roach's assertion that theater studies must reinvent itself and engage with new methodologies and new subjects of study and "no longer pour over 'Sam Shepard's entrails'" (Wade 1997: 4), and the appearance of parodies of Shepard's work, such as Chicago's Theater Oobleck's celebrated *The Slow and Painful Death of Sam Shepard* (1988) and Christopher Durang's *Stye in the Eye* (1994). It was evident that Shepard's cultural moment was slipping away or at least undergoing rigorous scrutiny.

The "Shepard fatigue" was further detailed in *The Village Voice* by Shepard biographer Don Shewey. Attending the Brussels-held 1993 international symposium on Shepard, entitled "Between the Margin and the Center," Shewey pondered if Shepard was becoming "the new version of Jerry Lewis or Mickey Rourke, marginal American pop figures elevated to cult status" (Shewey 1993: 103) by European audiences. During the two-day event organized by Shepard scholar Johann Callens, Shewey determined that "as hot as Shepard's critical reception had been in the '60s and '70s, it was now stone cold" (1997: 221). Though Europeans view Shepard's work—even his recent plays—as unique platforms for experimentation, many American scholars determined that Shepard's excursion into "realism" with the family cycle was unpromising, conservative, and pedestrian.

Shewey was amused by the conference, commenting that "the whole enterprise . . . [was] comically pathetic" as a "hotel conference room the size of an average university classroom could house the 'Shepard industry'" (1993: 103). Perhaps most telling was a Shepard scholar wondering aloud, "Are we dancing around the grave" of Shepard? (Shewey 1997: 221). Undoubtedly, the symposium was an indicator of the decline in interest in Shepard and his work and served less as a celebration and investigation and was more akin to a funeral.

A number of scholars have attempted to explain Shepard's inability to critically or popularly regain his status from the cultural moment (1979–85) during this later period (1988–present). Leslie Wade explains that

> from the vantage point of the mid-1980s, when Shepard's status in the American theatre reached its apogee, the trajectory of his

carccr cngendered assumptions that he would continue to produce
the challenging, often daunting works expected of the country's
most prominent playwright. In the 1990s these expectations went
unfulfilled. To all but the most loyal of Shepard devotees, it seems
that the playwright has entered into a state of decline, at best a state of
transition. (2002: 257)

Wade, who has chronicled Shepard through various articles and
works, has attempted to explain and theorize aspects of Shepard's
steep critical decline following *A Lie of the Mind*. Following that play,
Shepard worked almost solely in cinema and did not return to the stage
until 1991 with *States of Shock*, which demonstrated a radical shift in
Shepard's aesthetics and concerns, confounding critics and the public.
Wade notes that

> to facilitate the work of his biographer, Shepard should have ended
> his career with *A Lie of the Mind*; its epic scope and lofty ambition
> would have served well as a point of closure for the writer's life in the
> theatre. . . . Shepard has not since that time equaled *Lie of the Mind*,
> either in quality of writing or in intensity of audience response.
> (1997: 157)

Indeed, *A Lie of the Mind* (1985) does signal the end of a period (his
cultural moment) and a cycle of plays (family centered works). I agree
with most scholars and critics that Shepard's writings for the stage
following *A Lie of the Mind* leave much to desire, and I concur that
A Lie of the Mind serves as a summation of sorts regarding Shepard's
various themes and aesthetics. That said, it is integral in understanding
Shepard as a writer and cultural icon to consider these late works,
regardless of the works' various levels of quality. Though these works
from the late period may never receive, or even deserve, the critical
and popular accolades bestowed upon Shepard's writings from his
cultural moment, these late works do provide unique glimpses of a
playwright grappling with his own legacy, exploring new subjects and
approaches, and attempting to resolve certain issues and concerns
from earlier works.

Bluntly, Wade explains that "in attempting to contextualize Sam Shepard in the last decade of American theater history, one finds that he is rather a man out of time" (2002: 274). Wade poses a number of questions regarding the work of Shepard in this late period that follows his cultural moment. Wade asks,

> Is his decline in critical regard a result of his meager output, or the result of audience fatigue with his high-octane machismo? Or is there an implicit desire for the old Shepard, which prejudices reception of his more recent work? Has his interest in new relational modes been as yet unable to find compelling dramatic form? Can Shepard successfully develop his dramatic vision in a way that recognizes the hauntings of the American male without feeding the very demons he wishes to expel? (2002: 260)

Wade attempts to answer these questions, while also investigating some of the other elements that may have contributed to Shepard's critical wane. According to Wade, "American theatre of the 1990s embraced new concerns, new orientations, and consequently favored different imaginings of cultural consciousness. One may consider Paula Vogel and Tony Kushner as the decade's book-end dramatists, Vogel the representative of the decade's conclusion, Kushner its beginning" (2002: 274). Indeed, Shepard seems "out of step" (Wade 1997: 156) with other playwrights of the 1990s and 2000s, as "Shepard's plays have almost exclusively been concerned with the male experience, the European immigrant past, and the heritage of the West" (Wade 1997: 156). In contrast to such playwrights as Vogel and Kushner, as well as Suzan-Lori Parks and August Wilson, "Shepard's plays can appear to be sentimental, mournful of a lost American plenitude" (Wade 1997: 156) which are less central to the post-1980s cultural and ideological consciousness. Scholar Susan Harris Smith concurs with this observation, explaining that the "growing moves to pluralism and multiculturalism in American drama which, with feminism, point to a paradigm shift away from the loner male in a state of angst on the existential prairie" (1998: 37). Indeed, by this time other playwrights from a broader swath of the American populace, representing diverse perspectives of the American experience, gained their rightful and deserved positions as major dramatists.

An intriguing component of the descent of Shepard's critical reputation in the late period would be the ascendancy of other playwrights often working within the quasi-Shepardian territory. The American playwrights David Mamet and Tracy Letts and the Irish Martin McDonagh have met with great critical and popular success through their thematic and aesthetic concerns that connect to Shepard's corpus. During the Late Style of Shepard, these playwrights address many of the same elements associated with Shepard, yet these playwrights often achieve much more satisfying results. Though Mamet and Shepard hail from the same generation, when Shepard's cultural moment waned, Mamet ascended and he has been able to remain a writer whose new work—for the most part—engages audiences and critics. Mamet has not had to struggle to receive major productions of his work in New York City, yet Shepard, ever since 1992's *States of Shock*, has met with great difficulty in the mounting of new works in the city. 1994's *Simpatico* and 2001's *The Late Henry Moss*, despite Shepard's cache, were plagued with difficulties in their New York productions. *The God of Hell* (2004) also met with disinterest from many investors and producers. Eventually, it was produced in collaboration with the Actors Studio Drama School at the New School. *Kicking a Dead Horse* (2008) and *Ages of the Moon* (2010) received initial productions not in the United States, but in Ireland at Dublin's Peacock Theatre. *Heartless* (2013) and 2014's *A Particle of Dread* (*Oedipus Variations*) were both produced in New York, but failed to ignite much attention.

Unlike Shepard, Mamet has also been able to successfully navigate the tumultuous territory of cinema and television, penning numerous screenplays, consistently directing motion pictures, and even helming a television series. Shepard's time as a writer and director in film seemed to initially hold promise, but it never approached the critical and popular success enjoyed by Mamet. As with Shepard, Mamet remains focused on issues of identity, gender, and masculinity, yet Mamet's recent forays into political writings have raised the ire of even his staunchest artistic supporters.

Letts, like Shepard, concerns himself with the dingy motel rooms and caustic family relations found in the forgotten regions of America. His characters booze, abuse, and destroy one another in a Shepardian fashion. As with Shepard and Mamet, Letts has found success in cinema, as adaptations of his plays have met with great critical adulations. In addition, Letts earned the Pulitzer Prize for *August: Osage County* (2008). Unlike Mamet, yet very much like Shepard, Letts has begun to perform as an actor in high-profile roles such as his turn in the 2012 revival of Albee's *Who Is Afraid of Virginia Woolf?*[7]

Similar to Shepard's rapid rise on the New York theater scene in the 1960s, the Irish playwright Martin McDonagh gained the attention of the theater establishment as the *enfant terrible* of the London boards in the 1990s. Like a young Shepard, McDonagh often revealed a willful ignorance of—and at times, hostility toward—theater. McDonagh's violent plays, like Shepard's work, investigate sibling relationships and masculine codes. Also, McDonagh has moved from theater to cinema. McDonagh earned an Academy Award for his 2005 short *Six Shooter* while still being practically an unknown outside of theater circles. He wrote and directed the films *In Bruges* (2009) and *Seven Psychopaths* (2012) which garnered rave reviews, if not popular success. In all, it is quite telling that in the last ten years, Mamet, Letts, and McDonagh have had little to no difficulty receiving major productions of new works in New York City, often on Broadway. For Shepard, Broadway is reserved for revivals of his family plays.

Over the past twenty years, Shepard has met with great success in the production of short stories. Unlike Shepard's plays and screenplays from this period, which often received withering reviews, Shepard's volumes *Cruising Paradise* (1996), *Great Dream of Heaven* (2002), and *Day Out of Days* (2011) garnered unanimous acclaim. Indeed, perhaps the most satisfying and successful writing produced by the former "Great American Playwright" is to be found in these collections. Unlike Shepard's plays, productions, and written films, these volumes allowed for a wide circulation of Shepard's writings. For many outside his textual community, Shepard was primarily recognized as an actor, and if he was known as a writer, it was based solely upon his plays from the family cycle. With his volumes of stories and tales, Shepard emerged once again as a writer recognized beyond theatrical circles. The mounds of positive critical reaction to Shepard's prose collections seem to indicate that for critics Shepard is a writer whose talents are perhaps no longer best suited for the stage or screen, but are rather most effectively utilized and realized in short prose.

Another concern in terms of Shepard's decline is not just negative critical reaction to his plays or even other playwrights working in his "territory," but also the overall quality of his Late Style work. I wholly agree with Wade's assessment that "*States of Shock, Simpatico,* and *Eyes for Consuela* by and large [are] failed attempts" but that "Shepard's work retains vitality and spurs curiosity (though not satisfaction)" (2002: 258). In the wake of the triumph of his family plays and success as a film actor in the mid-1980s, Shepard found himself facing less than rhapsodic reviews of his plays. As noted, his collections of tales did gain positive notices, but Shepard would not receive nearly unanimous critical adulations of a stage work until 2008's *Kicking a Dead Horse.* Wade contends that Shepard's "plays of the 1990s may evidence a wiser, more reflective, more philosophical playwright, one more open to ethical responsibility, but that sort of rumination—in Shepard's case—may simply not translate into the creation of compelling drama" (2002: 276).

Concerning critical reception of Shepard's late work, Wade explains that "there are conversely those apologists invested in Shepard criticism who recognize no decline and labor to manifest the writer's ingenuity and brilliance, despite the unremarkable impact of his recent work" (Wade 2002: 258). For example, Rosen, commenting upon Shepard's Late Style, notes that critics "who seem to have tired of Shepard, much as critics in the past grew tired for a while of Miller, Williams, and Albee, the other great American playwrights who earned the scorn of critics for nothing less than the crime of becoming known for a singular voice, a singular view" (2004: 199). What Rosen is neglecting to note is that Shepard's "singular" view is no longer as sharp or dynamic. Though the hyperbolic praise of Shepard in the 1970s and 1980s seemed to reflect an incessant need for the proverbial "Great American Dramatist," the cultural moment of Shepard did indeed occur when the playwright was at the height of his dramatic abilities. The Late Style of Shepard, among other dynamics, reveals a writer working across different media, renegotiating his persona, and attempting to offer solutions to previous dilemmas from other works, but in all, the work itself is inconsistent in quality. Though the work from this late period may never achieve the adulation awarded to Shepard's family cycle, these writings do indeed offer significant insight into the entire Shepard corpus.

Though Wade offers perspective regarding Shepard's decline, I do take issue with his contention that "the world Shepard establishes offers no reimagined possibilities, ethically or socially" (2002: 275) as offered by other successful playwrights. Indeed, as detailed throughout this book, it is precisely this Late Style that attempts to provide solutions, essentially "reimagined possibilities" to dilemmas and crises from his earlier work. The Late Style, specifically, serves to instruct the audience "how" to act and perform toward a resolution.

In all, Shepard's late career critical reputation as a playwright seems to result from a multitude of factors, namely: that his subjects (for many) seem antiquated and irrelevant; other playwrights address the concerns of contemporary Americans more insightfully and efficaciously; the subjects and concerns of Shepard have been taken up by other writers who have met with greater success across various media; and, the quality of Shepard's work is no longer at the level exhibited during his cultural moment.

Though there is a bulk of scholarship on Shepard, primarily focused upon his family cycle and those works that precede it, there are few scholarly projects that explore the Late Style, and none that comprehensively consider his late work. That said, there are indeed certain scholarly works that inform this manuscript. Stephen J. Bottoms' *The Theatre of Sam Shepard: States of Crisis* serves as a central text in this project. The book examines Shepard's dramatic works, seeking to place them within a larger, cultural context of American theater and within Shepard's dramatic legacy. As the work was published in 1998, it chronicles Shepard's plays up to *Simpatico*.

Also of significance to this project is Carol Rosen's 2004 text *Sam Shepard: A "Poetic Rodeo."* As an entry in Palgrave's Modern Dramatists series, Rosen's work offers an analytical overview of Shepard's dramatic work. Rosen also theorizes that Shepard works within specific, definable stages of expression. It is this component of Rosen's survey that provides a useful, if at times reductive, approach to Shepard's writings. Rosen argues that Shepard's work can be delineated into five distinct phases, essentially "early plays celebrating myth," "hero plays," "family plays," "play[s] of cataclysm," and "plays of bold and broad strokes" (2004: 7).

Shepard's most recent phase, which is the subject of this manuscript, is what Rosen terms "the plays of bold and broad strokes" (2004: 7) and what I refer to as the Late Style. Rosen argues that these works are sporadic in quality and notes that these plays serve as "slapstick tragedies, displaying the gusto and outrageousness and, yes, also the spontaneous devil-may-care looseness of the youthful plays" (2004: 7). In this book, I propose an alternate vision of Shepard's periods of work signaled in part by his evolving persona. This project recognizes the Late Style as a distinct period in which Shepard explores new subjects and aesthetics, expresses himself through various media, and attempts to provide resolutions to problems posed in earlier periods. In fact, any consideration of Shepard's work from the Late Style must account for his explorations of expression beyond the stage as well as his status as an icon in both popular culture and American drama and literature.

Also instrumental in the creation of this document are *American Dreams: The Imagination of Sam Shepard* (1981) edited by Bonnie Marranca, David J. DeRose's *Sam Shepard* (1992), and Leslie Wade's *Sam Shepard and the American Theatre* (1997). Marranca's collection of interviews, essays, reviews, and commentary offers an insightful perspective on Shepard's work and its critical reception in the 1980s.

Though I am concerned with the plays, stories, and screenplays that were created in the decade following this volume, *American Dreams* serves as a detailed overview of Shepard's work and position in American theater. DeRose's work seeks to differentiate itself from other contributions to the Shepard industry, which he disparages as being "focused with dulling repetition on [Shepard's] Americana image, treating Shepard more as a social and literary phenomenon than a theatre artist" (1992: ix). That being said, DeRose attempts to locate an understanding of Shepard's work through an interrogation of Shepard's theatrical and thematic intentions while considering the artist's "preoccupation with heightened or 'critical' states of consciousness" (1992: ix). Wade's volume stands as an exceptional work, chronicling and analyzing Shepard's work with a keen eye, yet as with most publications concerning Shepard, very little attention is paid to works from the writer's late period.

The Cambridge Companion to Sam Shepard (2002) not only further institutionalizes the author by its mere existence, but also includes a number of essays that meaningfully contribute to this project. Of note are Christopher Bigsby's "Born Injured: The Theatre of Sam Shepard," Leslie Wade's "*States of Shock, Simpatico*, and *Eyes for Consuela*: Sam Shepard's Plays of the 1990s," and Matthew Roudane's "Sam Shepard's *The Late Henry Moss*." Each essay offers critical engagement with Shepard's plays from his Late Style. Additionally, the collection includes short chapters on Shepard and the cinema as well as Shepard's prose works. Unfortunately, these two essays are limited in scope and do not attempt to align these nontheatrical excursions with Shepard's theatrical work.

Though this book is not focused upon literary and critical theory and the possibilities breached by such interrogations, Mike Vanden Heuvel's *Performing Drama/Dramatizing Performance: Alternative Theater and the Dramatic Text* (1991) and Jeanette R. Malkin's *Memory-Theater and Postmodern Drama* (1999) inform this project to a notable degree. Each work contains a section centering upon Shepard's work. Vanden Heuvel's volume considers the interplay between the written text and the performed text and the creation of meaning in Shepard's plays, while Malkin identifies the instability of memory in Shepard's work and pursues the notion that Shepard's characters suffer under the anxiety of erasure.

In sum, there is a scarcity of scholarly engagement with Shepard's Late Style, creating a gap of knowledge regarding one of America's most renowned playwrights. Without investigating Shepard's Late Style, it is impossible to fully consider Shepard's entire corpus of work. In this late period, Shepard revisits familiar territory, while also lighting out for new regions in media, form, and subject. The Late Style also provides resolutions to dilemmas introduced in previous cycles of work. Shepard, in his late career, is willing to reconsider familiar concerns and position himself as a pedagogue by providing distinct methods and approaches in which to solve stated dilemmas through his writings. Though this concept of a dilemma (as introduced in an earlier period) and resolution (as provided in the Late Style) serves as a through-line in this period, the Late Style is also notable for the maturation of Shepard's iconic persona as well as his newly found activist voice that engages the politics of the day. In all, Shepard's Late Style of 1988 to 2015 is an essential component of Shepard's corpus. This Late Style (1) alters the Shepard persona; (2) provides resolutions to dilemmas previously introduced in his work; (3) investigates new concerns such as politics and colonialism; and (4) utilizes various aesthetics and genres to create an interwoven tapestry of transmedial work. To examine the Late Style corpus of Shepard, it is essential to first analyze the dynamics of the Shepard persona in this period.

Notes

1 The title of this chapter comes from the play *Simpatico* (61).

2 The title of this chapter is a question posed to the audience in *Kicking a Dead Horse* (30).

3 A line from Act I of *Simpatico* (17).

4 These words are uttered by Frank as he appears as a newly brainwashed Neoconservative in *The God of Hell* (91).

5 Eamon MacCree screams these words as he is surrounded by the Kiowa "dog soldiers" in *Silent Tongue* (140).

6 Spoken aloud by the elderly Gramma in *Far North* when she realizes that their small Minnesota town has lost most of its male population (120).

7 In 2013, a film version of *August: Osage County* was released with Shepard cast as Beverly Weston.

.

1

"How Many Lives . . . Within This One?": The Performances of Sam Shepard

Discussion of Shepard's work often cannot resist exploring Shepard's biography. Perhaps because of the enigmatic quality of his early works or the emotional honesty of the family dramas, Shepard's biography has consistently been mined and excavated for hints, clues, and signifiers that may help to elucidate his work. A component of this biographical turn may rest in the persona of Shepard himself. Through interviews, writings, and performances, Shepard is often linked to many icons and paradigms popularly associated with being American. Shepard's seeming embodiment of traditional American notions of male handsomeness, along with his projections of rugged, salt-of-the-earth "authenticity," apparent even in the earliest profiles of him as a writer, link him to the American West and masculine ideals. With his reception of the Pulitzer Prize in 1979 and his 1983 Oscar nomination for *The Right Stuff*, Shepard became a highly regarded author, a respected film actor and, incidentally, a celebrity. He was profiled in *Rolling Stone, Newsweek,* and *New York* magazines and posed for celebrity photographers Annie Lebowitz, Herb Ritts, and Bruce Weber. He was also the subject of fascination for those in theater circles, as Shepard was chosen to grace the 1984 inaugural issue of the Theatre Communications Group's magazine *American Theatre.* In this time he also began a decades-long romantic relationship with the Hollywood performer Jessica Lange. As a result, the two became a Hollywood "It" couple in the 1980s and served as subjects for the paparazzi's ravenous gaze. As Shepard achieved wider recognition as a playwright and actor in the 1980s, essentially becoming a celebrity-artist, attributes associated with Shepard's persona became magnified and gained further currency through mechanical reproduction. As a result, a distinct Shepardian persona was cast. Undoubtedly, Shepard's persona has developed into a lasting contribution to his own legacy as an artist. Shepard's performance of self—regardless of whether it is seen in his depiction of his early persona as a country bumpkin lost in a metropolis or in his depiction of himself as an embodiment of the "Great American Playwright" who bridges Hollywood, mainstream theatre, and avant-garde experiments—is an integral component of his artistic corpus. As Don Shewey notes, "The theme of self-transformation turns up again and again in Shepard's writing—and his life" (1997: 6). In essence, Shepard has always developed a persona, but with his cultural moment in the 1980s, the persona of that period was communicated to a global audience through film and the press. In the 2012 documentary *Shepard and Dark*, Shepard concedes that developing a persona or identity is a process similar to writing. He explains in voice-over: "You're just changing the costumes and the sets and the dialogue and it's playwriting. . . . You write your own little play and then you act it out" (Trumveld). But, what is the persona of Shepard after his cultural moment? How does the Shepard persona alter and remake itself for the Late Style?

This chapter will define Shepard's performance of self during the period I have termed the Late Style and examine how Shepard's persona reaches toward—and becomes intertwined with—the various roles he accepts as an actor. This period ushered in a "new" Shepard persona that resonated with his previous incarnations and revealed a multitude of nuances not previously explored. Further, this chapter will analyze roles performed by Shepard in film, and in one instance a play, and how these roles—when analyzed as a whole—help to perpetuate the Shepard persona. Through work in films such as *Hamlet* (2000), *Black Hawk Down* (2001), *The Assassination of Jesse James by the Coward Robert Ford* (2007), and *Brothers* (2009), Shepard comfortably eased into a position in which he embodied a paternal force in his roles, offering guidance to younger characters, while also retaining elements of his masculine, Western persona. During the early part of the twenty-first century, Shepard returned to the stage as an actor for the first time in almost three decades for Caryl Churchill's *A Number* (2004). In this performance, Shepard not only bolstered his persona by inhabiting yet another paternal character, but also grasped for an authenticity of experience often associated with theater. In sum, Shepard's roles as an actor, performances as a celebrity, and his literary output interweave with one another to create a specific performative aspect of his corpus. Though present in his earlier phases, this dynamic is fully pronounced in the Late Style. Indeed, to fully consider Shepard's projects—literary or otherwise—the scholar must take into account not only his work as an author, but also his acting projects and performances of self. Though the persona of Shepard has been addressed in the few biographical treatises on the author, there have been no examinations of the transmedial iterations of Shepard's persona in this late period.

In examining Shepard's projected persona it is useful to turn to Richard Poirier's "The Performing Self." The essay devotes considerable time to the performances of the authors Henry James, Robert Frost, and Norman Mailer. Mailer, like Shepard, projected a masculine heterosexuality, often portraying himself as a "tough guy," which is analogous in many ways to Shepard's "cowboy" image. Mailer, like Shepard, pursued many forms of expression, from the novel and journalism to filmmaking, criticism, and politics (even running for political office). Like Shepard's citations of jazz, rock, Jack Kerouac, and Jackson Pollock, Mailer perpetually tied himself to the masculine writings and posturings of Ernest Hemingway. The persona of Mailer was a persistent presence in American culture in the 1960s and 1970s, as he continuously attempted to write (and rewrite) himself into American history. Mailer was aware of—and celebrated—his own persona and superstardom. Mailer even claimed that he was "involved in an act of historical as well as self-transformation," for as Mailer noted, the "first art work in an artist is the shaping of his own personality" (Poirier 2003: 8). Unlike Shepard, Mailer never seemed to question his persona or the codes he embodied. Poirier explains that "there's something lovably, even idealistically youthful in Mailer's aspiration for fame. He wants to make himself an 'art work' which will provide the protective and illuminating context for all the other works he will produce" (2003: 16). Mailer, who does embody a familiar male archetype, represents a romantic attachment to fame and glory. His celebrity is a component of his own corpus, and he is not hesitant in proclaiming it as such. Shepard, in contrast, performs the role of the artist who resents celebrity, yet realizes that such status grants him extraordinary freedom in artistry.

As Shepard is a celebrated actor and playwright, it is also useful to call upon two notions theorized by scholar Joseph Roach. Roach specifically invokes the term "effigy" as a performance—or material piece of culture—that serves as an "image thus synthesized into an idea" (1996: 17). The Shepard persona works as a flesh effigy, yet that effigy possesses a certain degree of mutability as the Shepard persona is subject to variations of interpretation. For some, Shepard is the corporeal effigy that is interpreted to be the manifestation of a conservative, white, masculine heterosexuality that seems to have been placed under erasure during the 1970s. For others, Shepard serves as a sly, countercultural pose that simultaneously evokes and criticizes post–Second World War masculinity. Regardless of the persona performed, the public extract their own meaning from Shepard's corpus.

A more obvious connection between Roach's writings and Shepard resides in the concept of "It." Roach initially describes "It" as "a certain quality, easy to perceive but hard to define, possessed by abnormally interesting people" (2007: 3). This "It-ness" includes "characteristic manifestations of public intimacy (the illusion of availability), synthetic experience (vicariousness), and the It-effect (personality-driven mass attraction)" (2007: 3). Shepard certainly displays and embodies qualities associated with possessing "It," so much that he is indeed a "role-icon" that "represents a part that certain exceptional performers play on and off stage, no matter what other parts they enact from night to night" (Roach 2007: 39). Roach utilizes Marvin Carlson's notion of "ghosting" to further explain certain aspects of those who possess "It." Carlson describes ghosting as being "entrapped by the memories of the public, so that each new appearance requires a renegotiation with those memories" (Roach 2007: 6). Not only does Shepard seemingly "ghost" certain "role-icons" of American history (the cowboy, for example), he also "ghosts" other "role-icons" of Hollywood history (Gary Cooper and Burt Lancaster, actors often associated with the Western genre) while also "ghosting" his own various roles and his own biography. For example, Shepard's turn as the alcoholic, war veteran father in the film *Brothers* "ghosts" Shepard's previous work in *The Right Stuff* and *Black Hawk Dawn* (roles concerning military men), while also citing Shepard's biography (for those who belong to the Shepard textual community) concerning his own alcoholic, war veteran father.

Though decades removed from his cultural moment, Shepard remains one of the most recognized of all American playwrights. This recognizability resides not solely in his literary work, but can be primarily attributed to his visibility as an in-demand actor. Because of the interplay between Shepard's writing, acting, and persona, an investigation of Shepard's Late Style must take into account how these factors influence one another. Though other playwrights have written across the disciplinary divide of film and theater, no playwrights—and perhaps no authors—have achieved such popular and critical success as both a writer and actor. Indeed, some of the American public may recognize the names David Mamet or Neil Simon, yet very few could identify their image. For these writers, their photographic image does not hold a vital importance in understanding their work. Certainly, many aficionados of drama know of Mamet's early beret-wearing, cigar-chomping, Brechtian-posing days in Chicago or his later, *uber*-masculine poses with his hand-built writing cabin. Yet still, these images of Mamet have very little circulation outside the communities of contemporary American theater. Contrastingly, Shepard has been known by the general public over the past two decades as an actor.[1] Shepard is perhaps the only recognizable American playwright currently working. Eugene O'Neill, Tennessee Williams, and Arthur Miller were widely known in their day, though Shepard is primarily recognized by the public for his acting roles, not his writings. Indeed, from this summation, the unrecognizability of America's playwrights in a celebrity-oriented pervasive electronic media reveals how contemporary theater and its dramatists are marginalized in the United States. Indeed, the noncelebrity status of America's current top-tier playwrights may indicate that theater is no longer recognized by many as a vital component in our cultural landscape.

There are other notable writers from theater who have successfully crossed over to cinema as actors, such as Anna Deavere Smith, Wallace Shawn, Eric Bogosian, John Leguizamo, and the late Spalding Gray. Smith and Shawn are almost exclusively known as character actors, though their plays are widely studied and performed. Bogosian, Leguizamo, and Gray are primarily associated with live solo performances and carry the resulting persona with them to the screens of the cinema. In addition, these performers have had motion pictures produced that chronicle or adapt their monologues. Though Shepard has only once performed in a cinematic adaptation of his own stage work (1985's *Fool for Love*), Shepard's writings, persona, and acting career are carefully interwoven into a transmedial fabric. Within this cross-stitching of the literary, the performative, and the theatrical, these various dynamics inform one another. Indeed, to fully consider Shepard's position within American culture, and specifically within literature, theater, and film, the scholar must consider these various components that are inextricable from one another. As this project concerns Shepard's explorations in the latter phase of his career, the present chapter elucidates the connections between Shepard's honed persona and how that persona is further developed and underscored through his various acting projects.

Moreover, to ignore the interplay between Shepard's literary, acting, and performative work would result in scholarship that drastically reifies disciplinarian norms and privileges the literary, while most importantly, disregarding a component of Shepard's artistic output that is key to assessing his later period work. Indeed, Shepard may represent one of the last American embodiments of the "playwright-as-celebrity" phenomenon as typified by O'Neill, Williams, and Miller. As Shepard is known primarily by the public as an actor in cinema—and not as a playwright—perhaps he is no longer a celebrity-playwright, but rather a celebrity-actor who still happens to write plays, films, and prose for a limited audience.

This chapter will first trace the various "personas" the man born Samuel Shepard Rogers has inhabited since his arrival on the New York theater scene in the early 1960s. Then, the characteristics of Shepard's Late Style persona will be addressed. This phase is characterized by Shepard's performance of self as an American "man of letters" conscious of his own legacy, as well as an artist who continues to write and act well into his later years. Shepard inhabits a world of both literary and cinematic celebrity. As a result, the notion of celebrity and the artist's struggle to locate authenticity within the crucible of the marketplace is fully pronounced in this period, running through both his writing and his acting. In addition, this latter phase features Shepard moving into paternal roles in a number of films—both as a father character and a mentor to a younger generation of artists in theater and film. During this period, Shepard also ruminates on his own placement within the genealogy of theater and literature, positioning himself in direct connection to those authors that have influenced his own work. Though Shepard inhabits a different version of his persona for this most recent phase, there are certain traits and signifiers that serve as constants through his various persona phases. These core conceits to the Shepardian self serve as a through-line that connects the various personas. That said, there are certain traits in this most recent incarnation of self that stand in contrast to the earlier personas. Shepard's most recent persona emerges not only through interviews and documentaries, but also through his many motion-picture acting roles that directly reflect and reify his Late Style persona. As it is duplicated and amplified through various media, and emerges as distinct and recognizable across his works, Shepard's persona serves as an integral entry point for examining the interplay between an understanding of "Sam Shepard" and his various artistic explorations. Through analyzing Shepard's persona as promulgated through his various works, a more comprehensive understanding of both the persona and Shepard's work emerges. Finally, Shepard's position at the cultural convergence point of literary and cinematic celebrityhood serves as an intriguing location for examining the dynamics of the contemporary writer/actor within the realm of literary, theatrical, and popular culture.

So, what are the performed personas of Sam Shepard? There are certain traits of the Shepard persona that serve as a through-line from the 1960s to the 2010s. Paradoxically, a consistent theme of these various phases is the push toward "authenticity," as well as a romantic attachment to the American Southwest, a fascination with codes of masculinity and patriarchy, a wide knowledge of American history, the rejection of the "intellectualization" of writing, and a disdain for most theater. Considering the persona and the body it inhabits, Shepard has consistently projected a calm, reserved perspective, as if healing some unknown, internal wound. Shepard's persona as an actor falls into the lineage of such cinematic performers as Gary Cooper, Burt Lancaster, and Henry Fonda. This persona stands as essentially strong, virile men who represent the prototypical "salt-of-the-earth" American male associated with the cinema of the 1930s and 1940s. This archetype could be described as a tough, thoughtful man of action and few words who is a perpetual loner, uncomfortable in society. Perhaps the closest approximation of the Shepard persona is the Kirk Douglas hero of *Lonely are the Brave* (1962) based upon the 1956 novel *The Last Cowboy* by southwestern novelist Edward Abbey. In the film and novel, "Jack" Burns is a man whose loner status and subscription to a valiant, yet outdated cowboy code of the world comes into direct conflict with the progression of society. Not surprisingly, Burns, separated from his horse, is killed in the film's conclusion by a machine of the modern West: a truck. Shepard's persona also stretches beyond Hollywood into the elements found in the traditions of American literature. The persona is Emersonian in its proclamations of individualism and autodidacticism and Whitmanesque in its celebration of the self in relation to landscape, geography and nation and its privileging of the "barbaric yawp" of emotional expression over intellect.

Shepard's phases of persona are best understood in conjunction with his writing. As this chapter explores, the development of the Shepard persona is closely connected to his work. I have segmented Shepard's corpus into six distinct phases reflecting both his persona and his writings. The first phase is "artist as naïf" who produces "imagistic plays" (1964–66), followed by the "cosmic cowboy" composing "rock and roll plays" (1967–71). Shepard's time in Europe from 1972–75 is the "American abroad" engaged with "aesthetic explorations." Shepard's return to the United States transforms him into the "company man" writing "West Coast operatics" in 1976. With 1977's *Curse of the Starving Class* Shepard begins a move toward the "family cycle" and his tenure as "'The Great American Playwright.'" This phase serves as Shepard's "cultural moment" and concludes with 1985's *A Lie of the Mind*. Finally, Shepard inhabits the period which is the study of this project. The "Late Style" (1988–2015) is marked by Shepard's varied experimentations with theatrical forms and subjects, a move across various media and the posing of resolutions to dilemmas explored in earlier works. The persona of Shepard in this Late Style is that of a mature artist considering his position in the canon while also performing in acting roles that continue to reflect upon his obsessions with authenticity, gender, and the patriarchy.

But to examine the current Late Style persona, it is essential to survey the various phases of the Shepard persona within the larger Shepard corpus. When Shepard arrived in New York City from California in the early 1960s, he delighted in posing as "the artist as naïf," yet he was conscious of his own crafting of a self-image. For example, he dropped his birth name (Samuel Shepard Rogers III, but everyone knew him as "Steve" prior to New York) and used his rural "aw shucks" appearance to differentiate himself from countless other artists. Though he had performed in plays and had written a short dramatic piece before his arrival, Shepard painted himself as the naïve savant who bungles into artistic success: a country bumpkin of sorts who can break the rules of theater because he is not aware that any rules even exist. Photographs from this period show a dark-eyed, brooding Shepard with floppy bangs, often dressed in a long dark coat with a cigarette dangling from his lips. His scowling eyes and mischievous expression seem to hint at a higher intellect than one presented by the pose. This pose is an amalgam of James Dean "cool" with a weariness associated with the French Existentialists and the American Beats. As with subsequent phases of his persona, the image of Shepard becomes a vital component to his artistic corpus as a whole.

Shepard certainly represented an urban-chic-meets-stylized-rural-figure. The pose of the "country rube" differentiated himself from many of his peers. According to Shewey, Shepard "enjoyed playing the role of the hick from the sticks, an urban cowboy long before the days of designer jeans." (1997: 31). Among other attributes of Shepard, it was during his early days in New York that the Shepard persona was first noted for exuding a quiet charisma. Max Weber recognized the term charisma as a trait in which a figure within a tribal culture is designated or perceived as a leader, causing others to submit to that individual's will. This charisma is "a certain quality of an individual personality by which he [sic] is set apart from ordinary men and treated as endowed with supernatural, superhuman or at least superficially exceptional qualities" (Dyer 2007: 82). Shepard's initial ascendancy was among a subculture of artists working in New York City, which fostered a tribal mentality. Within this configuration, Jack Gelber's terming Shepard a "playwright as shaman" (1976: 1–4) seems appropriate. During this period Shepard wrote his first plays, often defined by their stunning imagery, such as the centrality of a man in a bathtub (1965's *Chicago*), the battle of flinging paint in *Fourteen Hundred Thousand* (1966), and the bleak whiteness of the set in *Red Cross* (1966).

With a pinch more of this "rustic" persona combined with an ever increasing consumption of drugs, Shepard transformed into a sort of "cosmic cowboy" during the late 1960s and early 1970s. Working with musicians such as the Holy Modal Rounders and Patti Smith, Shepard cut the image of a slim, cowboy hat–wearing psychedelic explorer who desired success and recognition as a rock star. Wild, unhinged, bizarre plays accompanied Shepard as he became more involved with the music scene in New York City. 1967's *Melodrama Play* concerns a rock and roll hit maker quarantined and forced to write a new song. Shepard performed as the not-so-thinly veiled autobiographical Slim in 1971's *Cowboy Mouth*. Written with Smith, the play concerns a confused and addled rock musician who yearns for both authenticity and celebrity.

When Shepard retreated to England, he further pursued music, ceased (or slowed) his drug intake, and wrote plays such as *Geography of a Horse Dreamer* (1974) and *Action* (1975), both of which helped to reform and then focus Shepard's aesthetic. I have termed this persona the "American abroad" and the work produced as "aesthetic explorations." The persona of this period is the (somewhat) sober and wide-eyed American casting a new gaze on his home nation. Living outside of the United States gave Shepard a new perspective on his nation and culture, allowing him to experience his own brand of *Innocents Abroad*. In fact, Charles Marowitz described the twenty-eight-year-old temporary London resident as "the personification of that conquering charm that is sometimes bred in the southern and western sections of America. . . . He remains Huckleberry Finn minus the fishing rod" (1972: 1–4).

With his return to the United States, Shepard transitions from the expatriate observing his home nation from across the pond to the maturing writer and "company man." Shepard locates an artistic home at San Francisco's Magic Theatre and becomes the company's playwright, composing what I term "West Coast operatics." These elaborate works, such as *The Sad Lament of Pecos Bill on the Eve of Killing his Wife* (1976), *Angel City* (1976), and *Suicide in B Flat* (1976) utilize both acting and extensive musical performances to explore elements as diverse as American folklore, the commercialization of art, and film noir. There, Shepard would begin to develop the plays that would bring him both critical and popular success, such as *Curse of the Starving Class* (1977). As his success as a dramatist grew, Shepard began acting in motion pictures, as in Terence Malick's *Days of Heaven* (1978). Suddenly, Shepard had a vastly larger stage to perform his persona. This popularity also ushers in the iconic Shepardian persona, namely the cultivating of

a curious mystique as a modern-day cowboy who exudes an understated yet unmistakable erotic presence that women especially find both exciting and disturbing. His attraction stems . . . from a kind of charismatic authenticity that harkens back to an earlier era . . . His reputation as a literary adventurer and his screen image as an archetypal American make Sam Shepard a unique combination of Ernest Hemingway and Gary Cooper. (Shewey 1997: 4)

During the 1980s, with appearances on magazine covers as well as in tabloids, Shepard projected a tender masculinity, earthiness, and authenticity that appealed to both men and women. As his popularity and critical acclaim ascended in the 1980s, he represented a powerful "double-punch" of artistry: Shepard was both a critically acclaimed playwright and film actor. As a result of the glow from a cultural moment consisting of celebrated plays and performances, Shepard was shackled with the designation of "Great American Playwright" with works such as *Buried Child* (1978), *True West* (1980), and *Fool for Love* (1983). It is during this period that Shepard's family cycle of work seemingly taps into the *zeitgeist* of the era, as the United States became fascinated with rural life and country and Western music. Americans of this time snatched up records in surprising numbers by Dolly Parton and Kenny Rogers, Outlaw Country musicians such as Willie Nelson were top concert draws, and audiences flocked to films such as *Urban Cowboy* (1980) and *Coal Miner's Daughter* (1980) and even country-twanged stage musicals like *The Best Little Whorehouse in Texas* (1978). Shepard's cultural moment coincided with a cultural moment for country and western music. Shepard's rise also paralleled the ascendancy of another actor performing the persona of a cowboy: Ronald Reagan. Shepard's plays, in some respects, offer a brutal interrogation of Reagan-era "family values." As Reagan performed the role of "paternal cowboy" of the nation, perhaps it is fitting that Shepard's work criticizing the patriarchy of American family—coupled with nuanced, revealing, and at times ironic performances of such American icons as jet pilot Chuck Yeager—became emblematic of an era in which the United States often blindly celebrated its status as "a city on the hill." Shepard projected this persona through the conclusion of his family cycle, which ends with *A Lie of the Mind* (1985).

If we are to inscribe ideological functions to our stars—such as Ronald Reagan performing the role of the "cowboy president"—what ideological function does Shepard perform in his cultural moment? Shepard as both an actor and playwright serves as an avatar for the individual. In essence, conservatives may have welcomed the emergence of Shepard the actor as a reinstatement of traditional leading men, while liberals perhaps recognized the former cosmic cowboy's mainstreaming as an indication that the counterculture could work within the confines of Hollywood. As scholar Susan Harris Smith points out, "Sam Shepard is a cultural phenomenon who fulfills national expectations and roles that have a high place in our desiderata: he is a figure who seems to embody the emergent opposition to commercial theatre and bourgeois hegemony and yet is attractively packaged as a movie star" (1998: 36).

For some, Shepard's rise as a celebrity film actor seemed as a reaffirmation of white, conservative, protestant, heterosexual values. The 1970s were marked by the ascendancy of nontraditional leading men in Hollywood films. Actors such as Al Pacino and Robert DeNiro projected a dangerous and masculine heterosexuality, yet they were marked by their "ethnic" background and assumed Catholicism. Dustin Hoffman and Richard Dreyfus often portrayed roles characterized by a tender and thoughtful heterosexuality, but their "Jewishness" served as a distinct departure from leading men of previous decades. With the rise of feminism, gay rights, and identity politics, Shepard serves, to a degree, as a "whitening" and "straightening" of the leading man paradigm. In the 1970s and 1980s, Shepard was often compared to such actors as Gary Cooper and Burt Lancaster, indicating that Shepard was a "throwback" of sorts to the days of traditional leading men who projected masculine heterosexuality that was uncomplicated by issues of ethnic and sexual identity. This equation also carries over to Shepard's writings. For some conservatives, Shepard's plays seemed to affirm heterosexuality and the patriarchal order. For some liberals, his plays worked as sly assaults upon the patriarchy and the American family.

To examine Shepard's persona in this latter period, it is useful to survey the details of his career in this Late Style. Indeed, Shepard's persona and writings are inextricably bound in his corpus. Following the play *A Lie of the Mind* (1985), Shepard added yet another hyphenate to his moniker of writer-actor. This time, it was the culmination of a lifetime of fascination with cinema. Shepard was now a film director.

When Shepard seemingly abandoned theater for film, hopes were high. Many critics believed that "film for Shepard may prove to be the final frontier, and American audiences may find that the writer regarded as the pre-eminent playwright of his generation may conceive the master works of his maturity not for the stage but for the silver screen" (Wade 148). But, that prediction would not become reality. When his directorial debut appeared, the film was met with critical confusion, inevitable head-scratching, and tepid box office. Shepard acted upon his artistic capital gained through work in theater and Hollywood and in turn produced a regional film focusing upon a family of women. *Far North* (1988) was the culmination of the desire to work with his domestic partner Jessica Lange. Gone were the violent confrontations between fathers and sons. Gone were the mythical imagery drawn from the American West. Gone were the expected "Shepardian" elements that had gained so much circulation in the textual communities appreciative of Shepard's theatrical endeavors. In all, *Far North* was an unexpected turn for Shepard.

Shepard's cinematic directorial debut *Far North* elicited little critical enthusiasm. Writing in *The New York Times*, Janet Maslin noted that "passages are more awkward, shapeless and uncertain. There is less sense of what the muted, oblique *Far North* actually is than of what it might have been" (1988). Indeed, Maslin's lamentation of the proverbial "missed opportunity" (1988) seems to predict subsequent critical assessments of Shepard's work from this period. Overall, Maslin concluded that "much of *Far North* is less weighty . . . though it never relaxes enough to become as fanciful as it apparently means to be" (1988). *The Village Voice*'s Katherine Dieckmann recognized that "unlike most of his plays . . . there's no sense of underlying rage, or even strong sentiment, save a warm-milk nostalgia for family (even if they're all nuts) and the good ol' days" (1988). Years later, *The New York Times'* Caryn James passingly referred to the film as a "facile comedy-drama" (1994). Overall, the film failed to establish Shepard as the next "Great American Film Director," yet the film marks the beginning of Shepard's Late Style.

Shepard's second attempt at directing found him creating a film with many of the elements one would expect from Shepard. Set in New Mexico territory during the late nineteenth century, *Silent Tongue* (1994) is a gothic period piece that utilizes familiar Shepardian tropes (father and son conflict, unexpected violence, the "reality" of mythological assumptions about history) to subvert and indict the cinematic Western genre. Caryn James of *The New York Times* praised the Western period piece as "eerie, inventive, poetic . . . Mr. Shepard's vision of the 19th century plains is unlike any other film maker's" (1994). For James, the film "signals a gigantic leap beyond" *Far North* and with *Silent Tongue* "he truly becomes a filmmaker" (1994). As the film was delayed in its release, James pointed out that "any picture that takes so long to be released arrives under a cloud of suspicion. This is the rare case in which the delay does not reflect how bad a film is, but how uncompromisingly good" (1994). Ann Powers, writing in *The Village Voice*, was not as rhapsodic, explaining that "Shepard's climaxes carry neither the strength not the intricacy the film demands" and that "it's all too operatic for the medium" (1994: 57). Highlighting what would become a concern with scholars regarding *Silent Tongue*, Powers explained that Shepard's desire to explore Native American women and their revenge upon men "falls short, because [Shepard's] heart remains with the pathetic fathers and their failing sons" (1994: 57).

Though *Silent Tongue* impressed many critics and played at the Cannes and Sundance Film Festivals, its subject matter and esoteric approach made it inaccessible to many. In addition, the death of actor River Phoenix (who portrayed the mentally unstable Talbot) before the film's release and the long shadow cast by the critically revered Western *Unforgiven*[2] (1992) perhaps contributed to its unenthusiastic reception by audiences. Following the commercial failure of *Silent Tongue*, it seemed as if Shepard's short tenure as a film director had suddenly been halted.

Though Shepard's experimentation with film directing was eventually viewed by many as a failure, his reconsideration of familiar themes through a media different than theater resulted in meaningful ruminations upon both gender (*Far North*) and colonialism (*Silent Tongue*). Indeed, as the Late Style of Shepard features nontheatrical media exploration and a reconsideration of issues previously established in his repertoire, these films serve as an intriguing opening point for his late career.

To many, it seemed as if Shepard had turned his back on theater to try his hand at directing in Hollywood in 1988. Though Shepard's two films failed to earn critical or popular adoration, Shepard's ventures into screen acting were much more celebrated. In all, Shepard's tenure as a screenwriter and director was much less illustrious than his career as a playwright, or even that of a motion-picture actor. When he returned to writing for the stage from his self-imposed exile to Hollywood, Shepard's cultural moment had not only waned, but it had fully passed. As if to signal a break from his previous family cycle and to boldly announce his return to theater, Shepard created the 1991 "Vaudeville Nightmare" play *States of Shock*. Never again would Shepard gain the popularity and critical adulation that he experienced during the family cycle. Indeed, Shepard's unsuccessful turn as film director and his less than celebrated return to playwriting with *States of Shock* marks the beginning of his Late Style, but within this period, we also see a shift in the Shepard persona itself.

Before his hiatus from theater, Shepard was cast as a leading man. Following his excursion into film directing, Shepard matured into other roles, most notably fatherly characters reserved for middle-aged men. The persona Shepard performs during this Late Style is a vital component of this period. Previously, the Shepard persona had traveled through various iterations, but still retained a few core conceits. The Shepard persona could be understood to be performatively masculine, seemingly self-reliant, out of step with the contemporary world, grounded in manual labor, reverential toward rural America, in praise of the authentic, dismissive of pretense, and scornful of the intellectualizing of art. These core components of his persona are further amended during the evocation of his Late Style persona. Though Shepard took a brief hiatus from playwriting, he never ceased performances in motion pictures. As a result, the Shepard persona continued in some form as a presence in American culture.

When he returned to playwriting with *States of Shock* (1992) he exhibited a calm, mature persona who accepted his role as an aging "man of letters." While he transitioned into more mature acting roles, primarily that of father figures, his Late Style fatherly persona is further supported by professional and personal relationships with younger filmmakers and actors such as Michael Almereyda and Ethan Hawke. Though Shepard is not as prolific a writer for the stage as he once was, he has published collections of prose and even became the recipient of honors bestowed on esteemed writers, including recognition from PEN, La Mama, and the Chicago Humanities Council. It is apparent that Shepard has comfortably settled into the paternal "man of letters."

A key component to understanding the Shepard persona, as previously noted, is rooted in his performances as an actor. Though Shepard originally worked in theater as an actor in the early 1960s, he first garnered acclaim in the medium as a playwright. He returned briefly to the stage with Patti Smith in *Cowboy Mouth* (1971), but avoided live stage performance for more than thirty years following that play. In *Cowboy Mouth* Shepard portrayed a young musician who falls under the spell of a mysterious woman (Patti Smith). Shepard and Smith wrote the play together and it more or less chronicled their own tumultuous affair that had strained Shepard's marriage. In essence, art and life intersected on stage in a calamitous fashion for all in the New York theater scene to witness. Following that aborted production, Shepard (with his wife in tow) fled to Europe.

As previously discussed, as Shepard wrote the more accessible family cycle plays of the 1970s and 1980s, he began to work regularly as an actor in motion pictures. Shepard's ascendancy as a "Great American Playwright" paralleled his success as an actor on-screen. At this time, Shepard moved from being a supporting actor (*Days of Heaven*) to a leading man (*The Right Stuff*, *Baby Boom*, and *Fool for Love*). He also occasionally served as a supporting character in adaptations of plays, such as the film versions of *Crimes of the Heart* (1986) and *Steel Magnolias* (1989). As noted, Shepard took a hiatus from writing for the stage to pursue film writing and directing. During this time he also shifted his on-screen persona from that of the cool, composed, and rugged Gary Cooper-type to that of a father figure. This transition is notable in two otherwise unexceptional films: *The Pelican Brief* (1993) and *Safe Passage* (1994). In *The Pelican Brief*, based on the legal thriller by John Grisham, Shepard portrays law professor Thomas Callahan. Though far older than his student Darby Shaw (Julia Roberts), Callahan continues an affair with her until he meets his demise through a car bomb. In this role, Shepard simultaneously portrays the love interest and a father figure/mentor to Roberts.

In *Safe Passage*, Shepard makes the full transition from leading man to father figure. The film stars Susan Sarandon as Maggie Singer, the matriarch of a family completely composed of males. Shepard is the neglectful husband that Sarandon is considering leaving. When the family learns that a son has gone missing during the bombing of a US Marines barracks, the clan comes together over the loss. As the often absent patriarch, Shepard comforts the family, offers advice, and emerges as a solid caring force, emotionally available both to his wife and to his sons. Elements of the film (a missing son/soldier, a family on the home front, a homosocial environment) would be later echoed in *Brothers* (2009). In both *The Pelican Brief* and *Safe Passage*, Shepard abandons his filmic persona of a leading man, love interest in favor of that of a mentor and father.

A unique paradox of Shepard in this late period is that he gained wide recognition and currency not through his writings, but through his acting in film. Prior to analyzing specific roles that help to construct the late Shepard persona, it is beneficial to address how the dynamics of the

Shepard persona interplay with both Shepard's writings and Shepard's performances. Through his various turns in supporting and character roles in motion pictures, ranging from Hollywood blockbusters and mediocre direct-to-video films to prestige motion pictures and celebrated independent productions, it is safe to assume that most viewers of a film that features Shepard are unaware of his voluminous literary output. That said, it is also safe to assume that most audience members who attended New York productions of *The God of Hell* and *Ages of the Moon* were not among the vast audiences clambering to see the multimillion dollar, critically panned film *Stealth* (2005). That said, even a film such as *Stealth* contributes to the construction of the Shepard persona.

The motion picture *Stealth* centers upon jet pilots and their battle with an out-of-control artificial intelligence piloting a jet. Shepard is featured in a major supporting role as a commander of the elite pilots, Capt. George Cummings. Those who occupy a position in the Shepard "textual community" can find their understanding of Shepard's corpus enriched through an intertextual reading of Shepard products. For example, Shepard as a pilot in *Stealth*, regardless of the film's unabashedly low-brow intentions, ties directly with Shepard's acclaimed work as the legendary test pilot Chuck Yeager in *The Right Stuff*. These roles as pilots also directly link to Shepard's own biography, as Shepard's father was a pilot. Shepard as Cummings is essentially an aged and mature Yeager. Once interpreted within these various interconnecting texts, Shepard's role in *Stealth* emerges as yet another figure that links with dynamics that seemingly fascinate Shepard, such as codes of masculinity. Indeed, beyond Shepard's role as a pilot, the film itself has echoes of Shepard's own written work. *Stealth*'s premise concerns a military-developed, renegade technology that threatens humanity. This concept connects directly to Shepard's 1969 play *Operation Sidewinder*, which featured— among many other elements—a giant, mechanized snake developed by the military that threatens humanity.

A film that helped to further establish the later Shepard persona is 2001's film *Black Hawk Down*, based on the nonfiction work by

Mark Bowden, which concerns a disastrous excursion by the US military in Somalia. Within this military setting, the film divides the men into two groups: the officers and the soldiers. The officers remain at the base, far from the conflict, while the soldiers are on the ground engaging the enemy. This is further delineated through the casting, as the officers are inevitably middle-aged men, while the soldiers themselves are youthful and inexperienced. Visually, this contrasts the two generations of characters, as well as actors. In *Black Hawk Down*, Shepard portrays Major General William F. Garrison, a man of great power and responsibility who is the commander in charge of the mission. Like the Shepard persona, Garrison is cool, calm, and fatherly. Garrison remains steady and professional even in the face of disaster. Depicting these men under pressure allows Shepard to exhibit the Howard Hawkes-ian credo of professionalism as a virtue of masculinity. This professionalism is an expectation in the military, as well as a cherished ideal in the Hollywood Western. Through Shepard's nuanced, emotional minimalism, the viewer understands the conflicted nature of Garrison: he has sent young men into a hostile environment and is unable to extract them and bring them to safety. As a father figure he remains couched in a masculinity that reveals little emotion. The biographic element of the Shepard persona—that Shepard's own father was a military man—informs his performance and the archetype of the military father figure that would be further explored in *Brothers*.

The year 2000 brought forth an intriguing role for Shepard: he was to perform in a Shakespeare production. Michael Almereyda's interpretation of *Hamlet* features a coterie of Hollywood actors and updates the play to the then present day-world of high pressure finance in Manhattan. Shepard appears briefly in the film, portraying the ghost of Hamlet's (Ethan Hawke) father. When he utters "Remember me," members of the Shepard textual community cannot help but interpret his ghostly turn as a reanimating of Shepard's own father as well as an intertextual link to Shepard's other fathers across various writings. Shepard's plays and prose have often centered upon the tension between a father and his son. This is evident in such early plays as

The Rock Garden (1964) as well as later work such as *States of Shock* and *The Late Henry Moss*. This is further informed by Shepard's tumultuous relationship with his own father, which has been detailed in multiple biographies, as well as in *Motel Chronicles* and the documentary *This So-Called Disaster*. Shepard's father was an abusive alcoholic and much of the playwright's work reflects his father and their relationship. Through playing theater's most famous dead father, Shepard once again involved himself in the dyadic relationship between father and son, while adding to the intertextuality of his own corpus. The performance can also be read as an extension of the ghost father figure from *Fool for Love* (1983). In many ways, Shepard portrays a variation of his own father and his theatrical patriarchs, making unreasonable demands and voicing expectations to a faithful, but confused son. Yet, this *Hamlet*'s New York setting and Shepard's wearing of dark clothes (such as a trenchcoat) are also a reference to those widely circulated photographs of the dark, existential Shepard of the early 1960s. Indeed, the paradox of an actor associated with "American-ness" and open vistas reciting Shakespeare among the skyscrapers of Manhattan creates a unique effect that not only underlines the "out of time and space" (or as Hamlet states, "out of joint") quality of the Shepard persona in this setting, but also harks back to his early days in New York City as a young playwright. Indeed, the mixture of the "old" and the "modern" qualities of the production correlate effectively with the Shepard persona. Shepard in *Hamlet* serves the persona as pointing toward the familiar (father and dress), while the timbre and echoes of the Shakespearean utterances are unfamiliar.

As with *Black Hawk Down*, Shepard finds himself cast alongside multiple generations of actors. This cinematic adaptation of *Hamlet* itself would lead to two very fruitful collaborations. The director, Michael Almereyda, would eventually film the rehearsals and performances of *The Late Henry Moss* and construct the documentary *This So-Called Disaster: Sam Shepard Directs "The Late Henry Moss"* (2004). Also, the actor portraying Hamlet, Ethan Hawke, has long been associated with Shepard productions, from his turns in the New York stagings of *Buried Child* and *The Late Henry Moss* to his directing of the 2010 revival of *A Lie of the Mind*. In a sense, the persona of Shepard has shifted from that of a young man to that of a father figure both on the screen and among other actors and filmmakers.

The Assassination of Jesse James By the Coward Robert Ford (2010) serves as a fusion of various elements integral to the late Shepard persona. The work itself is based on the critically revered 1983 novel by Ron Hansen that explores elements of the historical Western figure Jesse James. Shepard portrays the older brother Frank James, who serves less as a sibling and more as a father figure in the outlaw's life. Though Jesse is the leader of the gang, Frank is a revered advisor and voice of sensibility. As Jesse James, Brad Pitt is at times relaxed and fun-loving, but also violent and moody. As Frank, Shepard once again embodies a "professionalism" of the character. Frank James, historically speaking, was educated, dallied in intellectual pursuits, and was recognized as a "gentleman" of sorts. Shepard's interpretation of the character conveys a grimacing seriousness and stolidity that counters Pitt's smiling and reckless wild child. As in *Black Hawk Down*, Shepard's father-like character advises the young, but witnesses through clinched teeth the mistakes that bring about their destruction.

Of this late period, perhaps Shepard's most revealing performance is the film *Brothers*. *Brothers* concerns two siblings: Captain Sam Cahill (Tobey Maguire) and Tommy Cahill (Jake Gyllenhall). Their father Hank Cahill (Sam Shepard) is a hard-driving, hard-drinking former military officer who proudly basks in Sam's military service, while dismissing the ne'er-do-well Tommy. When Sam is deployed, Tommy remains stateside. Sam goes missing while on a mission and is presumed dead. Sam's wife eventually falls in love with Tommy. Having assumed that he is dead, the family is shocked to learn that Sam is actually alive. When Sam returns home he is forced to reckon with his own post-traumatic stress disorder and confront the seeming betrayals by both his brother and wife.

Certain tropes in this film reflect upon Shepard's work as an actor as well as his work as a writer. The film centers upon a conflict between two brothers, as well as the conflict between sons and a father. This intertextual, thematic reference reminds the textual community of *True West* and *The Late Henry Moss*, among other works depicting sibling combat. The father-son conflict recalls Shepard's own biography as well as plays such as *Curse of the Starving Class*. The film also concerns the military, a homosocial environment in which assumed masculine attributes are viewed as mandatory. An element of Shepard's character also surfaces in Hank's alcoholism. Eerily reminiscent of Shepard's own father, Hank is an ex-military man who now drowns his sorrows in hard liquor. A pivotal scene of the film centers upon the drunk and mourning Hank confronting his son Tommy. In the eyes of Hank, Tommy has not fulfilled his promise as a man. The father believes that the "better" son was killed. Shepard's role is key to understanding the film. Indeed, the relationship between the sons and their father offers further commentary on the differences between the war in Vietnam (of which Shepard's character is a veteran) and the invasion of Afghanistan and Iraq.

Brothers recalls other military roles portrayed by Shepard (such as in *Black Hawk Down* or *Stealth*) while also allowing Shepard to assume the role of the grieving father whose son has disappeared as a result of a military incident (as in *Safe Passage*). In addition, his father role echoes that of the Colonel in *States of Shock*. In both, the father is proud of his "dead" son. When the son in each work is revealed to be alive, both fathers endure a form of shame and disgrace. In *States of Shock*, the Colonel's disappointment at his own son's survival is voiced in dialogue and action. In *Brothers*, the father is relieved that his son is alive, yet this is tempered by the embarrassment and disgrace of his son's psychological state. Like the colonel in *States of Shock*, Hank is not able to appropriate the traditional, nationalistic narrative of the father who valiantly sacrificed his son for the nation. In fact, the returned Sam is caught in a limbo of sorts—he is physically present, but psychologically absent. The narrative of the father who sacrifices his son for the nation gains admiration, while the narrative of the son returning either physically (*States of Shock*) or psychologically (*Brothers*) damaged is regarded as shameful. The pride of the father, following a code of masculinity, allows for the sacrifice of the son to be seen as a great symbol of devotion and fidelity to one's nation. When that son returns, the "glorious" narrative of war and sacrifice is ruptured and the idealism of battle and conflict collapses into the reality of "dead" limbs (*States of Shock*) and "dead" minds (*Brothers*).

Since 2009's *Brothers*, Shepard has acted in more and more high-profile and critically lauded films. Of these, *Blackthorn* (2011), *Mud* (2012), *Out of the Furnace* (2013), and *Cold in July* (2014) stand as projects that not only exhibit the depth of Shepard's performance abilities, but also serve to further solidify the Shepard persona while tying his own legacy to a subsequent generation of performers. In essence, Shepard's presence in these films not only grants the productions a sense of artistic credibility and "authenticity" but also serve to boost the cache of performers who wish to also cement their legacy as "artists" rather than celebrities.

Though the film *Blackthorn* does not attempt to align Shepard with a younger performer grasping for artistic integrity, the film does connect the legend of Butch Cassidy, the subject of the film, to Shepard's persona. The motion picture emerges as a kind of *uber* intertext of Shepard's work. Though Shepard himself did not write the screenplay, his enthusiasm for the project (he is quoted as stating that this was one of the best screenplays he had ever read) and its references to the author/actor's corpus make the film one of significance within Shepard's late career.

In the film, Shepard portrays the famed outlaw Butch Cassidy. Historically, Butch Cassidy was a bandit who targeted big banks and corporations, not individuals. In addition, he and his partner went out of their way to avoid violence. As a result, Butch Cassidy achieved a certain amount of celebrity in his own lifetime. As many filmgoers know, Butch Cassidy has a filmic life of his own, embodied by Paul Newman in George Roy Hill's (1969) *Butch Cassidy and the Sundance Kid*. The film, a light-hearted celebration/spoof of Westerns, achieved both critical and popular success and forever linked Newman and Robert Redford to those cinematic roles. Hill's film concludes with a freeze frame of Butch and Sundance storming out a door to face the Bolivian army, with their fates unknown.

The on-screen text preface to *Blackthorn* explains that in 1908 Butch Cassidy and the Sundance Kid were supposedly killed in Bolivia, yet recent DNA tests upon the presumed bodies have revealed no linkage to present-day descendants of the two men. In flashbacks interspersed throughout the film, we are shown what happened after their supposed deaths. In fact, according to *Blackthorn*, Butch and Sundance escaped the siege. Sundance later died of injuries, but Butch drifted into anonymity, assuming the name James Blackthorn to work quietly as a horse breeder in rural Bolivia.

The film opens in 1927 with Butch composing a letter to his nephew, whom we later learn is actually his son. Butch is preparing to leave his adopted home of Bolivia and return to the United States. He goes to town, retrieves his money from the bank, and, on his return, is ambushed in the middle of the desert. Butch's horse—which has all of his money—flees in fear. Butch finds a desperate Spaniard who is on the run from a group of men. He explains that he has stolen money from a corrupt mine owner and exploiter of local indigenous people. If Butch assists in his escape to safety, the man will award Butch a sizable amount of the money.

Many trademark images from Shepard's work are presented in the film. Of course, there is the recurring thematic aspect of duality and friendship. The audience learns that Butch lost his identity with the death of Sundance. When the Spaniard enters his life—and proposes a deal to earn a great heft of money—Butch relocates his true identity within a partnership. As with many of Shepard's written characters, a man can only find a definition of himself through bonding with another man. And, as in many Shepard-penned works, this friendship involves faith, but also betrayal. Regardless of the enmity, the protagonist must have a counterpoint—be it friend (as in *Ages of the Moon*) or enemy (as in *When the World was Green*)—that gives his own life meaning. Unlike with Sundance, who reciprocated the emotions, we learn that the Spaniard's quest to wrestle money from a wealthy industrial miner has been a façade and in actuality, the Spaniard has stolen the money from the peasants themselves.

There are also sly elements recognizable to the Shepard cult, such as Shepard riding his own horses, speaking Spanish, and strumming a guitar and singing a little ditty with the refrain "Kiss my ass—I'm Samuel." These are all actions that the Shepard persona regularly performs. The imagery reminds one not only of the iconic images from the Western genre, but also specific images and concepts seemingly culled from Shepard's plays. These include: the dead horse and stranded man in the desert from *Kicking a Dead Horse*; the predictive nature of horse breeding from *Simpatico*; the lush green flora from *Eyes for Consuela*; the absent father who has abandoned the family from *The Late Henry Moss*; and, indigenous people initially interpreted as a threatening Other, only to be realized as less "savage" than the forces of modernity as in *Silent Tongue*. Butch's independence—as with so many Shepard characters—is eventually valorized. He says, "I've been my own man. Nothing richer than that." In addition, the casting of frequent Shepard collaborator Stephen Rea in a supporting role further solidifies the binds between this work and Shepard.

The deleted scenes of the film reveal that *Blackthorn* originally possessed yet another intertextual link to Shepard and his persona. In an excised ending, the final shot of the film concluded with a close-up on a grizzled Butch on horseback. As the camera pulls back, the audience realizes that this is a Butch who is a little older and he is actually part of a gang high up in the mountains. The camera pulls back even further to reveal that this is the set of a silent film and Butch is now a bit player in the motion-picture industry. Butch did indeed survive and made a return to the United States and has presumably located work portraying a Hollywoodized version of himself. In all, *Blackthorn* reveals itself to be a motion picture that resonates with elements from Shepard's corpus, be that his written work, his previous performances, or even his iconic persona.

Directed and written by Jeff Nichols, 2012's *Mud* takes place on the Arkansas banks of the Mississippi River. Mud (Matthew McConaughey), a fugitive from the law, has escaped and now lives in a makeshift boat on an island on the Mississippi. He is discovered by two boys, Ellis and Neckbone. The boys, drawn by Mud's passion for his former love Juniper, agree to help him. Mud, they learn, killed a man drawn to Juniper. Unfortunately, that man was connected to organized crime and the crime family has descended upon the area looking for Mud. Shepard portrays the grizzled Tom Blankenship, a man with a mysterious past who once served as a father figure to Mud. Blankenship lost both his wife and child during childbirth and took to mentoring Mud during his formative years. The film, which works as a modern rumination on elements culled from *The Adventures of Huckleberry Finn*, involves issues of masculinity and maturity wrapped into a crime thriller. The world itself features icons of Shepard's own works: cheap hotels, a rural setting, boots, guns, criminals, fishing, motorcycles, inexpensive housing (such as motorhomes and house boats), boys exploring nature, and men rebelling against the conventions of society while relishing the freedom of the natural world. Indeed, thirty years ago the character of Mud could have easily been portrayed by Shepard himself.

The film also resonates with father/son dynamics. Ellis and his father argue and fight about issues of duty and maturity; Mud and Blankenship work through their differences and regret; even the crime family from Texas, in which a father is seeking vengeance for his now dead son, meditates on such relationships. Indeed, the dynamic between Ellis and his father resonates with a Shepardian tension. Ellis longs to assert his own identity and seize his freedom while his father is quiet, passive, reserved, yet loving. Only when the father's masculinity is threatened by his wife—and the quality of his role as a father questioned—does the father react with anger, asserting his masculinity.

The Blankenship character is archetypal of recent turns by Shepard, in that he is an older man with military experience, a tragic loner who finds himself making demands of other men when they do not live up to his personal code of masculinity. Blankenship scorns Mud for his obsession with Juniper and his plan to escape to the Gulf of Mexico by way of a repaired boat. Begrudgingly, Blankenship helps Mud with his scheme and eventually saves Mud's life through his expertise with a rifle. As with other men portrayed by Shepard in film during this most recent period, masculinity must be proven through a test of sorts. At the conclusion of the film, it is believed that Blankenship and Mud have perished in the siege perpetrated by the crime family. A short epilogue shows Blankenship and Mud—prodigal son and father figure—commandeering a rickety boat from the Mississippi into the vast open waters of the Gulf of Mexico, assuring both of the men freedom.

Shepard returned as a "father figure" in director Scott Cooper's *Out of the Furnace*, a 2013 crime drama set among the workers of Pennsylvania steel country. Shepard portrays the father figure Gerald "Red" Baze, uncle to Russell (Christian Bale) and Rodney (Casey Affleck, a former castmate of Shepard in *The Assassination of Jesse James by the Coward Robert Ford*). Russell holds down a job and Rodney goes on various military tours to the Middle East, even as their father ails as a result of his decades at the steel mill. Rodney suffers from the physical and emotional injuries of combat, as evidenced by the long scar that snakes down his chest (similar to the torso scars seen in both *States of Shock* and *Heartless*). Rodney is also haunted by visions of atrocities he witnessed.

Arrested and sentenced to prison for manslaughter following a drunken automobile accident, Russell is separated from his family. When Russell emerges from prison, his father has died and his brother Rodney has fallen into serious gambling debt. To help defer the costs of his gambling, Rodney has turned to illegal bare-knuckle boxing. In desperation, Rodney cuts a deal with a rural New Jersey organized crime syndicate, led by Woody Harrelson, to take a dive in a match. Though Rodney takes the fall, he is killed by the gang. Russell, learning that his brother has disappeared, recruits "Red" (Shepard) to head into the mountains to investigate. Once the perpetrators are discovered, Russell and "Red" devise a plan to enact vengeance.

Out of the Furnace reunites Shepard with former collaborators (Affleck and Harrelson), while also forging a new screen relationship with Christian Bale. Bale, known to cineastes for his intense approach toward acting, is familiar to the larger public as the face behind the cowl of Batman in Christopher Nolan's *Dark Knight* trilogy. Like McConaughey, Bale is asserting his authenticity and building artistic credibility by appearing on-screen with Shepard in a "serious" piece of cinema. The film also wades into the familiar themes of Shepard's own work, with the battle between two brothers and the impact of violence upon a family.

As with *Out of the Furnace*, Jim Mickle's *Cold in July* (2014) features men working together to right some wrong of violence through their own acts of violence. Based on Joe Lansdale's 1989 novel of the same, *Cold in July* takes place in East Texas. A mild-mannered picture framer Richard Dane (Michael C. Hall) awakens one night to a sound emanating from his living room. He nervously grabs his handgun and creeps into the den only to discover an intruder. Richard shoots and kills the man. The police assure Richard that the victim was a known criminal named Freddy Price. The police are also surprised that "a man like" Richard "had it in" him to take a man's life. For many in the community, the soft-spoken Richard is seen—at least by East Texas standards—as masculine-deficient. To complicate matters, Freddy's father Ben (Sam Shepard) has just been released from prison. Sure enough, the aggrieved father begins to stalk the family, threatening to take the life of Richard's son as retribution. There are break-ins and bullets left in the child's bed. While visiting the police station, Richard eyes a wanted poster for Freddy Price. Richard notices that the photograph on the flier does not match the man he killed. Ben is taken into custody. Now suspicious of the police, Richard stakes out the police station.

Late one night, Richard watches as the police escort Ben to a train track, knock him out, and leave him there to be killed by a train, only to be discovered as an "accident." Seizing the moment, Richard pulls Ben off the tracks and takes him back to his cabin. Skeptical of Richard's assertion that the man he killed was not Freddy, the two dig up Freddy's grave and discover that the corpse is not Freddy's. Feeling the draw of a masculine adventure, Richard pledges to help Ben locate his son. As a result, Ben grows to be a father figure of sorts for Richard and Richard, in turn, morphs into the son Ben has never known. With the help of private investigator Jim Bob (Don Johnson), the trio track Freddy to the Houston area. In a freak accident outside of Freddy's home, the men discover a VHS tape. The videotape features Freddy—very much alive—killing a woman.

Upon viewing the snuff film, Ben realizes that he no longer desires to reunite with his son, but rather that he must now kill his son. Ben, an ex-con, has his own code and Freddy's murder of women violates that code. Learning that Freddy is part of a witness protection and relocation program, the men decide to track Freddy and murder him. In a mission similar to that found in *Out of the Furnace*, the men tactically invade a compound and murder all present. Ben saves Richard's life but Ben is killed, as is Freddy. As the film ends, Richard returns home, forever altered by this test of masculinity.

In sum, *Cold in July* serves as a further exemplification of Shepard's persona written across the screen. A hardened, wise—and at times threatening—presence that serves as a mentor to a younger man enduring trials of masculinity. These trials are almost always enacted through violence. Further, these late screen presences create a genealogy of sorts, pairing popular actors (McConaughey, Bale, Affleck, and Hall) with Shepard not only builds the younger performers' artistic credibility, but also allows Shepard, in a sense, to help mentor, forge their artistic identities. As of early 2015, Shepard was a cast member on the critically lauded Netflix series *Bloodline*, alongside such acclaimed younger actors as Kyle Chandler, Ben Mendelsohn, and Norbert Leo Butz. The drama chronicles the Rayburn family, a wealthy Florida clan whose troubled, prodigal son has returned. His reappearance exposes long-buried secrets from the past and exposes ruptures between the many family members. With its focus on family tensions, a powerful patriarch, and sibling conflict, the series is a further development of Shepardian themes, while allowing Shepard as a performer to hone his character—and in turn, his persona—over multiple episodes.

Beyond restructuring his persona during this phase into a father figure perpetually demonstrating a calm, restrained masculinity,

Shepard also returned to live theater for the first time in decades in the 2004 New York City production of Caryl Churchill's *A Number*. By associating himself with Churchill, Shepard (1) furthered his acting persona as a father figure and (2) associated himself with one of the most intriguing dramatists of the day. A tertiary effect of Shepard's performance was a new American attention directed toward Churchill. Though she has achieved acclaim and notoriety through plays such as *Cloud 9* (1979), Churchill has never been a playwright with popular, wide recognition in the United States. In the 2000s, productions were mounted that brought Churchill to large audiences in New York City. Most notably, Manhattan Theatre Club's 2008 production *Top Girls* featured Marisa Tomei and Martha Plimpton, while *A Number* heralded Shepard's return to acting on the stage. *A Number* is short and minimal. It concerns Salter (Shepard) who clones his son. Through the various encounters between the father and the cloned sons, the nature of identity and individuality is investigated and the play carefully deconstructs the notion of fatherhood. The play asks certain questions, such as "What is a father?" and "How are relations between father and son determined?" In addition, the play probes the hereditary influence of the father upon the son. In essence, the play performatively analyzes how a son may be doomed to repeat the actions of the father through biology. The power of genetics may not allow a son to veer from the destructive past of his father. This notion certainly reverberates through Shepard's own plays.

Prior to performing the role of Salter in the 2004 New York Theatre Workshop's production of Caryl Churchill's *A Number*, Shepard had previously confessed to a fear of performing before a live audience as an actor, explaining that he found the experience of confronting large groups of people "too spooky." Shepard's return to the stage as an actor after more than a thirty-year absence garnered stellar reviews. Ben Brantley termed Shepard "terrific" and concluded that Shepard "turns out to be an ideal interpreter of Ms. Churchill's disjunctive prose. . . Her fragmented dialogue flows from him like blood from an opened vein" (2004).

With his return to the stage, Shepard is once again engaging in an investigation of notions of authenticity. Live theater has long held a more esteemed cultural position than either film or television. For example, the trade paper *Variety* tallies the theater reviews and box office reports under the banner "Legit." When film and television actors are eager to prove their "chops" (i.e., talent, artistic integrity, or authenticity as a performer), they often seek out work on the stage. The stage serves to provide the celebrity with a venue to demonstrate their abilities without the mediatization afforded by film and television. For Geraghty, stage work by the celebrity-actor "takes on a particular importance as a way for film stars to claim legitimate space in the overcrowded world of celebrity status" (2007: 104). By returning to the stage, Shepard demonstrates a willingness to challenge himself as a performer, who is now, presumably, accustomed to film acting. Shepard's age also comes into this equation, as Geraghty notes in the following remarks:

> The emphasis on performance works well, in fact, for the aging star since it has the added merit of valuing experience and allowing a career to continue well beyond the pin-up stage. . . . The revival of Al Pacino's career and the continuance of De Niro's owes much to the sense of older performers displaying well-honed skills and passing on their knowledge to the younger actors around them. (2007: 104)

As noted, by seizing this opportunity Shepard has been able to add this role to his corpus, reaffirming his position as an investigator—not only as a writer and film actor, but also a stage performer—of the dynamics between father and son. The stage work also allows Shepard to demonstrate his "authenticity" as an actor. Though Geraghty contends that the stage acting endeavors by mature actors allow them to pass their skills to the subsequent generations, this influence is already seen in Shepard through his working with such next-generation performers as Sean Penn, Woody Harrelson, and Ethan Hawke. Indeed, through Shepard's extensive work with Joseph Chaikin, and then Shepard's own involvement with directing, Shepard has enabled various approaches to performance to be conveyed to a younger generation of theater makers. In essence, as Shepard eased into the roles of fathers on-screen, he was also enacting a type of artistic fatherhood for young actors. Previously, Shepard developed relationships with actors that were in close proximity to his age, such as Ed Harris and James Gammon. Even today, Shepard himself continues to possess great artistic capital beyond his cultural moment of the 1980s, able to attract a wide array of acclaimed performers willing to sacrifice wages simply to work with him, regardless of whether the work achieves a prestigious production. For *The Late Henry Moss*, Shepard directed younger actors such as Sean Penn and Woody Harrelson. In addition, even younger actors such as Ethan Hawke, Vincent D'Onofrio, Phillip Seymour Hoffman, and John C. Reilly have gravitated toward Shepard's work in revival. In a sense, Shepard's unofficial tutelage of these actors has allowed certain folkways and approaches (such as Joseph Chaikin's transformative exercises that Shepard learned at the Open Theater) to filter, both directly and indirectly, into a new generation of film, television, and theater actors.

Beyond acting as a father figure to various "sons" in the theater (as they are almost all exclusively male), a trait of Shepard's Late Style is that he provides resolutions to dilemmas previously encountered in his work. With this period, Shepard has moved into father roles and is in reality himself a father. Shepard's earlier work examined the strife between the petulant, rebellious son and the overbearing father. Indeed, Shepard himself has a strange and conflicted relationship with the notion of his own role as a father in its many iterations. Shepard's father was abusive and alcoholic, but—according to Shepard—also had moments of wisdom and clarity. The late Shepard persona continues to interrogate and examine the notion of the father, but Shepard has now transformed into the father figure himself. Though these later works continue to feature rebellious sons (*The Late Henry Moss* and *Don't Come Knocking*, for example), the father figures are developed with more empathy. Though fathers have long represented a destructive force in Shepard's plays, this Late Style allows for a nuanced interrogation of the father, and in some instances allows for the father to reckon and reconcile with past sins and actions. The supportive, healing vision of the father is visualized on the cover of *The Great Dream of Heaven* in which a father is fishing on a pier with a child. Fathers are no longer the embodiment of destruction, but can also function as teachers and peacemakers. As Shepard has matured into fatherly roles, the patriarchs of his writings now emerge as textured, yet not wholly sympathetic.

As stated, Shepard is not as prolific as in his early days, but he still regularly writes and stages new plays and has published a number of short prose works. The Late Style of Shepard is also marked by bold experimentation in dramatic modes as well as genre. Like Tennessee Williams, whose later works (until their recent resuscitation) were dismissed as imitative of avant-garde European plays, Shepard continues to explore various forms for the stage. In all, the late career Shepard has written a farce, political works, an extended monologue, an adaptation of a Mexican short story, a Brechtian inspired "nightmare" play, a few Beckettian pieces, and even another family saga. During this period he has also written screenplays, songs (with Bob Dylan), poetry, and numerous short stories, while also revisiting (and revising) such works as *Tooth of Crime* (1972). In addition, Shepard's contribution to the New York scene of the 1960s and 1970s gained new resonance as his persona of "Slim" was an integral component of Patti Smith's revered memoir *Just Kids* (2010). In all, the Late Style Shepard is an artist who has passed his cultural moment, yet still engages his artistic talents in new and exciting ways.

During this period, Shepard has also begun to carve out space for himself within literary and theatrical genealogy. The Shepard persona before the Late Style often displayed a certain antipathy toward the theater. For example, a 1971 program note from the playwright reads, "First off let me tell you that I don't want to be a playwright. I want to be a rock and roll star" (Bottoms 1998: 66). More bluntly, Shepard has also stated, "I hate the fucking theatre" (Wade 1997: 138). Part of this suspicion of theater resides in an anti-theatrical prejudice couched in Shepard's understanding of theater as antithetical to the authentic. This is a result of his valorization of rock and roll culture's notion of authenticity and the assumption of inauthenticity present in theater, as explored in the next chapter. In addition, Shepard's evocation of a masculine, instinctual, and heterosexual writer seems at odds with certain intellectual and queer aspects of theater. In the program notes for *Cowboy Mouth*, Shepard explains, "A lot of people think playwrights are some special brand of intellectual fruit cake with special answers to special problems that confront the world at large. I think that's a crock of shit" (Bottoms 1998: 270). Indeed, Shepard has consistently positioned himself outside of theater and stage culture.

In this Late Style, Shepard seems to have embraced his work in the theater. Regarding his former dream of rock stardom, Shepard noted in 1994 that being a rock star is the "last thing I'd want to be now" (Brantley 1994). In 2004, Shepard even walked back those earlier, abrasive comments regarding theater, noting, "It's a little brash to say I hate theatre. I don't make it a regular habit of going to theatre" (Shewey 2004: 23), adding that "I'm not quite sure who goes to the theatre anymore" (Shewey 2004: 82). That said, in that same interview, Shepard showed that he was hopelessly out of touch with contemporary theater, noting that he did not know the work of Suzan-Lori Parks and that his idea of political theater was Clifford Odets. Once again, Shepard has positioned himself as an outsider, aloof to the events of contemporary theater. Through the decades, Shepard seems to have made some sort of peace with theater, explaining that "the relationship between actor and audience; that moment-by-moment hanging in the balance, the terror of the moment . . . theater combines everything, for me, anyway" (Brantley 1994). This was reaffirmed ten years later when the playwright told *American Theatre*, "I can't think of another art form that combines so many elements and has so many possibilities" (Shewey 2004: 23).

Though Shepard has continued to portray himself as outside theater, he has never been reticent in citing his influences. That said, Shepard's many influences are not limited to the literary or theatrical world. Reflecting his deep affinity with notions of authenticity and a fascination with American history, Shepard often cites rock and jazz musicians, as well as abstract expressionists and mythic figures from both pop culture and American history as inspiration. This citationality stretches from his earliest works to the present. Yet, these citations have grown and altered from his early days to the present. His early, wildly heterogeneous and esoteric citations are rooted in Shepard's attempt to "explor[e] the writing of plays through attitudes derived from other forms such as music, painting, sculpture, film, etc. . . . I've been influenced by Jackson Pollock, Little Richard, Cajun fiddles and the Southwest" (Rosen 2004: 30). His text of 1969's *Operation Sidewinder* included an inscription dedicating the work to "Michaelangelo Antonioni, Crazy Horse, The Rolling Stones and Gabby Hayes" while in *Cowboy Mouth* (1971) the character of Slim, originally portrayed by Shepard, proclaims, "I love horse racing and stock cars. I love the Rolling Stones. I love Bridgette Bardot. I love Marlon Brando and James Dean and Stan Laurel and Wilson Pickett and Jimmie Rodgers and Bob Dylan and The Who and Jesse James and Crazy Horse and the Big Bopper and Nina Simone and Jackson Pollock and Muhammud Ali" (Shewey 1997: 74). In *Hawk Moon* (1973), Shepard rejects standardized grammar and writes, "Rock and Roll made movies theatre books painting and art go out the window none of it stands a chance against The Who The Stones and old Yardbirds Credence Traffic The Velvet Underground Janis and Jimi" (55). In the late period of 1988–2015, the influence and citations have moved from the popular and decidedly nontheatrical to the literary and theatrical. As explored later in this project, Shepard—just as he had earlier in his career aligned himself with rock musicians and rebels—has in this Late Style purposefully aligned himself with those two titans of twentieth-century theater—Beckett and Brecht.

Though Shepard long struck the pose of a naïf who stumbled into literature, the late Shepard is quite conscious of how he is inscribing himself into the annals of American letters. Shepard had previously utilized elements that specifically referenced other writers or artists, but Shepard's first play of this late period (*States of Shock*) consciously appropriates elements from Beckett's *Endgame*, most notably the use of a wheelchair and the dynamic between the infirm and the caregiver. Unlike Beckett, Shepard uses devices and techniques often associated with Brecht (such as shrieking whistles, thunderous drums, and bright flashes of light) to disrupt and shatter emotional continuity to push the audience/spectator to reflect upon the action depicted on stage. In more recent plays of the Late Style, Shepard has tied himself to Beckettian imagery and modes of stagecraft. Shepard summons elements from Beckett during this period in *Kicking a Dead Horse* (a man alone in the desert) and *Ages of the Moon* (two worn-out men waiting for a lunar event).

Shepard's appropriation of Beckett is not manifest on the stage alone. As Boris Kachka in a *New York* magazine article pointed out, the late Shepard is "looking not quite so countrified as you'd imagine"; instead, "as Shepard ages, he looks more and more like Beckett—the squinting eyes, the deep furrows, the air of shrugging amusement" (2008). The article concludes with Shepard remarking that Beckett's "mind is awesome. . . . Beckett turned my head around about thinking about theater. It doesn't have to be realistic, it doesn't have to be buried in this cause and effect, it doesn't have to be . . . dull" (Kachka 2008). Shepard aligns himself further with Beckett by including a quote of the latter at the beginning of his collection *Day Out of Days.* The quote, "That's the mistake I made . . . to have wanted a story for myself, whereas life alone is enough" is from Beckett's "Text for Nothing #4," yet Shepard neglects to cite the work, allowing the quote simply to float unadorned. This leads one to believe that Beckett himself uttered this, instead of a character in a prose piece. That said, Shepard may be making a move that is similar to what some critics and the public tend to do to Shepard: collapsing the voices of the characters into the literal voice of the author.

Critics also took notice of the connections between Shepard and Beckett. *The Village Voice* termed *Kicking a Dead Horse* "[Shepard] in a Beckettian mode" (Soloski 2008: 28) and considered the work "an homage to Shepard's hero, Beckett" (Soloski 2008: 33). In essence, Shepard is both acknowledging Beckett in his writing and interviews and embodying elements of Beckett in his presence and persona.[3]

Perhaps the strongest evocation of Beckett in reference to Shepard is in Stephen Rea's "Forward" in the 2008 publication of *Kicking a Dead*

Horse. Rea, an Irish actor who previously worked with Shepard on the original productions of *Geography of a Horse Dreamer* and *Action*, has also acted for two major writers of twentieth-century drama: Samuel Beckett and Harold Pinter. Rea argues that "three writers dominate late-twentieth-century drama: an Irishman, an Englishman, and an American—Beckett, Pinter, and Shepard" (2008: ix). For Rea, Shepard's work is the American incarnation of Beckett's lineage, for "Pinter and Shepard acknowledge freely this influence on their work, and no writers have seized upon Beckett's legacy with such willingness" (2008: ix–x). Rea contends that what Shepard has done "is to claim the Beckettian existential space and re-create it in rooms, ranches, prairies, badlands. . . . The characters of . . . *Fool for Love* and *A Lie of the Mind*, like Hamm and Clov in *Endgame*, are doomed for eternity to petrified noncommunication" (2008: x).

Irish playwright Conor McPherson further developed Shepard's connections to Beckett in the "Introduction" to 2012's *Fifteen One-Act Plays*. McPherson states that "Shepard's plays mark the scorch marks of European drama more than those of any of the other great American playwrights . . . an iron drive like Beckett's; . . . a dream world as disconcerting as Pinter's" (2012: xii). The resulting effect of having Rea and McPherson—two revered Irish practitioners—make such links between Shepard and Beckett allows for Shepard to be positioned within the lineage of celebrated playwrights.

Beyond being positioned within this legacy, this Late Style of Shepard's work also has him exploring further literary modes. Though Shepard had previously published prose works, such as *Hawk Moon* (1973) and *Motel Chronicles* (1982), the Late Style features Shepard publishing collected works of prose (*Cruising Paradise*, *The Great Dream of Heaven*, and *Day Out of Days*). These works distinguish themselves from Shepard's earlier nondramatic writings in that most of the pieces contained within the volumes conform to the strictures of short story writing. *Hawk Moon* was a collection of tales and ramblings, while *Motel Chronicles* is a semiautobiographical collection of sketches and snippets. The volumes of this later period are not seemingly random collected bits and pieces, but rather the works contained in each book construct an overall impression of certain themes and concepts. In fact, stories of this latter period have been singled out for publication in the *New Yorker*, the arbiter of literary taste and the venerable promoter of the modern short story. In fact, when Shepard rolled out his most recent collection of prose work *Day Out of Days*, the author graced the cover of *The New York Times Book Review* section and the work was the featured review of the week. Though Shepard's cultural moment has passed, there is a continuing interest in his writings.

Adulations and commemorations of Shepard's work also continued during this period. In 2009, he was recognized by PEN with its Master Playwright Award. At the ceremony, he was given, appropriately enough, a first edition copy of Jack Kerouac's *Lonesome Traveler* (1960). In 2010 he was awarded the *Chicago Tribune* Literary Prize. In 2011, he was recognized by the legendary La Mama Theatre, becoming the first recipient of the Ellen Stewart Award. That year he was also honored by the Chicago Humanities Council. At the end of 2011, Shepard became a fellow at the Santa Fe Institute (SFI) at the invitation of Cormac McCarthy. The SFI is, according to its website, an "independent, transdisciplinary scientific institute" that engages with "complexity research expanding the boundaries of science." Shepard explains that the organization is "mostly scientists . . . Nobel Prize winners . . . we all meet everyday. It's a way of seeing there's a dialogue between different [disciplines]. There's a lot of discussion about complexity theory and neuroscience, how things control human behavior. You run across people with different areas of expertise. It's very cool" (Gritten: 2012). Not comfortable to rest on his laurels, the late Shepard continues to foster a persona that evolves, simultaneously referring to his past while he pushes forward into a new territory. Though Shepard's cultural moment has passed, he no longer seems at odds with being a member of the "establishment."

The 2012 documentary *Shepard and Dark* is a unique depiction of Shepard. It chronicles the relationship between Sam Shepard and Johnny Dark and their decades-long correspondence. Directed by

Treva Wurmfeld, the film features the two men as they review their letters and share autobiographical episodes. The film itself is an excavation of their correspondence and their relationship. We follow them to a Denny's (in similar fashion to "The Great Dream of Heaven") in which they sift through various letters. This excavation, inevitably, leads to a confrontation with the past. Indeed, the film serves as a meditation on history, memory, and art. Early in the film, Shepard reads from a letter, stating, "I've always set myself up as a great enemy of sentimentality but now I see that time brings a certain yearning towards past experiences" (Wurmfeld). Through these forty years, their relationship is detailed.

Shepard touched upon familiar concerns once again in 2013's *A Particle of Dread* (*Oedipus Variations*). The work serves not as an adaptation of *Oedipus Rex*, but rather a rumination and reflection on fate and destiny that appropriates elements from the classic tragedy. The play itself opens with a gruesome, horrific scene. Otto (an analogue to Oedipus) is mopping up an enormous amount of blood on stage. Annalee (an Antigone-like character) has a violent husband. This husband has raped and killed a babysitter—leaving the splattered remains for Otto to clean. We learn that in this world, emotion is a chemical presence that can be detected in blood. And, at the crime scene, the blood reveals the rage of the man mixed with the fear of the victim. As in other works from the late Shepard, here too a disposition toward action—be it abandonment or violence—seems to be biologically and genetically programmed into the male. There is much concern of how this violence—once again, a traumatic event—will impact Annalee's children. Annalee resists the suggestion to abandon her children in the wake of their father's murderous frenzy.

A Particle of Dread (*Oedipus Variations*) duplicates and remixes the Oedipus myth, while generating and constructing a piece that unfurls in a seemingly different time and place. Sophocles' tragedy has been referred to as the "first whodunit," and Shepard takes this notion further by literally importing detectives to investigate these crimes. In a sense, Shepard is playing with classical mythology while infusing it with recognizable figures from popular culture (crime scene investigators) and from his own work (the investigators of *Suicide in B Flat*) to pursue the role of destiny and fate in our own contemporary lives.

Critics, for the most part, were baffled by the play. Ben Brantley, writing in *The New York Times*, prefaced his thoughts by explaining that Shepard's "work has always had a mythic cast, as well as plenty of pity and terror for the human condition" (2014). For Brantley, Shepard "is plowing those fields seeded by Sophocles and Freud. Using a centuries-spanning arsenal of devices to consider the case—from soothsayer-readable entrails to DNA analysis"; he concludes, however, that Shepard "doesn't dig up much in the way of new insights" (2014). Bewildered, Brantley notes that the play "often comes across as an anti-intellectual puzzle, suggesting a Rubik's cube being twisted every which way by a highly precocious kid" and serves as "a restless riff on ancient themes that ultimately says more about its creator than its subject" (2014). Tom Sellar in *The Village Voice* termed *A Particle of Dread* a "lethally muddled production, a pauseless procession of inaccessible characters who talk at us without allowing us fully into their psychic spheres" (2014).

Though Shepard has seemingly accepted his position within the canon of American drama, as evidenced by *Day Out of Days* and *A Particle of Dread (Oedipus Variations)*, he continues to provide the Shepard textual community with new material both as a writer and actor. Though Shepard proudly continues to brand himself as a luddite regarding new media, hilariously asserting in August 2012 that "I don't have a computer. I don't have an [sic] Internet. I don't have the [sic] e-mail. I don't have any of that shit" (Watkins: 2012), he does have an "unofficial" website. Operated by a fan under the production moniker Coymoon Creations, www.sam-shepard.com was established on November 5, 2005 (Shepard's birthday), and its stated mission is "to become the Net's most comprehensive site for all things Shepard." It is an aggregator of news as well as announcements and updates regarding Shepard's films, plays, projects, productions (both in New York and in regional theaters), appearances, and readings. In essence, the Shepard textual community, though not as large or pervasive as during Shepard's cultural moment, has a presence online, allowing for the textual community to be accessible to all with a connection to the internet.

A method of monitoring and assessing the circulation of Shepard's persona is to consider the content of the book covers of his published works. When Shepard began to rise in popularity as an actor, it seemed an intriguing marketing ploy to use his face on the cover of the volume. The pocket edition of *Seven Plays* (1981) features a dirty and disheveled Shepard looking across the plains. In this Shepard, we have the dustbowl farmer who is surveying his dying crop. The image, a still from *Days of Heaven*, revels in the virile, serious, and "salt-of-the-earth" persona Shepard was stoking in the late 1970s. In bold, the cover reads "America's Most Brilliant and Irreverent Young Playwright."

Following his reception of the Pulitzer Prize in 1979, the popularity achieved through higher-profile acting roles and the requisite flashing bulbs of the paparazzi, Shepard's visage—perhaps even more than his name—became instrumental in the marketing of the writer, his persona, and his works. The mid-1980s reissue of *Seven Plays* features a tense, unsmiling black-and-white image of Shepard staring directly at the viewer. The back cover features a dizzying accumulation of rapturous accolades and hagiographic superlatives. This volume contains some of his earlier plays as well as pieces from the family cycle of his career. As Shepard closed out the family cycle, *A Lie of the Mind* was published in a stand-alone volume with no image whatsoever, but with the title of the play in alternating colored letters.

The first work published in the Late Style was the 1993 text *A Play and Two Screenplays*, which contains the screenplays of *Far North* and *Silent Tongue*, as well as the script for *States of the Shock*. The cover features a photograph of Shepard that undoubtedly signals the beginning of a new period. Instead of a close-up of a scowling, simmering writer, the cover is a full body shot of Shepard. He retains his signifiers of the persona—a cowboy hat, jeans, and boots—yet his positioning and his demeanor reveal a new development in the persona. Instead of embodying the confrontational and perhaps even violent and tortured

writer, Shepard looks to the side, averting the gaze of the reader. Instead
of a snaggly scowl, Shepard sheepishly grins off into the distance, as if
he is silently chuckling at a private joke. Instead of a collared shirt—or
even rural working regalia—Shepard's t-shirt depicts varieties of trout.
Beyond references to his established persona (hat, jeans, and boots) and
a newly found sense of jocular levity, it is precisely what Shepard sits
upon that reveals the intentions of his new identity. Shepard resides in a
folding director's chair amid the rock and dirt of some far flung filming
location. This is Shepard not as the rebellious, cow-licked naïf or as the
rock star or even as the intense man of letters. Rather, this is Shepard
fulfilling a long-harbored ambition: this is Shepard at the beginning
of his career as film director. Of course, his film directing was greeted
with less than enthusiastic responses. By this time Wim Wenders' *Paris,
Texas* (based upon elements from *Motel Chronicles*) had garnered the
Palm d'Or at Cannes and Shepard's stock as an actor had risen, but
Shepard's two excursions into helming films were viewed by many as
disappointments. The films (*Far North* and *Silent Tongue*) are revealing
and insightful to a textual community familiar with Shepard's work,
but beyond that cult audience, the films are often considered merely
intriguing experiments or dismissed as long-winded trifles.

When Shepard's image returns on the cover of a play, it is *Simpatico*
(1994). The image is a close-up of Shepard (as in the reissue of *Seven
Plays*). Instead of black and white, and as with *Seven Plays* and *A Play
and Two Screenplays*, this image is bathed in a sepia tone evocative of
a distant era. Gone is the Stetson, but what remains is the beguiling
grin. Once again adorned in a t-shirt, Shepard seems to have just run
his hand through his resilient hairline, pushing back a few strands
while smiling about some humorous notion regarding the absurdity
of appearing on the cover of a published work. Indeed, this would be
the last play of Shepard's (until 2012) to be published with the writer's
image on the cover.

In moving from Shepard's cultural moment to his Late Style, in
which Shepard shifts his persona from rugged leading man to that of a
caring father figure, Shepard's image becomes less and less central to the

marketing of his published work. The 2002 collection featuring *The Late Henry Moss, Eyes for Consuela,* and *When the World was Green,* does not attempt to capitalize on Shepard's image. Rather, the cover features a disheveled Sean Penn crumbling on the floor against an antiquated refrigerator. Reminiscent of *True West* in its imagery of a crushed man in close proximity to a kitchen appliance, the figure central to the photograph is the actor Sean Penn from the original production of *The Late Henry Moss.* Shepard has literally been supplanted on the cover by another, younger actor/director who has come to represent artistic integrity, authenticity, simmering intensity and dedicated craftsmanship.

The next play Shepard published was *The God of Hell.* Instead of an image of the writer, or even an image from the production, the volume features the title of the play emblazoned over a photograph of a mushroom cloud. The cover is elusive and ambiguous and does not connect with the imagery utilized in previous publications. *Kicking a Dead Horse* returned to a definite, concrete image. Once again, Shepard does not grace the cover, but a still image from the original production has replaced the image of the author. This photograph—this time in color—features the actor Stephen Rea on the set of the play. Rea has much less theatrical currency and celebrity capital in the United States than Penn, and Shepard for that matter, yet the image signifies a bevy of Shepardian elements. A man, alone in the desert, adorned in vague Western wear, looks weary and contemplative. Immediately, the viewer of the cover realizes that this image simultaneously evokes elements associated with both Shepard and Beckett. The image falls directly in line with critical interpretations of the work, as well as Shepard's references to Beckett during this portion of his career.

In 2012, *Ages of the Moon* and "Evanescence" were published (along with reprints of various other Shepard works) as *Fifteen One-Acts Plays.* In a curious move, the publisher—for the first time since the softcover release of 1993's *Simpatico*—decided to feature an image of Shepard emblazoned on the cover. Of course, the image is an older photograph depicting a decidedly younger Shepard as a James Dean/Johnny Depp like bohemian with the requisite cigarette dangling from his lips.

A preface by playwright Conor McPherson further links Shepard to Beckett.

Day Out of Days features one of the most telling images from Shepard's corpus. On the cover is a child—perhaps five years old—astride a horse. The image itself appears to date from the 1940s or 1950s. The regalia adorning the child is a mythic and Hollywoodized version of the cowboy. His outfit has much more in common with Roy Rogers than the historical cowboy. The child raises his hat up in a celebratory fashion, as often seen at the conclusion of Western films and as demonstrated at the end of *Don't Come Knocking*. Upon further investigation, the child on the cover is revealed to be Shepard himself. To add to this sense of levity, the image of the mature Shepard on the inside of the back jacket reveals an older gentleman who is smiling and laughing in a state of joy and humor. Both the child on the cover and the old man at the back of the book work as repudiations of Shepard's stern and aggressive persona exhibited on the covers of his works (and in the media) from the 1970s and 1980s.

Just as these photographs have functioned as "controlled" or "mediated" images of the Shepard persona, photographs that have appeared during this period partially work to unmake the Shepard persona. The photographs include a paparazzi shot of Shepard walking the streets of Manhattan. Gone are the cowboy boots, trench coat, dark clothes, and scowl. In their stead, Shepard holds a shopping bag, dressed in prototypical cullings from the LL Bean catalog. But, it is what is in his hand that works to dismantle the old image. Shepard, the writer who still proudly works in long hand and on a typewriter, who retreats to his cabin for composing his work, and who spends time with horses, is hoofing the streets of New York City with a cellular phone pressed against his ear. Indeed, in *Simpatico* the cellular phone represents the greed of 1990s yuppiedom, yet in 2010 a very urbane Shepard stalks New York City with a Nokia in hand. Much less levity can be associated with another photograph that surfaced that same year. Shepard was arrested in Illinois for driving while intoxicated. Scrawled across celebrity gossip sites was Shepard's mug shot. For the first time, Shepard—who obviously has no control of his image in this setting—looks no longer like the once "future of American Theatre" or even the "Great American Writer" but rather simply appears to be a befuddled and disoriented old man. Though the Shepard persona has been simultaneously entranced and repelled by the looming shadow of his father, in this one moment Shepard becomes a facsimile of his own dad. A comparison between the mug shot of Shepard with the candid photographs of Shepard's father included in *Motel Chronicles* reveal that the writer's nightmare of becoming his father has—in some sense— become reality. The mugshot reveals an aged Shepard embodying what he has feared throughout his life. His 2011 piece "Normal (Highway 39 South)" depicts a narrator's time in a drunk tank in Illinois, not so dissimilar from Shepard's own experience. In May 2015, Shepard was once again arrested for driving under the influence (DUI), this time in New Mexico. Though looking less like his father in this mugshot, the image further bolsters Shepard's valorization of authenticity. The writer who composes "masculine" works has seemingly proven his authenticity through his *authentic* tangling with the law. Even as a senior citizen, Shepard's outlaw image remains intact, and in a sense, is enhanced by the incident.

In sum, the Shepard of the later phase of his career involves the development of a new persona. The persona of Shepard from this period is paternal. This is evidenced from both his acting roles in this phase and his status as an elder statesman of American theater. Shepard in his late persona no longer solely performs the role of naïf or cosmic cowboy; rather, Shepard has attempted—or is attempting to—reconcile with his own image as well as with his position in literary history. Shepard's latter persona—perhaps the last persona of his storied career—reveals an artist who has passed his cultural moment, but remains active in a variety of art forms. From acting and directing to writing, Shepard has seemingly made peace with himself, his art, his legacy, and his persona. Shepard has reconciled his present persona with his past persona. In essence, Shepard's persona is now the reserved, yet empathetic father, a kinder, gentler alternative to the destructive patriarchs that haunt Shepard's corpus.

Shepard seems to have accepted theater, as he no longer cites rock musicians as his primary influences, but rather comfortably evokes the playwright to whom he feels he holds the most debt: Samuel Beckett. The late Shepard persona to a degree still revels in being an "outsider" to theater as he has relentlessly pursued experimentation in his stage works. Though his cultural moment has passed, Sam Shepard's persona continues to resonate through his interviews, acting work, and writings. He no longer holds the exalted position as the proverbial greatest American playwright of the age, but he still presses forward, reflecting both upon his own persona as well as his legacy. Within this legacy, Shepard has often struggled to reconcile the concept of art with the idea of authenticity. Indeed, the Late Style of Shepard interrogates the interplay of authenticity with art. It is this interrogation that is the subject of the next chapter.

Notes

1   Indeed, in the process of writing this document, I discovered that many people outside the textual communities of contemporary drama did not know that Shepard was indeed a writer in addition to being a film actor. To further this point, a fellow scholar recently asked me, "Does Shepard even write plays anymore?"

2   In 2012, Shepard revealed in an interview that he had originally been cast in the Gene Hackman role in *Unforgiven*, but had passed on the project. *Unforgiven* is recognized by many critics, along with *High Noon* (1952) and *The Searchers* (1956), as one of the most important Western films of all time.

3   In addition, Shepard also aligns himself with Brecht in both writings and persona. In April 2012, a posed photograph of Shepard emerged in which he sports a black leather jacket and chomps on a stogie. Both the jacket and the cigar are signifying elements that refer to Brecht. Beyond carving his own persona, Shepard continues to refer to Beckett and Brecht in both craft and persona.

2

"What's Beyond Authentic?": Authenticity and Artistry in *Don't Come Knocking* and *Kicking a Dead Horse*

An intriguing area to explore when studying Shepard is the intersection between his obsession with authenticity and his role as a literary, theatrical, and film artist-celebrity. Can a celebrity be authentic? According to Richard Dyer, authenticity is an integral component of certain strains of celebrityhood. Indeed, for some celebrities "authenticity" is prized, for within the celebrity there can be a desire for "sincerity or authenticity, two qualities greatly prized in stars because they guarantee, respectively, that the star really means what he or she says, and that the star really is what she or he appears to be" (2007a: 11). Throughout his entire corpus, Shepard has consistently explored and performed authenticity. These are not only components of his persona, but also traits found within the roles he performs on screen and the situations he crafts in his writings. Indeed, even Shepard's first play *Cowboys* (1964)[1] centers upon the notion of what is "authentic." Plays such as *Cowboy Mouth* (1971), *Angel City* (1976), and *True West* (1980) consciously explore and interrogate the position of the artist and the compromises necessitated when the artist is subjected to the machinations of capitalism and the marketplace. In *Cowboy Mouth*, a young musician comes under the hypnotic sway of a woman who wants to transform him into a "rock n roll Jesus with a cowboy mouth" (Shepard 1984a: 157). *Angel City* centers upon a young writer brought to Hollywood as the motion-picture industry wishes to capitalize on his skills. Before the end of the play, the "Hollywood-types" are revealed to be literal demonic creatures seeking to prey upon the writer. Finally, *True West* ponders (among a multitude of ideas) the authenticity of the Western film and the conflict between two brothers warring to create an "authentic" vision of the West. This ongoing investigation by Shepard centers upon how authenticity can be signified, demonstrated, and performed and the ability (or inability) of the individual to achieve an authentic existence. This is further complicated by Shepard's position as a recognizable celebrity and commodity who continues to perform in films for consumption by the global market.

This chapter considers the dynamics of authenticity and analyzes the concept in the film and screenplay *Don't Come Knocking* (2005) as well as the play *Kicking a Dead Horse* (2007). The analysis of these works will yield the understanding that Shepard recognizes that authenticity, in its many iterations, holds a tenuous, nuanced, and even at times ambiguously compromised relationship with the production of art. In these writings, authenticity emerges as a valorized trait. These works reveal the compromise and reconciliation required of an artist striving for authenticity, yet *Don't Come Knocking* and *Kicking a Dead Horse* offer different conclusions regarding the path to—and the attainability of—authenticity.

The focus of this chapter is an examination of authenticity in Shepard's Late Style. In essence, this chapter investigates how the character of the artist grapples with the urge to regain authenticity. In previous periods, Shepard analyzed these dynamics, yet did not offer resolutions to the dilemma. In this Late Style, Shepard once again takes up the theme of authenticity and the artist, yet Shepard positions the artist as much older and experienced. He also provides two possible solutions to the friction that can exist between authenticity and artistry. As with other concerns in Shepard's work, the Late Style provides a collection of commentaries and conclusions to questions raised throughout his previous phases. The examination of the artist and the artist's relation to authenticity is significant to Shepard. He returns to this concern in the Late Style and posits two methods in which the artist can resolve the simultaneous pulls of artistry and authenticity in the face of the demands made by the marketplace. In sum, this chapter will examine the dynamics of the artist (in old age) struggling toward authenticity and demonstrate options for the artist or individual to reach a reconciliation between authenticity and artistry.

Shepard's valorization and privileging of authenticity in relation to artistry can be traced to many influences, such as Jackson Pollock's performances of uninhibited expression resulting in dripped canvases, Jack Kerouac's "spontaneous prose," and the improvisational stylings of Charlie Parker and John Coltrane. These processes of creation allow for the unencumbered and unimpeded emotional exhalation and creative expression of the artist. As a result, the artist is understood to be expressing an essential core of his/her artistic vision, allowing for the viewer/audience to gaze into the "authentic" process, the end result a product of an uncompromised artist who remains faithful to his/her vision. The authentic artist possesses a visionary instinct that engages in an unfettered process that results in an authentic product, be it a painting, a novel, or a jazz performance.

Shepard's belief in unimpeded expression can date to a poet who also wrestled with the sometimes conflicted nature of American identity. Whitman's "barbaric yawp" privileges the unimpeded, unfiltered expression of the artist and such a concept gained great currency in jazz, and the visual and literary arts of the mid-twentieth century. As Shepard was the son of a sometimes jazz drummer, the roommate of Charles Mingus, Jr. (son of the celebrated bassist Charles Mingus), and worked in a jazz club during the early 1960s in New York City, the musical form and its relevant concepts found their way into Shepard's work and persona. Shepard often bragged that he never revised a work until the 1970s. Like an improvisational solo in jazz, Shepard reveled in the unexpected, the surprising, and the immediate. Indeed, part of the intriguing element of Shepard's work from the 1960s is its unfiltered, unrefined, and unrestrained imagistic expressions of pain, confusion, and violence. In that conception of creativity, revising would be a betrayal of the instinctual artistic process. As Shepard found influence in jazz for theater, he also located jazz's impact on literature.

Jack Kerouac, along with other writers associated with the Beat Generation, sought to replicate elements of jazz in poetry and prose. Kerouac,[2] a major influence upon Shepard, valorized the immediate and spontaneous elements of artistic expression and attempted to recreate these notions from music in his writing. Kerouac's novels such as *On the Road* (1957), *The Dharma Bums* (1958), and *The Subterraneans* (1958), like Shepard's own work, celebrate aspects of the United States often neglected by mainstream American culture. Beyond Whitman, jazz, and Jack Kerouac, American painter Jackson Pollock[3] also holds great influence upon Shepard. Pollock, famous for his massive abstract expressionist paintings, developed a type of "action painting" in which the artist would drip and hurl paint at canvases, often dancing to blaring jazz in the process. Remarkably, these works capture elements of Pollock's violent and tempestuous interactions with the canvas and serve as the tangible, material by-products of Pollock's unique artistic process. Pollock, like Whitman and later Kerouac, extolled the virtues of unhindered expression, considering it a method to access authentic artistry. As Bottoms explains,

> The idea of creating a seamless flow between artist and artwork, of somehow expressing one's very essence in the act of creation, became crucial to the new generation: the abandonment of conscious attempts to structure art was seen as a kind of guarantee of the primal authenticity of the work. Jack Kerouac, for example, believed that the first draft of a piece was invariably the truest. . . . Shepard was clearly heavily influenced by this holy art attitude. (1998: 31)

Though Shepard would eventually distance himself from his earlier works and adopt practices that required multiple revisions and rewrites, Shepard's idealization of authenticity and expression would continue into the Late Style.

With rock and jazz music's influence upon Shepard—long professed by the writer himself—I look toward studies in rock music and popular culture to further elucidate the dynamics and concept of authenticity. The term authentic postulates "Real. Honest. Truthful. With integrity.

Actual. Genuine. Essential. Sincere" (Moore 2002: 209). Authentic in rock music involves the "rejection of music that is labeled contrived, pretentious, artificial, or overly commercial" (Barker and Taylor 2007: ix). In addition, "authenticity is linked with the romantic bent of rock culture, in which rock music is imagined to be truly expressive of the artists' souls and psyches" (Auslander 2008: 81). Authenticity, of course, is not fully determined by the artist or performer, but rather by the consumer of the music or performance. That said, the artist will at times attempt to present his or her identity and the artwork produced as equally authentic. Yet, attempts to perform authenticity recognize that the artist considers himself or herself inauthentic and must appropriate elements and poses to perform authenticity. It is the authenticity branded upon the artist and the artwork that grants the artist integrity. The establishment of artistic integrity, in turn, resists the traps of commercialism, for the authentic artist will express a "true" voice or vision regardless of economic pressures. Because of this, Hollywood or the so-called entertainment industry is seen in many of Shepard's plays as a corrupting force that strips the writer or artist of integrity and authenticity. In music, as in Shepard's writings, the commercial can be understood to stand in opposition to the authentic. Though postmodernity contests essentialist notions such as the authentic, Shepard's concept of the authenticity of expression, with its multiple points of origin and influence upon his writings, is a notion that weaves throughout his work. Indeed, it is Shepard's Late Style that so eloquently considers the relationship between the artist and the authentic and recognizes possible options for achieving an authentic existence. Like Shepard's persona, his Late Style works play in an area located between the authentic and the inauthentic.

As with rock music itself, Shepard's later work struggles with resolving the assumed conflict between authenticity and commercialism. With authenticity viewed as a stale relic of high modernism, Shepard's later work contests that fetishization of the authentic. For some critics, as noted above, "postmodernism may seem incompatible with authenticity" (Moore 2002: 213), yet in Shepard's Late Style world, authenticity is perpetually forced to negotiate its own meaning and relevance within the societal and economic forces of late capitalism. Shepard's later work, as with the larger discourse regarding art and postmodernity, meditates upon these binaries and interrogates their utility in the world. In Shepard's world of the Late Style, the protagonist mourns the loss of authenticity while simultaneously wondering if it ever existed at all.

That said, Shepard's artists of the Late Style find themselves struggling to reestablish their lost authenticity. To establish this authenticity, they must push against inauthenticity. This results in "authenticity of positionality," in which "authenticity [is] acquired by performers who refuse to 'sell out' to commercial interests" (Moore 2002: 213). But, many of the characters in this period of Shepard's work have indeed "sold out," or as the more enterprising would contend, "bought in." It is this complicity in which the artist accepts the institutionalization of their art that emerges as a central concern in Shepard's work. This "incorporation thesis" in rock music posits that "the institutionalization of rock implies a failure of its 'authentic' meanings" (Regev 1994: 87). In essence, rock musicians who "sell out" and become incorporated into the mechanism of capitalism lose their authenticity. Undoubtedly, Shepard and his work have achieved "institutional" status, and the late Shepard features an inward turn to further investigate the notion of authenticity when the artist himself has become incorporated into the firmament of the "establishment." Further, Shepard's work of this period not only meditates on the loss of authenticity, but also mourns the devaluation and impossibility of authenticity in the twenty-first century. The period also provides resolutions to the dilemma posed to the artist in earlier plays such as *Tooth of Crime*, *Suicide in B Flat*, *Angel City*, and *True West*. In these works writers and musicians violently grapple with the forces of creativity attempting to achieve authenticity through performance and artistry. Yet, these works provide no satisfactory resolution to the conflict between authenticity and inauthenticity. As with other works from Shepard's Late Style, *Don't Come Knocking* and *Kicking a Dead Horse* point the way toward a method of resolution and reconciliation to dilemmas previously explored in earlier works. Both these works propose solutions to the dilemmas concerning authenticity and artistry.

In 2005, Shepard starred in the Wim Wenders-directed *Don't Come Knocking*, a film for which Shepard also provided the screenplay. The film is quite dissimilar from their previous collaboration, the acclaimed *Paris, Texas*. Though both *Don't Come Knocking* and *Paris, Texas* are set in the vast spaces of the American West and concern the reunification of a nuclear family, the tones of the films differ substantially. *Paris, Texas* earnestly concerns the struggles encountered by a man who abandons his family and nearly a decade later emerges from the desert to locate them. In contrast, *Don't Come Knocking* is a light, yet highly uneven, burlesque of Hollywood, as well as a gentle spoofing of Shepard's own persona. The film concerns the aging Hollywood star Howard Spence (Shepard) who flees from the set of his newest Western film. Howard returns to the world of his youth in Elko, Nevada, reuniting with his mother, as well as tracking down an old flame near Butte, Montana. Through this search for his old, authentic self, Howard learns that he fathered a son decades ago, as well as a daughter. The daughter's mother is now dead. Because of this attempt to recover the authenticity of youth and reckon with his past, Howard eventually locates an authentic life through the creation of a new family.

Though not an actor, Hobart Strother, the protagonist of *Kicking a Dead Horse*, does have a connection to both the arts and authenticity. Hobart has recently suffered a moment of crisis similar to Howard. Hobart, a wealthy New York art dealer, has capitalized on the authenticity of his origin (he is originally from the Southwest) as well as the authenticity of his artifacts. In his line of work, Hobart scours the Southwest for items imbued with a sense of authenticity. He then sells the item—and its accompanying authenticity—to wealthy, East Coast patrons. Like Howard, Hobart has begun to realize the corrupting influence of commerce upon authenticity. Hobart flees the trappings of the metropolitan environment that he believes has corrupted his authenticity. In an attempt to reconnect with his now-vanished authenticity, Hobart has taken to the desert with minimal supplies and his horse, in a bid to demonstrate his authenticity as a man of the West. When the play begins, Hobart's horse is dead and he is alone in the vast landscape of a desert. In this isolation, Hobart interrogates and reckons with himself, demanding answers to the nature of authenticity.

Reviews and reactions to *Don't Come Knocking* and *Kicking a Dead Horse* were oppositional: critics viewed the film as an underdeveloped travelogue, while the play garnered Shepard his best notices in years. Unlike *Paris, Texas*, *Don't Come Knocking* failed to entrance audiences and critics. *The Village Voice's* Michael Atkinson correctly noted that the film

> meanders through predictable and emotionally undemanding territory, with Shepard himself grumping up center stage as a menopausal jerk searching for meaning we're never sure is there. . . . What all this has to do with moviemaking, stardom, substance abuse, paternity, middle age, Montana, or America, I could not say. (2006)

The New York Times' Stephen Holden proclaimed *Don't Come Knocking* "visually majestic but dramatically inert" with "elliptical, stagy dialogue" that "hems and haws, spinning its wheels trying to work up enough momentum to go somewhere, but never budges" (2006). As for Shepard, Holden recognizes the actor/writer's iconic maturation, noting that

> Shepard has physically aged into a symbol of the stubborn, cranky individualist who has been a constant presence in his plays and films. Nowadays, he merely has to squint into the camera to suggest a tired, suspicious cowboy who has spent decades riding the range, roping steers and peering into the horizon for signs of trouble. ("Another True West")

The film suffers from a variety of missteps, most notably a collision of aesthetics between Wenders' unapologetically romantic vision of America and Shepard's dialogue of the downtrodden. The film features much less squalor and hellish suburban imagery than *Paris, Texas* as Wenders constructs a film of wide vistas and Edward Hopper–inspired images of desolate towns. Yet Wenders' camera undercuts the irony of

Hopper's paintings, overwhelming Shepard's script with an epic scope. In all, Wenders' concept for the film clashes violently with Shepard's script. The result, as most critics noted, was a motion picture with tonal shifts and unjustified grandiosity that seemed to be an empty and shallow exploration of themes familiar to both the writer and the director. Indeed, a reading of the screenplay reveals a story quite different from that which reached the screen. It is a small, character-based script that meditates upon memory and redemption, yet its filmic incarnation is confused and bloated.

After a decade and a half of reviews ranging from the scorching to the mixed, Shepard earned uniform praise for *Kicking a Dead Horse* (2008). *The New Yorker's* Hilton Als recognized the work's position within the Shepard corpus, explaining

> Sam Shepard's *Kicking a Dead Horse* . . . feels like a summing up of sorts, though not an ending. Given Shepard's protean skill as a writer, a performer, and a director, it's difficult to imagine him coming to the end of anything; he simply moves through the artistic phases and challenges he creates for himself, incorporating what he has done before, while hinting at what is to come. (2008)

The critic also hailed the dialogue, noting that the play "contains some of the most poetic and metaphysical writing Shepard has produced since the seventies" (2008). For Als, with *Kicking a Dead Horse* "the playwright reconfigures himself—a Midwestern boy who dreamed of a West that no longer exists, if it ever existed—into the form of a man who dreamed of a different kind of life for himself, before ending up lost in the brush, another gone critter in the sad purple light" (2008).

The Village Voice's Feingold concurred, also placing the work within Shepard's corpus, noting that

> recent Shepard plays have felt like perfunctory strolls through familiar material, not to be compared to his best work. . . . *Kicking a Dead Horse* shows Shepard back on form, not merely recapitulating old motifs but reimagining them, in ways that are often amusingly sly. (2008: 34)

The play also served as an occasion for extended articles on Shepard himself and his legacy in *The New Yorker*, *The Village Voice*, and *New York Magazine*.

As noted, *Don't Come Knocking* serves as a burlesque of Hollywood and Shepard's own persona while *Kicking a Dead Horse* works as a meditation on the interplay between commerce and art, and the inherent compromise of integrity and authenticity under the demands of market forces. Both the actor Howard and the art dealer Hobart have achieved success through the marketing and selling of authenticity. Howard is desired for Western films because of his authentic persona while Hobart can easily acquire Native American artifacts or Frederic Remington paintings for his customers. Howard, like Hobart, hails from the Southwest. Howard is not a trained actor or artist, but rather a cowboy who fell into acting on a lark. As a result, he is viewed as a "real" cowboy. It is Howard's authenticity, demonstrated through his horseriding and various traditional cowboy performative activities (such as handling a lariat or wielding a six-shooter), as well as his rugged handsomeness that makes him a valuable commodity for makers of Western films. Paralleling Shepard's own relationship to Western films, a "real" Western film can be branded as such if Howard is a member of the cast. It is precisely Howard's authenticity that is the worth of his participation in a feature film.

Though Howard performs this authenticity on film, he himself has determined that he is indeed no longer authentic. It is this perceived authenticity that has become commodified. In a sartorial moment, Howard bolts from the set of the film. Howard has reached a point of crisis in which he loathes and despises his present inauthentic self. This inauthentic self is a corruption of his former, authentic identity. Howard is inauthentic in that he no longer lives on the range, but is now the prototypical "Hollywood-type," concerned with sexual conquests, copious consumption of narcotics, and living the flash-bulb blinded life of a celebrity. When an investigator for the film studio's insurance company surveys Howard's now-abandoned trailer on the film set, he finds "all kinds of dope, sex, alcohol and debauchery" (Shepard nd: 3).

The investigator concludes amid the groupies and lines of cocaine that "there is every indication that Mr. Spence was engaged in a totally irresponsible and self-indulgent lifestyle" (Shepard nd: 12). This behavior is indicative of how far afield Howard has strayed from his former authentic self.

Yet, Howard is anything but an A-list celebrity. In a car after leaving the film set, Howard hears a radio DJ wonder aloud, "Anybody remember the old shoot'em up star from the seventies called Howard Spence? Well, it seems he 'up and skedaddled' from his most recent flick. . . . Where are you, Howard?" (Shepard nd: 12). So, it is apparent that the compromise he made between his authentic self and the promise of celebrity has resulted in neither personal fulfillment nor sustainable celebrity for, as indicated by the DJ, Howard is a "has been." He is an actor who has passed his cultural moment, but now finds himself in a state of crisis and wishes to regain his authenticity. When visiting his mother, he thumbs through a collection of tabloid clippings she has kept, documenting his various romantic affairs and outrageous behavior. Howard explains that "I never did any of that stuff. . . . Things just sort of took over. . . . Things came up" (Shepard nd: 26). As a young man, Howard was an authentic cowboy who worked on the range. As an aging man, he has lost his authenticity and has been relegated to performing an inauthentic variation of his former identity. Howard's authenticity and integrity have been compromised by the commercialization and commodification of his authenticity.

Hobart, like Howard, not only has the authentic pedigree of coming from the West, but the items he sells guarantee the buyer possession of a material good with the aura of authenticity. Hobart wheels and deals in the high-powered world of the New York City art scene. Through exploiting the authenticity of himself and his artifacts, he has gained, like Howard, material wealth and prestige. Hobart, through his commercializing and monetizing of authenticity through art, has himself become detached from authenticity. For Hobart, like Howard, authenticity is a condition that was attained at one point in the past, but it has since been compromised through celebrity and commerce. Hobart's conundrum concerning authenticity is spurred by his profession, that being an art dealer. More specifically, Hobart has poached artifacts from the American Southwest and sold them for a great deal to art patrons, essentially giving Easterners a totem of perceived authenticity from the West. It is the authentic totem that is corrupted and profaned by this commercial exchange. This corruption also taints Hobart's sense of self. In the worlds of both Howard and Hobart, art and commerce comingle, but when each of the men achieves professional success, it costs them their authenticity.

Like the actor Howard, the art dealer Hobart finds his present, compromised life intolerable. He states, "All I can tell you is that I had become well aware of my inexorable descent into a life in which, daily, I was convinced I was not intended to be living" (Shepard 2008: 15). Hobart longs for his past, authentic self, "when I worked for an honest living. Back in the days of AUTHENTICITY, when I 'rode for the brand,' as they say: mending fences, doctoring calves, culling cows" (Shepard 2008: 41). Both men feel that they have "sold out" and long to return to the authenticity of their former selves. These former selves are authenticated through geographic location—both men valorize the rural, indicating that the city (Los Angeles for Howard and New York City for Hobart) connotes inauthenticity. Their former selves are also authenticated by occupation—acting and art are viewed as inauthentic or illegitimate, and legitimate work within their understanding of masculinity entails manual labor, often involving nature, via the earth (farming) or animals (ranching). What makes their own predicaments more detestable is that Howard and Hobart have both capitalized on the perception of their authenticity, resulting in a compromised, inauthentic life. Through these works, Shepard takes a mature, complex view of the dynamics between artistry, authenticity, and commerce. At the conclusion of each work Shepard provides two possible avenues for the artist attempting to regain authenticity. As a result, both men must literally and figuratively journey to confront their present self through evoking their past.

Howard is forced to trace his past through his journey. His flight from the film set results in a visit to his mother, with whom he has not spoken for decades. He also visits the grave of his father. Though Howard physically searches out his past and engages with the present to reconnect with his lapsed authenticity, Hobart psychically confronts his past through the performances of dialogue with himself. During the play, there is only one other figure that appears onstage: a silent, mysterious, and unnamed girl. Like Howard, Hobart has fled, but he must face his past through memories and a performance with himself.

Howard and Hobart view their lives in binary terms. The binaries are comprised of two separate periods. Essentially, Howard and Hobart each had an authentic period prior to compromising their authenticity for material and professional gain. Then, for the bulk of their lives, they embraced inauthenticity. In their advancing age they seek to revisit their past in an attempt to recapture the essence of their authenticity, or perhaps at the least, to reconnect with the period of their lives in which authenticity existed in a pure, unexploited, and uncompromised form. Howard's past authenticity is referenced in *Don't Come Knocking*, but it is visualized through the use of still photographs. Throughout Shepard's Late Style, still photographs are utilized extensively in his stories ("Self-Made Man"), plays (*Simpatico*), and films (*Silent Tongue*) to literalize the past. For Howard, these photographs appear first in his mother's home. Howard "sees an old photo of his father in an Army uniform, then another photo of his father horseback on the family ranch, holding up two dead bobcats and smiling at the camera. . . . He picks up a photo of himself as a small boy on a pony, watching ranch hands branding calves. He tries to recognize himself in the young innocent face" (Shepard nd: 29). These photographs help to shape memories as they are authenticators of a past and serve as documentation of a time and place. When he stumbles into the M&M bar, "his eyes fall on one of the posters from his old westerns, the first film he did, thirty years ago. . . . The shock of seeing himself in the past registers on his face. . . . There is one of him and Doreen [his ex-girlfriend and mother of his son] in the old M&M with his arm around her and a beaming, beautiful smile on her face" (Shepard nd: 64). As Howard attempts to regain his authenticity through tracing his own past, Hobart takes on a much riskier proposition. He chooses to "test" his own authenticity by pitting himself against nature. Only through abandoning the inauthentic trappings of the metropolitan area and venturing into the authentically dangerous desert can he prove his authenticity.

For the men of these works, authenticity exists as a conceit often determined by the self, but it is reflected by the exterior trappings of the individual. In essence, the characters must signify their authenticity through various markings, posings, and behaviors. Most obvious of these markers of authenticity are the methods in which these characters costume themselves. When *Kicking a Dead Horse* opens, we are told that Hobart wears a "rumpled white shirt, no tie, sleeves rolled up, no hat, baggy dark slacks, plain boots for riding but not cowboy boots.... There should be no attempt in his costume to make him look like a 'cowboy.' In fact, he should look more like an urban businessman who has suddenly decided to rough it" (Shepard 2008: 9). Though Hobart once existed as an authentic manifestation of the West, he has traded that identity for monetary success. In a moment of crisis, Hobart takes to the desert to prove his ability to recapture his authenticity. Because of this, Hobart does not adorn himself in the expected regalia, but rather appears in modified business clothes, signaling that this expedition is (1) his current self without any costumed pretensions at being a "cowboy" and (2) perhaps not fully planned and organized, but rather a result of an impulsive decision.

As Hobart's excursion is an attempt to reconnect with his past self in a pursuit of (re)attaining authenticity, *Don't Come Knocking's* Howard flees the fabricated and simulated world of a film set. On set, Howard is dressed in a decidedly Hollywood vision of the cowboy. Howard is adorned in a "White western hat, fringed leather jacket, chaps, spurs, boots" and armed with "pearl-handled pistols" (Shepard nd: 4). Though the script also indicates that this is "all the traditional cowboy paraphernalia" (Shepard nd: 4) it is worth noting that the scene in the film exaggerates the costume, for no cowboy who ever truly existed in the West wore such an outrageous and garish outfit. In fact, the only cowboy to wear such duds would be located in spoofs of the Western genre, such as *Cat Ballou* (1965), *Blazing Saddles* (1974), and *The Villain* (1979). The inauthentic nature of the motion picture that is being filmed within *Don't Come Knocking* is further (humorously) emphasized through the histrionic acting of the performers as they are filmed and the erotic fetishization of the Southwestern landscape in the background. As Howard descends into a crisis of self and identity as he realizes that he has become disengaged from his previous authentic self, he now exists as an inauthentic version of himself, exemplified by his willingness to exploit his past authenticity for financial gain and celebrity fame. It is quite telling that when Howard flees the simulated American West of the movie set, one of his first actions is to dispose of his costume. Shedding the ridiculous costume is his first move in attempting to reconcile his present self with his past self. Howard stops and immediately exchanges outfits with an old ranch hand. In essence, Howard has traded his signifiers of his inauthentic identity for the regalia of an authentic cowboy.

Certainly both Howard and Hobart are in the midst of their own identity crises. When Howard learns that he is a father, this gives him an immediate, authentic role and familial connection that he cannot deny. Hobart is more fractured, enacting various conversations with himself. He even admits, "After a whole lifetime of being fractured, busted up, I'd suddenly become whole?" (Shepard 2008: 29). For Hobart, authenticity equals a sense of wholeness, which includes a unity of mind/soul/ body to form an authentic identity. Yet, Hobart—through the endless conversations with himself—enacts and performs this disunity. If Hobart were able to unify these separate selves, perhaps he would move closer toward authenticity.

At the conclusion of *Don't Come Knocking*, Howard enacts a blatantly inauthentic—yet romantic—pose. Like many other cinematic cowboys, Howard pulls his horse back and it stands on its hind legs. In a glorious action, Howard waves his hat and once again bolts from the film set. This time, Howard is not merely running away from his identity as he did at the beginning of the film. Instead, Howard is running *toward* his new identity as a father to his son and daughter. Howard has accepted his role and has united the past with the present, fully realizing his authenticity in the role of a father.

A less reductive and explicit conclusion to the quest for authenticity is achieved by Hobart. Through the dialogue exchanges with himself—in which his seemingly older, authentic self interrogates his present, inauthentic self—Hobart remains "stuck" and unable to act upon either impetus. Should he revoke his authentic roots or should he return to them? Should he forfeit his success and wealth or should he recognize the compromise necessitated by the pairing of art and commerce? Hobart has placed himself in a position in which he must demonstrate his authenticity to remain alive. If he cannot act upon his old and weathered authentic skills, he will perish. Granted, when Hobart headed into the desert, his horse was alive which allowed for an "out" in this test of authenticity. Once the horse dies, the test of authenticity gains much higher stakes. Instantaneously, this excursion has taken on the potential for disaster. Hobart must indeed rely on his authenticity from the past to survive this predicament in the present.

When Hobart considers his death, he imagines the headlines: "'Prominent Art Dealer Found Dead in Badlands with Dead Horse.' There was no apparent sign of struggle" (Shepard 2008: 64). Though Hobart does not forfeit the battle for life, it is apparent that the achievement of authenticity in one's life may be an impossibility. As experiences and perceptions combine to assist in the creation of one's identity, the authenticity of one's personhood becomes more convoluted. Hobart realizes that achieving absolute authenticity is impossible, but striving toward authenticity—instead of truly giving oneself over to the inauthentic as an action of resignation—is a worthy pursuit. But this desire, or as Hobart puts it, a "hankering" for authenticity, has taken a grave turn as he faces death in the desert. As Howard has located authenticity not in his past, but in the product of his past (his new family), Hobart never truly achieves authenticity, but he does achieve a type of enlightenment, for as Rea notes in his introduction to the play, "Hobart Strother realizes the futility of his quest for AUTHENTICITY" (2008: xii). As Howard reconciles with himself, his past, and his offspring, Hobart faces death in the desert, yet his desire for authenticity—and his actions to test his authenticity— retain a noble quality. Perhaps it is in his assumed demise—and the recognition that Hobart is truly authentic in death—that Hobart has achieved authenticity. Authenticity in the end is in part attainable for Howard through the reconciliation with his past and the assumption of responsibilities as a father. Hobart values the quest for authenticity, but realizes that authenticity itself is elusive, and such tests of authenticity are futile. In the end, Hobart can only fully achieve authenticity through his own demise in an authentic environment.

Through these works, Shepard also interrogates authenticity and its relation to the American West. For purveyors and subscribers to the mythos of the West, such traits as self-reliance and authenticity are often viewed as fundamentally required attributes. As with authenticity, Shepard has repeatedly returned to the West as fodder for his work. And in the Shepard corpus, the notion of the West and its perceived link to authenticity and artistry has been previously contested in *True West*. Stephen Rea, writing in his foreward to *Kicking a Dead Horse*, explains that with the play "we watch with some shock as Shepard dismantles the imagery" of the American West and the audience experiences "the urgency of the wider American crisis: the collapse of a sense of history and maybe America itself" (Rea 2008: xii). Though I contest Rea's generous reading of the play as concerning itself with the "collapse of a sense of history" as being too inclusive and broad, I do agree that the play does serve to undermine assumptions regarding authenticity and the American West. Yet, both *Don't Come Knocking* and *Kicking a Dead Horse* investigate authenticity while simultaneously paralleling the inability to attain authenticity with the differences between the authentic and inauthentic.

In sum, Shepard posits two resolutions to the dilemma of authenticity. Through Howard, authenticity is seemingly achieved through forming relationships with others, be it a community or family. With Hobart, authenticity is a concept that was at once attainable, yet attempts to regain authenticity are futile. In death, the mythic narrative surrounding the deceased can promulgate authenticity, as alluded to in Howard's dead father or in the presumed narrative that will arise following Hobart's expected death. For Hobart, authenticity is unobtainable and only resides in the past. As Howard has accepted his role in connection with the community that he has formed, Hobart remains alone in the desert, struggling to define himself. Howard has achieved authenticity of a sort, yet Hobart has not—the only authenticity he will achieve is through his own demise in an authentic environment. With embracing life and community, Howard achieves authenticity; by seemingly embracing death, Hobart will also achieve authenticity. For, what is more undeniably authentic than a corpse? Indeed, perhaps Hobart's inevitable demise will answer his own question, "What's beyond authentic?" (2008: 30). As the memory of the former authentic self is central to the crises experienced by Howard and Hobart, there are much more serious and traumatic memories explored in Shepard's Late Style. It is the interplay between memory and trauma that is explored in the next chapter.

Notes

1 The text of this play no longer remains, yet it was rewritten in 1967 (with trace elements from *Cowboys*) as *Cowboys #2*.

2 Kerouac was also a great influence on Bob Dylan. During the 1975–76 Rolling Thunder Revue tour, Dylan, Shepard, and poet Allen Ginsberg journeyed to Kerouac's headstone in Lowell, Massachusetts. The image of the three men hovering over the marble marker is emblematic of the direct linkage between the Beats (Kerouac and Ginsberg), folk/rock and roll (Dylan), and American theater (Shepard).

3 Shepard did write the 1977 play *Jackson's Dance* based upon the painter, yet because of legal tension with Pollock's widow Lee Krasner, the play was abandoned before production.

3

"One of Us Has Forgotten":
Memory and Trauma in *Simpatico*,
The Late Henry Moss, and
When the World was Green

As noted, protagonists of both *Don't Come Knocking* and *Kicking a Dead Horse* find themselves in crises concerning authenticity. Both Howard and Hobart are haunted by the memory of their former authentic selves. As with many other elements of Shepard's work, the concept of authenticity is itself related to the notion of memory. A consideration of both memory and authenticity leads to investigations as to what exactly constitutes an "authentic" memory. Indeed, can the "authenticity" of a memory be empirically determined or confirmed? Memory itself evolves and morphs through time and space, so such perceptions are subject to alterations, modifications, and erasure.

Not surprisingly, a major thread throughout the work of Shepard is the dynamics of memory. Shepard's meditations on memory move throughout his artistic output, regardless of the media. As previously noted, the persona of Shepard embodies a variety of signifiers. For some, Shepard is the incarnation and embodiment of long-forgotten codes of masculinity, a persona that connects to a memoried and mythologized period of American history. For others, he stands as a self-aware parody, rooted in the ethos of the 1960s counterculture, scrutinizing the destructive allure of the patriarchal order and indicting the selective memory of a culture fed by its own pop mythology. In either iteration, Shepard the author and performer stands as a signifying being, simultaneously evoking the alternative theater scene of the 1960s and the grandeur of the American West, both of which are based upon presumed "authentic" memories. As such, Shepard's persona and work—what I refer to as his corpus—are distinctly tied to memory.

Much of Shepard's earliest work, such as *The Rock Garden* (1964), is haunted by the specter of memory. This play and his other imagistic explorations from that period appear to be constructed as dreamscapes filtered through hazy memories of the American past. Shepard's family cycle is also connected to notions of memory, often centered upon a traumatic event or past transgression uncovered or revealed. Works such as *Buried Child* (1979) and *A Lie of the Mind* (1985) concern the dynamics of remembering and forgetting and how the dynamics of each impact familial relationships.

In sum, the links between memory and the interplay of remembering and forgetting in Shepard's work reside in the notion of trauma. In plays preceding his Late Style, Shepard was not able to offer performative strategies through which issues involving trauma and memory could be resolved. With *Simpatico* (1994), *The Late Henry Moss* (2000), and *When the World was Green* (1996), Shepard analyzes—and proposes solutions to—the effects of memory-based trauma.

The field of trauma studies has been well-established through the scholarship of both Shoshana Felman and Cathy Caruth. Felman's essay "Education and Crisis, Or the Vicissitudes of Teaching" and Caruth's "Unclaimed Experience: Trauma and the Possibility of History" helped to designate the field. These, and other related works, examine and argue that the

> site of trauma is the fact that literature as an art form can contain and present an aspect of experience which was not experienced or processed fully. Literature, in other words, because of its sensible and representational character because of its figurative language, is a channel and a medium for a transmission of trauma which does not need to be apprehended in order to be present in a text. (Ramadanovic nd)

This chapter is not focused on the overtly political or theoretical dimensions of trauma, but rather is concerned about how the clinical characteristics of trauma and post-traumatic stress disorder—and their interplay with memory—are represented in Shepard's Late Style writings. These traumas and stresses and their relations to memory are specifically quarantined in interpersonal relationships, be it within a friendship (*Simpatico* and *When the World was Green*) or within a family (*The Late Henry Moss*).

According to the *DSM-IV*, Post-Traumatic Stress Disorder (PTSD) occurs when a person has "experienced, witnessed, or was confronted with an event or events that involved actual or threatened death or serious injury, or a threat to the physical integrity of self or others" and the reactions and responses to the trauma include "intense fear, helplessness, or horror." In addition, the traumatic event may be reexperienced through "recurrent and intrusive distressing recollections of the event, including images, thoughts, or perceptions" or through the "acting or feeling as if the traumatic event were recurring (includes a sense of reliving the experience, illusions, hallucinations, and dissociative flashback episodes, including those that occur upon awakening or when intoxicated)." Following the trauma, the victim may have an "inability to recall an important aspect of the trauma" as well as "irritability or outbursts of anger." Shepard's Late Style concerns remembering/forgetting, and the work examined in this chapter is directly tied to trauma and its reverberations upon the individual in the present.

This chapter examines the dynamics of memory in the plays *Simpatico*, *The Late Henry Moss*, and *When the World was Green* as well as in selected short stories. These works thematically concern the issues of remembering and forgetting, but they also enact and embody the actual process of memory. These writings can certainly be termed "memory works," but through closer examination, these writings demonstrate *how* memory works. The plays and stories analyze the mechanics of remembering and further consider how the processes of performance and reenactment allow individuals to reckon with their own personal narratives.

These works also provide resolutions to the dilemma of the traumatic memory. As much as Shepard's previous work is haunted by the past and plagued by a traumatic event, Shepard rarely sought to provide a successful method of confronting the past prior to the Late Style. In this cycle, Shepard dramatically illustrates methods in which to make peace with the past and provides possible actions for the individual to take in an effort to reconcile with trauma. *The Late Henry Moss* and *When the World was Green* reveal that the reenacting of an event—or the reenacting of a moment of creation—can lead one to reconciliation with a past trauma. In contrast, *Simpatico* dramatizes the peace one attains when confronting and "letting go" of the past in comparison to the suffering of those who refuse to relinquish their memories.

The probing of trauma and memory in the Late Style is not solely necessitated by the present gap in scholarship.[1] The significance of examining how memory works—and how trauma is confronted— resides in the concept that Shepard is seemingly "working through" the questions and concerns explored in earlier phases of his career. As a trait of the Late Style, Shepard attempts to provide solutions to dilemmas previously left unresolved. This phase of Shepard's work— and his attention to these concerns—reveals the rewards and possible consequences of revisiting the memory of a traumatic event while simultaneously providing a methodology for reexamining the past.

Over the past twenty-five years, scholarship concerning the intersections of memory and theater has developed extensively. Texts such as Patricia R. Schroeder's *The Presence of the Past in Modern American Drama* (1989) approach plays through dramatic criticism to reveal the properties and dynamics of memory. Memory has also informed works concerned with cultural and intercultural notions of remembering and forgetting, such as Spencer Golub's *The Recurrence of Fate: Theatre and Memory in Twentieth Century Russia* (1994) and Diana Taylor's *The Archive and the Repertoire: Performing Cultural Memory in the Americas* (2003). The present chapter is primarily informed by three works concerning the elision point between memory studies and theater studies, namely Jeanette R. Malkin's *Memory-Theater and Postmodern Drama* (1999), Marvin Carlson's *The Haunted Stage: The Theatre as Memory Machine* (2001), and Attilio Favorini's

Memory in Play: From Aeschylus to Sam Shepard (2008). This chapter extends the analysis of remembrance and forgetting to these Shepard works that conceptualize the notion of memory as a trauma that must be confronted and resolved.

Malkin's text situates itself at the intersections of memory, theater, and postmodernism, examining both the thematic elements of memory present in plays and the memory structures enacted through the various works. Malkin contends

> that the way memory is conceptualized has changed in postmodernism and that, indeed, the terms used to discuss memory share a common ground—and often overlap—with the terms we have come to associate with postmodern aesthetic. (1999: 1)

Malkin pursues this further by contending that "postmodernism is crucially bound up with agendas of remembrance and forgetting, serving, at least in part, to re-call the past from repression or from its canonized 'shape' in order to renegotiate the traumas, oppressions and exclusions of the past" (Malkin 1999: 1). *Memory-Theater and Postmodern Drama* includes an extensive consideration of memory and trauma in Shepard's plays *Cowboys #2*, *The Unseen Hand*, *Operation Sidewinder*, *Action*, *The Tooth of Crime*, and *Buried Child*.

Carlson uses the metaphor of "hauntings" to examine the ghosting and residual traces that occur during and following theatrical performances. Carlson's theory of such spectral tracings was also briefly touched upon in reference to Shepard's persona in Chapter 1. In *The Haunted Stage: The Theatre as Memory Machine*, Carlson analyzes the haunted stage, text, body, production, and (of course) house. The final chapter concerns "Ghostly Tapestries," which deals with how the play of signs and signifiers in postmodern performance creates a multitude of meanings, effectively tapping into the audience's individual, cultural, and institutional memories. These memories, in turn, are combined and construct a heterogeneous array of perceptions that evoke memory while also duplicating the processes of memory. Carlson's text serves the section of this project by providing a method in identifying signs and signifiers that play with the phenomenological perceptions of the audience member. Also, Carlson recognizes the intertextual potentiality of elements on stage that reverberate with the audience's memory, referencing the audience's own past and how that past relates to the performance.

Favorini's work examines how theatrical and dramatic constructions of memory interplay with understood processes of memory, focusing upon "how playwrights represent memory and how they dramatize the memory/history binary" (2008: 1), from which Favorini coins the term "memographer" to designate those concerned with analyzing memory. Favorini not only references Shepard in the title of his work, but also includes an extensive reading of *A Lie of the Mind* within the context of memory studies. Utilizing these works as models of methodological approaches, this section will first summarize Shepard's memory writings from the Late Style. Then, Shepard's conceptions of memory and trauma will be examined. Finally, the chapter will explain how Shepard views performativity as a method of confronting, understanding, and possibly resolving trauma.

The 1994 play *Simpatico* concerns the nature of friendship and how the present is dictated by past events. As the play opens, we are introduced to Carter and Vinnie. Carter has flown from his stately Kentucky home to visit his former gambling partner Vinnie who lives in a skid row hovel in Cucamonga. While Carter has found great financial success through the breeding and racing of horses, Vinnie has achieved only abject failure. Decades ago the two performed small-time cons on the horse racing circuit. To land a big score, the young Carter and Vinnie blackmailed a horse racing official. The blackmailing incident involved photographing the horse racing official (Simms) when he was in the throes of an extramarital affair. To lure the official into such a compromising position, Vinnie's wife at the time volunteered for a one-night stand with Simms. After the partners succeeded in their con, Carter absconded with both Vinnie's wife and his beloved car. Vinnie has retained the photographs and other ancillary evidence from the crime for years, hoping to use the items as leverage. He has threatened to reveal these materials to ruin Carter and as a result, Carter has served as a source of money for Vinnie for decades. Vinnie agrees to hand over the evidence if Carter is able to convince Vinnie's ex-girlfriend Cecilia to return to him. Vinnie—now dressed similarly to Carter—has left for Kentucky to locate Simms. He presents the photographs and evidence to Simms, but the man explains that he has reinvented himself and no longer wishes to revisit the past.

Vinnie then calls upon his ex-wife (and Carter's current wife) Rosie. Through dialogue, Vinnie realizes that both Carter and Rosie's lives have also been ruined and destroyed by their attempt at the "big score." Vinnie returns to Cucamonga to find Carter in his apartment, dressed in his shabby clothes, apparently suffering from a psychological breakdown. In essence, Carter and Vinnie have switched clothes and positions. Carter grovels for Vinnie to help him—even to exchange identities to offer some semblance of stability. Vinnie leaves while Carter uncontrollably shakes and shivers on the floor of the filthy apartment.

Following the blistering critical reception of the 1991 one-act *States of Shock*, 1994's *Simpatico*—Shepard's first full-length stage work in almost a decade—signaled a return to seemingly familiar territory: a quasi-realistic play concerning the stress and struggle of two men. Unlike *States of Shock*, which critics almost uniformly dismissed, critics were split as to what to make of *Simpatico*. *The New Yorker's* John Lahr most pointedly asked, "For almost thirty years, Shepard's plays have been a defining part of American theatre. So what's happened?" (1994). *Time's* Richard Zoglin termed *Simpatico* "a pretty arid stretch of land" (Roudane 2002: 267) while Michael Feingold of *The Village Voice* noted that the play "feels less like a Shepard play than a B-movie script by someone who's read a lot of Shepard" (1994: 77). Vincent Canby of *The New York Times* was more forgiving of *Simpatico*, heaping the work with praise, proclaiming it a "fine, seriously funny new play" and the "the most compulsively watchable, most entertaining collection of rascals, scalawags and fools to be seen on any New York stage in a long time" (1994). Canby continued, extolling the "breathtaking succession of surprises in the writing" and proclaiming that "with the exception of David Mamet, no American playwright of his generation matches Mr. Shepard in the creation of characters that are immediately so accessible and so mysterious" (1994).

Six years after *Simpatico*, Shepard utilized memory as a method to explore a well-trodden territory of his corpus: the family play. *The Late Henry Moss*, produced in 2000, and inspired by the death of Shepard's own father, opens with two brothers, Earl and Ray. The estranged siblings have been out of contact with one another and their father for many years. Both have come to Bernalillo, New Mexico, learning that their father—Henry Moss—has recently died. The two men sit in their father's home, while their father's corpse resides on a nearby bed. Through dialogue, the audience gathers that there was a past traumatic incident that forever changed the dynamics of their family. This event is commonly referred to as the "big blow-out." Years ago, their father came home intoxicated and violently abused their mother. Ray resents his older brother Earl for not defending their mother and for fleeing the family never to return. As the brothers discuss Henry, Ray is determined to reconstruct the last days of his father. Ray's probing inquiries further aggravate Earl. Earl responds by beating and thrashing his younger sibling. Ray calls in a witness to Henry's last hours on earth: the taxi driver who transported Henry just prior to his death. The taxi driver explains how Henry and Conchalla (Henry's girlfriend) spent their last night. In a reversal of roles—and in a reenvisioning of the past—Earl comes to the home intoxicated and Ray viciously beats him. Slowly, the past and the present begin to meld and the two brothers find themselves face to face with their father. Through the collapsing of space and time, the brothers recognize their shared trauma and how the specter of their own father has haunted their lives.

The Late Henry Moss was first mounted in San Francisco in 2000 with a celebrity cast and Shepard as director, and then in New York under Joseph Chaikin's direction. As it concerned familiar Shepardian tropes—warring brothers and the haunting spectral menace of their recently deceased father—many critics hoped for a return to form for Shepard. But, as with his previous play, 1998's *Eyes for Consuela*, critics found little promise in the work. Charles McNulty in *The Village Voice* found the play a "plodding, mixed-bag" (2001: 67). John Lahr explained that *The Late Henry Moss* is "all attitude, no texture" (2001) and Robert Brustein in *The New Republic* surmised that "it does not seem to have any compelling reason for existence other than to provide opportunities for a few fine actors" (2001). Even Shepard's staunch defender Brantley described the play as "long, plodding and diminishingly crowded with echoes from stronger works" and that it further devolves into a "big moment of self-confrontation regularly found in dysfunction-of-the-week television movies" (2001). Brantley concluded the review, accusing Shepard of having "tamed and fenced in an imagination that was born to run wild" (2001). Evoking the recent sense of national mourning in the wake of the September 11 attacks and placing the New York production within that context, Brantley longs for "the sort of authentically American voice that is so much to be cherished right now" and hopes that it "is still somewhere inside Mr. Shepard," demanding that the playwright "let it loose again" (2001) and reemerge as an important voice in American theater and culture.

Upon their initial productions, *Simpatico* and *The Late Henry Moss* were criticized for being essentially "retreads" of elements found in Shepard's earlier *True West*. These three works do share many similarities beyond the prototypical Shepardian scene of two men physically abusing one another. *True West* ends in a figurative and literal stranglehold between brothers Austin and Lee, offering not a defined resolution, but rather an indication that this conflict will continue.[2] *Simpatico* and *The Late Henry Moss* point toward other possible outcomes and methods of resolution in such a conflict between men.

A third play from Shepard's late period that concerns memory and trauma is *When the World was Green (A Chef's Fable)*. The work is a collaboration between Shepard and his longtime mentor and friend Joseph Chaikin. Shepard and Chaikin have collaborated on a number of works, including 1979's *Tongues* and 1985's *The War in Heaven*. *When the World was Green* is a series of moments shared between a figure identified only as the Old Man and a woman designated as the

Interviewer. The Old Man is being held in prison, presumably awaiting execution. Through the Interviewer's interrogations, the audience learns that generations ago, in a locale designated as the "village of Ameda in the mountain region" (Shepard 2002: 225) a neighboring clan poisoned the Old Man's family mule. Even though the neighbors were related to the Old Man and his family, it did not matter. From that point, the two clans waged war on one another. As a result, when the Old Man reached the proper age, he was told that he would kill Carl, a member of the enemy family. After tracking his target for years, the Old Man—who is a chef—finally poisoned Carl. After the incident, it was revealed that the Old Man did not murder Carl, but was rather an innocent man. The audience begins to conclude that the Interviewer's father was the victim of the Old Man. The Interviewer visits the Old Man one last time and brings him the materials to create a final dish. The Old Man recognizes that his life—separated from his relentless pursuit of Carl—has lost its meaning, yet he momentarily overcomes the trauma of his life through the reenactment of creation, instead of destruction. That creation is the preparing and cooking of a meal.

When the World was Green was met with critical ambivalence and indifference. In *The Village Voice*, critic and Shepard biographer Don Shewey termed it a "play for healing" (1996: 71). Brantley commented that "the play glimmers with Shepardesque themes: the falseness of memory, the gulf between men and women and, above all, the uncertainty of identity" 1996).

In addition to these three plays, there are multiple short stories and writings from this period that concern memory. The title story from Shepard's collection *Cruising Paradise* centers upon two teenage boys, the narrator, and Crewlaw. Crewlaw's father has recently died in a fire. To confirm the incident, the two boys locate the father's partially burned mattress. It serves as a totem of sorts. The two boys take the mattress and light it on fire. Through this action, Crewlaw seemingly exorcises the failures of his father. In "See You in My Dreams," Shepard offers a narrative of a father's last days before death. From the location (Bernalillo) to the neighbor (Esteban), the tale works as another interpretation of the events chronicled in *The Late Henry Moss*. "Dust" concerns a man's horseback trip through a section of the desert in which time and space collapse, and the present and past seemingly intersect. And, the piece "Self-Made Man" details an internal, genealogical journey a man takes when he considers the variety of photographs that document his family's history.

Regarding Shepard and memory, Favorini contends that the author "sees American history as procedural, engaged in an ongoing attempt to rebuild consciousness in the face of trauma—to heal itself" (2008: 221). This notion of healing is especially applicable to his Late Style. To explore the notions of memory as experienced by the characters of these works, it is important to first establish the "past" as perceived by the characters. This past may be experienced, remembered, forgotten, or even fabricated. Once elements from the characters' pasts have been delineated, it is possible to examine the dynamics of memory through the methods of accession. These works concern and depict memory, but as noted they also operate within the syntax, grammar, properties, and predicates of memory. As a result, these works enact the dynamics of memory. This process of memory is not limited solely to the performers and characters, but is also extended to the audience and the reader. Shepard utilizes familiar tropes and aesthetics and even sensory stimulation to yank the audience into a psychic participation with the memory process of the works.

Regarding *A Lie of the Mind*, Favorini states that "virtually every character is engaged in a dance of remembering and forgetting" (2008: 219). This concept can also be extended to the works considered in this chapter. The characters of these Late Style works exist in a space that requires constant negotiation between the past and the present, as well as an interrogation of the truth of the past as filtered through the unstable dynamics of memory. As a result of this back and forth between the past and present, the characters are unable to authentically exist within the present as they cannot fully shake off the influence of the past. For example, in *Simpatico*, Carter's entire empire (of the present) is built upon the con and blackmailing (of the past). As Carter ascended, Vinnie plummeted. Carter seemingly drew the lucky hand, not only landing Rosie but also effectively capitalizing on their horse con. For Carter, Vinnie, and Rosie (as well as Simms), the con job and blackmail serve as a traumatic experience that impacts their current lives. For estranged brothers Earl and Ray in *The Late Henry Moss*, the return to their dead father's home is an attempt to reconcile with a traumatic event from their shared past. This event—like Carter and Vinnie's scam—exerts unflinching influence and control over their present-day identities. Similarly, one's identity defined in relation to another as formed through memory is at the heart of *When the World was Green*. The Old Man, now imprisoned, has spent his entire life planning to destroy Carl. The Old Man cannot fulfill the prophecy— and erase his own trauma of being condemned to murder a man— except through the enactment of yet another trauma. When he kills the wrong man, the Old Man's attempt to reconcile with his past and fulfill a familial proclamation has only resulted in a trauma for the Interviewer, perpetuating a cycle of memory and trauma.

Within Shepard's plays, there is a proliferation of properties that can be termed memory objects. Essentially, these are physical properties that are invested with a meaning tied to a past experience. These material objects can be placeholders for an experience or serve as a totem that can cause a memory to unexpectedly flood through a character's mind. Indeed, there are certain properties and objects that appear and reappear throughout Shepard's work. These are recognizable to members of the Shepard textual community who are aware of such intertextual weavings. The presence of these properties helps to construct a meaning and significance of the object as it recurs again and again throughout the writer's corpus.

These objects can also serve a practical purpose in furthering the action of the play. Quite literally, the mementos of Vinnie and Carter are legal evidence that remind the men of their conspiracy against Simms. These negatives, photographs, and letters serve as incriminating evidence, comprising a material narrative of the con and blackmail. According to Vinnie, "It's all in a shoe-box. It's all stacked very neatly in there. Not a speck of dust on anything. I check it all on a regular basis. . . . Some of the letters take me back" (Shepard 1995: 34). Of course, Vinnie obsesses about the past and the con itself and these mementos are daily reminders of Vinnie's complicity in the crime. Because of his complicity, he lost both his best friend and wife. The photos themselves depict Rosie seducing Simms. The images are sexually explicit and viewing the mementos in the box immediately transports the various characters to their shared past. It is a unique point in their personal histories in which all their lives intersected. The photographs for Vinnie indicate the power he wields over Carter, yet they also represent the moment in which his idyllic existence was shattered. Vinnie, Carter, and Rosie had created their own unique family of sorts, traipsing up and down the California racetracks, but the feeling of being a family is shattered through their desire for the "big score." For Carter, the photographs represent the incident that helped to establish him as a powerful horse breeder and broker, yet they also remind him of when he betrayed Vinnie. For Rosie, who denies that she is even in the photographs, the images are read as a marker of what she sacrificed for monetary and social success. Finally, for Simms, who also initially denies his presence in the photographs, the images signify the collapse of his former life, but also the moment in which he rebirthed himself as a man focused on the present and future. The box of evidence is used to bend Carter to Vinnie's wishes, but as a whole it represents the objects that forever altered the lives of the characters in the play. When Cecilia confronts Carter about the nature of his friendship with Vinnie, she asks, "How can you identify your friendship? How is that possible? Do you have pictures of it or something? The two of you holding hands. Displaying strings of trout?" (Shepard 1995: 42). Indeed, how does one substantiate or authenticate a friendship? In a reversal from the standard use of photographs to identify relationships, the photographs do not verify a friendship but rather document the splintering of characters from one another. In other words, while photographs can serve as a marker of authenticating an action and situation, the photographs that reside at the center of *Simpatico* are not necessarily a reflection of reality.

Cecilia contends that the "pictures didn't lie. I can tell you that much" and continues that Vinnie "showed me a couple of pictures of this guy that were presented as evidence against him" (Shepard 1995: 49). But, the photographs do indeed lie, as they were staged to entrap Simms. So, as memories are unstable and cannot always be substantiated, memory objects—material objects instilled with associations of past events or traumas—are similarly unstable and do not always substantiate the truth of the past.

The importance of such mementos, especially photographs, is not lost in *The Late Henry Moss*. The play opens with Earl flipping through a family photo album while Ray rummages through their late father's tool chest. The photo album and tools are former possessions of their dead father. The photo album is a document of the past, a reminder of their lives before the "big blow-out." The tools serve as a reminder of their father's emphasis on traditional masculine roles. They also instill hope for the future as Earl compels Ray to keep the tools, in case he ever has "the urge to be useful again!" (Shepard 2002: 13). For Earl, Ray, and Henry, the ability to use tools is an indicator of masculinity. The tools, as items passed down to sons, serve as a lasting reminder of the expectations upon a man within the traditional roles of the patriarchy. In addition, the tools represent the skills and "usefulness" a father would traditionally teach his sons. That Ray gives these tools away indicates the value he places on his father's legacy as symbolized by the tools. In a sense, the tools reflect a concern with repairing the past and present and with building for the future. The tools also work to highlight the values their father placed on men's perceived roles and their ability to use their hands to "fix" objects. Paradoxically, neither Henry, Ray, nor Earl are able to "fix" themselves and their relationship to the past. Only at the conclusion of the work do the two brothers move toward confronting their past trauma and with that confrontation, they begin to "fix" their relationship and their selves.

The audience learns that mementos were sent through the ensuing years from Earl to his brother Ray after Earl left the family. These gifts included "Socks. T-shirts. Rubbers. I sent you Camels once"

(Shepard 2002: 11) which all hint at the masculinity tied to both Henry and Earl. In a small way, Earl has sought to appease his brother, yet also provide material objects that seem to usher Ray into manhood. Yet, Ray disparages these weak gestures of giving, branding the gifts "Tokens. Tokens of guilt" (Shepard 2002: 11). These items sent to Ray were meant to transition him into manhood, yet they only served as reminders of Earl's absence.

When an emissary from the outside world arrives in the guise of Taxi, the driver who transported Henry during his last few hours, both the photo album and the tools become properties of contention. When Taxi enters, he immediately begins to handle both the photo album and the tools. As a result, Ray becomes annoyed, then enraged at the man's lack of manners. Ray explains to Taxi that "when you're a stranger in somebody's house, you don't automatically assume you can sit down at their table and fool around aimlessly with their father's possessions" (Shepard 2002: 53). Ray is now protective of these objects for they stand as material items that connect him to Henry. Prior to the entrance of Taxi, Ray seemed ambivalent about the items, yet with an intruder upon family affairs, these items are now imbued with great importance. They stand as material connections that link the sons to their father. After Taxi leaves, the audience and Earl learn that Ray has given both the photo album and the tools to Taxi. Earl is shocked when he is told that the photo album and tools are gone, for it was Ray who initially blasted Taxi for touching the mementos. Earl asks, "What the hell are you doing giving away our father's belongings to a complete stranger?" Ray responds, "I didn't think they meant anything to you" (Shepard 2002: 91). Earl harangues Ray even further, explaining, "There were photographs in there going back to the turn of the century. Those photographs are irreplaceable. Now some total stranger's got ahold of them. An outsider!" (Shepard 2002: 91). Ray explains that Taxi "can always make up some kind of a story about them" (Shepard 2002: 91). This reveals Ray's contempt for the veracity of narratives and their inability to authenticate past actions or events. As with the photographs in *Simpatico*, the images have an unstable relationship to the truth of the past, for it is the narrative that frames and contextualizes the images, giving them specific meanings. These photographs do not necessarily have to be tied to a specific narrative but rather they can be used to substantiate new meanings, or narratives, regardless of whether they are true. In essence, anyone can construct a false personal narrative with memory objects, be it Taxi or Earl.

In addition, Ray has lost any type of value for the items. Ray retains the memories of his father, yet uses the expunging of the memory items as a method through which to anger Earl, for Earl places great meaning on material objects (as exhibited through the gifts he has routinely sent Ray through the years). Ray has chosen to sever the material connections to Henry, yet Earl is unwilling to do the same. Through this action, Ray is attempting to exorcise the traumatic experiences of his past by ridding himself of the reminders of his father. Consequently, these objects serve as reminders of the brothers' traumatic past, yet these items also possess the potential to inspire a narrative. Ray strangely explains, "maybe [Taxi]'s got no family. Maybe he needs to make one up" (Shepard 2002: 92) and the conclusion is that Taxi could use the album as a type of "authenticator" of a false family and the site for the creation of a new, imaginary family. The tools, also, can be implemented quite literally in the creation or repair of an object. For Ray, the authenticating properties of the photo album only dredge up traumatic memories. Though Earl mourns that the materials were given to a stranger with no connection to Henry, it is true that both Earl and Ray have no real connection to their father beyond the biological and the traumatic. By forfeiting the album and tools, Ray has successfully cut the brothers off from their familial history, an action that seemingly halts the inevitable repetition of their father's actions. By abandoning the goods, Ray has attempted to avoid becoming his father. With both Earl and Ray eventually role-playing as their father within the play, they both reckon with their past and construct a new familial future.

In Shepard's prose pieces, essentially collected sketches, stories, and dialogues, the concept of memory and the process of remembering are primarily rooted in memory objects. The story "Self-Made Man" features the title character tracing his genealogy from material objects. These items provide a link to his past. The man specifically focuses upon photographs. Like the photo album in *The Late Henry Moss*— or, to a lesser degree, the incriminating evidence of *Simpatico*—these images provide material evidence of lives. The man in the tale observes "tintypes going back to the Civil War" (Shepard 1996: 3) as well as the numerous photographs that line his mantel. These photographs relate not only to the man's familial history, but also indicate aspects of a larger cultural history. The man observes a photograph depicting Westerners during railroad expansion. In the photograph are

> railroad men riding cowcatchers, waving derbies; blasting their way through granite mountains; unstoppable in their absolute conviction of Manifest Destiny. The later generations, where the mysterious glint of doubt begins to creep into their eyes. (Shepard 1996: 3)

These images distill the uncorrupted idealism of the nineteenth-century frontier and document a romantic vision of the West. The man in the tale would "sit with the portraits on his lap and dust them softly, long with his blue bandana" (Shepard 1996:4). For him there seems to exist a connection to these photographs of his ancestors, who appear "more real than imagined. More real than his living relatives, who were now scattered to the far ends of the country" (Shepard 1996: 4). Through these photographs, the connection to the past is more vibrant and defining than his relation to the present. Indeed, the man's identity is biologically bound to his genealogy. Instead of as a product of his time, the man views these images as direct links to his familial past.

Many of the pieces contained in *Day Out of Days* (2011) are essentially prose sketches of photographs. Indeed, Shepard himself confesses in the documentary *Shepard and Dark* that "a photograph, in many ways, is much, much more powerful than the writing" and that "a photograph is—right now . . . emotional. . . . It's like music" (Wurmfeld 2012). In "Kitchen," the narrator describes the images that overlook the food preparation area at his home. The walls are adorned with "snapshots of different sons in different shirts doing different things like fishing, riding mules and tractors. . . . Postcards of nineteenth-century Lakota warriors . . . Henry Miller with a walking stick . . . sinking ships. Slaves in sepia tones . . . pix of hawks and galloping horses" (Shepard 2011: 3). Indeed, the kitchen—the location of creation for the chef in *When the World was Green*—is also the space in which memories are created through reflection upon images.

These memories are also mined—and perhaps created—through engagements with photographs. In "Pea Ridge Battlefield, Arkansas," the narrator remembers a photograph of his "second great-grandfather . . . [who] had his left ear blown off right here. . . . I have a picture of him, back home in my kitchen" (Shepard 2011: 48). The narrator of "Choirboy Once" analyzes a photograph of his younger, pubescent self adorned in choir robes. In a Proustian moment, the narrator is yanked back into a world of women, religiosity, and sexuality, all intertwined. He thinks of "fingernails of the Virgin Mary, raw smell of pussy. . . . Going down on Jesus" (Shepard 2011: 113). As with his other references to photographs in *Cruising Paradise* and *The Great Dream of Heaven*, prose allows the narrator to describe and contemplate a photograph, documenting the swirl of memories, emotions, and sensations attached to the image.

Beyond photographs, characters in Shepard's prose seek to commune with objects imbued with meaning through memory. Some of these objects must be sacrificed while others have the potential of transforming the individual. "Cruising Paradise," a story in the volume of the same name, is a first-person piece that details a young man and his friend's quest to dispose of a significant mattress. The narrator's friend (Crewlaw) has recently experienced a tragedy. According to the narrator, "Crewlaw's dad had burned himself up in a motel bed. That was the story. . . . I couldn't quite picture it, although Crewlaw related it as though he'd been a witness to the whole event" (Shepard 1996: 37). Crewlaw explains that "'we're not gonna do anything with it. I just wanna see it'" (Shepard 1996: 40). Crewlaw only wishes to see, to witness, and to touch the remaining memory object associated with his father's death. They take the mattress and attach it to the roof of Crewlaw's hot-rodded '48 Mercury. The narrator explains that "the loud headers on the flathead Merc rumbled down through the floorboards, out into the immaculate aisles of lemon trees and oranges. I had a definite sense of somehow being a passenger in an evil vehicle cruising through Paradise" (Shepard 1996: 41–2). The boys take the mattress, throw it into an empty aqueduct, and proceed to burn it. During the ritualized immolation, Crewlaw states, "'Now, he's *all* the way gone'" (Shepard 1996: 43). When Crewlaw returns home, his aunt angrily tells him that he is doomed to repeat the fate of the father, "'Layin' up in some Christ-less flophouse just like yer oldman. Staring at the cracks in the plaster. Wondering what ever became of your life'" (Shepard 1996: 46). This harsh condemnation echoes *The Late Henry Moss*, as Henry did indeed spend the final days before his death pondering what had happened to his life and how it had become so miserable. In addition, Henry's sons role-play the actions of their father and it is this role-playing that allows them to slip away from the cycle of repetition and abuse. With the torching of the mattress, Crewlaw is honoring his father and ritualizing the recognition of his death. At the same time, Crewlaw is destroying a material connection he has to his father and signaling a willingness to relegate that relationship to the past.

Though Crewlaw successfully disposes of the material object, memory objects can also lead to transformation. Certainly, Crewlaw's actions can be viewed as ushering him into independence and adulthood. Yet, in the piece "Dust," the discovery of material, authentic objects leads to a wholly different type of transformation. When the protagonist Price meets with a man (Lowell) and his daughter for a horse ride in the desert, the two tell Price of some odd findings in the area. Lowell explains that

> me and the daughter have made some strange discoveries out here. Found us an old buffalo robe in a cave once that had three carbines wrapped up in it. All rusted out and the stocks were eaten away by the

wind, but they dated back to the 1890s. . . . Found a locket too, with
an old faded photograph of a young girl. Couldn't hardly make out the
face, but there was a shank of yellow hair in there with it. (Shepard
1996: 127)

These artifacts foreshadow the unique transformation that awaits
Price. As he rides with Lowell and his daughter, Price slowly becomes
separated from his companions and, in a foreshadowing of imagery
from *Kicking a Dead Horse*, finds himself alone in the desert. The man
is consumed by the landscape and eventually the past. Price finds
himself transformed into a man from the past astride the horse. He
looks down at his hands and finds that the "knuckles seemed to be
standing out, more prominent than usual. The broad fingernail on his
index finger seemed even broader and the bulging callus beneath it"
(Shepard 1996: 131); he morphs into the body and figure of a man who
is—quite literally—from the past. Price "felt himself dissolve" (Shepard
1996: 131). Now lost in both space and time, he accepts the uncanny
predicament, and

> thought that if he wandered long enough, he'd get good and lost. He'd
> get so hopelessly lost that he'd be forced into some part of himself that
> he'd never known before. Some part he'd be forced to meet up with. The
> proposition thrilled and terrified him. (Shepard 1996: 132)

Yet, Price is not a man immediately transplanted by the geographic and
cultural memory of a locale. Rather, he seems to exist in limbo between
the past and present. Though the man wishes to give himself over to
the memory of the past and of the place, "it was the mind that wouldn't
cooperate. He couldn't control the picturings" (Shepard 1996: 132).
Price cannot completely abandon his own time and place. His romantic
inclinations regarding the self versus the elements of nature found in the
desert are naïve and potentially deadly, for Price—like Hobart in *Kicking
a Dead Horse*—is wholly unprepared to survive such conditions. He has
found himself locked in the past, haunted by the cultural memories of
bravado, violence, and supposed liberation.

Though not transformational in the same sense, "See You in My Dreams" is an autobiographical piece that serves as a reflection on Shepard's own father as well as a template for *The Late Henry Moss*. The piece details the narrator's visit to his deceased father's home. Like a detective, the narrator attempts to piece together his long-estranged father's life through the objects and items that remain in the house. These material objects are evidence of a life lived.

> The walls, collaged with pictures torn from magazines. . . . Loretta Lynn; Dolly Parton; English settlers galloping across an ocean of emerald lawn; Hank Williams' tombstone . . . curled up photos of me and my sisters in our 4-H uniforms, showing sheep at the county fair . . . cans of half-eaten tuna fish and a crusty bowl of Esteban's black bean soup. Stacks of *National Geographic*, *Look*, and *Life* . . . . A peanut butter jar on the floor, half filled with brown water and soggy cigarette butts. Piles of letters he'd written and never sent. (Shepard 1996: 146)

These images detail that the father appreciated country music and kept the narrator in his thoughts as indicated through the photograph of the siblings. The bowl of soup reveals that his neighbor was indeed serving as a caretaker, as in *The Late Henry Moss*. The magazines indicate an interest in science and current events. Most telling are the letters written, yet never sent.

The narrator locates a letter addressed to himself and it reads

> You may think this great calamity that happened, way back when—this, so-called disaster between me and your mother—you might actually think it had something to do with you, but you're dead wrong. Whatever took place between me and her was strictly personal. See you in my dreams. (Shepard 1996: 146)

The son, whose father left after an abusive episode similar to the violent "big blow-out" in *The Late Henry Moss*, realizes that his father also suffered from his actions, and that the moment of the "so-called disaster" served as a traumatic episode for all, an incident that forever splintered the family, perpetually punishing the victims as well as the perpetrator.

In *Day Out of Days*, Shepard continues to address the lingering memories of the "big blow-out." A narrator's depiction of a similar traumatic event recurs in "One Night in the Long-Ago." The narrator states, "The father came home late and smashed every window in the house with a claw hammer? Is that it? . . . Ripped the front door off its hinges and then set fire to the backyard? . . . You'd think he'd be over it by, (sic) now, wouldn't you?" (Shepard 2011: 22). Shepard seemingly answers this rhetorical question by approaching the paternal figure many times throughout the volume. The fear of repeating the mistakes of the father—the curse of resenting one's father, yet being destined to become that same kind of patriarch—haunts Shepard in this stage of writing. In "She," a woman tells a man that "he'll wind up just exactly like his old man. Dead on the side of the road with no witness. I can see it clear as day" (Shepard 2011: 165).

The anxiety and fear of developing into one's own father is pursued to a greater degree as Shepard seemingly theorizes that violence and cruelty are embodied in the male body and inevitably passed from father to son. In "Things You Learn From Others," the narrator confesses that "what you don't learn, though, is how to protect others from your own manifestation of cruelty and malice which you've learned so insidiously through skin and blood" (Shepard 2011: 250). Violence and cruelty are biological and genetic. The individual has no agency in concerns of lineage and ancestry and is held hostage to one's disposition as determined by the past. This shadow of a dead father still haunting a narrator continues in "Bernalillo," in which the narrator details how his father died, and "Lost Coin," which chronicles a visit to his father's grave.

Perhaps the most evocative passage regarding a son's tangled history with his father is from "Orange Grove in My Past." The narrator explains,

> I thought I had done my level best, done everything I possibly could, not to become my father. Gone out of my way in every department: changed my name, first and last, falsified my birth certificate, deliberately walked

and swung my arms in exact counterpoint to the way he had; picked
out clothing the opposite of what he would have worn, right down
to the underwear; spoke without any trace of a Midwestern twang,
never kicked a dog in the ribs, never lost my temper over inanimate
objects . . . and never hit a woman in the face. I thought I had come a
long way in reshaping my total persona. I had absolutely no idea who
I was but I knew for sure it wasn't him. (Shepard 2011: 172)

The passage is further elevated to prominence within the Shepard
canon, for it is recited by Shepard himself in a voice-over in *Shepard
and Dark* as the writer drives through Bernalillo, the location of his
father's death.

The narrator of "See You in My Dreams" yearns for more material
to explain his father, yet only his uncle's "stories became like small links
for me in the mystery of my father" (Shepard 1996: 147). Through
this collection of material objects, the narrator is able to partially
construct the biography of his father. By the time of *Day Out of Days*,
Shepard's narrators have seemingly abandoned efforts to comprehend
and understand their father, but rather continue to wrestle with the
influence a figure and a traumatic event from the past can have on the
present.

As material objects can serve as reminders of a past, place can also
be an evocative location in stirring or retaining memories. In *The Late
Henry Moss*, Earl decides to retrace Henry's last night. This results in
Earl visiting a variety of bars and watering holes frequented by his
father. When Earl returns drunk from this expedition, Esteban explains
to the now-intoxicated Earl, "You wanted to go to those bars, Mr. Earl.
You wanted to visit all of Henry's old bars. That's what you told me"
(Shepard 2002: 83). Esteban believes that "maybe you thought you
would—discover something. . . . Something about Henry" (Shepard
2002: 83–4) through following his last excursion in the town. In a type
of reenactment—a dynamic explored later in this chapter—Earl traces
his father's visitations and is transformed into a partial incarnation of
Henry through intoxication. The power and pull of place in relation

to memory is also expounded upon in *Ages of the Moon*, as examined in Chapter 6, when a character speaks of carrying his dead wife upon his back throughout town as a type of revisiting of places that loomed large in their shared memory. Earl is unable to retrace these steps with the corpse of his father, but Henry remains a presence, not far from Earl's mind. By the play's conclusion, the importance of place—and its connection to memory—is also evident to Ray. After Ray and Earl have experienced a sort of catharsis as well as an understanding and reconciliation through reenactments and a flashback, Ray tells Earl, "I'm gonna stay awhile. . . . I feel—some kind of connection here" (Shepard 2002: 89). Though Ray has never visited this home, he realizes its significance—his own father lived and died there, and also, perhaps more importantly, it is the location in which he made peace both with his brother and his past.

Once the characters of these works have accessed the past, be it through the handling of a memory object or by communing with the essence of a place, they must inevitably confront traumatic memories. Some characters essentially "live in the past," allowing the actions of the past to consume their thoughts in present. Characters can consciously evoke the past for nostalgic reasons, or as an attempt to reconcile with a past event. Others may mourn the events that have occurred. The concept of past also relates to those characters who wish to forget events. Others simply deny that incidents from the past even occurred. Further, some characters misremember the past. Finally, there are characters who desperately attempt to forget the past but are unsuccessful. They are haunted by the past, unable to suppress the traumatic memories of events that have long since passed.

At the beginning of *Simpatico*, Carter and Vinnie confront one another and argue about how their scheme determined their subsequent lives. Carter resists such a discussion, saying, "We are going backwards, Vinnie" (Shepard 1995: 10). Vinnie wants to relive and reexamine the past, but Carter explains that "there was a time and place for risks and that time has passed" (Shepard 1995: 10). Carter asks Vinnie, "You're not still harboring something, are you Vinnie? That's not healthy. That's the kind of thing that leads to cancer and insanity" (Shepard 1995: 93). Of course, Vinnie is indeed harboring resentment regarding his past, but he is also concocting a plan to seize the present and the future, and to wage retribution against Carter.

As Carter seemingly holds the power in the relationship, and has put the past behind him, Vinnie continues to perseverate on the past, namely on how he could have retained both his friendship with Carter and his marriage to Rosie. He is ruled by regret. Carter refuses to publicly confess and "own up" to his role in the con and ensuing blackmail, an action which would threaten Carter's identity as a respectable member of the upper class. In retribution and in a desire to remake the past, Vinnie decides to take the evidence to Simms, and then to Rosie. When Carter agrees to meet with Vinnie's girlfriend Cecilia, Vinnie urges Carter to stress the old days when they ran horses. Vinnie compels Carter to emphasize "how I used to be. . . . Back—you know—when we were runnin' claimers. In the old days, you know. . . . Tell her how we used to swap those two geldings around—you know. How the money was flying" (Shepard 1995: 31). Vinnie's personal peak was achieved when he was with Carter and Rosie. Once Carter and Rosie left him, Vinnie began a rapid descent into failure and Carter simultaneously ascended to success. Vinnie views Carter's success and fortunes as something that he himself could have achieved. Because of that, Vinnie is obsessed by the moment of the trio's schism and wishes to return to that point in time to remake his life.

When Vinnie travels to Kentucky on this quest to rewrite his personal history, he visits Rosie. At first, she denies her relationship to Vinnie and the events discussed. Eventually, she acquiesces to their shared past. When he begins to plead his case to Rosie, she and the audience immediately realize that Vinnie is attempting to begin anew by metaphorically returning to the moment of the schism and having Rosie stay with him. Vinnie understands that the moment of the trio's splitting (as a result of the con and the blackmail) had solidified their eventual identities. The three had agreed to congregate after the con and blackmail were completed. Instead, Carter and Rosie left Vinnie.

Vinnie was abandoned as Carter absconded with his wife and car. In essence, Carter had become the beneficiary of the con and blackmail, taking Rosie, Vinnie's car, and presumably a good deal of the cut from the con.

With the box of evidence, Vinnie plans on destroying Carter. Obviously delusional, Vinnie goes to Rosie in a sad effort to reclaim the past. Vinnie attempts to romance Rosie with the nostalgia of their younger days. In those days, they would "read the form 'til two in the morning sometimes. Picking long-shots. Clocking works . . . . Slept in the truck bed. Listened to the tin roof flap on the shedrow" (Shepard 1995: 98). This vagabond lifestyle of decades past is now beyond reach for both of them, yet that does not halt Vinnie from attempting to start over with Rosie. Vinnie confesses, "I had this idea in my head. I had it all cooked up. I was gonna get another Buick. Just like the one I had. . . . I was thinking maybe we could still run off together" (Shepard 1995: 101–2). Rosie, now the wealthy wife of a respected horse owner in Kentucky, exclaims, "Oh Jesus, Vinnie. Give it up! Everything has already happened! It's already taken place. This is it. There's no 'running off' anymore. It's a done deal. You're in your little hell and I'm in mine" (Shepard 1995: 102). Rosie rejects Vinnie's offers and Vinnie is forced to return to California. By the end of the play it is assumed that Rosie continues as an alcoholic, bitter woman who seemingly regrets her past actions. Indeed, the trio gambled their identities on the success of the con. The con was successful, but it forcibly changed each character's identity, destroying their lives in the process. Paradoxically, it seems that only Simms, the blackmail victim who has made peace with his past, is now able to lead a fulfilling life.

Unlike Vinnie, who is both haunted by and perseverates on the past, Simms has reconciled with the past and looks only to the future. This ability to examine the past, yet focus on the future, is manifest through Simms' obsessions with horse bloodlines. The bloodlines are the family trees of horses and are key to identifying and predicting the ability of a horse to win races. Vinnie and Carter's blackmailing of Simms drove him from his position of power. Because he cannot change the past,

Simms attempts to predict the future. For Simms, bloodlines are "an endless chain. Never get to the bottom of it . . . the glaring truth of it all reaches up and slaps you right on the face" (Shepard 1995: 104). For Simms, bloodlines—as well as the human condition—are "all in the genes. We've got nothing to do with it. It was all decided generations ago. Faceless ancestors . . ." (Shepard 1995: 109). This pursuit of bloodlines allows an individual to partially predict the future. Even though this future cannot reverse the past, even a semblance of prescience allows the individual to prepare for future events. Because of this obsession with bloodlines, essentially past biological conditions that have been forged and are unchanging, Simms no longer ruminates on the past and looks only toward the future. This notion of ancestry, inheritance, and genealogy also recalls "Self-Made Man" in that humans, by the logic of that tale, are merely organic products that serve as a link in a great chain of temporal and generational existence.

As Vinnie obsesses about the past, Simms has simply allowed his own past to fade away. Like the ancestors of the horses he studies, the past has occurred and it is cemented—one can only confront the present and partially predict the future. In fact, as Simms has changed his name and relocated, it is as if the incident has given Simms a sense of rebirth. He explains to Vinnie that "you could put the past to death and start over. Right now . . . vengeance appeals to you more. . . . Why is blood more appealing than re-birth?" (Shepard 1995: 61). In fact, Simms believes the blackmail and con that ruined his former life gave him the opportunity of a second life. Simms explains that "loss can be a powerful elixir" (Shepard 1995: 65). Yet, Vinnie is not completely willing to allow the past to fade away, for his desire for vengeance against Carter keeps him obsessed with the past.

Carter later sends Cecilia to visit Simms to try to retrieve the box of evidence. When she recognizes him from the blackmail images, Simms explains the situation, once again extolling the virtues of relinquishing the past. Simms says, "Well, some of us get caught with our pants down and some don't. I was one of the lucky ones. . . . I got over it" (Shepard 1995: 118). Unlike Vinnie, who is obsessed with reclaiming the past to create a new life, and Carter, who is obsessed with reclaiming the evidence to preserve his present life, Simms is willing to allow the past to remain safely in the past.

At the conclusion of the play, both Vinnie's and Carter's positions—in relation to one another and the past—have reversed. Vinnie has apparently been able to sever his present identity from past events and holds the power in the relationship through the box of evidence. He accepts the present, yet Carter is now the one "going backwards." Carter explains, "I'm going to change my name. . . . I'm going to disappear. . . . I'm going to stay here with you. . . . We could maybe start up with the claimers again" (Shepard 1995: 131) to which Carter responds, "Those days are over, Carter. Long gone. Give it up" (Shepard 1995: 132). Carter even proposes that "I'll take your place and you can have mine. . . . You can have it all. Even Rosie" (Shepard 1995: 132). Vinnie has erased Carter's identity by holding the evidence over him. Carter now finds himself in the stranglehold of the past. Carter fears that the revelation of the con will destroy his present identity as a respected horse breeder. Simms' advice to Vinnie has apparently allowed Vinnie to escape from the traumatic events of his past.

Ray and Earl in *The Late Henry Moss* must also confront their own memories of the past to reconstruct their identities. At present, they are both damaged individuals in the process of reckoning with the "big blow-out." Unfortunately, they often misremember events from their past. Memory is tenuous, unstable, fleeting, and can be fraught with inconsistencies as time between the incident and the present increases. The focus of their disagreement is the "big blow-out." This violent episode involved Henry viciously beating his wife in front of their young sons. As the audience learns toward the end of the play, Earl fled during the abuse and Ray resents his older brother for refusing to protect him or their mother. When Ray first asserts his version of the events, namely that Earl ran away during the "big blow-out," Earl dismisses the memories as being altered by time, for "things get embellished over the years" (Shepard 2002: 9). To Ray, who witnessed the traumatic event and still suffers from its resonances, the memories are "still very vivid with me" (Shepard 2002: 8). Ray contends that Earl did indeed run away during the incident, yet Earl will not or cannot admit to his flight years ago. The audience—and Ray—are unable to know if Earl honestly does not recall leaving his brother and mother to Henry's violence. It is possible that Earl, as a result of the embarrassment about his inability to defend his mother, has chosen to misremember the past. When Ray accuses Earl of running, Earl responds that "it's no good carrying the wrong pictures around with you the rest of your life. They're liable to get more and more warped as time goes on. Pretty soon you'll forget how it really was" (Shepard 2002: 10). Both Ray and the audience are compelled to question the exact events of the "big blow-out," yet only in the concluding act of the play is the truth of the trauma revealed through the brothers reenacting the event.

Both brothers seemingly misremember the past, offering demon-strations of the subjective nature of memory. After being reunited at the beginning of the play, Ray and Earl have a conversation about a car. Earl contends that Ray was always under the hood of car, working on the car's engine. Ray responds that he never possessed a car. This moment of confusion reveals Earl's inability to accurately remember events, yet this is also true of Ray.

Ray tends to collapse his older brother (Earl) and their father (Henry) into one entity. This is first alluded to when Earl sings a profane ditty to which Ray responds, "I remember him singing that." Earl retorts, "That was me!" (Shepard 2002: 7). When the subject of the "big blow-out" is first discussed, Ray states that he recalls Earl's presence and "I remember windows exploding" (Shepard 2002: 8). Alarmed, Earl explains, "That was him, not me. That was him doing that. . . . You're getting me mixed up with him" (Shepard 2002: 8). For Ray, who experienced the trauma of both witnessing physical violence against his mother and enduring abandonment by his older brother, his own memory seems stable. In reality, Ray continually misremembers the actions of Earl and their father, often weaving them into one singular entity.

Yet, Ray is not the only character who begins to meld Earl and Henry into one figure. In Act III, Esteban cooks in the house as Earl sleeps off a vicious hangover. When Earl awakes, Esteban makes the mistake of comparing the son to the father. This comment angers Earl, who responds, "I am nothing like the old man!" (Shepard 2002: 83). Earl erupts at Esteban's comment. The truth is that Earl's alcohol abuse, tempestuousness, and potential for violence has him becoming more and more like Henry. This is literalized in the reenactment of the "big blow-out" when Ray attacks Earl. During the attack, Earl pleads with his brother, "That wasn't me that was doing that! That wasn't me! That was him!" (Shepard 2002: 100). Because of Earl's refusal to defend his mother from Henry, Earl has become complicit in the incident. In the moment of lashing out, Ray is simultaneously physically punishing both his father and his brother. To Ray, Henry and Earl are responsible for the traumatic "big blow-out" and its resultant consequences as both represent forces that traumatized Ray's early life. This trauma has lingered in Ray and continues to impact his life.

In all these works, the characters are metaphorically haunted by ghosts that act as constant reminders of the past. In *Simpatico*, as Carter presumably lives a charmed life, Vinnie believes that his own existence is a type of death. Vinnie complains that Carter never gave him a chance to fully live his life. Carter only offered him the "option to disappear . . . to perpetually change my name and address . . . to live like a ghost" (Shepard 1995: 15). To Carter, Vinnie is "dead . . . locked away" (Shepard 1995: 16). When Carter fled with Rosie and the Buick, ending their friendship, Vinnie became a victim held against his will by the events of the past. Only through vengeance, reconciliation, or exposure can Vinnie hope to commute this life sentence. Vinnie possesses the evidence, but he is unsure as to how to act upon it. He also realizes that the present is not fully constructed by events in the past. Through Simms, Vinnie learns of the opportunity for rebirth and resurrection. Perhaps to bury the past, one must give up on the quest for authenticity (detailed in Chapter 2) and embrace the ability to invent and reinvent the self to one's own desire. At the beginning of the play, Vinnie simply wants Carter to confess to authorities about his involvement in the blackmailing of Simms. In the end, Vinnie has forfeited this desire and recognizes the potential for a new beginning through the recreation of the self.

Throughout these works, the characters—as well as the audience—are conflicted as to the nature of the truth as connected to memory. When Carter arrives at Vinnie's apartment, and their argument ensues, Vinnie demands that Carter be truthful. To that, Carter responds, "The Truth! The Truth! And only one of us is able to have a handle on that I suppose" (Shepard 1995: 17). Vinnie, eagerly cutting closer to the disputed truth, responds, saying, "One of us is a helluva lot closer to it than the other one! . . . One of us has forgotten" (Shepard 1995: 17). The "one" referred to is, of course, Carter. The truth becomes even more contentious when the audience learns that Vinnie has also created a false identity for himself. Carter, having used the power and money accrued through the con and blackmail, has become a respected member of the gentry class. This identity betrays the truth of his background and ignores that the new "persona" of Carter is built upon a foundation of crime. But, Vinnie—who the audience is led to believe can see the past in much clearer terms—has also created a false identity. In his relationship with Cecilia, Vinnie has concocted a romantic backstory. He explains to Cecilia that he is a private investigator, and even uses the box of evidence and incriminating photographs as a type of "proof" of his occupation,[3] explaining to her that this is the evidence he has gathered.

In *Simpatico*, the audience must piece together (in a fashion similar to a private investigator) the truth as conveyed by the various characters. In *The Late Henry Moss*, the truth is "presented" to the audience through flashbacks. Once the media in which the narrative presented is altered, the essence of truth alters as well. In the play *Simpatico*, there are no literal, dramatized flashbacks. The audience must weave together the past events, cobbling together bits and pieces to construct an understanding of the con and resultant blackmail. In contrast, Matthew Warchus' 1999 cinematic adaptation of *Simpatico* literalizes the past.[4] Through flashbacks in which different actors play younger versions of Carter, Vinnie, and Rosie, the audience experiences the events as undisputed fact within the narrative. This is further stressed by the method Warchus employs for the flashbacks. Events from the past are preserved as "found footage." In essence, when the past is depicted, the action is often documented through grainy, unrefined filmstock and is shot as if it were the friends' own home movies from the time. Through this, the past is stabilized for the audience. The past is no longer variations of truth altered through narration and interpretation, but rather the truth exists as unquestionable evidence neither clouded nor compromised through memory. This stabilizing of the past works against the dynamics of memory as explored in the play.

As noted, *Simpatico* is preoccupied with notions of memory and truth, as well as with the investigation of the past. Vinnie, as previously mentioned, presents a false narrative of himself as a private investigator. In a later conversation with Vinnie, Simms bemoans the loss of great detective films. He even asks, "Whatever happened to the great plots?" (Shepard 1995: 56). Though Simms is referring to film plots, as in the story of a film, he himself was entangled in a "great plot" that drove him from the horse racing industry. After all, Simms was the victim/ mark/subject of a "plot" that concerned a con and blackmail. The idea of investigators and a "plot" is further pronounced in production. The stage version of *Simpatico* implicitly involves the audience in the detective work. Unlike the film, in which the past is presented and enacted through "found footage," the play requires the audience to piece together the clues, evidence, and testimonies to reach a conclusion. At times, these testimonies contradict one another, and the audience must construct an understood "truth" regarding events that occurred decades ago. So, the audience—like the characters—must construct their own version as to what they deem to be the truth.

In *The Late Henry Moss*, the narrative of the past becomes central to Ray's comprehension of his father. As Earl arrived at Henry's home just prior to his father's death, Earl is the keeper of the narrative of Henry's last days, yet Ray doubts the veracity of Earl's narrative. At the beginning of the play this skepticism is evident and becomes more pronounced as the action progresses. Ray does not believe Earl's narrative of the "big blow-out" trauma and has his own doubts about the validity of the narrative describing the last days of Henry. Referring to these final days, Ray asks, "Earl, would you mind going back through the whole story for me one more time? . . . There's some stuff that doesn't make sense" (Shepard 2002: 22).

Earl resents Ray's attempts to dig further and further to reveal the truth. Ray eventually calls in Taxi as a witness to testify regarding Henry's last days. Earl comments to Ray that "you thought maybe you'd get to the bottom of something—clear things up? Make some big reconciliation" to which Ray responds, "I don't need any reconciliation! I don't need it with you either!" (Shepard 2002: 44). Ray seems less interested in reconciliation than grasping an explanation of his father. Yet, when Taxi unspools the narrative of Henry's last day, it is Ray who resents the narrative. Ray condemns Taxi, accusing him of being related to liars: "Your whole family's a pack of liars. They were born liars. They couldn't help themselves" (Shepard 2002: 68). This accusation also reveals Ray's fear that one's past (genealogy) determines one's future. For Ray, the individual cannot shake the predetermined qualities generated through one's lineage, be it a penchant for fabricating the truth or a tendency toward alcohol-fueled violence. This is a source of fear, as well, for both Ray and Earl—like so many other Shepardian sons—are terrified of transforming into a variation of their father, a figure feared and despised, yet paradoxically respected. Taxi responds to this interrogation by attempting to flee, but Ray contends that Taxi now owes him a story. Up to this point, Ray has held fast to all the material possessions of Henry and now he craves the narrative. The narrative stands as intangible evidence of Henry's life, a testimony to his existence and death. Like *Simpatico*, a narrative of a past event must be constructed and shared as a method of reconciling with the past.

When Taxi shares the story of Henry, Ray still denies its veracity, noting that there is no way to prove the events. Ray compares Taxi to Earl, explaining that Taxi is just like his brother, a compulsive liar, willing to fabricate narratives. Ray believes that there must be an unquestionable, undeniable truth that can be accessed about the past, be it the distant past (the "big blow-out") or the recent past (Henry's last days before death). When Taxi narrates the events of Henry's last hours on earth, these are reenacted by the actors portraying Henry and his girlfriend Conchalla. The audience must engage the narration and the reenactment via flashback and make a conclusion regarding the truth of what did indeed occur. After taking in Taxi's narrative, Ray constructs a "truth" about both Henry's last hours and the "big-blow-out," telling Earl that he now has a metaphorical "clue" as to the actual occurrences. For Ray, the narrative has solidified his remembrance of the truth of the "big blow-out." In *Simpatico*, the past is not embodied, rather only narrated. As a result, the past remains nebulous to the audience. In *The Late Henry Moss*, the narration of Taxi is presented and performed through a flashback, but the characters are unsure if it is solely Taxi's interpretations of the events or that the narration accurately reflects the past.

When Earl returns after Taxi's exit, he becomes concerned that Taxi's story does not correlate to his own narrative of the events of Henry's last night. Earl complains that Taxi would attempt to "confuse the issue . . . the perdicament (sic)" (Shepard 2002: 90–1) to which Ray calmly responds, "I didn't know there was a perdicament (sic) here, Earl" (Shepard 2002: 91). Ray explains that "he just told me what happened, that's all. Simple story" (Shepard 2002: 91). Ray believes he now possesses the "truth" of Henry's final night. As this truth conflicts with Earl's characterization of Henry's last night, it threatens the integrity of Earl's narrative of the traumatic event. As before, Ray does not believe Earl's narrative of the "big blow-out" or of Henry's last days. After listening to Taxi's testimony, Ray no longer refers to his father as "Henry" but now calls him "Dad." Through Taxi's narrative, Ray has grown to further understand and perhaps even empathize with his father. With this knowledge of his father, Ray now assumes the power in the relationship. There is a reversal that occurs, for Ray now holds intimate knowledge of their father and the "big blow-out." Ray possesses the "truth" regarding the event. Earl is still paranoid about the narrative Taxi has shared, frightened that the truth may be revealed.

With the reversal of power and Ray possessing an intimate knowledge of their father, the younger brother now professes a closeness to Henry. As mentioned, this is the point in the play when Ray begins to refer to Henry as "Dad." This will eventually lead to speculation upon the nature of cruelty and its inheritability as well as the ability of survivors of trauma to reckon with their past through reenactment.

In these works, each character has endured—or is in the process of enduring—a trauma. In *Simpatico*, Vinnie's traumatic experience occurred when Carter and Rosie abandoned him. Carter was not traumatized by the event, but he is currently toiling with a trauma as Vinnie allows Carter to suffer under his own delusions, paranoia, and anxiety. Rosie's trauma can be located in the moment when she seduced Simms. This seduction, and its record in photographs, exists as a moment in which she sacrificed her dignity for the advancement of Carter and Vinnie. Of course, these actions and her subsequent flight with Carter helped to mold her resultant identity.

The Late Henry Moss, like *Simpatico*, revolves around a traumatic experience. Decades ago, Earl and Ray's father viciously beat their mother. During the incident, Earl fled the house. Earl is traumatized not only by witnessing Henry almost kill their mother, but he is equally plagued by the guilt that haunts him regarding his own inability to protect his mother. Ray is traumatized by witnessing the abuse and by his brother's abandonment. The trauma in *When the World was Green* is much less defined. There are specific moments, particularly when the Old Man explains the gory effects of war that impacted his village. The lingering effects of witnessing such brutality is certainly considered trauma. It can also be argued that his entire life was composed of traumatic events, as he was perpetually stalking another human and planning his demise. The most defining trauma of the Old Man's life was when he was given the order to execute Carl. The order cast his identity for the remainder of his life. The paradox in *When the World was Green* is that the action that serves as a sort of liberation for the Old Man functions as trauma for the Interviewer. When the Old Man murders the man he assumes is Carl, he is momentarily liberated from the hunter/hunted relationship. Yet, without that dyadic relationship, the Old Man's identity has now lost its definition. When the Interviewer learns of her own father's death, she is traumatized. For the Interviewer, that trauma is transformed into the impetus to learn as much as possible about her mysterious and ever-absent father.

Like the Old Man, Ray endured a significant trauma as a child. Ray confesses that he does not remember details from the "big blow-out" but he tells Earl that I "remember you leaving. That's all I remember. . . . When you first left. When the big blow-out happened" (Shepard 2002: 7). A moment later, Ray reveals that he actually remembers more of the incident, explaining, "You know what I'm talking' about. . . . That's very vivid with me. Like it happened yesterday. . . . I remember windows exploding . . . Blown out. Glass everywhere" (Shepard 2002: 8). Ray recalls little to reconstruct a coherent narrative, but he does possess sensory details from the event, explaining, "I remember it as a war or something. An invasion" with "Explosions. Screaming. Smoke" (Shepard 2002: 9). Ray has endured a traumatic event, an event that comparatively seems similar in its effects to that of a soldier during combat. As a result, Ray suffers from symptoms associated with PTSD. Earl's initial testimony of the events focuses not on the violence or sensory, impressionistic details, but rather couches it in terms of actions, and within that, Earl tends to place blame upon his mother as the instigator of the "big blow-out." Earl explains that their mother "locked [Henry] out of the house. . . . Set him right off. Went into one of his famous 'Wild Turkey' storms" (Shepard 2002: 9). As Earl has successfully hidden his own PTSD from Ray and others, the conclusion of the play reveals that Earl—like Ray—has suffered long-term effects from the incident. Throughout the play Ray continues to gather more clues, evidence, and testimony, and is able to further reconstruct the incident. A precise, factual narrative of the event becomes the goal for Ray as it has defined his identity. For Earl, we initially believe that the "big blow-out" has had little subsequent impact. At the conclusion of the play, the audience learns that the incident struck both men in differing, yet equally damaging ways. Their attempts at understanding the event work to further develop their relationship with one another and each's ability to form a cohesive identity. Essentially, the brothers must confront the shared trauma of the past, but in that, they are forced to reckon with one another and their father.

In *When the World was Green*, it is the originating event that has given both the Old Man and his family a sense of purpose. The event occurred "many, many years ago when the world was green, my great-great-great-grandfather was working in an open field with his mule . . . [and] the mule fell over dead in front of my grandfather's plow. He just dropped dead" (Shepard 202: 190). The Old Man contends that the mule was poisoned because "he'd been breaking out of his pen and eating the neighbor's crops" (Shepard 2002: 191). It is revealed that the neighbors poisoned the mule, but these neighbors were part of the Old Man's extended family. According to the Old Man, the family was "related to us, but they became our enemy on that day. They have always been our enemy. All this time" (Shepard 2002: 191). The Old Man explains that he wasn't even born when the original events transpired. In fact, many years have clouded the details regarding this century-old conflict, yet the past continues to haunt and, to a degree, control the present.

The Interviewer was subject to trauma at a young age when she was abandoned by her father. Her subsequent life has been a prolonged negotiation with that trauma. The trauma resonates throughout, for she defines herself by the pursuit of the mysterious man who is her father. For the Old Man, the trauma has also been prolonged. As the Old Man was born into a conflict between two families, the trauma has been a constant companion. His only hope of moving past the trauma of the hunting of his own cousin is to locate and dispatch the cousin. The Old Man must fulfill his destiny to rid himself of the traumatizing burden. Both the Interviewer and the Old Man are attempting to reckon with the trauma of their lives through the locating of another individual. The Old Man wants to find Carl. The Interviewer desires to learn more about her father. When these connections are made, the lingering effects of the trauma can be presumably resolved. The Old Man was indeed "born into it" and has little choice, yet this makes remarkably little difference with the predicament of the Interviewer. Though the Old Man was destined to hunt Carl, he did not learn of this mission until he was five years old. The recognition of his purpose in life can be seen as the traumatic event, while the subsequent pursuit and murder are extensions of that trauma. The Interviewer was abandoned by her father at the same age. By resolving their respective traumas, both risk eliminating the obsessions that gave their lives meaning and substance.

The Old Man confesses that he is unable to sleep at night. He is haunted not by images of his victim, but rather "Pictures . . . . Birds. Faces. Crowds of people fleeing. Wind. The open sea. Things like that" (Shepard 2002: 199). The Old Man is plagued by images that he perceived through his life, a life that was defined by (1) his relationship to Carl and (2) his familial obligations. Throughout his life, the Old Man has desired to create and transform through cooking, rather than fulfill his destiny as an appointed destroyer. When the victim is revealed not to be Carl, the Old Man realizes that his existence has been predicated on one sole purpose: to murder Carl. When the Old Man is denied the fulfillment of what he suspected was his destiny, he is placed in a position to no longer act on those expectations (as he is in prison). The realization that his life has had no meaning beyond the stalking of Carl becomes a retraumatizing event. As a result, he gains no pleasure from anything—including his beloved culinary delights—as he withers away in prison.

As in *Buried Child*, these works hinge on a "truth" that is usually secreted away from the various characters and is revealed toward the conclusion of the play. In that play, the audience learns about the murder and burying of the young child. Similar secrets are disinterred and brought forth in these three works. In *Simpatico*, the audience discovers that it was indeed Rosie who seduced Simms and posed for the incriminating photographs. In *The Late Henry Moss*, the audience learns what really occurred at the "big blow-out." Finally, in *When the World was Green*, the audience learns what the Interviewer has suspected, the Old Man did indeed murder her father.

For characters in *The Late Henry Moss* and *When the World was Green*, the process of reenacting is essential to the understanding of past events, specifically those events that can be understood to be traumatic. The process of reenactment within the context of the play allows for the past to be reanimated, resuscitated, reclaimed, and reperformed. Characters unconsciously/consciously reenact events from the past and these reenactments become vital to their memory and understanding of the past. In *The Late Henry Moss*, Ray and Earl experience the last days of their father through the testimony of Taxi and Esteban. In addition, they both reenact the persona of their father. In the first act, Earl attacks his younger brother, reenacting the violence of their father. At the end of the play, the power relations are reversed and Ray becomes the abusive patriarch. Both sons perform the role of their abusive father. Only through this reenactment do they both understand the transgressions of their father. It is through this reperformance of trauma that the brothers are able to reconcile with their past and one another. In contrast, *Simpatico* does not include a reenactment of traumatic events as a method of confronting and reconciling with the past. There is indeed an action, but roles are reversed. Carter and Vinnie reverse the power relationships, yet they are still caught in a perpetual "identity dance." At the conclusion of the play, Carter is obsessed with retaining his position in high society and seems to be descending into madness, while Vinnie returns to his false profession as a private investigator. Seemingly because they cannot reenact the trauma, and in turn reassess the events that determined their respective fates, they are doomed to remain in their destructive symbiotic relationship. There is no reconciliation. There is no moving forward, away from the past. The past will continue to haunt their present-day lives. This "identity dance"—like a tango with the leader position alternating—will continue, with no resolution.

As the Interviewer seeks answers and explanations regarding the murder of her father, the Old Man offers a compelling narrative of his life and exploits. When the Old Man cooks a meal for the Interviewer in the closing moments of the play, a sense of purpose, self, and identity is returned to him. In addition, he momentarily becomes a stand-in for the Interviewer's long-absent father. For the first time, after agreeing to the reenacting of his cooking, the Old Man can establish an identity independent of Carl. After the murder of an innocent man and his subsequent incarceration, the Old Man has abstained from cooking. The Old Man has been liberated from his symbiotic relationship, but he no longer has a sense of identity independent of Carl. The action which was to liberate him, based upon a long-forgotten trauma from the past, has resulted in a new trauma for the young woman whose father was murdered. Seemingly, the method to exorcise the demons of the past is to confront the trauma through performance and action. It is only under the Interviewer's insistence does the Old Man agree to prepare one last meal and it is through the actions of this process that he is able to commune both with the food and the Interviewer, bringing a sense of mutual peace to both characters. The process of reenacting a common practice from the Old Man's life allows the Interviewer to understand and forgive her father's murderer. In turn, the Old Man is momentarily allowed to revel in his craft and—for once—exist as an individual, independent of his familial obligations, creating rather than destroying.

All these reenactments posit notions regarding the ability of individuals to reckon with the memory of a past traumatic event. These notions include the efficacy of purging trauma through embodiment, the inescapability of replaying and reenacting the past and the agency an individual possesses in such reenactments. These notions in turn lead to questions such as: Are humans forever entangled in the "identity dance" with themselves and others? Do victims of familial abuse inevitably become "players" in reenactments in which they themselves become perpetrators? Can reenactment purge the individual of traumatized emotions and lead to a better understanding of their past?

The Late Henry Moss concludes with this exchange:

> **Ray** "You know me, Earl—I was never one to live in the past. That was never my deal"
> **Earl** "Yeah. Yeah, right. I remember." (Shepard 2002: 113)

With this utterance, there is an implicit understanding now between the brothers. They have recreated and reexperienced the trauma of their father's abuse. Both Earl and Ray have taken turns being "Henry," in the process inflicting violence. They have arrived at an agreement about the narrative of the events. Because of this reenactment, in which both men slipped in and out of the role of the father, they both have some understanding of their father's violence. Through the reenactment of traumatic events, the two have grown to better know their father and each other. It has allowed the event to be jarred open for further analysis and discussion, which leads to a reconciliation with the past, their father, and one another.

As noted, key to Earl and Ray accessing and comprehending the nature of their shared trauma is the reenactment of the events, with each man assuming the role of their father. In Act I, Earl inherits the mantle of his father when Ray interrogates his older brother about the "big blow-out." Ray states, "I'm not gonna give it up, Earl. You know why? Because I'm your witness. I'm your little brother. I saw you, Earl! I saw the whole thing. . . . I saw you! I saw you run!!" (Shepard 2002: 45). This assertion, which is later revealed to be true, questions Earl's loyalty to his brother and mother and insults Earl's courage. Earl pummels his younger brother, throwing him across the room and repeatedly kicking him in the gut. Earl apologizes to the shocked Esteban, stating, "I'm sorry about all this, Esteban. I truly am. I hate this kind of thing, myself. Family stuff" (Shepard 2002: 45). With such a comment, Earl further normalizes familial violence.

Later in the play, following Taxi's testimonial, Ray steps into the "Henry" role and abuses Earl. Ray has now become the inheritor of his father's tendencies toward violence. When Ray berates Earl, he repeatedly kicks him in the ribs. Ray says, "If I'm gonna be living here I'd like to have a little order. Scrub the floors maybe. The windows. Brighten the place up a bit. . . . You got a bucket around? A mop? . . . This is my house now. So I want it clean" (Shepard 2002: 95). This is an explicit channeling of Henry's persona. Ray forces Earl into the "mother" role in this restaging of the "big blow-out." The stage directions read "*Ray grabs Earl by the hair, shoves the apron into Earl's face and drags Earl over to the tub*" (Shepard 2002: 96). Earl must accept the subservient role of the mother. Ray orders Earl to "Scrub every inch of this floor till it shines like new money" (Shepard 2002: 96). With such an action, Earl cleans and removes the grime of the years to reach a "cleaner" understanding of the events. Ray screams, "You remember how mom used to work at it, don't ya? . . . You remember how she used to scrub, day in and day out. Scrub, scrub, scrub" (97). While Earl is forced to clean like their mother, Ray shouts, "All those hours and hours, slaving away—Slaving away. It was for him. . . . And then—here he'd come! Bustin' in the door. You remember." And the stage directions indicate that "*Ray rushes to the door, opens it slams it, then turns himself into drunken Henry*" (Shepard 2002: 98). Ray assumes the guise of Henry in this unconscious experiment in role-playing as a way to get at the truth regarding Henry and the "big blow-out." As Ray imitates Henry, he also narrates the action. As Ray channels Henry, Earl continues scrubbing, screaming, "I don't remember any of that" (99). Ray violently refutes those notions, yelling, "You were there, Earl. You were there the whole time" (Shepard 2002: 99). During Henry's abuse of their mother, Ray constantly "thought Earl's gonna stand up for her." (Shepard 2002: 99). Earl continues to deny his presence at the incident, explaining, "I wasn't there for that!" (Shepard 2002: 99). Ray continues, saying, "I barely came up to his waist. . . . He was kicking her, Earl! He was kicking her just like this!" (99). The script directs the actors in the following action: "*Ray starts savagely kicking Earl all over the stage*" (Shepard 2002: 99). As Ray abuses Earl, he continues screaming,

> And every time he kicked her his rage grew a little bit and his face changed! His eyes bulged out. . . . And her blood was flying all over the kitchen! . . . I kept thinking . . . Earl's gonna stop him. . . . I saw your car—your little shit Chevy. Kicking up dust the whole length of the hay field. (Shepard 2002: 100)

Ray has performed the role of Henry, while Earl has become their mother, the victim of Henry's wrath.

This reenactment stirs their memories of Henry, and the audience and the brothers experience Henry's recollections of the "big blow-out." Yet, Henry also suffered from this trauma. A resurrected Henry explains, "The day I died—She was on the floor. . . . I can see the floor—and—her blood—her blood was smeared across it. I thought I'd killed her—but it was me. It was me I killed" (Shepard 2002: 112). Following the reenactment, the brothers understand the guilt felt by Henry, but they do not justify or excuse his actions. The brothers understand that the alcohol abuse following the "big blow-out" served as a long, extended process of gradual suicide for their father. Yet Henry, ever a despicable person, still attempts to foist blame upon Earl, even from beyond the grave. Henry exclaims,

> You were there. You were there watching the whole time. I remember your beady eyes peering out at me from the hallway. You saw the whole thing. . . . I looked straight at you! You looked straight back. Your mother was screaming the whole time! . . . You coulda stopped me but you didn't. (Shepard 2002: 113)

To this, Earl explains, "I was—just-too-scared" (Shepard 2002: 113). Through reenactment, in which both brothers take turns in the role of the abusive father, they have both learned about themselves and their father. As a result, the two men, who now have a clear view of the truth regarding the "big blow-out" can begin the process of healing the decades-old wounds inflicted by the trauma.

Shepard's notions of memory and trauma are present throughout his corpus. Yet, it is only in his late work does Shepard offer methods of grappling with the past and its memories to transform the individual. Memory and trauma weigh heavily on Carter, Vinnie, and Rosie. Though the past is reckoned with, there is no conclusion, and Carter and Vinnie will be caught in a perpetual tango of identity and power controlled by their memories and the past. The reenactment of an event from the past, be it an action of creation or trauma, allows for a reckoning of the individual with his or her past. In essence, the character must "perform" to better understand their past and to comprehend their current identity and relationships with others. With the transformation of trauma through performance and reenactment, Ray and Earl and the Old Man and the Interviewer, respectively, have engaged their past and have reached a sense of peace with themselves, others, and their own trauma.

Notes

1 To a minor extent, trauma is explored in Katherine Weiss' short piece "Cultural Memory and War Trauma in Sam Shepard's *A Lie of the Mind, States of Shock* and *The Late Henry Moss*."

2 As previously noted, Shepard has commented that "a resolution isn't an ending; it's a strangulation" (Bottoms 3).

3 The idea of a man "impersonating" a private detective to impress women is the focus of "Thin Skin" in *Cruising Paradise*.

4 Though Shepard did not formally participate in the writing or production of the film, Warchus is a longtime theater director known primarily for his celebrated 2000 mounting of *True West* with Phillip Seymour Hoffman and John C. Reilly.

4

"I Miss the Cold War So Much": Interrogating Masculine and Conservative Narratives in *States of Shock* and *The God of Hell*

Elements of trauma appear in *States of Shock* (1992) and *The God of Hell* (2005), yet both works are notable for their peculiar position in Shepard's corpus. Both are emblematic of the playwright's willingness to experiment with aesthetics and content in this later stage of his career and are reflective of the writer's newly found political voice. Unlike previous work, both *States of Shock* and *The God of Hell* unabashedly engage with political issues and offer commentary on broader concerns of the contemporary world. Though much of Shepard's work during the late 1970s and the 1980s centered upon fathers and families, these two plays explore how these tropes interact with the larger concerns of macro-politics. *States of Shock* reveals the horror of war and the destructive influence of American foreign policy and masculine codes. *The God of Hell* indicts the George W. Bush Administration and its power overreach following the events of September 11, 2001, while meditating upon the persecution of those who opposed the so-called "War on Terror." At the time of *The God of Hell*'s production, Shepard, who has often been silent on his political views, exclaimed that "we're on the biggest losing streak we've ever had. How many people come home from Iraq with limbs missing? Yet we're supposed to be victorious in this thing. It's a fucking nightmare. Every day it's brainwashing, that this is a heroic thing we're involved in. It's unbelievable bullshit" (Shewey 2004). Shepard subsequently described *The God of Hell* as a "takeoff on Republican fascism, in a way" (McKinley 2004).

States of Shock and *The God of Hell* were created in the wake of other Shepard works that garnered the writer attention. Intriguingly, both *States of Shock* and *The God of Hell* seemingly jettison all the traits of their immediate forbears. *States of Shock* was Shepard's theatrical follow-up to *A Lie of the Mind* (1985), one of the author's most revered and controversial works. *States of Shock* is a sharp turn away from the subject matter, tone, and aesthetics of *A Lie of the Mind*. *The God of Hell* served as a return to the stage following the media-scrutinized, much-publicized, and thoroughly celebritized *The Late Henry Moss* (2000). *The God of Hell* is a dark farce that explores not families, but rather the effects of George W. Bush's so-called "War on Terror" upon rural Americans. Both *A Lie of the Mind* and *The Late Henry Moss* seemed to reify and reassert long-held notions regarding Shepard's work, namely his plays' focus on fathers, sons, and familial violence. Though these themes certainly creep into *States of Shock* and *The God of Hell*, both plays defy expectations of what Jill Dolan calls "a Shepard" (1986: 113). Both *States of Shock* and *The God of Hell* rebuke critical assumptions regarding the consistency of Shepard's aesthetic and his inability to be a politically engaged writer. Indeed, with each Shepard invokes a seemingly "new" aesthetic to reflect his "new" political voice.

Within theater studies, Shepard has been understood to be an apolitical writer, though the Late Style of Shepard challenges this notion. Indeed, just as Shepard experienced a "cultural moment" in the 1980s, he has experienced a "political moment" in his Late Style. Though his works can be discussed in terms of the politics of gender, Shepard himself has very rarely commented or written on political issues. As a major defining trait of the Late Style, Shepard emerges as a playwright explicitly engaging with the political concerns of the age. With *States of Shock* and *The God of Hell*, Shepard has created two works that lampoon and criticize American conservative politics of the early 1990s as well as the so-called "War on Terror" in the early twenty-first century. Though Shepard has not previously explored such political issues, questions, or concerns, the Late Style cycle poses questions and posits possible resolutions regarding the conservative turn in American politics. Namely, Shepard examines the "conservative narrative" of the United States, interrogates its dynamics and offers possible resolutions to the issue. With these plays, Shepard is explicitly exposing the corrupting narrative promulgated by conservative politicians and ideologues. As with other concerns in the Late Style, Shepard offers methods through which to resolve such a dilemma. Indeed, in these works Shepard interrogates the conservative narrative of the United States and illustrates methods in which to undermine, subvert, and even eliminate this destructive vision.

Though the politics of gender are a central topic in Shepard scholarship, there are few investigations of Shepard's considerations of broader American political concerns. This chapter is the first investigation of the political works from his Late Style. This chapter examines these works in light of Shepard's political turn and argues that they are indeed significant works within the corpus of Shepard and, as with all works from the Late Style, provide a resolution to a dilemma. As *States of Shock* represented his first foray into explicitly political work, Shepard has no previous political dilemmas to resolve in this late stage. Rather, both works pose dilemmas and provide solutions within the plays themselves. Further significance of such an investigation resides in the notion that Shepard has once again reinvented himself and his work. No longer working within a secluded world of obsessions and familial conflict, the Late Style heralds Shepard as a political writer specifically working toward the subversion of conservative hegemony. Fittingly, Shepard links the corrupting codes of masculinity with these destructive forces of conservatism. Finally, both works reveal another trait of the Late Style: an eagerness of Shepard to explore new aesthetics on stage. Both *States of Shock* and *The God of Hell* are formal experimentations—unlike even his experiments in the 1960s and 1970s—that require the audience, in a quasi-Brechtian sense, to reevaluate the politics of their own day.

The God of Hell opens on a Wisconsin farm. A married middle-aged couple, Frank and Emma, lead a seemingly non-eventful life. Frank tends to his beloved cows, while Emma keeps home and lovingly raises plants. This pastoral scene is disrupted when a mysterious figure from Frank's college years arrives looking for temporary residence. Frank has not seen or heard from the visitor Graig Haynes since college. In fact, Frank reveals that he believed Graig was dead. When Graig emerges from the basement for breakfast, he stresses that no one must know that he is at the farmhouse. Shortly after Graig arrives, a suited gentleman comes to the door, attempts to charm Emma, and eventually makes his way into the farmhouse. Emma is disturbed by the intruder, for he seems to know intimate details regarding both Emma and Frank. The man suspects that the couple is harboring a fugitive. The intruder is revealed to be Welch, an unspecified agent from the government who has arrived to return Graig to the mysterious and ominous Rocky Buttes. Welch contends that Graig has been contaminated and is a carrier of some sort of radiation. Emma notices that their houseguest occasionally emanates blue sparks from his fingers. Eventually, Welch locates the fugitive and tortures both the scientist and Frank. Frank transforms into a supporter of Welch. The farmer now wears a suit, acts in a manner similar to Welch, and has agreed to sell his cows. Welch reveals a plan to drop the now contaminated cows into an area in the United States, creating a national emergency that will allow the government to seize even more control. Led by Welch, Graig emerges from the basement on a leash. He is barefoot and hooded with electrodes attached to his genitals. The agent marches both men from the farmhouse to their next mission. As Welch leads his two new devotees, he urges Emma to "get in step." As Emma watches them disappear, her plants begin to glow a bright blue, akin to the sparks that shot from Graig's hands.

Critics were neither uniformly condemnatory nor congratulatory of *The God of Hell*, but the play did spur a number of interesting commentaries regarding the role of American theater in the wake of the events of September 11 and the so-called "War on Terror." After disappointment with *Eyes for Consuela* and *The Late Henry Moss*, Shepard stalwart Ben Brantley found that that the playwright "is in an encouragingly feisty mood these days" and that *The God of Hell* is "neither a smooth nor subtle play, at its best has an absurd and angry vigor that brings to mind Mr. Shepard's salad days as the ultimate wild dramatist of the 1960s" (2004). That said, Brantley explained that though it is "pretty standard agitprop," Shepard still demonstrates a "gift for finding deadpan surrealism in bucolic speech" (2004). *The Times Literary Supplement*'s John Stokes was generous, opining that despite the play being "at once too blatant and too theatrically literate to provoke spontaneous political comment" and that it "seems like one step forward and two steps back," it is reassuring to know that "Sam Shepard, after a period of relative inactivity, is imaginatively on the move" (2005). John Lahr in *The New Yorker* concluded that "Shepard doesn't have the structural prowess to turn his situation into genuine farce, but he manages a confident and unsettling scenario of surreal doom" (2004). Robert Brustein praised the play, placing it within the continuum of timely political New York City theater, with its ability to efficaciously respond to the so-called "War on Terror." For Brustein, *The God of Hell*

> represented a powerful indictment of how our conduct toward prisoners abroad was influencing government behavior at home. . . . In short, after a long period when American political theater was primarily devoted to issues of social injustice and unequal opportunities regarding women, gays and lesbians, blacks, Latinos, and other minorities, it is now beginning to look outward as well, examining our responsibilities toward the world. (2005)

Equally as politically engaged, 1992's *States of Shock* opens in Danny's, a family restaurant and diner. A waitress, Glory Bee, tends to a couple dressed in white, identified as White Woman and White Man. Throughout, the couple comments about the events of the play and draw attention to their passivity. Stubbs, a distant and injured young man, emerges in a wheelchair pushed by the older and embittered Colonel. Stubbs' wheelchair is adorned with American flags and other nationalistic paraphernalia, while the Colonel is dressed in an amalgam of militaristic symbols, such as war medals and a Civil War–era sword. The two men sit at a booth. It is revealed that Stubbs was severely wounded when protecting the Colonel's son during a battle and the two are at the restaurant to memorialize his death. Stubbs and the Colonel argue about the details of the battle. Stubbs refuses to conform to the Colonel's narrative of the events. The Colonel beats the wheelchair-bound Stubbs. The audience begins to realize that Stubbs is the Colonel's son and the Colonel is embarrassed that Stubbs did not valiantly perish in battle. With support from Glory Bee, Stubbs stands, while the Colonel collapses into the wheelchair. Seizing power over the Colonel, Stubbs takes the sword and prepares to decapitate his father as the lights go to black.

If reactions to his previous play (1985's *A Lie of the Mind*) were rapturous, the responses to Shepard's return to the New York stage with this Brechtian-Beckettian hybrid were absolutely condemnatory. Indeed, the six years between *A Lie of the Mind* and *States of Shock* reveal a shift not only in Shepard's aesthetic, but also critics' attitudes toward his work. The most insightful criticism regarding the play came from *The New York Times'* Frank Rich. Rich began his review by stating, "Sam Shepard has been away from New York theater for only six years—since the epic *Lie of the Mind*—but *States of Shock*, his new play at the American Palace, could lead you to believe he has been hibernating since his East Village emergence in the Vietnam era" (1991). For Rich, the play devolves into "narrow preaching" as well as "repetitive incantations and images that define the play's territory with didactic rigidity" resulting in a work that "does not really go anywhere intellectually or theatrically" but settles upon imposing "typical Shepard conceits" (1991). Rich concluded that with *States of Shock*, "Mr. Shepard seems to have shifted his customary creative process into reverse" (1991). In 1994, *The New York Times'* Ben Brantley, himself a self-confessed Shepard aficionado, reflected upon *States of Shock*, noting that it was "speared by critics" and led to "speculation that the playwright's skills had been left fallow for too long."

Aesthetically, *States of Shock* seeks not to replicate the assumed "realism" of previous plays such as *A Lie of the Mind* or *True West*. Rather, the play imports a nightmarish, Beckettian quality. The play also utilizes elements culled from happenings, expressionism, and surrealism. The imagery and performance techniques employed in *States of Shock* seemingly reveal the influence of Beckett and Brecht. Shepard has long noted Beckett and Brecht's impact upon his work. Such references by Shepard serve as citations to demonstrate their influence upon his dramaturgy. In turn, Shepard is inserting his work into the genealogy of revered twentieth-century playwrights. Shepard has revealed that he truly became interested in theater after reading *Waiting for Godot*, while on numerous occasions, Shepard has referenced Brecht as an inspiration.[1] *States of Shock*'s use of a character in a wheelchair consciously connects the play to *Endgame*, yet Shepard's vision is a reversal of the power dynamics utilized by Beckett. In *States of Shock*, it is the younger man that is bound by the wheelchair. These power relations are reversed by the conclusion of the play. In addition, there are further textual and performative connections to Beckett. Both the White Woman and the White Man appear to be escapees from a Beckett work. The White Woman and White Man are "white and pallid, like cadavers" (Shepard 1993: 5), occasionally slip into a "trance state" (Shepard 1993: 22), and are adorned "completely in white, very expensive outfits" (Shepard 1993: 5), perhaps an allusion to Beckett's use of the pallid, corpse-like characters in a number of plays and dramaticules. The couple's obsession with convenience and consumerism—and their inability or unwillingness to recognize the reality and dire situation that surrounds them—directly connects to Winnie and her husband in *Happy Days*. The White Woman's "wide-brimmed straw hat and elaborate jeweled dark glasses" (Shepard 1993: 5) further emphasize that connection. Though scholars have debated the "realism" of numerous Shepard plays, there is no doubt that *States of Shock* is working in a mode akin to surrealism and draws attention to its own artifice. *States of Shock* is appropriately subtitled "A Vaudeville Nightmare" and is an explicit departure from perceived notions of Shepardian "realism."

In general, Shepard's celebrated work only superficially obeys the strictures of realism. According to Susan Harris Smith, "Despite what the critics have seen as his drift towards realism, I would contend that Sam Shepard remains an experimentalist and that, though he fulfills the traditional American literary need for a masculine and autochthonic mythologizer, he continues to remain well outside the dominating discourse of realism" (1998: 39). Scholar John Glore has termed Shepard's work "nova-realism." For Glore, "nova-realism" indicates "not only newness, but also the process whereby the newness is attained—a regenerative decimation of stuffy, old-fashioned realism in the service behind forms, behind surfaces" (1981: 57). Bottoms employs the term "subjective expressionism" to describe Shepard's brand of realism in which characters perform "externalizations of raw emotion" (Bottoms 1998: 42–3). Vanden Heuvel terms Shepard's aesthetic as "modified domestic realism" (1991: 212). Beyond this concept, Vanden Heuvel suggests that Shepard employs such "performance gestures to undercut or ironize the realist framework" and through such actions "suggest that within even the status quo lies the potential for transformation and difference, the possibility of 'another kind of world'" (1991: 214). William Demastes has further problematized notions of "naturalism" and "realism" in Shepard's work in *Beyond Naturalism: A New Realism in American Theatre* (1988) and the Demastes-edited volume *Realism and the American Dramatic Tradition* (1996).

The God of Hell operates in a world much closer to "realism," but this reality is brought into discord through the introduction of a power or ability that defies normal human capabilities. In that sense, *The God of Hell* works as a piece of science fiction. Scholars have turned toward Brecht to better explain the effect the science fiction genre has upon readers. As a result, this evocation of science fiction and Brecht are appropriate when considering the dynamics of *The God of Hell*. When approaching science fiction as a literary genre, Istvan Csiscery-Ronay's theory of *novum* and Darko Suvin's *cognitive estrangement* aid in the deconstruction of the form. The concept of the *novum* can be described as the "innovation or novelty in [a science fiction] text from which the most important distinctions between the world of the tale from the world of the reader stem" (Csicsery-Ronay 2003: 119). For Suvin, science fiction creates the unique effect of *cognitive estrangement*. This can be described as a reality made strange or bizarre, but one that casts light on contemporary issues. Similar to Brecht's distancing or alienation effect (*Verfremdungseffekt*), science fiction's *cognitive estrangement* "allows [the audience or reader] to recognize a subject, but at the same time make it seem unfamiliar" (Suvin 1978: 60). This mode allows Shepard to stage an interrogation of the politics of torture by having the audience actually witness reenactments of brutal procedures on stage. The science fiction elements make the experience simultaneously familiar and new.

The God of Hell, like Shepard's comfortably apolitical *Geography of a Horse Dreamer* (1974), takes a scenario that seemingly reflects reality, then introduces a *novum* that destabilizes that understood notion of reality. For example, much of the events at the beginning of *Geography of a Horse Dreamer* seem to occur in reality. The element (*novum*) introduced into this reality is the soothsaying power possessed by a young man, Cody. He can predict with shocking accuracy the winner of horse races. As a result, he is being held captive by a gang and forced to share his visions so that they can place winning bets. Eventually, the play devolves into a torrent of garish, Sam Peckinpah-inspired violence. Similarly, *The God of Hell* begins in reality, until an outsider (Graig) is introduced. Graig has been infected with a type of radiation and it has consequently granted him mysterious powers manifested through blue bolts that fly from his hands. Unlike many of Shepard's plays, where minor elements of the play seem to work against assumptions of reality, the *novum* of *The God of Hell* (the mysterious blue bolts) immediately moves the work into an unsteady realm that resides somewhere between science fiction, farce, and political satire. As with Shepard's refusal to abide definitions and delineations while engaging with various media, Shepard also resists the stability of genre. Like *Geography of a Horse Dreamer*, *The God of Hell* also devolves into a scenario of stylized and ludicrous behavior. As *Geography of a Horse Dreamer* begins with a "realistic" scene and concludes with a bloodbath, *The God of Hell* starts as a "farm saga" (like *Curse of the Starving Class* or *Buried Child*) and closes with manic, military steps performed by men with electrodes attached to their genitalia. With the *novum* introduced, the destabilized expectations of the audience in relation to the archetypal Shepard play are further problematized. The intertextual relations between Shepard's work and influences are allowed to reverberate, creating intriguing amalgams of imagery and aesthetics that offer an incendiary critique of American policies.

Shepard invokes Beckett and Brecht in a multitude of ways in this pair of political plays. Beyond the imagery utilized, the characters of *States of Shock* also echo Beckettian figures through verbalizations, such as the Colonel's absurdly protracted pronunciation of "MAROOOOOOOOONED" (Shepard 1993: 45) which harkens to Krapp's relishing of the word "Spoooool" in *Krapp's Last Tape*. In a Beckettian fashion, Stubbs also incessantly repeats phrases such as, "Become a Man!" (Shepard 1993: 27). Perhaps the noteworthy Brechtian element located in *States of Shock* is the use of periodic disruptions. *States of Shock* employs musical cues, dance, drumming, projected imagery, whistles, and absurd violence to periodically disrupt the audience in defiance of the allure of character and emotion to remind the audience of the recent Gulf War. This forces the spectator to consider the events and dynamics of the world beyond the walls of the theater. As much of Brecht's work explicitly addressed politics, perhaps it is fitting that Shepard would appropriate Brechtian aesthetics for his first overtly political work.

Shepard himself draws attention to this dramaturgical device. The Colonel notes that Stubbs has "suffered a uh—kind of disruption" (Shepard 1993: 6). Similarly, the spectators undergo a series of disruptions. These disruptions prohibit prolonged empathy with characters and remind the audience of the war at the time. But, the disruptions also convey the televisual nature of Gulf War I as the military action became a "theater of war" for CNN's incessant coverage from Iraq and Kuwait. Finally, these explosions of visual and sonic dissonance replicate and theatricalize the disruptions experienced by Stubbs. In essence, the play in performance mimics and enacts the phenomenological experience of the returning veteran who suffers from a variation of post-traumatic stress syndrome. The experience of the performance duplicates the experience of sensory overload endured by the physically and psychologically damaged former soldiers.

But, what are we to make of these performative references to Beckett and Brecht? Certainly, these works confirm the efficacy of imagery and performative aesthetics gleaned from Beckett and Brecht. Also, the invocation of such imagery and aesthetics allows Shepard to scribe himself into the genealogy of playwrights. In addition, as Shepard is moving into new concerns (politics) within his corpus, he seemingly appropriates aspects and elements from other playwrights. In turn, these elements serve as aesthetic stabilizers as Shepard ventures into a new thematic realm. As mentioned in a previous chapter, Shepard's work of this later period often draws comparisons to Beckett's work. As a result, the use of this Beckettian imagery and Brechtian aesthetics does indeed reveal Shepard's willingness to "light out for new territory," yet this new territory, in the broader sense of theater and performance, is well-trodden. Indeed, Shepard's use of Beckettian and Brechtian elements perhaps reveals less about the playwright's willingness to experiment than the monumental impact Beckett and Brecht had upon playwrights who matriculated and matured during of the 1960s. But, it must be said, Shepard appropriates these elements and combines them with some of his own thematics that have resonated throughout his work, such as masculinity. In the Late Style, Shepard investigates the consequences of masculinity further, examining its impact upon American military interventions, conservative narratives, and policies regarding torture.

As masculinity and concerns of the male appear throughout Shepard's work, perhaps it is no surprise that many of the plays themselves include references to phalluses. This is true of the Late Style political plays. Indeed, *States of Shock* and *The God of Hell* not only center upon political concerns, but also use a physical signifier of traditional masculinity—the penis—as an entry point for discussing male codes, patriarchy, and ideology. The tensions and conflicts associated with codes of masculinity are a well-trodden theme in Shepard's corpus, but they are pursued to a darkly comic extreme through explorations of the significance of the penis to one's conception of masculinity and the connection between masculinity and politics.

Both *States of Shock* and *The God of Hell* repeatedly reference male genitalia. In these plays the phallus becomes a target of the masculine codes, and by extension, conservative ideology. The position of power is held by men (the Colonel and Welch) who possess undamaged or non-distressed genitalia. They both retain power through either mocking or damaging another man's genitals. As the penis can be a physical identifier of male identity, it also becomes the location of contention for power in the dynamics of various relationships. The characters in the plays wage a battle that can result in emasculation through genital mutilation or victory through the reclamation of virility. In both plays, the threat to the penis—and by extension, the male—is enacted by conservative forces representing outmoded codes of masculinity. For example, Stubbs is revealed to be impotent as a result of his injury. This injury is a direct result of his attempt to enact the masculine ideals put forth by the Colonel. In *The God of Hell*, both Frank and Graig undergo genital torture when they refuse to conform to the masculine codes aligned with conservative ideology espoused by Welch. In both plays, the penis becomes a vital link between the character, his identity, and the relationship to the prevailing power dynamics of politics.

In *States of Shock*, Stubbs reveals that "when I was hit I could no longer get my 'thing' up. It just hangs there now. Like dead meat. Like road kill . . . MY THING HANGS LIKE DEAD MEAT" (Shepard 1993: 12). The Colonel has rejected Stubbs because of his inability to enact the ideals of the masculine code in battle. Stubbs has been injured and the signifier of his manhood (the ability for his penis to become erect) has been negated. Stubbs collapses this virility into his own identity. Only toward the conclusion of the play, when he reclaims his masculinity through the ability to achieve an erection, does Stubbs seek to destroy the Colonel.

This reversal of power is not achieved in *The God of Hell*. Frank and Graig are victims of a type of transformative behavior modification in which Welch preys upon their fear of emasculation. The Colonel also attempts to control Stubbs' behavior through medication and bribes, as well as threats to reveal his erectile deficiency to the patrons of the entire restaurant. When the Colonel notices that Stubbs and Glory Bee seem to have a mutual attraction, he squashes Stubbs' hopes and confidence by pointedly asking, "What're you going to do when she finds out about your 'thing,' Stubbs?" (Shepard 1993: 37). This power-play continues to undercut any sense of virility—or autonomy, for that matter—that may be growing within Stubbs. With such actions, the Colonel easily slips into the abusive father archetype so familiar within Shepard's work. The Colonel not only consistently degrades Stubbs, but conveys the embarrassment he feels at Stubbs' mere presence. Stubbs is a living reminder of the destructive reality of war and a blow to the outdated, conservative narrative of the heroism of war. The Colonel's actions toward Stubbs cause the young man to question, "Why are you so determined to abandon me? . . . Is it my impotence?" (Shepard 1993: 36). This impotence is a reference to Stubbs' literal impotency, but it also refers to his inability to enact and perform the masculine ideals put forth by the Colonel's code.

Stubbs' sexual impotency is also viewed as a "hollowness" at his core, not only figuratively, but also literally. Stubbs' injury, displayed to the audience throughout the play, is indicated as a "massive read scar in the center of his chest" (Shepard 1993: 7). He later states, "The middle of me is all dead. The core. I'm eighty percent mutilated. The part of me that goes on living has no memory of the parts that are all dead. They've been separated for all time" (Shepard 1993: 14). Stubbs later explains that "it went straight through me and out the other side. It left a hole I can never fill" (Shepard 1993: 24). As with Stubbs' impotency, the Colonel views this "emptiness" as an indicator of the loss of masculinity, and Stubbs' only hope—according to the Colonel—is to appeal to the Colonel's sense of masculine charity. The Colonel states, "The hole through your middle. The rotting core. The limpness. There's no way you can disguise something like that. Your only hope is to throw yourself at my feet and beg for mercy. Imitate my every move. I'm your only chance now" (Shepard 1993: 41). For Stubbs, the hollowness in his chest parallels the damages to his genitals. Stubbs is emotionally (chest/heart) and sexually (genitals) damaged. For Shepard's men, the heart, genitals, and politics seem to be tightly interwoven. The only way to overcome emasculation is to perform, enact, and embody—like the Colonel, like Welch—the masculine code as prescribed by the conservative American patriarchy.

Similarly, when both Frank and Graig are unwilling to conform to the demands of the agent Welch, and by proxy the patriarchal government that he represents, electrodes are attached to Frank and Graig's penises. Once the genitals are placed in pain—essentially sexual torture—the individual can be controlled. In both *States of Shock* and *The God of Hell*, penises are seen not only as direct links to male identity, but also as vital conduits to male thought processes. Through the genitals the man's self and brain can be accessed. When Welch attempts to transform Frank and Graig into his minions, it is through the torture of the genitals. When Act II opens, Frank "enters from outside through the porch door dressed in suit and ties exactly like Welch's and carrying an attaché case exactly like Welch's. He walks very bowlegged and sore as though something visible has happened to his genitalia" (Shepard 2005: 77). It is revealed that Frank performs according to Welch's demands precisely because of the genital torture he endured. Later, in a conversation with Graig, Welch references the "long, tedious procedure. The intensive training. The sleepless nights. . . . What would happen to your body now if you had to undergo the same ordeal? The same stress to your appendages. . . . The pain to your penis, for instance?" (Shepard 2005: 72–3). It is obvious that the "training" referenced by Welch involved accessing the brain of Graig through inflicting pain upon the penis. After Frank appears in the decidedly Welchian regalia, he announces to Emma that he has sold his beloved heifers and has fully subscribed to Welch's ideology. Welch has been successful in rewiring and rewriting Frank's brain and identity through torturing his penis.

Contrastingly, such approaches to reifying masculine codes and patriarchal hegemony fail in *States of Shock*. As the Colonel continues to lord over the infirm Stubbs, it is the injured soldiers' genitals that are referenced as an indicator of his failed masculinity. Though the Colonel attempts to control Stubbs through the penis—and the degradation of Stubbs' virility—the Colonel is not completely successful, which allows for Stubbs to reassert his virility and destroy the embodiment of patriarchal power. In sum, masculine codes and conservative ideology threaten the physical indicators of masculine identity. Through torture, fear, and intimidation, forces of conservatism, as represented by the Colonel and Welch, attempt to stomp out any opinion that can be perceived as rebuking or undermining the conservative narratives of history, masculinity, and the nation.

In *The God of Hell*, Emma, being the sole woman of the play, is seemingly immune to the actions of Welch. He threateningly demands for her to "get in step" (Shepard 2005: 98), yet Welch cannot force her to enact the masculine codes of the ideologically conservative government. Welch can only control a male, for he forces the male to submit to masculine codes by threatening the victim's identity and corporeal signifier of masculinity. Similarly, Glory Bee is able to resist the masculine codes of the Colonel and even assists in Stubbs' usurping of the patriarchy. Key to the proliferation and retention of the patriarchy is the instillation of fear upon subjects. The attempt to force Stubbs to concede to male codes through degradation is reversed when a newly virile Stubbs seizes power from the Colonel. The conclusion is much more dour in *The God of Hell*, for the masculine code embodied by the conservative ideology of the government seems to be victorious over men, yet women are left with a choice to either comply or resist the patriarchy. Apparently, the key to retaining the patriarchy and masculine codes is through the proliferation and reproduction of masculine codes that are enforced through instilling fear in others. This reproduction of the code calls for a type of adherence and continual enactment of the codes of masculinity, yet these codes can be contested and resisted by women who refuse to subscribe to such an ideology.

The threats to masculinity—and an attempt to force the subjugated into conforming to masculine codes—result in both psychological and physical torture. The Colonel punishes, humiliates, and tortures Stubbs in an attempt to have the injured soldier conform to masculine codes and the conservative narrative of war. In *The God of Hell*, Welch threatens various forms of tactics for extracting information. When Emma offers resistance to Welch, he threatens that "we could resort to high-priority tactics if we were forced to" (Shepard 2005: 63). When he locates Graig, Welch taunts him, rhyming Graig's last name (Haynes) with "brains, maims, flames, chains" (Shepard 2005: 67). These terms, as presented in such a series, hint at some of the cruelty Graig has previously endured. Eventually, torture is utilized on both Frank and Graig as a way to punish and modify/transform them. *The God of Hell* also considers the larger implications of the use of torture by Americans upon "enemy combatants." Historically, George W. Bush, the Central Intelligence Agency, and the Department of Justice used actions deemed by the Geneva Convention to be torture. The Bush Administration used the term "enhanced interrogation," yet these actions included waterboarding, sleep deprivation, and sensory overload which are indeed understood to be torture.

The God of Hell also utilizes visual elements to evoke a historical event that was revealed during the Bush presidency. When Graig is marched out on stage following his basement session with Welch, Graig is described as "now in T-shirt, bare feet, and old khaki pants. He wears a black hood on his head" and a "cord runs directly into the fly of Haynes's pants" (Shepard 2005: 90). Welch is using the cord as a type of leash to lead the man around. This image echoes the photographs that accompanied Seymour Hersh's journalistic expose of the Abu Ghraib prison. In Abu Ghraib, prisoners were stripped, hooded, humiliated, wired to electrodes, and led by leashes. Shepard uses the imagery of Abu Ghraib to draw attention to the willingness of those representing an ideologically conservative government to use torture and related techniques, perhaps even against its own citizens, especially on those who question or oppose the government's ideology. Further, Shepard's depiction of these techniques through performance forces the audience to witness torture. Such a performance offers a live depiction of torture and demonstrates the dehumanizing cruelty that became obscured by the various political debates surrounding the Abu Ghraib scandal.

Prior to the revelation of the actions at Abu Ghraib, the American public was engaged in a debate regarding the use of torture on prisoners of war. Though torture has not been proven to be an efficacious interrogation method, the Bush Administration pushed for the use of controversial techniques through the now infamous "Torture Memos." A portion of that debate centered upon the definition of torture. When Emma initially sees the hooded Graig (and the traumatized Frank), she asks if Welch is torturing Graig. Welch denies torturing the man, claiming, "We are not in a Third World nation, here. . . . This isn't some dark corner of the Congo" (Shepard 2005: 87). But indeed Welch, like many other conservative zealots, has seized the narrative and terminology that describe the events in an effort to counteract any claims of torture.

In practice, the torturer debases the victim. This debasement "transforms" the victim of torture into an obeying creature. In essence, torture serves to "train" the victim. Welch is attempting to force Frank and Graig to comply with his demands and to "get in step" with the ideology of the government. This transformation of the subject is akin to the "training" of a dog. When Emma sees the hooded and wired Graig, Welch offers her the "leash" that leads Graig and states, "It's just like holding the leash of a well-behaved dog" (Shepard 2005: 90). Though torture is physically inflicted on the individual with the purpose of extracting information or punishing, a secondary reason for its use is the display of the tortured. The individual who undergoes torture and interrogation serves as a reminder to others of the consequences of opposing the dominant power. At the beginning of Act II, Frank has been transformed by Welch into a "believer" through torture. Frank can now subscribe to the ideology of Welch while the audience witnesses the "transformation" through the torture of Graig.

But to what end are the Colonel and Welch attempting to control the men of *States of Shock* and *The God of Hell*? These enforcers of the patriarchy and defenders of politically conservative values seek to control and remake Stubbs, Frank and Graig through humiliation and domination. This humiliation and domination are centered upon the men's genitalia, as the minds of Stubbs, Frank, and Graig are accessed through their penis. As the men's notions of masculinity and identity are physicalized through the presence of the penis, it serves the Colonel and Welch in their differing power stuggles to target the penis in an attempt to alter the mind. But why alter the mind? Both the Colonel and Welch demand that their victims conform to masculine codes, and in these masculine codes reside the valorization of certain notions linked to politically conservative narratives of manhood and national identity. In essence, both the Colonel and Welch are attempting to "remake" the men into their visions of what it means to be masculine and American, and by an assumed natural extension, a man who subscribes to a conservative ideology. Of course the tactics utilized by both the Colonel and Welch have differing results, yet an analysis of their demands of conformity to a politically conservative, patriarchal narrative reveals how the forces of masculine codes are not only destructive, but can spread and contaminate beyond the borders of personal and familial relationships.

States of Shock and *The God of Hell* depict an assault by masculine, political conservatives (The Colonel and Welch) upon potentially subversive forces (Stubbs, Frank, and Graig) who deign to question or deny the supremacy of the grand, patriarchal narrative. Because of their inability to "get in step" as Welch states, these dissenters are subjected to humiliation and torture in an attempt to force them to subscribe to the grand, patriarchal narrative. If the masculine, conservative narrative resides at the center of this contention present in both works, what indeed is this narrative? There are glimpses and images dropped throughout both works, but a prime indicator of this narrative can be located in a line shared between the two plays. In *States of Shock*, Glory Bee, in initial agreement with the Colonel's lament of the present, proclaims, "I missed the Cold War with all my heart" (Shepard 1993: 41). Similarly, the recently "transformed" Frank announces, "I miss the Cold War so much" (Shepard 2005: 91).

How could the Cold War be central to this masculine, conservative narrative vision of the United States?

Many Americans view the Cold War era as the moment when the United States decisively asserted its role as a hegemonic superpower. Following the Second World War, the United States (along with the Soviet Union) emerged as the two dominant global powers. Elements of the American Empire (through cultural, military, political, and economic hegemony) stretched from Japan and the Philippines to the Caribbean and Germany. This reach and domination allowed for the solidification of the United States' status resulting in a direct competition/conflict with the Soviet Union. The world itself was placed into a binary—nations and cultures were deigned to be either capitalist or communist. This binary was part and parcel of the narrative of the imperial, patriarchal forces leading the United States at the time. In addition, this resulted in the myth of American exceptionalism— essentially, the concept that the United States' assumed supremacy over other nations was justified by God. By this extension, the United States viewed itself as a sort of "holy land" with its own saints (the "Founding Fathers"), creeds ("The Pledge of Allegiance"), and holy documents ("The Constitution").

Indeed, the post–Second World War era did lead to economic expansion and growing fortunes for some American citizens. But, under such opposition to the Soviet Union, and the subscription to a binary worldview, conformity and nationalism were the doctrine of the age. Though the Cold War involved such horrific occurrences as the Vietnam War, the Cuban Missile Crisis, McCarthyism, and the prevalence of Jim Crow laws in some areas of the nation, for many political conservatives it remains a period of unparalleled strength and greatness. Political conservatives, producing their own narrative, can easily view the 1950s and early 1960s as the "Good Old Days." This essentially ignores, negates, and dismisses the importance of youth, counter- and subcultures, civil rights, social justice movements, feminism, gay liberation, sexual liberation, and the seeds of identity politics. These various political movements would emerge between the early 1960s and the 1980s and seek to dismantle the white, heterosexual privileged patriarchy that continued through the immediate aftermath of the Second World War.

With such romance for the Cold War, perhaps it is not shocking that political conservatives utilize moments of national crisis to reassert masculine and nationalistic narratives borrowed from the Cold War era. *States of Shock* was written during Gulf War I, which began under the presidency of George H. W. Bush. *The God of Hell* was written during the aftermath of the attacks upon the World Trade Center, which led to Gulf War II, under the presidential term of George W. Bush. These two wars allowed for the nations to harken to the Second World War and the Cold War, eras driven by the often termed "Greatest Generation." Certainly, the Second World War and the Cold War are ripe periods for nostalgic waxing. The conservative narrative of that period of history often evokes white picket fences, families attending church, American flags proudly displayed, children properly dressed, kitchen-bound women baking casseroles, and men unwinding with a Scotch after work. This idealization and valorization of the Cold War allows the conservative to assert the importance of (heterosexual, white) "family values" to American identity. According to the conservative narrative, with the "decay" of "family values" in the mid- and late 1960s, the United States entered a period of decline. With Gulf War I and Gulf War II (along with the USA Patriot Act and the rise of the religious right within American politics), the conservative narrative was once again proclaimed to be the "authentic" history of the United States. With both *States of Shock* and *The God of Hell*, Shepard seizes upon periods (Gulf War I and 9/11/Gulf War II/"War on Terror", respectively) in which the conservative narrative was once again held as the history of the nation, and individuals who sought to question this narrative were denounced, silenced, or "transformed" into subscribers to that narrative.

A central conflict of *States of Shock* circulates around a battlefield narrative. The Colonel explains that he and Stubbs are at the restaurant to memorialize his son who, according to the Colonel, was killed in battle. The Colonel refuses (1) to acknowledge that Stubbs is actually his son and (2) to believe the true narrative of the events that led to the physical injury of Stubbs. The Colonel retains and holds fast to a mythic narrative of war and is unwilling to accept the reality of the battlefield. The Colonel demands that Stubbs retell the story of the battle, yet he refuses to believe the experiential testimony offered by Stubbs. Stubbs provides an "authentic" depiction of events, while the Colonel wishes only to hear about a battle that reifies his masculine and conservative beliefs; that the Colonel wishes for Stubbs to reenact the battle with toys indicates the infantilism of such a conservative vision of war. Rather than something akin to "The Charge of the Light Brigade," Stubbs offers a narrative that centers upon the reality of war. Stubbs explains,

> It's very clear what happened. We were back to back. . . . I could feel his spine trembling on my spine. There was nothing we could do about fear. We couldn't bargain with fear. . . . It was friendly fire that took us out. That's what it was. . . . It was coming straight at us. . . . It was friendly fire. It smiled in my face. I could see its teeth when it hit us. I could see its tongue. . . . There was a face on the nose of the missile. They'd painted a face. You could see it coming. . . . We opened our arms to it. We couldn't resist its embrace. We were lovers when it hit us. We were in heaven. (Shepard 1993: 32)

This narrative unmakes a variety of conservative assumptions regarding war and battle. Stubbs is injured and his fellow soldier is killed not by the enemy in a heroic stand-off, but as the two quiver in fear. This subverts the "macho" narrative of the soldier defending himself and fellow troops. The two men consider praying, yet they do not know how to pray and they don't seem to believe in God. This further undoes the conservative belief that God is on "America's side" when the nation is at war. The men are hit by a missile painted with a garish smile that is sent by their own forces by mistake. Once again, the idea of friendly fire is an anathema to the masculine, conservative narrative, for it calls into question the efficacy of American warfare and soldiers and represents the most ridiculous and absurd type of casualty. The painted missile or bomb reveals the inability of the military to recognize that the weapon deployed will, if it functions as intended, undoubtedly take lives. That the victim's last image seen before death is a cruel painting upon a missile adds a sinister tone to an already disturbing action. Finally, there is the revelation of a metaphorical queer space created between the two victims. In the last moments—before death—the two men, "quivering" become "lovers" in death, a complete refutation of the heteronormative assumptions engendered by conservative, masculine narratives of the military. Combined, Stubbs' "authentic" narration of the war upends and undercuts the Colonel's desired mythic and masculine narrative of battle.

As the play continues, Stubbs refuses to submit and accuses the Colonel of familial crimes: "You had my name changed. YOU INVENTED MY DEATH" (Shepard 1993: 44). With his "son" dead, the Colonel can assume authorial power over the narrative of the event and control the ideological meanings derived from such a narrative. In addition, this allows the Colonel to assume the role of a "sacrificing father" who "gave" his son for the "nation"—another trope of conservative, nationalistic, and American masculine codes.[2] Because the Colonel's son has survived, he—and others—must recognize the brutal, savage reality of war and the "authentic" narrative of battle as told by those who have endured it.

When the Colonel hedges, and admits that they may "be somehow remotely related" to Stubbs, he demands that Stubbs give him "some sign of total, absolute, unconditional submission" and he "might" consider adopting Stubbs. Only if the young man "swear[s] on a stack of Bibles to submit" (Shepard 1993: 42) will the Colonel finally recognize Stubbs as his son. The Colonel will claim Stubbs only if Stubbs rejects the "authentic" narrative of the injury/metaphorical death and accepts the conservative, masculine codes, and narrative.

Through the aforementioned monologue describing the horrors of war, the Colonel attempts to disrupt the narrative, yet he cannot force Stubbs to relinquish control of the testimony. The Colonel has already attempted to squelch Stubbs' narrative through pills, humiliation, and threats. Later in the play, when Stubbs refuses to acquiesce and still rejects the Colonel's narrative of war, the injured soldier is subjected to brutality. The Colonel in a rage, attempting to force Stubbs to accept the masculine, conservative narrative, thrashes the young man with a "spanking," a type of punishment often reserved for children (of parents who subscribe to "conservative" methods of discipline or behavioral control).

The Colonel's specifics of the conservative narrative are revealed in a monologue that positions Americans as victims to atrocities throughout the centuries. Of course, American domestic and foreign policy through the centuries has also perpetuated such crimes. The litany rattled off by the Colonel includes

> Torture. Barbarism of all sorts. Starvation. Chemical warfare. Public hangings. Mutilation of children. Raping of mothers. Raping of daughters. Rapings of brothers and fathers. Executions of entire families. Entire generations of families. Amputation of private organs. Decapitation. Disembowelment. Dismemberment. Disinterment. Eradication of wildlife. You name it. (Shepard 1993: 24)

This list of crimes and atrocities touches upon the horrors of American history, yet the Colonel is seemingly unaware of his own implication (as protector of masculine codes and patriarchy) in the continuance of such slaughter under the justification of nationalism/patriotism, which itself is an extension of masculine codes and the concepts of patriarchy. This narrative, which positions America as resilient continues, as the Colonel reminds Stubbs that

> We can't forget we were generated from the bravest stock. The Pioneer. The Mountain Man. The Plainsman. The Texas Ranger. The Lone Ranger. My son. These have not died in vain. . . . We have a legacy to continue, Stubbs. It's up to us. No one else is going to do it for us. . . . Here's to them and my son! A soldier from his nation. (Shepard 1993: 24)

When the Colonel evokes these members of the "bravest stock" who helped to create the nation, the Colonel is perpetuating a narrative of the conqueror. The "types" that he mentions could also be seen as violent intruders into the lands of the indigenous peoples of North America. The Texas Rangers were used, in fact, to rid Texas of Native Americans. The Colonel's ridiculous myth as history narrative reaches absurd heights when he collapses the historic "Texas Rangers" and the decidedly mythic "Lone Ranger" into what he argues is the "authentic" narrative of the United States. In essence, the conservative narrative of history often ignores empirical historical evidence in favor of mythology, which is often promulgated through Hollywood and popular culture.

Similarly, in *The God of Hell* Welch also references the conservative "heritage" of Americans. After he tortures Graig and "controls" him through electrodes attached to his penis, Welch proclaims, "Some things do come back, don't they? Some things do manage to penetrate all the false heroics, all the flimsy ideology. We're suddenly stung by our duty to a higher purpose. Our natural loyalties fall in line and we're amazed how simple it is to honor our one true heritage" (Shepard 2005: 73). This notion of "one true heritage," which valorizes and privileges a primary "heritage" or narrative, presumably one constructed by Christian, white, heterosexual males, is similar to the "history" as presented by the Colonel. This is the "clean," uncontested vision of American history as written by the dominant members of society. It is a history from "top-down." It is a history that unquestionably champions Manifest Destiny, Horatio Alger inspired "bootstrap" economics and the infallibility of the United States.

As Stubbs is primarily concerned with retaining the narration of the past and present, Welch seizes upon the present to control the future. At the conclusion of *The God of Hell*, Welch angrily says, "Everything has been building to this. . . . We are going to deliver you to your Manifest Destiny" (Shepard 2005: 96). Like the Colonel, when he is presenting the narrative of events, Welch (according to Emma) is not "the least bit interested in . . . The Truth" (Shepard 1993: 58). As with the Colonel, Welch is only interested in a "reality," "truth," or "narrative" that confirms his ideology.

Through these plays that jettison subtlety and ambiguity in favor of provocation, Shepard interrogates conservative narratives that attempt to valorize American masculinity and nationalism. Shepard—by posing the question of how to confront such ideologies and narratives—reveals two very specific actions that can result in the dismantling of that late twentieth-century brand of conservatism. In *States of Shock*, the play ends with Stubbs raising a sword above the Colonel's exposed neck. Literally, Stubbs will behead the beast that promulgates such a destructive ideology. That, a radical call to action, reveals that there is no negotiation with conservative forces. Indeed, the conservative, patriarchal worldview can only be overcome through metaphorical violence. A less blunt, but more practical and reasonable resolution to the issue of conservative narratives and ideology is offered by *The God of Hell*. At the end of the play, Emma remains untransformed. The men were easy prey, yet Emma still possesses the power to resist and subvert the conservative ideology put forth by Welch. So, resistance to such conservative, patriarchal dogma may reside in the strength of women.

Early in *The God of Hell*, it is revealed that Frank is apolitical. He knows next to nothing of politics and metaphorically refuses to "choose sides." Such willing ignorance results in Frank becoming transformed by conservative forces, even though Frank and Emma assumed they lived beyond the reach of politics. Yet, if Frank were aware of the political scenario of the day, he could have resisted Welch's intrusions and eventual seizing of power. Once Frank is transformed, he no longer possesses agency or free-thought. As with other works in the Late Style, Shepard's political plays offer resolutions to dilemmas, instead of concluding with ambiguity. In essence, Shepard posits through these two works that conservative ideology can be defeated through (1) direct action (*States of Shock*), (2) resistance by women (*The God of Hell*), and (3) the responsibility of one to be politically aware and engaged. With these plays, Shepard is succinctly offering three distinct methods in which the conservative narrative (and subsequent worldview) can be contested and combated in the United States.

Notes

1 In Michael Almereyda's film *This So-Called Disaster*, a documentary on Sam Shepard and the rehearsal process of *The Late Henry Moss*, Shepard humorously explains Brechtian techniques to an eager and enthusiastic, but at times confused, Woody Harrelson.

2 As noted previously, this concept is explored in the motion picture *Brothers* (2009) in which Shepard portrays the patriarch of a military family.

5

"Surrounded by My Primitive Captors": Hybridity and Hegemony in *Silent Tongue* and *Eyes for Consuela*

Beyond considering the policies of the United States regarding military interventions and "enhanced interrogations," the Late Style also positions Shepard as an artist engaged with the legacy of colonialism. This indeed is a form of political writing and engagement, but Shepard's intentions and aesthetics with these works are quite different.

Shepard has—and still—cuts the image of the mythical cowboy. Shepard often wears boots, can be seen with a Stetson atop his head, and has an unyielding passion for horses and the American West. His writings have often concerned both the American West and the mystique of the cowboys, and as an actor, Shepard is a steady presence in the Western film genre. That said, before this later phase of his writings, Shepard had rarely explored the narrative of the American West from the perspective of indigenous peoples. One of Shepard's most complex and challenging works, *Operation Sidewinder* utilized specific elements of Native American culture in production and performance. Shepard sought not to casually appropriate random components of "Indian" culture, but rather to explore elements of the culture in a faithful and respectful manner, as a way to draw attention to the historical plight of Native Americans. That said, its depiction of Native Americans is highly problematic. Though Shepard intended to authentically depict Native Americans, the play tends to idealize them as politically engaged activists who uniformly possess a "spirituality." In essence, Shepard's depiction of Native Americans conformed to the general move by the counterculture to romanticize First Nations' cultures.

The Native American people and their culture were popularly fetishized and appropriated by elements of the counterculture that rose to prominence in the late 1960s and early 1970s. Theater practitioners also utilized Native American elements in production. Native American elements were blatantly appropriated in such works as the musical *Hair* (1967), and The Living Theatre's *Paradise Now* (1968). With proclamations of tribalism, both works further popularized the counterculture's fascination with Native Americans. Other works at the time also utilized components of Native American culture. Playwright Arthur Kopit sought to reinscribe the narrative of Manifest Destiny and problematize the mythology of the American West with 1969's *Indians*. The cinema was also beginning to reconsider Native Americans. Arthur Penn's 1970 cinematic adaptation of the 1964 novel *Little Big Man* attempted to further investigate the treatment of Native Americans. The medium of the motion picture was appropriate for such a consideration, for American cinema has long promulgated a colonial narrative of the Indian Wars of the 1800s and helped to enshrine that narrative through the Western.

This project's consideration of Shepard's investigation of hybridity and hegemony is informed by Chadwick Allen's essay "Indigenous Literatures and Postcolonial Theories" which analyzes the "United States as a site of on-going colonialism *vis-à-vis* American Indian peoples." (2003: 3) This chapter also utilizes Deborah L. Madsen's *Beyond the Borders: American Literature and Post-Colonialism* as a model text that elucidates the depiction of the United States' colonialism and hegemony in American literature. This chapter extends these texts' concepts to two works by Shepard. Both the film *Silent Tongue* (1993) and the play *Eyes for Consuela* (1998) explore hybridity through interrogations of the relationships between the indigenous peoples of North America and the hegemony of American culture, be it in the nineteenth century (*Silent Tongue*) or at the close of the twentieth century (*Eyes for Consuela*). These two works serve as a counter-narrative to the oppressive, hegemonic cultural narratives of both the American West and the contemporary economic and cultural relationship between the United States and Mexico.

Prior to *Silent Tongue* and *Eyes for Consuela*, Shepard had included references and minor characters associated with indigenous peoples or traditions, but indigenous peoples had never been the focal point of his writings until this late period. For example, Native American concerns are explored to a minor degree in the short pieces "Left Handed Kachina" and "Can a ½ Ton Fly?" in *Hawk Moon*, while a "witchdoctor" character in *La Turista* represents an archetype of an indigenous shaman. These works, along with *Operation Sidewinder*, traffic in what DeRose terms "imperialist nostalgia." Though Shepard stipulates that the ceremonies included in *Operation Sidewinder* be authentic, writing that it should be "spiritual and sincere and should not be cartooned or choreographed beyond the unison of rhythmic patterns" (Wilcox 1993: 50). The effort smacks of "imperialist nostalgia" in that it includes

> an archetypal search for authentic and for spiritual origins in a modern and material world of technology and media-generated simulacrum. Nowhere else in his dramatic writings does Shepard so transparently attempt to acclaim the spiritual lifestyle of Native American culture as vastly superior to high-tech, militarized, and industrialized worlds of the modern white man. And nowhere else does Shepard go through such pains to "authentically" re-create and represent Native American legend and ritual ceremony. (DeRose 1998: 64)

The later works *Silent Tongue* and *Eyes for Consuela* attempt to move away from these romantic notions by offering textured characters attempting to reckon with the dynamics of hybridity and borders.

Following *Operation Sidewinder*, Shepard did not fully return to issues of Native American identity in his writings until the 1995 film *Silent Tongue*. This supernatural Western investigates issues of identity, borders, and gender during the late 1800s in the New Mexico territory, and in some ways, attempts to perform a corrective to the countless depictions of Native Americans on-screen. Shepard's 2000 play *Eyes for Consuela* (based on a short story by Octavio Paz) analyzes the contemporary effects of American cultural imperialism on the indigenous population in Mexico. In sum, Shepard's later cycle of work continues the investigation of indigenous cultures and imperialism begun in *Operation Sidewinder*, yet these works from the Late Style examine the issues with more nuance. Both *Silent Tongue* and *Eyes for Consuela* utilize issues of identity, hybridity, and borders to examine the legacy of colonial and imperial violence inflicted upon Native American populations. In this period, Shepard presents a more complex and intellectual engagement with issues concerning indigenous peoples. Shepard reexamines a historical period through a genre (Western) and medium (film) that has long disregarded the concerns of Native Americans. In addition, Shepard adapts an Octavio Paz short story to consider the contemporary tensions between the new colonial powers and the indigenous peoples in the aftermath of NAFTA (North American Free Trade Agreement) and the growth of the globalized economy. In a sense, Shepard has sought the voice of the "Other" to serve as the basis for his critique. With both works in different media, Shepard seeks to demonstrate that American history and cultural identity are inseparable from the historic and modern complexities associated with empire and colonialism.

In essence, these works by Shepard seek to draw attention to both historical and contemporary struggles between indigenous populations and the forces of hegemony. Though scholars have—to a minor extent—considered *Silent Tongue*, there has been no previous investigation of both *Silent Tongue* and *Eyes for Consuela* as works that interrogate historical and contemporary dynamics of hegemony.

As with other issues engaged by Shepard in the Late Style, Shepard utilizes *Silent Tongue* and *Eyes for Consuela* to posit possible resolutions to presented conflicts. The works question the moral implications of imperialism, in both the historical narrative and the contemporary global economy. In turn, Shepard provides possible avenues of reckoning and reconciliation that can undermine—and to some extent, dismantle—the legacy of imperialism that haunts both the United States' past and as well as its position in the contemporary world.

Shepard enacts this by investigating issues of identity and borders, while exploring methods in which the United States can grapple with the moral quandary of imperialism and hegemony.

The film *Silent Tongue* (inspired by the 1964 Japanese film *Onibaba*) is set in 1873 in the New Mexico territory. At the base of a tree is Talbot Roe (River Phoenix) who is mourning the recent death of his "half-breed Indian" (Shepard 1993: 126) wife Awbonnie (Sheila Tousey). The next morning Talbot's father Prescott Roe, (Richard Harris) arrives on horseback at a traveling medicine show to obtain a new wife for his son. Prescott seeks out Eamon MacCree (Alan Bates), proprietor of the medicine show, which serves as a traveling conglomeration of sideshow performers, circus acts, and "snake-oil" salesmen. Previously, Prescott had "purchased" Eamon's "half-breed" daughter Awbonnie for Talbot. Prescott and Eamon strike a deal and Eamon offers his second "half-breed" daughter Velada. When Velada (Jeri Arredondo), described as "only about seventeen with long black hair swirling around her like a hurricane" (Shepard 1993: 134), learns of her impeding sale, she bolts from the medicine show on horseback. Eamon's son Reeves (Dermot Mulroney) is angry that his father would sell his own daughter.

Through flashback the audience witnesses how Eamon met the mother of Awbonnie and Velada. Eamon and a group of men come upon a Native American woman who has had her tongue cut out. Eamon proceeds to rape the woman, who will be known as "Silent Tongue." Eamon takes Silent Tongue (Tantoo Cardinal) and she eventually gives birth to Awbonnie and Velada. In the present, Silent Tongue is no longer with Eamon.

Talbot continues to hold a vigil by the tree supporting the body of Awbonnie. Suddenly, the ghost of Awbonnie appears to Talbot and pleads for her freedom. Awbonnie threatens that if Talbot does not grant her the freedom owed, "a curse will fall on your father's head. . . . Your suffering is nothing compared to what your father will have to bear" (Shepard 1993: 168).

Prescott has set out in pursuit of the runaway Velada. During the night, Velada has a vision of knives plunged into Prescott's back. Velada believes that both her dead sister (Awbonnie) and her mother (Silent Tongue) are attempting to enact vengeance upon the men who have betrayed them. Velada meets Talbot, but Talbot believes her to be the ghost of Awbonnie. Eventually, Talbot accepts Velada. Velada has another vision, this of Awbonnie returning as a ghost and attempting to cut out her tongue, exclaiming, "You like bargaining with Whites, then you bargain with me, your sister" (Shepard 1993: 184).

Meanwhile, Reeves and Eamon are separated from the medicine show. Reeves resents his father for selling his half-sister into marriage. Eamon is eventually surrounded by Kiowa and Reeves abandons him. The audience learns that Silent Tongue fled Eamon a few years prior and has returned to her tribe. As the Kiowa encircle the men, Eamon pleads with the "dog soldiers," asking, "I don't suppose you'd know my former wife, by any chance? . . . Please impress upon her that I have now more than paid for her defilements. I am completely absolved! Will you tell her that?" (Shepard 1993: 198). Silent Tongue appears on the horizon, watching the encounter between her tribe and Eamon. The screen cuts to Prescott and Talbot, walking away from the tree that holds Awbonnie's corpse. Velada has presumably left for her own freedom, while vengeance is enacted upon Eamon.

As with *Silent Tongue*, Shepard turns toward adaptation to interrogate the dynamics of the "Other" in conflict with the hegemony of empire in *Eyes for Consuela*. The play, based on the one-page short story "The Blue Bouquet" by Octavio Paz, is set in present-day Mexico in a boardinghouse on the edge of the jungle. Henry, a middle-aged American man, has fled marital strife in Michigan. In front of the boarding house, there is an elderly man with a walking stick and an eye patch slowly moving back and forth in a rocking chair. This is Viejo. Throughout the play, a mysterious young Mexican woman periodically appears. She has skin that is "pale white and ghostly; jet-black long hair and red lips" (Shepard 2002: 120). Her most distinguishing accoutrement is the belt wrapped about her waist. The belt has "long leather thongs. . . . Blue eyeballs are attached to the end of each thong" (Shepard 2002: 120). This mysterious figure, who moves in and out of scenes as an apparition, is Consuela. When Henry ventures from the boarding house and explores the jungle, he encounters Amado. Amado is a thin man dressed in the traditional white clothes of the *bracero*. He is armed with a machete and wears a sombrero, which is often hanging down his back. When Henry asks Amado what he wants, Amado simply replies, "Your eyes, mister" (Shepard 2002: 124–5). Amado assures Henry that he will not kill him, but will simply cut out his eyes because the woman he loves desires a collection of blue eyes. Henry reveals that he has brown eyes. But this does not deter Amado from his mission. Henry is forced to return, under the threat of decapitation, to the boarding house, accompanied by Amado. Amado explains that he once crossed the border into the United States, became enthralled with material culture, and even married to become a US citizen; however, he always desired to return to Mexico. Amado then tells the story of his love for Consuela. The two fell in love in the same pueblo at the age of seven. When they were older, Amado and Consuela were celebrating at a festival. Amado fired a gun and it struck Consuela's father in the eye. Distraught, Amado pledged to care for Consuela's father, Viejo. Amado fled Mexico and entered the United States as an undocumented worker to earn money to pay Viejo's hospital bills. Amado reveals that he has cut out the eyes of sixteen men and that "each time I present these gifts to Consuela she will smile slightly. . . . These are the only moments when she smiles. I live for these moments" (Shepard 2002: 143). Henry speaks with Viejo and explains that he has had conversations with Consuela. Viejo reveals that Consuela is a "*sombra . . . un fantasma*" or a ghost or apparition. The old man explains that Consuela was his daughter and that she was shot by Amado and that "same bullet passed through my eye and left me with half a world" (Shepard 2002: 173). Henry realizes that he has become entrapped in a situation that defies logic and reason. In addition, Henry recognizes his fortune and the opportunities available to him at home and pledges to empathize with and seek to understand the sorrow experienced by Consuela and Amado. Amado—and Consuela—allow Henry to leave. Viejo assures Henry that when he returns to his state of Michigan, that Henry "will see the snow with new eyes" (Shepard 2002: 181). With a new-found appreciation for his own life and a new perspective on tension between the United States and Mexico, Henry abandons his possessions and immediately returns to his wife.

Critic Ben Brantley, who had heaped praise upon Shepard's previous full-length work *Simpatico*, found much less satisfaction with *Eyes for Consuela*, noting that the play stands as a "long, poetic metaphor-engorged two-act work that plays as if it were an early draft for a short, poetic metaphor-enriched one-act work" (1998). Brantley continued, explaining that the play "never generates a sense of urgency" and that it is "unusually torpid" and "not Mr. Shepard's dialogue at its finest," "95 minutes too long" and "painfully self-conscious" (1998). The review concludes with Brantley mourning that "nowhere evident are the discipline, maturity and insight of the artist" (1998) who wrote *Buried Child*, *True West*, or *Fool for Love*. An additional review in *The New York Times* by Vincent Canby noted that *Eyes for Consuela* is a "goofy though not funny meditation on a number of subjects" and it seems to be a "fragile, futile" play (1998).

Though Shepard bases his play on "The Blue Bouquet," it is worth noting that Paz's diminutive piece never overtly explores the political and cultural dimensions introduced by Shepard. Shepard has essentially utilized Paz's folk legend as a stepping-off point to envision the clash between the indigenous Mexican population and Americans in a contemporary world of inequality and exploitation. That said, *Eyes for Consuela* is problematic. The play may strike some as Shepard perpetuating the cruel stereotype of the indigenous Mexican peasant as bloodthirsty and superstitious, though Shepard does attempt to link the audience's sympathies, to varying degrees of success, with Amado.

Both *Silent Tongue* and *Eyes for Consuela* are concerned with the politics and signifiers of identity. These signifiers are utilized to separate and "other" populations. These identities are signified through markers that are nearly inescapable, such as eye color, dialect, or tribal affiliation. In addition, these identities are often hybridized. Almost all of the characters in *Silent Tongue* assume unstable, hybridized identities. Prescott Roe is Irish-born, but lives in the territories of the United States. His son Talbot is of Irish descent, so he is considered Irish-American. The same is true of Eamon, who was born and bred in Ireland, but now travels throughout the territories with his son Reeves who, like Talbot, is Irish-American. In turn, as the cultural Irish were colonized by the English, there is an extended sense of hybridization for the fathers. Essentially, they are from a colonized culture, but are now assisting in the colonization of an indigenous people. These two father figures also assume further hybridizations of their identities, signified through their demeanor and dress. Prescott is described as "well into his sixties but rugged as a boot. His eyes have the kind of inner stillness that comes from dealing with nature and horses not with human beings. He is an absolute extension of his horses. They all just flow along with him at the gallop" (Shepard 1993: 127). So, Prescott has unconsciously adopted the mythical stance of the "western cowboy."

More complicated and fraught with contradictions is Eamon's identity proclaimed through dress. Eamon has appropriated various elements from Native American culture, such as two long braids with beaded cinches and a beaded vest under an English waistcoat. He simultaneously signifies his "white" identity through a top hat, heavy trousers, and cavalry boots to the knee. Eamon carries a long-barreled navy Colt revolver on his hip and holds a gnarled blackthorn shillelagh. Eamon serves as a pastiche of Western identities, a combination of American, Irish, and Native American regalia. His use of Native American signifiers is ironic as Eamon brutalizes and exploits various indigenous peoples throughout the film. Further examination of Eamon's use of Native American signifiers reveals that his dress is a "costume" for his "character" that peddles faux medicinal remedies. In addition, Eamon has added a narrative to seemingly authenticate his identity. Eamon presents himself as "Doctor and Professor Emeritus of Herbal Prairie Medicines—The Honorable Eamon Monachain MacCree" (Shepard 1993: 139). Pushing sham elixir, Eamon has developed an origin and narrative that attempts to authenticate his identity and the product. Eamon is reputed to be "a man who was captured at a very young and tender age and taken into the hands of the dreaded Kiowa/ Comanche" (Shepard 1993: 138) who learned his "secrets" from an "authentic Medicine Man from the dreaded Kiowa/Comanche Nation" (Shepard 1993: 141). The "secret" was something "which no white man had ever been made privy to. A secret which I have brought with me here today to share with each and every one of you . . . . The Ancient Sagwa Serum, stolen from the Kickapoo!" (Shepard 1993: 141). As with the works explored in Chapter 2, "authenticity" in Shepard's Late Style can be elusive, misleading, or nonexistent. In essence, Eamon utilizes, appropriates, and exploits various traits from Native American culture to craft an "authentic" identity that will help sell his product.

All of the women in *Silent Tongue* also find themselves in hybridized identities. Even incidental female characters in the film are hybridized. When Eamon is first introduced, he is with a prostitute identified as "mixed-breed." Similarly, Silent Tongue and Eamon's daughters are also caught between cultures. The dead Awbonnie, the oldest, is described as a "half-breed Indian girl" (Shepard 1993: 126). Eamon condemns his own daughters, explaining that Reeves should "thank your stars you weren't born a half-breed like your demon sisters" (Shepard 1993: 164). Reeves contests Eamon's decision to "sell" Velada to Prescott, exclaiming, "What about Velada!" to which Eamon responds by saying, "She'll make do. She's Kiowa." Reeves retorts "She's your daughter!" to which Eamon says, "She's Kiowa first!" (Shepard 1993: 172). Silent Tongue had her tongue removed and was expelled from her tribe because she supposedly told a lie to the "headman" of her tribe. In turn, she is raped and taken by—and eventually married to—Eamon. Silent Tongue finds herself neither identifying with the culture that expelled her nor the culture that has enslaved her. All the men and women in *Silent Tongue* find themselves hybridized, yet unlike the men, women are not allowed agency in determining their own identity. The women are under the hegemony of the men. The indigenous tribes are exploited and abused by colonial incursion, yet in both realms women have little power. For example, Silent Tongue is mutilated by members of her own tribe, then raped by a white man.

Yet, even more signifiers are used to differentiate indigenous peoples from colonial interlopers. Both *Silent Tongue* and *Eyes for Consuela* are concerned with indicating difference through the sensory body parts. *Silent Tongue*, as the title reveals, features a Native American woman whose tongue has been removed. The tongue is a sensory organ in that it conveys taste to the brain, but also, the tongue is an indicator of language. Predominantly, the languages of Native Americans are uniquely tied to the tongue, for they are spoken, not written, languages. In contemporary parlance, one's "tongue" is a synecdoche for one's language. In addition, the Native American women in the film are identified not only through genealogy and appearance, but also through speaking a distinctive dialect of English as their second language. But, the Native American women are not alone in a dialect, for both Prescott and Eamon reveal their Gaelic roots through their distinctive, Irish lilt. Identity in *Eyes for Consuela* is similarly revealed through identifiers in characters. In fact, the eyes[1] referenced in the title are the most obvious signifiers. For Amado and Consuela, the color of eyes marks those who are identified as being different from outside the native populace of Mexico. Eyes reveal emotion, thoughts, and various aspects of the inner lives of humans. Beyond what eyes reveal, eyes serve as receivers of images from the material world. Eyes take in color, shape, texture, and distance, as well as light and darkness. Eyes also bring perspective to the individual, in both the literal and metaphorical sense. Indeed, *Eyes for Consuela* utilizes the metaphor of eyes to examine imperial hegemonic forces from both the perspective of the colonized and the colonizer. Henry, a representative of empire, is forced to "see" from the perspective of the subjugated, while revealing the personal politics of hemispheric hegemony.

When Henry cannot understand Amado's "perspective," he tells Amado, "I can't see you" (Shepard 2002: 153). Eyes are utilized when the perspective on an issue is askew, such as when Henry details how his marriage has been deteriorating because he and his wife "haven't exactly—seen things—eye to eye over the years" (Shepard 2002: 130). Seeing and eyes can also be associated with enlightenment or transformation through the gaining of perspective. As Henry approaches an understanding of his predicament in its many iterations, Amado tells Henry, "Maybe you are on the edge of seeing something" (Shepard 2002: 151).

But, it is precisely the *blue* eyes that become the focus of the play. Amado explains that Consuela's desire for blue eyes occurred to her in a dream. Blue eyes hold a variety of meanings within the play. They are in contrast to the brown eyes associated with the indigenous populations of Mexico who are descended from the Aztecs and Mayans. Blue eyes were traditionally associated with Europe, but with the rise of the United States as an economic and cultural power in the twentieth century, blue eyes also became associated with "modern" Americans. Blue eyes are also viewed as a trait that can lead to the promise of the United States. Upon looking at Henry's passport, Amado confesses, "Blue eyes and an American passport. There was a time when I might have killed for these two things" (Shepard 2002: 175). Amado would have killed for blue eyes for a multitude of possible reasons. Not only would he kill to fulfill the demands of Consuela, he would also murder out of resentment of the American economic exploitation of Mexico and its citizens, which he experienced first-hand in his time in the United States. Amado would also once have killed for possession of the passport, as an American passport could gain unfettered entrance to the United States. In addition, an American passport is a valuable commodity on the black market for it can be altered and can potentially stave off questions by American authorities. Amado continues to assert to Henry that he has blue eyes, but Henry, attempting to avoid the gruesome procedure, yells, "I DON'T HAVE BLUE EYES!! Why can't you get that through your head? . . . This is a total misunderstanding" (Shepard 2002: 149).

Though Henry contends that he has brown eyes, and even "places his fingers and thumbs around his eyes, stretching them wide open so Consuela can see their color"[2] (Shepard 2002: 168), this fact does not deter Amado from his mission. Amado has Henry look at the passport once again. Inexplicably, the eyes are now blue in the photograph. Mysteriously, the photograph has changed. Amado tells Henry, "You are blind now. Now! In this world. You do not see" (Shepard 2002: 179).

In essence, Henry is "blind" in Mexico. He is blind to the exploitation and abuse suffered by Mexicans, while he is simultaneously blind to the events within his own life. Consuela explains that Henry's eyes "are not blue. They have never been blue. They never will be" (Shepard 2002: 179). This reveals that Henry retains an element that allows him to view the world from both the "brown eye" perspective as well as the "blue eye" perspective. By viewing the world through both sets of eyes, Henry is able to confront the fallout of imperialism as well as the mistakes in his own personal life. As Viejo says, "When you return to Michigan, you will see the snow with new eyes" (Shepard 2002: 181). Through his encounter and conversations with Amado, Henry learns a differing perspective, a perspective imbued with empathy. Henry comes to understand the sorrow and desperation of those exploited. Toward the conclusion of his ordeal, he proclaims, "Because I'm in sympathy with [Consuela]! I know what her sorrow is all about! I know why she needs this" (Shepard 2002: 178). Henry has gained his "vision" through the trials of this encounter. He was forced to confront what he assumed about Mexico and the United States and about what he believed about himself and Amado. Amado explains to Henry that now "you will be able to step across the border. Into the light" (Shepard 2002: 179). Henry's "enlightenment" now allows him to view the world more fully and wholly, with empathy for those caught under the economic and cultural policies of an empire. Yet Amado, who is fulfilling the wishes of Consuela, explains to Henry that "you—have nothing to give me—but your eyes" (Shepard 2002: 132). The eyes not only serve as a gift to Consuela, but the acquisition of the eyes also works as an act of retribution that metaphorically forces the colonizer to view the world as a member of the colonized. The colonizer has previously forced a perspective upon the colonized subject. The colonized subject's action of seizing the eyes of the colonizer serves as a reversal of power.

In *Eyes for Consuela*, Henry can be read as representative of the economic and cultural influence of the United States upon Mexico. Henry describes himself as "just a plain old everyday average American man. . . . There is nothing—absolutely nothing inside me that can even begin to comprehend this stuff. . . . I simply want to return to the known world" (Shepard 2002: 172). Henry stands as a beneficiary of the United States' standing and position in the world, yet the preeminence of the United States can also be partially viewed as being built upon the exploitation of other nations and peoples. Though he is not aware of the conditions and sorrow of many of his hemispheric neighbors to the south, his culture of convenience and safety is partially made possible through American policies in relation to Mexico. His lifestyle is placed into relief when he encounters a representative of the indigenous underclass of Mexico.

Henry is indeed a representative of imperial power, yet he does not view himself as such. Henry explains that "I'm a U.S. citizen. . . . I've done nothing against you or your country. I'm a visitor! A tourist. I bring money into your country. Commerce! If it weren't for me and others like me, your country . . ." (Shepard 2002: 156). Though Henry is unable to complete the sentence, the harsh sentiment is conveyed. Henry views Mexico as a location for vacation, a temporary space for his personal recreation. Though Henry has not necessarily directly exploited Mexico, he has benefited from NAFTA and various free trade provisions put into place by the United States, as well as an American economy that is partially built upon the underpaid labor of undocumented workers. At this point, he is unable to "see" the world from the perspective of the colonized and exploited. Henry justifies his presence by placing himself in the position of the benevolent patriarch, essentially arguing that if it were not for Americans, Mexico would collapse.

Amado stands as a representative of the colonized and exploited. He explains that "there is no work in Mexico. Poverty is our prison" (Shepard 2002: 142). To gain money, Amado crosses into the United States as an undocumented worker. Once in the United States, he is exposed to a culture of convenience, affluence, and material gain. Amado details that in the United States there are

> many 'valuable things': Tennis shoes. T-shirts. Television. . . . Radios. VCR. Refrigerator. Ford Mustang. I even got the biggest prize of all . . .

A *gringa*! Yes. Blonde. Blue eyes. Very young. *Joven y dura*. . . . I wanted her light. So—we married. . . . Now, I was a citizen. A real American citizen with papers. Legal. I could come and go without swimming the Brazos. Without shame. (Shepard 2002: 133)

It is the American material culture that first seduces Amado. He explains that as he ran across the border "my lungs were screaming but my head kept dreaming of 'things'" (Shepard 2002: 133). Though Amado first comes to the United States to help pay for Viejo's medical bills, he falls prey to the darker side of American consumerism. The materialist culture transforms Amado into a man who values consumption, but also comes to view humans, in this case a woman, as "objects" to acquire. Amado's acquisition of a *gringa* signifies his attainment of socioeconomic success and stability in the United States. Amado further explains, "In America everything is easy. Food is easy. The roads are paved like silk. Money is easy. Sex. Movies. Drugs" (Shepard 2002: 149).

Yet, Amado's transformation into a *gringo* comes with a price. Amado explains that as one becomes enraptured with and hypnotized by American culture, it is easy to lose oneself, as there is always a yearning, and inner voice screaming, for a reunification with one's authentic identity. In the United States, Amado is an undocumented immigrant and serves as an "unseen" presence in American society. To be "seen" once again Amado returns to Mexico and to Conseula. This action works to reconnect Amado to his culture and his lost love. In Amado's estimation, Mexico represents a stability and authenticity that is unattainable in the United States. Mexico represents history, genealogy, and a sense of place. Indeed, Shepard himself has opined that "Mexico is what America should have been. Mexico still has heart, it still has extraordinary passion, it still has a sense of family and culture, of deep, deep roots. . . . There are places you go in Mexico that just make you feel like a human being. The Indian culture is what I think does it for me" (Roudane 2002a: 77). For Shepard, Mexico exists as a far more authentic locale than the United States. It is a nation and culture that still retains a vibrant connection to its past through its indigenous cultures.[3]

Amado pities Henry as an individual with no true home. As an American, Henry's identity is not tied to a specific location. Indeed, Henry has exhibited a certain rootlessness. Though Henry is originally from Texas, this does not necessarily differentiate him from modern American monoculture. Seemingly, modern America has forsaken its connection to geography, region, and space for commerce, emblemized by commuter culture. Amado reveals that he and Consuela grew up together in the same village/pueblo, yet Henry and his wife grew up separated by thousands of miles.

Henry attempts to characterize Americans differently for Amado. Henry, unironically and jingoistically, presents an imperial view of the American character. He explains, "You don't see us sneaking off into other people's countries. . . . We fight for every inch . . . come hell or high water!" (Shepard 2002: 166–7). Henry cruelly characterizes Mexicans as "sneaking off into other people's countries," yet it is Henry who has "escaped" to Mexico. He refuses to recognize the extreme lengths taken by undocumented workers to earn money for their families in Mexico. Henry is tied to the "idea" of the United States and has subscribed to the conservative narrative of "old fashioned grit" associated with Americans. In contrast, he does not recognize the tenacity and courage of Mexicans who come into the United States clandestinely. Amado explains that "I was a '*mojado*' once. . . . A 'wet.' I wanted 'things.' 'Valuable things.' I swam the river in the dead of night" (Shepard 2002: 133). The reason for the "sneaking" (as Henry terms it) is complex and indicative of the United States' economic policy and problematic policies toward Mexico.

Initially, Henry refuses to understand Mexico. When Viejo explains that "there are no emergencies here, my friend," Henry responds that "this whole country is one big fat festering emergency!" (Shepard 2002: 170). When Amado was in the United States, he was "bleeding for my homeland," yet Henry does not "bleed" for the United States, but he does seemingly value its material culture and lifestyle of stability and safety. Henry attempts to further "other" Mexico by differentiating it from the United States. Primarily, Henry contrasts the seeming "advancements" of technology in the United States with the assumed "backwards" actions of Mexicans. Henry argues, "Ghosts and sacrifices! Superstition and visions! We're approaching the millennium here! . . . Electricity has delivered us! We're on the verge of breaking into territories never dreamed of before. Things which will set us free so we don't have to be gouging each other's eyes out" (Shepard 2002: 172). In his attempts to cast a striking contrast between the two nations and cultures, Henry naturally assumes that technology is inherently beneficial to humans. He draws science and superstition into an oppositional binary, but the space created in the play does not exist in such an easily defined area.

Like *Silent Tongue*, *Eyes for Consuela* traffics in a space that accommodates both science and superstition. As demonstrated, the borders that seemingly separate identities and cultures are problematized in *Silent Tongue* and *Eyes for Consuela*. Also in these works, the metaphorical border between the scientific and the spiritual are transgressed, carving out a space in which the science of the colonizer is subverted by the beliefs of the colonized. In essence, science—as associated with the hegemonic forces of empire—is destabilized, while the mysteries of the spiritual world are the purveyance of indigenous peoples. Far from demonstrating a reductive belief in superstitions, Shepard argues that the supernatural and paranormal are valuable attributes to cultures that are under erasure by colonialism and empire. The science of *Silent Tongue*, as represented by Eamon's elixir, is suspicious and fraudulent, while the appearance of spirits and ghosts is recognized by the characters as events that have a profound effect upon living humans. The young widower Talbot is haunted by the specter of his recently deceased Native American wife Awbonnie. Amado is similarly haunted by his widow Consuela. In addition, each of these spirits is demanding certain specific actions to be taken within the corporeal world.[4]

Though the appearance of ghosts within these indigenous cultures (Kiowa for Awbonnie and Mayan for Consuela) carry specific, unique meanings, these ghosts can also be interpreted as haunting reminders of past powerlessness. As the issue of gender is a recurring subject throughout Shepard's work and is explored in Chapter 6, it is worth noting that it is only in the afterlife are these women able to achieve complete power and agency. These women have been marginalized through the patriarchy of their native culture and the patriarchy of the invasive cultures. During life, the women endured this double bind. The spirit world offers a space that is neither conquerable nor colonized. In essence, the spirit world is beyond the reaches of empire. It is a liminal, undefined space that seems to exist between the living and the dead. The afterlife has afforded Awbonnie and Consuela a type of agency not achievable in the corporeal world. In these works, women find liberation outside the patriarchal restrictions of corporeal life. Essentially, women cannot achieve true freedom within the patriarchy, but are afforded such beyond the realm of the scientific. In addition, both women were indirectly killed by men: Awbonnie died in the birthing of a child she did not want, while Consuela was killed by Amado's stray bullet. Men—consciously or not—are responsible for these women's deaths.

As larger signifiers, these ghosts refer to the violence and genocide perpetuated by the powers of empire. Awbonnie herself is quite literally a product of colonialism as her mother was raped by Eamon. Awbonnie was sold by her white father to a white man to wed. In addition, Awbonnie's father holds nothing but contempt for indigenous peoples. Consuela stands as a genealogical link to the Mayan, to whom many of the indigenous peoples of modern-day Mexico trace their heritage. Through their childhood in a pueblo—and through Amado's traditional regalia—it is unquestionable that both Consuela and Amado stand as contemporary connections to Mexico's native past. Consuela's death is certainly accidental, yet her demands are rooted in an animosity against empire. The conquest of the indigenous peoples of Mexico brought an influx of Spanish and those of European descent. Beyond language and dress, physical characteristics were traits that were seen as foreign by the indigenous peoples. These included light skin, light hair, and blue or light colored eyes. Though the audience is never given a specific reason why Consuela yearns for blue eyes, the most obvious reading is that this serves as a "lesson" for those that represent the forces of empire.

The acquisition of the blue eyes—signifying European or American—can metaphorically force the colonizer to view the world through the colonial subject's eyes. In both works, the concept of the ghost remains as a reminder of the violence and oppression associated with empire and colonialism.

The ghosts themselves are described by Shepard in very specific terms. The ghost of Awbonnie first appears standing over the corpse of Awbonnie, looking down at Talbot. The ghost is

> dressed in a long white gown. Her face is painted in a fierce war makeup with a wide white stripe running from top to bottom across her hose. One side of her face looks like the corpse of Awbonnie, and the other side is sneering and evil looking. (Shepard 1993: 150)

Consuela in her ghostly form is described as a young Mexican girl, "her skin is pale white and ghostly; jet-black long hair and red lips" (Shepard 2002: 120).

Performatively, Shepard assigns these characters actions and movements that differentiate them from those who exist in the corporeal world. Dressed primarily in white, the ghosts cut an angelic image, tempered by the grotesque (Awbonnie's "sneering and evil" face and Consuela's belt of eyeballs). Paradoxically, it is the men in the material world who conduct "demonic" actions, such as Eamon's rape of Silent Tongue and Amado's extraction of blue eyes.

The ghosts of Awbonnie and Consuela are not passive specters, but are rather active and at times vengeful manifestations of the resentment against empire. As Talbot mourns his dead wife and is unable to halt his vigil, essentially not fully releasing her to the afterlife, the ghost of Awbonnie demands her freedom. When all attempts to gain agency have failed, she warns that "if you don't do this thing I ask, then a curse will fall on your father's head. . . . Your suffering is nothing compared to what your father will have to bear" (Shepard 1993: 168). Later, Awbonnie's sister Velada endures a nightmarish image of Talbot's father being stabbed by a ghostly figure. The same spirit also grabs Velada by the hair, and in an intertextual allusion to *Buried Child*, violently pries her mouth open with her hands. The ghost pulls out Velada's tongue and holds it, as if to violently sever it. Velada screams that "my sister is sending you her thoughts! . . . She's my mother's weapon! She is moving on you now with vengeance" (Shepard 1993: 173). Apparently, Silent Tongue's resentment of the forces of empire (as represented by Eamon) are being channeled through the ghost of Awbonnie and directed toward Velada. Velada is targeted because she has agreed to be sold to Talbot, essentially capitulating to imperial hegemony.

The ghosts themselves are bound through mutilation. Awbonnie's mother was mutilated, while Consuela gives the order for mutilations. These mutilations serve as a reference to the dynamics of power and the logistics of sense organs. The extraction of the tongue negates the ability to communicate through spoken word, but also eliminates elements of taste. Without a tongue, the narrative is metaphorically ceased, yet a powerful message is sent reasserting power. The extraction of eyes eliminates the possibility for seeing, so the intake of information through sight is impossible. The tongue helps to convey and communicate a narrative, while the eyes serve as the organs that view and perceive events. Combined, the eyes and tongue serve to witness and testify to occurrences and actions.

The men of these works profess a love for the women that are now dead. Talbot is driven to madness by his sorrow for the deceased Awbonnie. Amado's love for Consuela is all-encompassing as her ghost commands him to perform inhumane acts. He admits that "each time I present these gifts to Consuela she will smile slightly. . . . These are the only moments when she smiles. I live for these moments" (Shepard 1993: 143).

In *Silent Tongue*, the ghost of Awbonnie confronts Talbot's father Prescott and warns him not to sell Velada into marriage. She orders Prescott to accept that his son is mad and that "he's far out of your reach. Far beyond you! He's in another world!" (191) and that a "replacement" wife will serve no purpose. The ghost contends that for Talbot, Velada will be just "another squaw! Another Kiowa dog, sold for horses!" (Shepard 1993: 191). The ghost's sentiments reveal that

Awbonnie did not reciprocate the affections directed toward her by Talbot. In addition, these demands indict Prescott for continuing the abuse of indigenous people for personal and selfish reasons, as Prescott simply wants another wife for his son to help him return to sanity.

As the love expressed by Talbot is not reciprocated by Awbonnie, the love experienced by both Amado and Consuela is all-consuming. It is a love that is linked to the destruction of both their lives. Consuela gains leverage over Amado in the afterlife, yet Amado continues to value the love he holds for Consuela. He asks Henry, "Do you believe that love comes cheaply? (Shepard 2002: 144). For Amado, love demands loyalty. As Henry contends to Amado, "You've become her slave." (Shepard 2002: 151).

This emotional bond is contrasted with Henry's own marriage, one in which his very much alive wife has become a metaphorical ghost. Though Henry's wife survives, his relationship with her is strained. Indeed, both Henry and his wife are "ghosts" of their former selves. It is precisely because of the stress from this relationship that he has found himself in Mexico. Henry says, "I don't know what happened exactly. How it changed. One day—it was—just gone. She became cold. Indifferent" (Shepard 2002: 145). To Henry, his wife and their marriage are dead. He is not "looking" to alter his perspective or even save his marriage, but through his experiences with Amado, he learns not only to view the conflict between empire and subject through different eyes, but also to view his personal relationships through new eyes. In conversations, both Amado and Henry discuss the relationships they possess with their wives. Amado explains that "if you met Consuela, you would not be able to speak. She would take your breath away . . ." (Shepard 2002: 149). It is this sense of love and passion that Henry has lost in the relationship with his wife. Placed into this situation, he learns the role of empathy not only in political and cultural concerns, but also in personal relations.

Shepard's ruminations on colonialism and imperialism circulate upon notions of hybridity and identity, borders, and the ways in which these demarcations are subverted and problematized. Shepard's late career ruminations on indigenous peoples and their relationship to hegemony and empire reveal a writer attempting to investigate not only the historical, but also the contemporary tension that arises between the subject and the subjugator. In *Silent Tongue*, the hegemonic power of empire and patriarchy must be dramatically overthrown. Shepard's proposal for contemporary conflicts, as explored in *Eyes for Consuela*, is a call for those in positions of privilege to consider the impact of broad economic policies upon the subjugated individual. Then, through the dismantling of oppressive power structures, indigenous peoples can efficaciously move toward resisting and refuting cultural and economic imperialism.

Notes

1   The concept and metaphor of eyes proliferate throughout the later phase of Shepard's work. In *The Late Henry Moss*, eyes and "seeing" become a relevant dynamic during the brothers' attempt to gain a different "perspective" on their father.

2   This exact action is performed in *The Late Henry Moss*.

3   The final piece, entitled "Gracias," in the collection *Day Out of Days* is a short description of a transcendent moment experienced in Mexico. In it, the narrator tells of visiting Mexico with his family and hearing a pianist playing a waltz on a backstreet. He concludes with the remark, "That was one of those days I remember" (282).

4   There is also a female apparition that appears in *Kicking a Dead Horse*, while a ghostly woman appears in *Heartless*.

6

"Where's All the Men?":
Men, Women, and Homosociality
in the Late Style of Sam Shepard

During his cultural moment of the 1980s, Shepard's work was undeniably polarizing within literary and theater scholarship. Hailed by the popular press as the proverbial "Great American Playwright," Shepard was also condemned by others as glorifying and perpetuating outdated modes of masculinity.

As a topic of focus within his work, gender in Shepard's family cycle has been duly covered by critics and scholars. The dynamics of gender have been scrutinized and examined by some of the field's most respected scholars. Surprisingly, little attention has been paid to the depiction of gender in his later work, specifically the writings that I have deemed the Late Style. This may be attributed to the Late Style's less problematic, and in turn sophisticated, depictions of gender. The scarcity of scholarship may also be the result of the reception of Late Style works by critics and the theatergoing public. Though Shepard's cultural moment has long since waned, work from his later period features unique perspectives on both women and men and include more nuanced explorations of the relations between the genders. This Late Style reveals how homosocial environments allow for the creation of a utopian existence for women, while the homosocial sphere for men inevitably results in disappointment and betrayal. This chapter serves as a critical intervention in Shepard scholarship. Most conclusions regarding Shepard's work and gender are based on the author's earlier works. As noted, there is little scholarly consideration of Shepard's Late Style, and as a result, there has been a lack of attention paid to issues of gender in Shepard's late work.

In the film *Far North*, the play *Ages of the Moon* (and to lesser degrees "Evanescence" and *Heartless*) as well as the stories "The Door to Women" and "Great Dream of Heaven," Shepard reveals homosocial worlds that serve as unique, microscopic explorations of gender. In *Far North*, Shepard takes the viewer to rural Minnesota to investigate the aging and outdated patriarchal (dis)order, while revealing a unique, thoughtful, and emotionally authentic "new" code devised by women. The film works as an intertextual burlesque of Shepard's previous work, yet my analysis will focus primarily on gender and homosociality. Indeed, it is curious that Shepard, for his film directorial debut, selected a subject matter (women), a location (Minnesota), and a tone (lightly humorous) which are in seeming opposition to the aesthetics of his family sagas. In addition, the film certainly plays as an excellent example of regional filmmaking, with particular attention paid to the uniquely Midwestern details of the film's *milieu*. Indeed, *Far North* stands as a pivotal moment in his corpus. Shepard turns away from the relatively consistent aesthetic of his family sagas and moves into the Late Style, which is marked by transmedial exploration, the posing of solutions to dilemmas, experimentation in form, and the investigation of new subjects. Prominent in the Late Style is a reconsideration of gender dynamics. Regardless of the dramatic and filmic efficacy of *Far North*, it serves as a unique text for analysis of gender, specifically female homosociality. In fact, by the end of the film, men have been exorcised from the space and the new homosocial order (composed of mothers and daughters) emerges as a utopian alternative to the patriarchy. *Ages of the Moon*, which is an extended dialogue between two men, further meditates upon the failures of male codes, but the play also reveals the salvation of the male through a meaningful and authentic loving relationship with a woman. "Evanescence, or Shakespeare in the Alley" is a short piece concerning a woman and the violence of love. *Heartless*, a return to the female homosocial environment, attempts to considers issues of gender within a matriarchal family. Similar elements are explored in two Late Style prose pieces. "The Door to Women" examines the apparent chasm between a grandfather and a grandson when a woman threatens to enter their homosocial environment. Finally, "Great Dream of Heaven" concerns two elderly men who have seemingly found comfort, enjoyment, and possibly desire in homosocial bonding. Only when a woman arrives is this homosocial world unexpectedly fractured.

This chapter will first survey and examine contentions made by scholars regarding gender in Shepard's work. The chapter will then explain the concept of homosociality. Next, the writings to be scrutinized in this chapter will be summarized. Then, the works *Far North*, *Ages of the Moon*, "Evanescence", *Heartless*, "The Door to Women," and "The Great Dream of Heaven" will be analyzed in light of the dynamics of homosociality. Finally, Shepard's new paradigms for men, women, and the relations between—which tend to be quite different from those of previous writings—will be explained. As with other dilemmas explored in earlier work, Shepard in this Late Style proposes a solution to the conflict he believes exists between genders. In sum, this chapter contests critical assumptions regarding gender in Shepard's work and argues that the Late Style reveals Shepard investigating gender through homosocial environments and envisioning a world liberated from the patriarchy and its antiquated codes of masculinity.

Before examining these works in reference to homosociality, a general overview and review of critical stances regarding Shepard and gender are necessary. In presenting an encapsulation of the scholarly criticism of gender in Shepard's work, I am neither attempting to valorize nor ostracize these contentions. Rather, I am merely seeking to *historicize*—and in some cases, respond to—the interpretations of scholars engaging with Shepard's depiction of gender. From this distillation, I will then move to demonstrate how the later works of Shepard grapple with gender through experiments with homosociality and how these same works yield intriguing (and at times problematic) conclusions regarding the dynamics between men and women.

To provide a glimpse of scholarship regarding Shepard and his depiction of women, I will summarize works by a number of scholars such as Sue-Ellen Case, Lynda Hart, Bonnie Marranca, and Ann C. Hall.

These critical engagements reveal some of the recurrent themes that run through readings of gender in Shepard's work. In the influential 1988 essay "Toward a Butch-Femme Aesthetic," Sue-Ellen Case documents the butch-femme role-playing performances of Split Britches. Case asserts that Split Britches' "freely moving, resonant narrative space" (1988: 290–9) works in opposition to the plays of Marsha Norman, Beth Henley, Irene Maria Fornes, and Sam Shepard. Case utilizes these playwrights as examples of heteronormativity through their aesthetics, while Split Britches' utilizes a decidedly queer aesthetic. In addition to Shepard's aesthetic, the playwright's treatment of women draws Case's attention. Case contends that

> the violence released in the continual zooming-in on the family unit, and the heterosexist ideology linked with its stage partner, realism, is directed against women and their hint of seduction. In *Lie of the Mind*, this becomes literally woman-battering. Beth's only associative space and access to transformative discourse is the result of nearly fatal blows to her head. . . . The closure of these realistic narratives chokes the women to death and strangles the play of symbols, or the possibility of seduction. In fact, for each of them, sexual play only assists in their entrapment. (1988: 297)

In performance, directors and actors are granted some degree of interpretive agency, often defying, subverting, or reifying authorial intent. For Case, both Shepard's aesthetic and the subject matter are problematic, as both the aesthetic and subject matter further support patriarchal assumptions. Certainly, *A Lie of the Mind* depicts brutality, and much of this brutality is directed toward Beth, who (barely) survives being beaten by her husband. As a result, she is brain-damaged and aphasic, but does achieve a form of transformation.

First, in response to Case, Shepard is not utilizing realism. I have addressed Shepard's notion of "realism" in Chapter 4. In fact, Case's seeming misprision of Shepard's aesthetics may have more to do with the elements of the production she attended (Case is not specific) or a cursory reading of the play. As with all of Shepard's plays, there are specific transformative dynamics that occur during performance that reveal the work to defy realistic expectations. Superficially, Shepard's aesthetic with *A Lie of the Mind* may be interpreted and reductively referred to as "realism." This, of course, ignores elements of Shepard's dramaturgy and minimizes the unique performative dynamics that occur within these plays.

Second, Case contends that Shepard's depiction of heterosexist ideology results in a literalized battered woman. This is indeed true, yet Case may be unnecessarily reducing this notion to a general condemnation of heterosexuality. Certainly, in *A Lie of the Mind*, the patriarchy, heterosexist ideology, and masculine codes are all bound together in an unceasing war against women. But, the only relief from the destructive stresses of the patriarchy are located in the moments shared between Beth and her mother, moments that work within Eve Kosofsky Sedgwick's explanation of female homosociality. These events in *A Lie of the Mind* seemingly predict Shepard's eventual call for a female homosocial utopia in *Far North* as an alternative to the violence and pathology of the patriarchy. The violence against women in *A Lie of the Mind* serves as a literalization of the corruption of the patriarchy, but it offers hope for women through homosociality. Shepard cannot be definitively characterized as subverting or championing masculine values, but rather depicting a dialectic that engages patriarchal hegemonic assumptions. As David Savran notes, "To suggest that Shepard simply denigrates women or refuses to give them a voice ignores the ambiguity which their status as supplement brings into play" (Savran 1984: 72).

In "Men Without Women: The Shepard Landscape" (1981), Florence Falk argues that in Shepard's dramas "any female is marginalized" (91) and forced to live vicariously through the men to whom they are attached. In these works, "survival is the name of the game, and women traversing the male frontier learn stratagems to stay out of the crossfire and endure quietly" (1981: 98). The women of "Shepard's plays are compelled to adapt themselves as best they can to the exigencies of the male world to survive" (1981: 99). Indeed, Shepard's women in Falk's view are forced to be industrious as a mode of survival in a violent, masculine world. This is true in the Late Style, yet Shepard also offers a vision that goes beyond mere survival.

Lynda Hart's explosive "Sam Shepard's Pornographic Visions" (1988) interrogates assumptions regarding the critical accolades bestowed upon the work of Shepard and attempts to clear a space for a feminist interpretation of his standing. She begins the essay by referring to Falk's essay and the resultant scholarly and critical silence. The piece begins:

> While the critical majority continues to celebrate Sam Shepard as the greatest living American playwright, a few dissident voices can be heard. Florence Falk's early essay about the absence of women in Shepard's plays made little impact on the critical establishment bent of valorizing Shepard. Falk's [writing] . . . did not decenter Shepard as the preeminent dramatic voice of America. No one, in fact, seemed to dispute Falk's claims. Evidently there is no contradiction or even recognition of a problematic issue here; on the contrary, the "true" spokesperson for America seems to necessarily speak from a masculine space where the feminine is always the absent Other. (Hart 1988: 161)

Indeed, Hart's piece certainly offers excellent insight into the dearth of women in Shepard's plays. Perhaps we can even view his later work with strong female presences (*Far North* or *The God of Hell*, for example) as a conciliatory gesture toward critics who took him to task for ignoring the potential of women within his work. Hart recognizes that Shepard is "debunking the oppressive myths of American culture," but concedes that the ambiguous tone of his work can be viewed as "a dangerous reinstatement of the very values he seeks to undermine" (Hart 1988: 163). Once again, Hart elucidates the at-times dangerous agency of interpretation inherent to theatrical productions. Authorial intent can never be guaranteed to be felicitously communicated to the actors and directors, and neither can the authorial intent always be efficaciously conveyed to the audience as a whole. This ambiguity also extends to the treatment of gender conflict. Hart notes that Shepard has explored the dynamics of gender relations in *Fool for Love*, *A Lie of the Mind*, and *Paris, Texas*, yet "what is alarming is . . . [that] the author's attitude toward his subject [gender conflict] is ambiguous at best" (Hart 1988: 165). Hart supports this claim of ambiguity regarding gender conflict by citing an interview in *The New York Times* in which Shepard notes,

> There's something about American violence that to me is very touching, In full force, it's ugly, but there's also something very moving about it because it has to do with humiliation. There's some deeply rooted thing in the Anglo male American that has to do with inferiority, that has to do with being a man, and always, continually having to act out some idea of manhood that is invariably violent. (Hart 1988: 165)

Of course, Shepard presents his work with levels of meaning, littered with signifiers that serve a multitude of purposes, not solely acting as commentary upon gender conflict. Granted, in the work of Shepard, it does "appear [that] the 'true' spokesperson for America seems to necessarily speak from a masculine space where the feminine is always the absent Other" (Hart 1988: 161). But, within the corrupted patriarchy of Shepard's family sagas, is it not the patriarchy that has attempted to silence the female voice? Haven't Shepard's male characters, heedlessly seeking the self through the enactments of outmoded masculine codes, destroyed themselves and others? Perhaps most intriguing regarding Hart's usage of Shepard's quote is that even at this time, the "persona" of Shepard, the "playwright" Shepard, and a "Shepard play" seem all to be collapsed into one cultural entity with a singular, monolithic meaning. With Shepard as an actor, celebrity, and "persona," perhaps such conflation is inevitable, disallowing for thoughtful interpretations of the dynamics between the various significations linked to Shepard. Hart concludes that "we need more critics . . . who ask questions that extend beyond boundaries of the sacred textual domain and call attention to the politics of the artist who creates these representations before we can assess Shepard's place in the American theater" (1988: 174). Though the consideration of a writer's politics (in all senses of the term) is not a new notion, it is intriguing. Shepard has proudly displayed his leftist leanings in the Late Style, in contrast to fellow "macho" playwright

David Mamet's conversion to right-wing conservatism following the events of September 11, 2001.

Scholar Bonnie Marranca edited and compiled the first collection of criticism centered upon the work of Sam Shepard. Entitled *American Dreams: The Imagination of Sam Shepard* (1981), the collection features essays, reviews, and interviews. In the essay "Alphabetical Shepard: The Play of Words" Marranca herself approaches Shepard through alpha-logocentric means, taking each letter of the English alphabet as a starting point for an insight regarding Shepard and his work. In the piece, "Z" stands for "The Zero Gravity of Women." In this weightless space, Marranca contends,

> One of the most problematic aspects of the plays is Shepard's consistent refusal or inability, whichever the case may be, to create female characters whose imaginative range matches that of males. . . . Women are frequently abused, and always treated as subservient to men, their potential for growth and change restricted. (1981: 30)

Marranca's assertion is correct, yet as she proceeds, she explicitly concludes that this demonstration of the corrupting power of masculine codes and the patriarchy is a valorization of such codes. Marranca notes, "Shepard's portrayal of women is as outdated as the frontier ethic he celebrates" (1981: 30). Yes, many of the female characters created prior to the Late Style lacked depth, but contending that these characters are related to some kind of authorial nostalgia for the "frontier ethic" is not well-founded. As Marranca states, "men have their showdowns or face the proverbial abyss while the women are absorbed in simple activities and simplistic thoughts" (1981: 30). These men are adherents to broken codes and marginalize everyone in their lives, forcing their families, friends, and loved ones to the brink of destruction in their personal pursuit of the masculine self. At this point, Marranca notes that "there is no expression of a female point of view in any of Shepard's plays" (1981: 30) and I agree, for the destructive weight of the patriarchy does not allow for a female point of view. In fact, that can be taken to be the point of many of the conflicts within Shepard's plays. Marranca continues, noting that the "heroism and strength of the cowboy is revered by Shepard but in actuality the men he creates are ineffectual, fearful, and emotionally immature" (1981: 30). Marranca, like many other critics of this period, collapse the various Shepardian manifestations and cultural products (persona, writer, script, etc.) into one unchanging, stabilized corpus. Once again, by stating that the men are "ineffectual, fearful, and emotionally immature," Marranca simultaneously proves Shepard's point. These men, according to Marranca, "show no strength or character or will, yet they are allowed to dominate because it is their due as men" (1981: 30). As a result, the abuses and corruption of the patriarchy are revealed. Marranca assumes that "Shepard has no apparent interest in the relations of men and women, preferring instead to write about male experience. He writes as if he is unaware of what has been happening between men and women in the last decade . . ." (1981: 30). In actuality, Marranca supports Shepard's point regarding patriarchy. Shepard is demonstrating the fallout from retaining patriarchal codes. Marranca continues by arguing that Shepard "has not radicalized the way women interact in dramatic form" and that "his female characters are much less independent and intelligent that (sic) many of those created by these forefathers a hundred years ago" (1981: 30–1). Marranca's contention that Shepard's women are not radicalized is true. His explorations of gender in the Late Style attempt to rectify some of his failings as a writer of female characters. Marranca concludes with a call for Shepard to incorporate the "landscape of the female body" and to plow a space for "a female language area" in addition to "all the other 'languages' he has mastered" so that "the silent voices in the plays will tell their stories" (Marranca 1981: 31). Shepard's women are virtually a non-presence in the pre-family cycle plays, but with the family cycle, we see more of an attempt to integrate women into the work. With *Fool of Love* and *Lie of the Mind*, there is a conscious effort to excavate the buried voice of the female, but it would be Shepard's *Far North*, his first cinematic effort of the Late Style, that would fully demonstrate the value of a female presence.

Jane Ann Crum's "'I Smash the Tools of My Captivity': The Feminine in Sam Shepard's *Lie of the Mind*" (1993) responds to Marranca's scholarship on Shepard by contending that Marranca "does not want 'the feminine' as a presence in Shepard's work so much as she wants female characters who speak and act with the authority of men" (197). But, as Crum points out, if the women were empowered within Shepard's plays, they would be compelled to participate within the patriarchy. This argument continues, as Crum contends that Shepard utilizes the Derridian concept of *differance* to "split open the binary opposition and revel in the pleasures of open-ended textuality" (1993: 197)—this also aligns Shepard's work with Cixous' notion of the *ecriture feminine*. *Ecriture feminine* "rejects binary opposition and challenges the power structures which result from phallogocentrism" (1993: 197). This fascinating line of analysis holds that "in *A Lie of the Mind*, whether consciously or unconsciously, Shepard embraces the feminine. Here is to be found what Marranca longs for, women with imaginative range, women endowed with a new language, and a substantial 'landscape of the female body'"(Crum 1993: 211). Crum argues that *"Lie of the Mind* offers . . . models of feminine revolution . . . methods by which the female characters liberate themselves from submissive roles and activities and achieve 'the landscape of the female body'" (1993: 197). With *Far North*, Shepard offers another revolutionary method of liberation for women: female homosociality.

The work of Ann C. Hall, particularly the article "Speaking Without Words: the Myth of Masculine Autonomy in Sam Shepard's *Fool for Love*" (1993) and the volume *"A Kind of Alaska": Women in the Plays of O'Neill, Pinter, and Shepard* (also 1993), serves as an intervention of sorts between the binary readings of Shepard's work. Hall neither castigates the author nor resorts to hagiographic praise, rather she deftly engages the work through a critical feminist frame. Her nuanced analysis of Shepard's work reveals dynamics regarding female characters and the patriarchy. Countering the criticism that Shepard's female characters are incomplete or underwritten, Hall notes that

> Shepard's characters are often inconsistent, rapidly shifting from persona to persona, from mood to mood, desperately searching for

the secure identity the realistic formula presumes. Since this technique precludes consistent characterization, searching for a complete, fully developed and consistent female characters in the plays of Sam Shepard is troublesome at best. (1993b: 152)

Shepard's characters are almost always in the process of transformation, a dynamic paralleled by the "transformative" performance styles of the actors portraying Shepard's roles. For Hall, these "incomplete" characters do not have to do with Shepard's inability to create characters with depth; rather

this shifting characterization, moreover, forces both feminists and non-feminists to reevaluate the means for defining accurate or acceptable means of female representation in a manner similar to Brecht's alienation effect—by representing conventional ideologies in unusual ways, we are forced to reevaluate those ideologies. (1993b: 152)

This is a generous reading of Shepard's female characters, no doubt. Hall also locates a linkage between the plays of Shepard, Pinter, and Miller in that "through these female characters, the plays expose the process by which patriarchy attempts to oppress women. . . . Moreover, the female characters resist such oppression and eventually encourage their audiences and their fictional male counterparts to reconsider female oppression" (Hall 1993a: 2). Once again, the dynamics of performance allow/disallow authorial intention to be conveyed efficaciously to the director and actors and consequently, the spectators/audience. Recognizing this slippery nature of drama to be interpreted through performance (with the resulting embodiment as well as signs created for the production) allows for Shepard's depiction of patriarchy and male codes to be either rightfully criticized or unfortunately celebrated.

Having sketched out some of the major critical concerns regarding Shepard and his depiction of women, I now turn to Shepard's depiction of the male. Shepard's plays "repeatedly return to the depiction of male violence and arrogant machismo" and connect such notions to "the very root of the ruthless self-aggrandizement which still holds sway at every level of American culture" (Bottoms 1998: 16). Shepard himself has been quoted as stating,

> Machismo may be an evil force. . . . I know what this thing is about because I was a victim of it, it was part of my life, my old man tried to force on me a notion of what it was to be a "man." And it destroyed my dad. But you can't avoid facing it. (Cott 1986: 172)

Granted, Shepard's plays are littered with fathers, sons, and brothers, as well as cowboys, drifters, drunks, loners, and brutes. But, within these depictions, there rests a critique of such performances of masculinity; yet, "Shepard himself frequently seems trapped within this same limiting view of masculinity" (Bottoms 1998: 17). These limiting perspectives marginalize and push to the borders all identities not white, straight, and male. I concede that the forced liminality of "Othered" identities in contrast to the patriarchy replicates some of the worst tendencies of the patriarchy itself, silencing and ignoring those with different perspectives. But, does the critique—and replication of structure—erode or solidify patriarchal notions and masculine codes? If so, does Shepard posit and envision an alternative to the destructive nature of masculine codes and the patriarchy? Perhaps, if we look further into Shepard's meditations on the homosociality in *Far North*, *Ages of the Moon*, "Evanescence", and *Heartless*, as well as the stories "Doorway to Women" and "Great Dream of Heaven" discussed later in this chapter, we may locate a proposed resolution to Shepard's belief in a conflict between genders.

As stated, scholars, particularly in the 1970s and 1980s, held that Shepard's female characters were problematic for a multitude of reasons. Namely, if present at all, women were often depicted as silent, abused, and helpless and defined by their relationship to men. Women within the patriarchy of Shepard's plays possessed little to no agency or voice. Granted, a central component of Shepard's dramatic project is the criticism of masculinity and male codes as enacted within the violent paradigm of patriarchy. Within this patriarchy, women were marginalized, yet Shepard would eventually have his female characters speak and grow and offer alternatives to the patriarchy. Shepard moved toward developing such female characters in the 1980s. With the Late Style that is at the center of this manuscript Shepard attempts to more fully investigate women. Susan Bennett contends that "Shepard has attempted—perhaps in response to the cumulative effect of these observations—to make some sort of reparation" (1993: 168) through integrating more female characters into his work, beginning with *Fool for Love*. Felicia Londre recognized that the "masculinization of America, as reflected in the [1980s] works of Sam Shepard, is an enlightened recognition of the feminine component at its full value" (1993: 169). During his "cultural moment," Shepard attempted to foster more developed female characters, but only his turn toward film directing would result in a satisfactory exploration of women.

Certainly, we can see a development of female characters through Shepard's corpus, from the integration of female characters into his plays of the 1980s to the gynocentric *Far North*. As this film serves as an entry point for the Late Style, Shepard's work moves to attempt to forge ahead in the fleshing out of female characters who inhabit identities that exist outside attachments concomitant to men. But, what caused this move to "light out for new territories" located in the "female landscape"? Scholar Leslie Wade contends that in the late 1980s, with plays such as *Fool for Love* and *A Lie of the Mind*, "the dramatist grew increasingly cognizant of the violence in his work and began to rethink the codes that had colored his outlook and guided much of his behavior" (1997: 120). Bottoms traces the emergence of what Shepard calls his "female side" or "female part" to an earlier location in Shepard's work, specifically the "strangely prophetic female characters" (1998: 147) from the late 1970s, found in such plays as *Angel City* and *Buried Child*. In the 1980s, Shepard conceded that he must engage the "other side" or the "female side" or "die a horrible death as an artist" (Wade 1997: 120). Shepard notes,

> You get to the point where you say, "But there's this whole other territory I'm leaving out." And that territory becomes more important as you grow older. You begin to realize that you leave so much out when you go into battle with the shield and all the rest of it. . . . You can't grow that way. . . . There just comes a point where you have to

relinquish some of that and risk becoming more open to the vulnerable side, which I think is the female side. . . . It's much more courageous than the male side. (Bottoms 1998: 234)

By taking "this leap into a female character" (Wade 1997: 121), Shepard recognized the necessity of including the perspectives of women to further undercut the patriarchy so prevalent in his dramaturgical worlds. Certainly, his plays in the family cycle stress the destructive nature of masculinity, male codes, and the patriarchy, but including a female perspective pushes that interrogation of men and their families into even more engaging areas. For Shepard, *Fool for Love* "is really more about a woman than any play I've ever written, and it's from her point of view pretty much" (Bottoms 1998: 196). For Bottoms, *A Lie of the Mind* "suggests an increasing exasperation with the foolishness of the doomed male, and the female characters begin to take over the center of attention: for the first time, Shepard offers a clear and positive alternative to masculine failure in the shape of the more resilient, and more genuinely rooted, female characters" (Bottoms 1998: 231).Wade notes that at the time of *Fool for Love* and *A Lie of the Mind*, Shepard was reconciling with his father, reestablishing familial connections with his sisters, and developing a relationship with Jessica Lange.

Over the decades, Shepard himself has offered insight regarding his work and its depiction of women. In a 1993 conversation with scholar Carol Rosen, Shepard noted that

the female force in nature . . . became more and more interesting to me because of how that female thing relates to being a man. You know, in yourself, that the female part of one's self as a man is, for the most part, battered and beaten up and licked to shit just like some women in relationships. That men themselves batter their own female part to their own detriment. And it became interesting from that angle—as a man, what is it like to embrace the female part of yourself that you historically damaged for one reason or another. (Shewey 1998: 79)

Shepard has explained that "the female side knows so much more than the male side. About childbirth. About death. About where it's at" (Bottoms 1998: 192). Is this Late Style of Shepard an embracing of his own "female part"? Shepard's Late Style doesn't necessarily revel in the exploration of women, yet it does reveal a more nuanced and empathetic attempt to further understand the role of women in connection to society and codes of masculinity.

In 1988, as *Far North* was being released, Shepard commented that "having fallen in love with Jessica [Lange], I took a tremendous turn in terms of my own vulnerability. My relationship with Jessica allowed this vulnerability to show itself" (Allen 1988: 114). *Far North* was certainly a "family affair" for Shepard and Lange. The motion picture has been termed an homage to Lange's family, as her father and uncle have small acting roles, her sister worked in wardrobe, and Duluth (the setting and filming locale) is Lange's hometown.

Though assuming these events and developments had discernible impact upon Shepard may be tilting too far toward linking art with biography as a traceable cause and effect dynamic, it is undeniable that Shepard was indeed attempting, with varying degrees of success, to allow the women in his work to be heard. In this Late Style of transmedial exploration, Shepard would do just that, but his reconciliation of gender conflict seems to reside in homosociality.

How are we to understand feminist theory, gender theory, or even masculinity within the context of discussing Shepard's later works? Before proceeding to discuss homosociality, it is valuable to explore the vocabulary and definitions of the terms employed in this study. In a general sense, critical feminist theory "undertakes to deconstruct the opposition man/woman and the oppositions associated with it in the history of western [*sic*] culture" (Culler 2011: 140). In addition, this serves as "a theoretical critique of the heterosexual matrix that organizes identities and cultures in terms of the opposition between man and woman" (Culler 2011: 140). This theoretical approach also works to subvert patriarchal structures, dynamics, economics, roles, and discourse. In addition, feminist critical theory can also envision alternatives to the patriarchal systemizing of society and culture. This can often lead to utopian constructs that exist outside the rigid confines and expectations of the patriarchy.

The patriarchy works as the explicit result of male masculine hegemony. Masculinity must be performed within the strictures and structures of the patriarchy, enacting expectations of the white, heterosexual male. This, in turn, works to support the structure itself. As a result, as male masculinity holds economic and material power in the society, the male masculine archetype becomes the "normative" position. Indeed, if "masculinity is performed successfully, its performer attains power and privilege that offer him a greater sense of self-determination, something not generally offered to the forced participants of femininity" (McDonough 1997: 5). But, one must not neglect the importance of ethnicity, material wealth, or social class within the patriarchy and the limiting effect these traits have upon the freedom to perform various iterations of masculinity. In fact, economics and ethnicity "limit what range of performances men are allowed if they hope to maintain their power" (McDonough 1997: 6). In other words, if the male performs the understood traits of (white, heterosexual, upper class) masculinity within the patriarchy, he will attain and consolidate a powerful, hegemonic position within the society. These performances of masculinity are often dictated by codes of masculinity, often privileging action over contemplation, instinct over intelligence, and stoicism over emotion. In addition, traditional male heterosexual masculine codes of the United States privilege self-reliance and physical strength, while offering contempt for both the queer male as well as women seeking to defy traditional male societal privilege. Of course these codes are not homogenous, but they do indeed include numerous core qualities that can be consolidated for analysis.

By extension, gender can be viewed as a slippery, unstable location of shifting and ebbing identities. Gender can be understood to be not what one is, but rather the culmination of acts and performances. These in turn serve as citations to one's gender identity. For Judith Butler, "there is neither an 'essence' that gender expresses or externalizes nor an objective ideal to which gender aspires, and because gender is not a fact, the various acts of gender create the idea of gender, and without those acts, there would be no gender at all" (1990: 140). In a Butlerian sense, gender is asserted and reasserted through the accumulation of repeated acts, a performative turn that connects Butler's theories directly to theater studies.

According to scholar Eve Konofsky Sedgwick, the term *homosociality* can be understood to be "social bonds between people of the same sex" (1985: 1). In Sedgwick's *Between Men: English Literature and Male Homosocial Desire*, male homosociality is connected directly to male homosocial desire within the patriarchy. Sedgwick defines patriarchy by deferring to Heidi Hartmann, who terms it as "relations between men, which have a material base, and which, though hierarchial, establish or create interdependence and solidarity among men that enable men to dominate women" (Sedgwick 1985: 3). Under the patriarchy, this desire is often prohibited or restricted. Male, heterosexual relationships allow for male bonding, but within the patriarchy, these relationships reject any (overt) similarities to same-sex desire. In fact, the homosociality of the patriarchy consciously attempts to distance similarities of its relationships from those of the relationships between queer men. Male homosociality within the patriarchy often takes the form of activities that demonstrate and embody masculinity in an effort to perform "straightness" and to minimize and marginalize homosocial activities that may be deemed "effeminate." In essence, these activities attempt to eradicate speculation that the men engaged in homosocial activity can be identified as queer. As a result, "male bonding" activities such as athletics, alcohol consumption, and barbequing can be read as assertions of both masculinity and heterosexuality while helping to solidify the patriarchal order.

As male heterosexual homosociality attempts to enact a contradistinction from male queer homosociality, Sedgwick reads female homosociality quite differently and details her methodology in the first section of *Between Men*. In fact, "the diacritical opposition between the 'homosocial' and the 'heterosexual' seems to be much less thorough and dichotomous for women, in our society, than for men" (Sedgwick 1985: 2). Sedgwick contends that "women in our society who love women, women who teach, study, nurture, suckle, write about, march for, vote for, give jobs to, or otherwise promote the interests of other women, are pursuing congruent and closely related activities" (Sedgwick 1985: 2–3). The bonds created between sisters, mothers and daughters, female friends, and women who possess same-sex desire are all related, so as a result, female homosociality is not necessarily dichotomized against "homosexual" homosociality, but rather holds a position on the same continuum. And, these female homosocial groupings (and consequently, spaces) can serve as powerful locations for contesting the patriarchy and envisioning a utopian geography.

Sedgwick contends in *Between Men* that the archetypal love triangle created between two men and one woman may be, in fact, the actions of two men attracted to one another, but the men are prevented from acting upon their desire. In essence, the woman is reduced to a placeholder between men who are prohibited from consummating their mutual attraction. Though this dynamic is not overt in the majority of Shepard's work, its tensions can be felt. Regardless, both male and female homosociality are indeed a recurring concern of Shepard in this Late Style.

Male homosociality in Shepard's Late Style can be seen as a natural extension of masculinity, male codes, and the patriarchy. The male homosocial space serves as a location for the confirmation and enacting of such beliefs. This space also tends to move toward gynophobia and is relentlessly narcissistic. For the men in Shepard's work, male homosociality works as an insular world in which the men attempt to explain and support one another, psychically propping up the patriarchy. For example, in *Ages of the Moon*, the character Byron achieves fulfillment by refusing to abide by the gender codes. Yet, his love for his wife does reassert the privileging of heterosexuality. Ames, in his reckless, selfish onanistic quests for sexual gratification, sacrifices the bond held with his wife. At the conclusion of the play, Byron understands the beauty and complicity of the bond forged with his now deceased wife. Ames is left, once again alone, unhappy, drinking on his porch, waiting for something, anything, to occur. Yet, these men rarely achieve a sartorial moment in which they realize the ridiculousness of their actions and the emptiness and destructive potential of masculine codes. Female homosociality under patriarchal systematics are also viewed as appropriate, and seem to be a natural extension of the close, societally approved bonds developed between sisters, mothers and daughters, and close female friends. Shepard's work of this later period explores these homosocial worlds in an intriguing, transdiscplinary manner that seems at odds with some of the early critical characterizations of his work.

Far North begins with the family patriarch Bertrum (Charles Durning) driving his horse-drawn cart down an empty country road in contemporary northern Minnesota. The horse Mel overturns the cart and Bertrum lands in the hospital. Bertrum has two daughters: Kate (Jessica Lange), a single, professional woman who has fled the rural area for the city; and Rita (Tess Harper), who has remained near the family farm. Visiting her father as he recovers in the hospital, Kate reveals that she is pregnant. As she is unwed, this unnerves Bertrum. He demands that Kate enact vengeance upon the horse. Kate must kill Mel. Kate is in town to attend the birthday celebration for her beloved Gramma. Kate and Rita's mother Amy revel in tales of the "old days." Their Gramma wonders about the curious absence of men in their community.

Kate returns to the homestead and shares Bertrum's request with her sister, Rita. Rita's husband—as with almost all the men in this area—is nowhere to be found. Rita's teenage daughter Jilly spends a great deal of time engaging in sexual escapades with the local boys. It is revealed that Jilly is performing the assumed role of the "aggressive male" in her numerous relationships. This is depicted in the film when Jilly (Patricia Arquette) violently seduces two boys in the back of a car. Rita learns of the plan to execute Mel and sets the horse free. Meanwhile, Bertrum and his drunken brother-in-law Dane (Donald Moffat) stage an escape from the hospital. Kate and Rita set off into the woods to retrieve Mel and the confused Jilly. The women eventually reunite with each other and the horse. While in the woods, they encounter the drunken, lost, and disoriented Bertrum and Dane. The women essentially "rescue" the clumsy old men. At the conclusion, Gramma blows out her birthday candles at the party and asks "Where's all the men?" while the film cuts to Bertrum, rifle in hands, slowly leading Mel up the side of the mountain to his presumed doom.

In *Ages of the Moon*, two male friends both in their mid-sixties (Ames and Byron), sit on the porch of an old house, sipping whiskey during the evening hours. Ames has called Byron to come and visit him. Ames reveals that he has recently been "banished" from his home by his wife. Ames' wife discovered that he engaged in a tryst with a young woman during a fishing trip. In an attempt to find some solace, Ames requested a visit from his friend who he has not seen in some time. As the two sit on the porch, awaiting the coming lunar eclipse, they speak about their experiences and confront their growing mortality. The supremely self-involved Ames is shocked to learn that Byron's wife has recently died. Byron explains that after her peaceful death, he hoisted her body onto his back and took the body on a sort of "farewell" tour of the town. Byron—grasping at his heart in pain—reveals that "something has come apart" and without his wife, he has little reason to live. The two men sit on the porch and calmly continue to wait for the "once in a lifetime" opportunity to witness a lunar eclipse.

As detailed in Chapter 1, the film *Far North* was deemed a disappointment by many critics. *Ages of the Moon* also failed to generate such critical enthusiasm, but it also did not earn condemnations. Rather, most critics grudgingly praised its minimalism and lyrical dialogue. John Lahr appreciated the play, but concluded that it is "more splash than sizzle" though the "play's charm is insinuating" (2010). Ben Brantley wrote that *Ages of the Moon* "exudes a contagious weariness" and that "longtime fans of Mr. Shepard should definitely see this play" as it "is a poignant and honest continuation of themes that have always been present in the work of one of this country's most important dramatists, here reconsidered in the light and shadow of time passed" (2010). That said, Brantley also warns that "the show doesn't exert that unsettling visceral charge you associate with Mr. Shepard at his best" and that "there's an inhibited quality here that keeps the production from catching fire. It's neither as funny nor as fierce as it needs to be" (2010). Michael Feingold referred to *Ages of the Moon* as a "ruminative mood piece like other recent Shepard works" yet it "lacks forward motion" and in all "it offers instead the serene circularity of a staged poem" (2010).

A short work, "Evanescence, or Shakespeare in the Alley" (2011) was written as a contribution to the "10 × 25" festival of ten-minute plays. The imagistic piece's aesthetic seemingly connects to his earlier work from the Off-Off Broadway days, yet its considerations of gender— specifically, womanhood—firmly place it within the continuum of the late works, serving as a thematic precursor of sorts to *Heartless*.

"Evanescence, or Shakespeare in the Alley" focuses on a single woman reflecting on the confluence of sexuality and violence she has encountered throughout her life. It opens with the Woman sitting in a rolling office chair. As with the male/female relationships in *Age of the Moon*, a dissolved relationship has led to an existential crisis, as identities of the two parties in the relationship had become inextricably intertwined. With their identities collapsed into one another, the severing of the bond leads to anguish, for meaning and solace for the Woman was evidently located in the relationship itself.

As the Woman further reflects upon her situation, meditating on suicide and remembering her father, watermelons begin to drop onto the stage accompanied by jarring "Duane Eddy-like" guitar riffs (Shepard 2012: 51). This Brechtian device serves to alarm the audience, ideally forcing them to extract themselves from the emotion of the moment and reflect upon the connections between the Woman and themselves. Not since *States of Shock* has Shepard experimented with such theatrical devices to "shock" the spectators out of passivity. Shakespeare then appears on stage, dragging a black Visqueen bag that contains the corpse of a woman. He approaches the Woman, and quoting from *The Comedy of Errors*, asks, "How comes it now . . . that thou art thus estranged from thyself? Thyself . . . being strange to me . . ." (55). The Woman longs for her partner, asking, "We are connected, aren't we? Always. In that way—I mean. We are—always. Aren't we?" As a minor work in the Shepard canon, "Evanescence, or Shakespeare in the Alley" does reveal that the author is now considering the implosion of a heterosexual relationship not just from the man's perspective (as in *Ages of the Moon*), but is attempting to have a woman voice her perspective, even though that voice is limited to a brief work.

Shepard further considered these themes in his next full-length work, 2011's *Heartless*. His first foray into a gynocentric homosocial environment since *Far North*, *Heartless* is at its core the story of a man who stumbles into the space of a Shepardian family, ruled not by a destructive patriarch, but rather by an unpredictable and eccentric matriarch. Indeed, just as *Ages of the Moon* concerns male friendship, *Heartless* meditates on a family that revolves around female relationships. Roscoe, a professor of Cervantes who has recently abandoned his own family, accompanies his much younger girlfriend Sally to visit her family. The family resides in a home once owned by James Dean. The family includes Sally's sister Lucy and their wheelchair-bound mother Mable. Also present in the home is the mysterious (and mute) Elizabeth who serves as a caretaker for Mable. Sally bears the scar of a heart transplant, and we later learn that Elizabeth possesses a similar scar. Roscoe is eventually drawn toward the ghostly Elizabeth and they make love. When Sally learns of the transgression, Roscoe is confronted by the women of the home and eventually flees. Sally closes the play by acknowledging her mother's wisdom regarding men.

The play received a mixed reaction from critics. Ben Brantley noted that the work "provides only flashes of the glorious theatrical glee and anguish that animate" Shepard's earlier work and for "a few delighted moments, you feel you've come back to Shepard country" (2012). That said, Brantley recognized that "for Shepard aficionados, *Heartless* offers a fascinating focus on a figure that this restlessly imaginative author—in contrast to other great American playwrights, like Tennessee Williams and Eugene O'Neill—usually doesn't pay much attention to: good old long-suffering, child-shaping, hearth-keeping Mom" but concluded that "Shepard has said all this before, and with more dramatic urgency and clarity" (2012). Brantley, however, hailed the turn by longtime Shepard performer Lois Smith and commented that "it's refreshing to find Mr. Shepard's usual gender ratio reversed in *Heartless*" (2012). *The New Yorker*'s Hilton Als recognized Shepard's ambitions regarding female characters, explaining that "unlike much of Shepard's work, 'Heartless' isn't nostalgic for the fantasy of the Old West, where the romance was between men—fathers and sons and brothers. Instead, it tries to dramatize what men imagine women are like when men aren't watching" (2012). Acknowledging his style, Als continues that "Shepard's great strengths are his Kerouac-like robustness, even silliness, and his poetic resistance to explaining his artistic impulses" while "he digs and digs to get at something that means something to his consciousness— especially his unresolved relationship with his father" (2012). Among this "wonderland of wounded women" Als asked, "Could it be that Shepard's ideal woman is some version of Dad?" (2012). *The Village Voice*'s longtime critic Michael Feingold confirmed that *Heartless* "is a Sam Shepard play" but sadly confessed that "the last work to strike me as a Sam Shepard play was *Fool for Love*, nearly three decades ago" (2012).

Like *Ages of the Moon*, the story "The Door to Women" also centers upon male homosociality. A boy and his grandfather live a cloistered existence away from all female contact. The grandfather has successfully driven all women from their house, "some by betrayal, others by neglect" (Shepard 2002: 43) and models a masculine code for his grandson. The grandfather has noticed that the boy has been receiving the affections of a young woman in the neighborhood. The boy denies feelings for her, or even thinking about her, confirming his compliance to the code. At the conclusion, the boy flees the confines of his grandfather's home and revels in the memory of the intimacy that he has shared with the young woman, a transgressive act that he has successfully hidden from his grandfather.

The tale "Great Dream of Heaven" concerns two male friends who have long since passed the days of youth. Dean and Sherman grew up together and now share a cinder block bungalow in Twentynine Palms. After the deaths of their respective wives and the maturing of their children, the two men relocated. They dress similarly in bolos and Stetsons and "the one great daily pleasure they both looked forward to was their walk down to Denny's by the highway for coffee and patty melt [sandwiches]. This was truly like heaven to the both of them" (Shepard 2002: 130). They both have affections for Faye, a waitress at the restaurant. The two men make "their appearance at Denny's each day at noon to remind Faye that her sort of beauty was a great blessing in the midst of all this sad madness" (Shepard 2002: 131). For Dean and Sherman, it seems as it "was luck to have an enduring friendship, a true partnership, at their age and not be condemned to some horrible blithering sentence of aloneness" (Shepard 2002: 132). One morning, Sherman wakes and notices that Dean is gone. When Sherman arrives at Denny's, Faye is not there. He is told that Dean came in early that morning and left with Faye. Sherman returns to their bungalow and finds Dean. Sherman feels betrayed by his friend. While Dean hopelessly attempts to explain that "it wasn't my idea, it was hers!!!" (Shepard 2002: 139), Sherman packs an old military duffle bag and begins walking until he disappears in the distance.

As stated, *Far North*[1] is a Chekhovian burlesque of Shepard's own explorations of gender. Centered upon the women of a family in northern Minnesota, Shepard gently meditates on the power and promise of female homosociality, while mocking the absurd failures of the patriarchy. The first shot of the film features the grizzled patriarch Bertrum commandeering a carriage being drawn by the horse Mel. The carriage itself is a strange *mélange* of the archaic and the modern—it is certainly a traditional carriage of sorts with buggy springs, yet instead of wooden wagon wheels, the contraption brandishes modern automobile tires. Like his mode of transportation, Bertrum's codes and beliefs are hopelessly out of date.

Mel as a horse complicates the binarial relations between humans and animals. When Mel defies Bertrum, he is violently rebelling against his subordination. In essence, Mel's "throwing off of the bridle" serves as a demonstration of one way of upending the patriarchy—a sudden, physical rebellion, a violent reaction akin to Stubbs' dispatching of the Colonel in *States of Shock*. The women of Bertrum's family demonstrate another strategy at subverting the patriarchy, that of establishing a female homosociality that strengthens communal bonds, while forging a less destructive and less antiquated code of behavior that serves as an alternative to male codes.

Just as Bertrum is identified as a man out of place (he is one of the few remaining men in the area) and out of time (as he is near death, he is literally running out of time, while his conservative values keep him entrapped in a time long passed), his daughter Kate is identified as a character of the modern world. When she first appears, Kate has just arrived from New York City and is an emissary of sorts from the modern metropolis. She performs the role of "modern career woman" which is indicated by her "fashionable big-city clothes" (Shepard 1993: 53). This contrast is further demonstrated as Bertrum, representative of old masculine codes, lies in a hospital bed with multiple tubes connecting to various locations on his body. The patriarchy is on its last leg and has required medical intervention to keep it alive. When the representative of modernity and womanhood (Kate) arrives, instead of a "heart-to-heart" conversation between father and daughter, Bertrum immediately "smells" that she is pregnant and bemoans that she is not married. He asks, "Is that still too old-fashioned for ya?" (Shepard 1993: 54). Bertrum further demands that Kate "make it a boy. . . . Too many damn girls in the family as it is. Family's thick with women. Never used to be like that. Used to be men. All men" (Shepard 1993: 54). Though Bertrum resents her "big-city-girl" ways, he makes a ridiculous paternal request: Kate must kill the horse Mel. In Bertrum's mind, this enacts a sort of vengeance and retribution against a creature who refused to remain in its "place." Bertrum demands that "Yer gonna have to shoot him for me" (Shepard 1993: 55). With his last gasp, Bertrum commands his daughter to exact vengeance upon the entity that defied the binarial order of (hu) man/animal. Bertrum further attempts to convince Kate of enacting this vengeance by proclaiming, "You were my last hope. What I deserve for not havin' a son" (Shepard 1993: 56). Bertrum needs someone to "avenge" him and the dishonor that the horse enacted. Kate attempts to counter Bertrum's demands, drawing attention to the obvious point that "it's just a horse, for Christ's sake! It's a dumb old horse! He didn't know what he was doing!" (Shepard 1993: 57), but Bertrum contends that Mel was aware of the action and as a result, the patriarch views the unsettling of the (hu)man/animal binarial relationship as a threat to the patriarchy and his own identity. Mel is aligned with the females of the family—this is evident in Rita's remark, "I can't let anything happen to Mel. He's part of the family" (Shepard 1993: 84). For the women, Mel is an integral member of the family; for Bertrum, he is merely a tool or a biomechanical machine to be used to achieve an end. In addition, for Bertrum, a woman is like a horse, in that "a horse is not an animal to be trusted" (Shepard 1993: 100). Like Mel, Kate will eventually defy the patriarchy and masculine codes by refusing the request to execute Mel. In addition, Kate and the other women of the family will enact and demonstrate a less violent undermining of the patriarchy through female homosociality.

But Bertrum is not the only withering male family member. Down the hospital corridor Kate finds Uncle Dane, Bertrum's brother-in-law. Uncle Dane claims that he is in the hospital for "just a little checkup" (Shepard 1993: 59), but his ailing health is most likely related to his vast consumption of alcohol. Dane does not wholly share Bertrum's codes. When Kate finds him, he is enraptured by a horse race on the television. With Dane, we seemingly find a man who takes great pleasure in the beauty and grace of horses, rather than viewing the animal as a simple tool or machine. In fact, when Dane learns of Mel's rebellion against Bertrum, he exclaims, "Serves him right. That horse shoulda killed him, way he treats animals. One a' these days a horse is gonna kill him. . . . He's got it comin'" (Shepard 1993: 59). Dane values animals, while Bertrum has contempt for them. We learn later that Bertrum has killed all the family dogs, essentially because he was mad. So, Bertrum's code is distinctly destructive, enacting its violence even on domesticated animals.

Toward the end of the film, as the two old men escape from the hospital, Dane confronts Bertrum about his wanton destruction and violence. As they wander along the train tracks during the night, Dane explains, "You never listen to reason, Bertrum. . . . Yer always gonna beat somethin' to death. Shootin' yer horse ain't gonna solve anything. . . . All you'll have is a dead horse on yer hands" (Shepard 1993: 98). Dane is pleading with Bertrum to reconsider his ways and how he deals with animals and people. Of course, such comments lead to Bertrum enacting violence, hailing a bevy of rocks at his brother-in-law. Paradoxically, Dane's pleading for "nonviolence" spurs Bertrum on to even more violence. But, in the end, it is the women who come to the rescue of both men.

In their escape from the hospital, the two geezers revert to enacting a male adolescent fantasy. Dane (crawling "marine style" nonetheless) sneaks into Bertrum's room with rum, celebrating the fact that he has "won today" from the races. Like two teenage boys, the men become drunk, secreted away from society and women. This perpetuation of adolescence is also displayed when Kate reveals to Bertrum that she cannot enact his desire to execute Mel. We are told that "Bertrum rejects her" and he "jerks his head back toward her. His eyes open. His face reddens. He seems on the verge of a temper tantrum, like he's about to explode" (Shepard 1993: 87). This infantile behavior is indicative of Bertrum's (and the patriarchy's) emotional, violent reaction when a request is refused. Any objection to a male request is read as a direct rejection of the (re)assertion of the patriarch's hegemonic power.

The first glimpse of female homosociality is when Kate returns to the family home and explains Bertrum's demands to her sister (Rita) and mother (Amy). Rita is shocked that Kate would even consider such a demand, claiming it to be "murder" and that "it's not the poor horse's fault," (Shepard 1993: 62) a statement which their mother agrees. According to Rita, their father Bertrum is "always wantin' to shoot somethin'. As soon as somethin' goes wrong, he wants to shoot it" to which Amy exclaims, "He's shot all our dogs" (Shepard 1993: 63). Even in this (somewhat) light-hearted take on gender relations, it is impossible to escape the violence of the male. This is stressed once again when Amy is awakened by the noise from Jilly fighting with her mother. Amy rushes out from the bedroom to attend to the commotion, saying that because "there was so much noise, I thought [Bertrum] was home" (Shepard 1993: 69). Not only has the patriarch regularly killed the family animals, when Bertum does come home, he often causes quite a ruckus, similar to other domestic disturbances instigated by returning, intoxicated fathers in *Curse of the Starving Class* or *The Late Henry Moss*.

The relationship between Kate and Rita is certainly complex. Kate has gone off to the city, while Rita has remained at home. Rita resents her father's favoritism toward her sister—as Rita notes, "You have always been on his side, haven't you?" (Shepard 1993: 113). Rita also resents Kate's attempts to control Jilly's libido. When Jilly is engaged in sexual activity with two boys, it is Kate—not Rita—who runs after the teenage boys with a gun. Kate does not understand that Jilly is the sexual aggressor. Finally, if Kate fulfills her mission to execute Mel, Rita will be betrayed. There are scenes when the two sisters share moments of intimacy. As the two have found Mel, they both ride him as the sun sets. Rita asks "So, you're gonna have it, eh?" (Shepard 1993: 99). This moment offers the potential for ending the pregnancy, certainly never an option under an all-powerful patriarchy that is now waning. As Bertrum says, "Used to be, when you got a girl in trouble that was it. You got married. That was all she wrote" (71). The promise of a woman's choice regarding sexuality and reproduction is once again referenced when Kate pointedly asks Jilly, "Did you use any protection?" (Shepard 1993: 103). The women, in the new, post-patriarchal world, have agency as well as command over their own bodies and sexuality. For many attempting to uphold the patriarchy, this aspect of feminism is the most threatening.

When Kate and Rita finally locate Jilly and place her on the back of Mel, we are given a unique vision of all three women, in nature, at peace (momentarily) with one another and with the horse. This image creates an image of serenity and beauty, quite at odds with other, more recognizable and iconic images from Shepard's work, such as the smashing of a typewriter in *True West*, a woman having her mouth forcibly penetrated by a man's hand in *Buried Child*, or a young man urinating all over his sister's school project in *Curse of the Starving Class*.

This image of the three women on horseback is contrasted with the bumbling, intoxicated violence of Bertrum and Dane. In a stupor, as they wander the train tracks, Bertrum assaults his brother-in-law with rocks, while Dane responds with a hurled beer bottle. Their juvenile violence escalates until the two continue waging a nocturnal war. Bertrum accuses Dane—as well as the women in his family—of being descended from Mongol hordes. Dane, Amy, and Gramma's side of the family are composed of immigrants from Finland, as revealed when Gramma gently sings a Finnish tune to herself and a Finnish song is performed at her birthday party. Bertrum blames Dane and the women in his family for an inherited negative quality. Bertrum says, "Nobody in their right mind would marry into eyes like that. They've all got it. They keep passing it on like some disease. BARBARIAN WOMEN" (Shepard 1993: 106). For Bertrum, there is an essentialized element to the women in his family that makes them distrustful and deviant.

This moment also offers a glimpse into the "real" code of masculinity as followed by Bertrum. When first glimpsed by Kate, Bertrum seems to be wearing a cape, appearing as a geezer in mock-heroic dress. In addition, Bertrum refuses to answer calls for help from his own daughter. When the men hear the call for assistance, Dane suggests, "Maybe we oughta see what the trouble is, Bertrum" to which his brother-in-law states, "I don't wanna know what the trouble is. I got plenty of my own. . . . And what're you gonna do about it, Mr. Hero?" (Shepard 1993: 113). Bertrum's code is marked by an inability and unwillingness to help others in need. In addition, the code is driven by fear.

Dane and Bertrum wander down the highway in the darkness of night. The three women are riding Mel calmly. They approach the two men and rescue them. This image reverses the archetype of a solo man rescuing a woman or a group of women while charging on horseback.

Rather, Shepard's vision of homosociality in *Far North* appears to be a group of women, calmly trotting down a modern highway to rescue two witless old men. The horse is in complete agreement with the women, a reversal of Mel's attempt to "throw off the reins" of Bertrum at the beginning of the film. As the viewer witnesses this image, Bertrum perceives something much more akin to his belief in the barbarism of women. Though it is simply three woman trotting on horseback, Bertrum sees his greatest fear. The script notes

> BERTRUM'S POINT OF VIEW. He sees a nightmare approaching. Mel has the white X painted on his face and he's in full gallop, sparks flying from his hooves. The women are all in primitive warpaint; strips of rawhide with skulls tied to them clatter around their waists. They brandish sickles and lances with banners streaming from them. They carry knives between their teeth. They scream savagely like demons from hell as they sweep down on BERTRUM.[2] (Shepard 1993: 117)

For Bertrum, the modern woman is literalized and embodied by a phantasmagoric vision of female "savages." Bertrum's distaste for the upending of the patriarchy strikes him with fear. Indeed, Bertrum and his antiquated code of masculinity are threatened. His codes are becoming irrelevant while there is an increase in the agency and social/economic power of women.

Within Shepard's work, female homosociality stresses the importance of the matriarchal family, independent of male influence. Women must assume both "traditional" male and female gendered roles. Gender within this sphere is much more flexible than in the male homosocial environs. The female homosocial realm exists within the larger patriarchy, but works stealthily, subverting male concerns and demands. Women do not necessarily assume the masculine stance, but rather develop their own codes and actions that are often at odds with male expectations of women. In *Far North*, when the daughter Kate refuses to execute the family horse Mel, rejecting codes of masculinity, she is effectively forging her own, new order in opposition to the patriarchy. This is further emphasized at the conclusion of the film when the matriarch of the family celebrates her birthday, and only women are in attendance. Bertrum foolishly hauls Mel out for execution while the women of the family celebrate and reassert the important bonds developed in the homosocial environment.

Shepard's celebration of the potentiality of the matriarchy reappeared in 2011's *Heartless*. As Shepard's fathers almost inevitably abandon their families, mothers seem to remain, often holding the family together. When Roscoe finally leaves Sally and her family, Sally turns to her mother and asks, "How come you saved me when you knew I was doomed? When you knew it was hopeless. How come you kept me going?" to which Mabel responds, "What are mothers for?" (Shepard 2013: 119). With *Ages of the Moon*, "Evanescence, or Shakespeare in the Alley," and *Heartless*, it seems as if Shepard in his late work has conceded that most men are incapable of committing to women in a way that agrees with their views of love and relationships. Indeed, homosociality seems to be the answer to Shepard's vision of the eternal division between male and female.

The geographic region of *Far North* has also become more and more homosocial through the disappearance of men. Bertrum and Dane wonder, "Where's the man?" (Shepard 1993: 71). Amy comments that the "only difference today is the notable lack of menfolk. There used to always be men. Always. . . . Where'd they all go?" (Shepard 1993: 77–8). Indeed, to where have the men disappeared? In turn, Gramma's centenary celebration reasserts the value and sorority of female homosociality with non-patriarchal codes of behavior and empathetic understandings of human dynamics. The scene is described as follows:

> A large throng of women gathered around Gramma's living room table for her birthday. They all sing a Finnish song for her. The remains of a gigantic breakfast in the plates in front of them. GRAMMA sits at the head of the table in her wheelchair. . . . She is surrounded by the family and their children—all girls. Not a man in sight. (Shepard 1993: 118)

Kate toasts "to our dearest grandma, Trenje—The Source of Us All!" (Shepard 1993: 119). This recognizes the primacy of the matriarchy, as the patriarchy fades from relevance. Gramma asks, "Where's all the men?" and the final shot of the film is Bertrum leading Mel into the woods with a gun. As the women continue to cement their familial and social bonds in the present and the future (as represented by the children), Bertrum—in an absurd and ludicrous act—reverts to his familiar behavior of violence and destruction. As bonds between women have strengthened and grown in the contemporary world, the violent behavior and destructive codes of the male have made him irrelevant and unnecessary for the components of life. Like a species aware—but in denial—of its own imminent extinction, the males of *Far North* trudge forward, retaining their codes as they slowly wither and expire as their own irrelevance becomes more apparent to everyone but themselves.

As stated, there is a certain lack of men in this region. Bertrum and Dane are seemingly the last remaining men. Their homosocial relation is one of desperation, convenience, and family rather than choice or pleasure. In fact, Bertrum and Dane are not even truly fond of each other, yet as remaining relics of the patriarchy, they gravitate toward one another. At the hospital, Bertrum confesses that "I never thought there'd come a time . . . when I'd stop missing women. I just don't miss them anymore" (Shepard 1993: 70). From this, Bertrum proceeds to complain about "these gals a' mine. These two daughters. Neither one of 'em's got a man. They got kids, all right. They get knocked up but they got no man. . . . Where in the hell is the goddamn man?" (Shepard 1993: 71). Bertrum goes on to blame modern men ("Used to be, when you got a girl in trouble, that was it. You got married") then shifts the blame to modern women, lamenting "who the hell knows what [women] do on their own these days. They go off away to the city, come back pregnant, and they got no goddamn man" (Shepard 1993: 71). The homosocial bond between Bertrum and Dane is strengthened through nostalgia for (more) fixed gender roles and a resistance to modernity. But Bertrum recognizes the powerful allure of modernity, as signified by the magnetism of the metropolis. Bertrum notes that "no man in his right mind's gonna stay up here in this Christless country"

(Shepard 1993: 71) when the big city beckons. The world "outside" of rural Minnesota is equated with the "modern" world. The old men's self-righteous entitlement resides in their accomplishments in the past ("A man who's fought in the trenches of Italy; in the slime of Korea; who broke his back on the railroad of Lake Erie!" (Shepard 1993: 74)) and in their resentments of the present (standard conservative American targets such as "big government-United Nations kind'a stuff" (Shepard 1993: 74)).

Far North features four generations of a family represented through four generations of women. There is Gramma, who is soon-to-be one hundred years old, and her daughter, Amy. Amy has two daughters (Kate and Rita) and Jilly is the daughter of Rita. Both Gramma and Amy retain a hold upon traditional gender roles evidenced through Gramma's "Where's all the men?" comment and Amy's incessant cooking throughout the film. Amy remembers grand feasts of women serving men and even awakes to glimpse an aged photograph of her and Bertrum at their wedding. In addition, Amy holds to the patriarchal gender roles of the past by asking the pregnant Kate, "Where's your man?" Rita and Kate have subverted the traditional roles that would have been assigned to them. Neither have men in their lives. So, they are single women. When Kate and Rita fight, Rita says, "Now you've got yourself knocked up and you don't even have a man, do ya, Kate?" to which Kate asks, "Where's your man?" Rita ends the conversation by screaming out, "I don't need a man!" (Shepard 1993: 113). Kate resides in a city, an apparently unheard of option for unmarried women in this rural patriarchal Minnesota subculture. Rita, we learn, knows the ins and outs of horse riding and firearms. While Kate considers executing Mel and exacting her father's wish, Rita mounts Mel and stages an escape. Rita has upended the wishes of her father as well as the patriarchy. When her sister attempts to enact those masculine codes, Rita resists those actions. Eventually, Rita attempts to draw her own daughter in resisting the patriarchy and masculine codes, imploring Jilly to join the quest "to save Mel. You and me" (Shepard 1993: 83).

As Rita's daughter, Jilly is the character who most radically upends and reverses traditional roles. In her various amorous dalliances with local boys, we learn very quickly that she (1) is the instigator of sexual escapades and (2) assumes the often male role of sexual aggressor. When Kate learns that Jilly is drunk and attempting to fellate two boys in the back of a car ("I don't give turns! I give head!" Jilly exclaims), Kate storms out after the boys with a gun. A nonchalant Rita tells Kate, "She's not getting raped, believe me. They're getting raped" (Shepard 1993: 66). Beyond assuming the male role in sexual relations, Jilly also consumes alcohol in a decidedly masculine fashion. She drinks and drinks fast, racing toward intoxication. In essence, "she drinks like a man."[3] Jilly's masculinity is defined by a combination of her aggressive sexuality and a fondness for intoxication. When Kate and Rita search through the forest for Mel, they stumble upon Jilly, once again having sex with yet another boy.

"Traditional" female roles are upended again when Kate is saddled with the responsibility of equine execution. Bertrum admits to her that "you were my last hope. What I deserve for not havin' a son, I suppose" (Shepard 1993: 56). In the absence of a male offspring, Bertrum places a "male" responsibility upon his daughter. Kate is caught in an identity crisis—can she remain a woman and enact an element of her father's violent male code? According to Bertrum, Kate "was the only one mean enough" (Shepard 1993: 73) to kill Mel. There are other indications that Bertrum wishes Kate to live up to his expectations and these expectations are those a "traditional" father would have for his son. With the men having gradually disappeared, only Kate is "mean enough" (which she is not)—there are no more men to enact the antiquated codes of masculinity.

For the family, Kate does seem be the heir apparent of her father's sense of masculinity. Kate has been the (sometimes) reluctant object of Bertrum's attempts to "engender" a sense of masculinity in her as "they've always had a strange relationship" (Shepard 1993: 76). Amy states that Kate is indeed "just like her father" (Shepard 1993: 76). Kate does possess loyalty to her father, confessing that the execution of Mel could serve as her "last chance. . . . Just to do something for him" (Shepard 1993: 73) and later explains to a doubting Rita, "Dad knows. He knows everything" (Shepard 1993: 99). When Kate decides against destroying Mel, Bertrum rejects her. Only when Kate agrees, does he smile with approval. Kate concedes that once Mel is executed, "maybe we can be friends" (Shepard 1993: 87). Through this agreed upon action, Kate is abiding by the patriarchal notion of loyalty to the father by rejecting both common sense and animal empathy.

But, we learn that this is only one of a series of tests of masculinity that Bertrum has forced Kate to endure. Kate tells herself angrily, "It's another one of your tests. . . . It's another one of your stupid tests!" (Shepard 1993: 89). In a montage of flashbacks, we see Bertrum throwing a naked baby from a dock into a lake. We then see Bertrum slapping a pony as a young girl "hangs on to the mane for dear life" while the pony "bucks" wildly. Finally, an adolescent Kate drives a John Deere tractor straight into a tree. About these tests, Kate proclaims,

> They never did me a damn bit a' good. I mean, I learned to swim on my own! I learned to ride on my own! . . . None of your tests did me a damn bit of good. Not one of 'em. The only thing it taught me was how to fight back! So I guess I owe you for that. (Shepard 1993: 90)

In essence, Bertrum's ridiculous tests of masculinity have taught Kate (like the horse Mel) to "buck" the patriarchal system.

But, Kate is not the only "student" of Bertrum's lessons. As he wanders with Dane, Bertrum explains, sounding ever-much like Willy Loman, "Trouble with you, Dane, see, is that you're never going to be a leader of men. That's your problem, you're too soft. You gotta learn to look life in the face and not knuckle under. Not run to the bottle . . ." (Shepard 1993: 100). Of course, Bertrum himself is neither a leader of men nor a teetotaler. In fact, Bertrum seems as much an aficionado of cheap liquor as Dane.

As the film concludes, the viewer is present at the homosocial birthday celebration for Gramma. As there are no men present, the conclusion of the film recognizes the importance of this homosocial communion and reasserts the irrelevance of men in this post-patriarchal world. This utopian vision of bliss and communalism is contrasted with Bertrum as he is shown holding Mel's reigns and leading the horse to the forest for execution. In the conclusion of the film, women are seen as ensuring longevity, community, and happiness, while men—still adhering to antiquated male codes—are seen as ensuring only vengeance and destruction.

Ages of the Moon also reveals a homosocial space, but this area is carved out for frank interaction and discussion between men. The audience quickly learns that Byron has been called to this remote location to console his friend Ames.[4] Ames was recently "banished" from his primary home when his wife learned of his dalliances with a young woman on one of his fishing trips. The two sip whiskey and wait for the total eclipse of the moon, scheduled to occur at 5.00 a.m.

As a two-person play, *Ages of the Moon* continues an exploration of explicitly Beckettian aesthetics as seen in *Kicking a Dead Horse* and in *States of Shock*. As *Kicking a Dead Horse* borrows elements from *Happy Days* and *States of Shock* references *Endgame*, *Ages of the Moon*, with its *non sequiturs*, Vaudevillian bits of "stage business," and the "act" of waiting for an expected occurrence reflects *Waiting for Godot*.

As the two men wait for the eclipse, they discuss mortality. Ames notes, "We haven't got all that much time left. . . . We're not exactly spring colts" (Shepard 2011: 12). But with age, much has changed. As Byron says, "Used to be we could talk about anything. The two of us. Years ago. There wasn't all this—judgement" (Shepard 2011: 14). Both men are looking to reestablish a friendship on the same terms shared in the past, but that is not possible. The two men's varying perspectives may indeed keep them apart.

Aging[5]—as indicated by the title—is referenced throughout the play. Both men are identified as being in their mid-sixties. "Four point six thousand million years. That's how old they reckon the moon is," Ames points out. When asked if he could picture that time, Ames confesses, "I can't even picture yesterday" (Shepard 2011: 45). Byron adds, "I remember the look of shock on your face when you saw me get off the bus. . . . How old I was. . . . How old I have become. . . . Eyes buried way back inside the sagging fleshy mask" (Shepard 2011: 46). This aging is further explored as the eclipse (literally, a shadow or darkness) approaches the moon. Ames states, "Starting to get covered up, isn't it?" (Shepard 2011: 62), making a parallel with the eclipse and their own approaching deaths. They are indeed decades away from their young years. When Ames attacks and chokes Byron, Ames remarks, "We were just having a little disagreement. A little scuffle. In the old days we used to beat the shit out of each other" (Shepard 2011: 57). Indeed, the men wish to reestablish a relationship founded decades ago, but as they have changed and altered through the years, both physically and emotionally, a reestablishment of the relationship on the same terms is impossible.

One of the ways in which Ames and Byron differ is their attitudes and actions toward women. In this homosocial sphere, the women seem almost supernatural and beyond comprehension.[6] Byron contends that women are "actually hooked up to [the moon], I mean—the cycles. You know" (Shepard 2011: 43). As a result, women have "a whole different-outlook" (Shepard 2011: 43). Ames seeks sexual gratification outside of his marriage, while Byron's loyalty to his now dead wife Lacey impresses even Ames. Byron, recognizing the ridiculous nature of Ames' dalliances, asks, "What's become of you, Ames?" (Shepard 2011: 16). Byron adds, "She [Ames' wife] doesn't like you drinking, I suppose" and chastises him for "drinking and chasing young snatch. At your age" (Shepard 2011: 16). As Ames explains his actions, we realize that he indeed loved his wife on their honeymoon and remembers intimate details. He tells Byron, "I was never so much in love. . . . I was. I never thought it would end" (Shepard 2011: 31). Ames also reminisces that "she always giggled in moments of crisis. . . . I can't get her out of my mind." Ames betrayed his wife and has been shunned. Byron is shocked that Ames would cheat on his wife, while Ames himself has turned to alcohol consumption to lessen the emotional pain. Byron notes, "You shouldn't let her get to you like that, Ames" (Shepard 2011: 41). When Byron later reveals his dedication to the dead Lacey, Ames realizes that he has indeed squandered the relationship with his wife. Byron notes,

"I'd never get myself into a jam like that. . . . I'd never run the risk . . . of losing her" (Shepard 2011: 48). Later, Byron's sorrow and sense of loneliness is so intense that he attempts to inscribe himself into the past of Ames so as to reexperience the moment of love. When Ames shares stories pivotal to the relationship with his wife, Byron attempts to convince Ames that he was there, too.

The audience also learns that Ames' wife was desirable to all men. When Byron admits to having feelings for Ames' wife, Ames reinscribes his own memories to reflect Byron's presence. As a result, Ames blames Byron for his own marital strife and begins to choke him. This leads to Byron clenching his chest, shouting that "something's come apart in there" and claiming that Ames has "destroyed" him.

But, it is Lacey's death that has truly broken Byron. He explains,

> Lying beside her. Watching her breathless face for hours. Right beside her. . . . All day. Watching her like that. All through the night. No breath. Her skin. Eyes glazed over. Nothing. Gone. I could never have imagined something like that. After all those years. Just-dead. In the morning like that. And the birds—going on outside like nothing ever happened. (Shepard 2011: 58)

After her death, Byron carried Lacey on his back around town and took her "to all the places we walked every day. . . . Nobody knew she was dead, Ames. Nobody asked" (Shepard 2011: 65). After his friend's monologue of poetic imagery, Ames is speechless at Byron's display of love and devastated by his friend's loss. Realizing his hubris, and the time that is ticking away, Ames reflects on his recent sexual tryst, confessing that "I don't even know who she was, Byron. Some girl. I can't even remember her face. Just some girl I picked up in a bar. Probably never see her again my whole life" (Shepard 2011: 66). Ames' betrayal of his wife seems all the more tragic when contrasted with Byron's devotion to his dead wife. The play concludes as Byron says "won't be long now" and the two huddle together and wait for the eclipse.

As *Ages of the Moon* concerns aging, references to the past—and memories of the past—figure prominently in the work. Byron accuses

Ames of living in the past, remembering when life was "better." Byron asks, "You're not going to suddenly gush nostalgic, are you?" (Shepard 2011: 21). But, Byron's perception of the past—as with the brothers in *The Late Henry Moss*—is subject to distortion. Byron contends that he was indeed with Ames and his wife on their honeymoon in New Mexico when they met Roger Miller, a singer associated with the tune "End of the Road," which reflects upon the thematics and dynamics of the play itself. In fact, it seems that Byron is attempting to place himself in Ames' past experiences. Ames argues with Byron, asserting, "You were never there! Believe me. This is something that happened to me that was entirely independent of your presence. Separate. An experience of my own" (Shepard 2011: 24). Byron is intruding in on Ames' memories, causing Ames to say, "Why do you keep trying to insinuate yourself into my past?" (Shepard 2011: 27). As stated previously, this reinscription by Byron is an attempt to place himself within a moment from the past that offered love and hope to Ames.

As with other males in Shepard's work, the men of *Ages of the Moon* reveal a friendship that ebbs and flows through the years. Even though Byron is the "friend that [Ames] called at three in the morning like a howling dog" (Shepard 2011: 37), Byron has not been emotionally honest with his friend. Byron has been unable to confess to Ames that his beloved wife is dead, and has been dead for some time. Though their relationship is (seemingly) found on emotional honesty, these two men are unable to achieve moments of exchange and revelation concerning their lives.

Male friendship, homosociality, and attempts at communion do not necessarily achieve happiness, but love brings happiness to Byron. For Ames, his own dalliances demonstrate a betrayal of his wife, even though he still longs for her and apparently still loves her. Ames took his wife for granted and squandered her love toward him through his infidelity. Byron's nearly Atlasian undertaking demonstrates a respect and devotion to his wife that is beyond Ames' comprehension. Though the two men assault one another in the course of the play, Ames—in an act of fraternal compassion—hoists Byron onto his back and attempts to carry him to the truck. This action reflects Ames' love for Byron and parallels Byron's act of hoisting Lacey upon his back.

Overall, *Ages of the Moon* reveals that homosocial relationships between heterosexual men should offer a space for conversation and honest reflection. But, this homosociality—especially of men of this "age"—can also revolve around regret. Byron finds meaning and fulfillment in his life only through a faithful, heterosexual relationship. Ames, acting upon his libido, finds only sexual gratification, but not long-term happiness or fulfillment. Ames' inability to attain fulfillment with his long-suffering wife contrasts with Byron's fierce dedication to Lacey. Ironically, Ames—who betrayed his wife—squandered the relationship, while Byron—who lost his wife—remains undefined and without identity in his wife's absence. Though this chapter focuses primarily on *Far North* and *Ages of the Moon*, it is worth noting that 2011's *Heartless* marks a return by Shepard to women as a primary subject.

In *Heartless*, Roscoe is witness to a familial world in which time and space seem to collapse as the past and the present meld. But, it is a wholly homosocial realm composed solely of women. The spectators/audience learns that Sally's family—like so many other families in Shepard's works—is unified by a past trauma that defines their present existence. Whitmore—Mabel's husband—fled the family and the children have memories of the police arriving amid domestic abuse. Whitmore's abandonment of the family—which parallels Roscoe's leaving his own family—reiterates Shepard's obsession with the inability of the father to remain with his family. Indeed, Roscoe is identified as "the one who just recently left his wife and children" (Shepard 2013: 15). As a parallel, Shepard, as revealed in *Shepard and Dark*, resents his father for his violence and his abandonment of the family. Shepard also suffers from the guilt of abandoning his own family when he fell in love with Jessica Lange in the 1980s.

The matriarch Mable is an intriguing creation, tailored for performer Lois Smith.[7] Mable's cognizance and coherence slip back and forth between the present and past, between memory and vision.

Physically, she appears grotesque, with her "hands seized up and clutched to her chest like claws, [and] her feet twisted up" (Shepard 2013: 44), yet she remains the wise—yet oddly eccentric—mother, loyal to her daughters, suspicious of men, and empathetic to the idealism of unconditional love. As with *Ages of the Moon*, *Heartless* examines the concept of selfless love while witnessing its destruction. Indeed, according to these plays—as voices in *Heartless*—women are seemingly searching for selfless love. "That's what we're all looking for, isn't it? . . . Unconditional loyalty . . . someone blind to our faults. Who only sees the angel in us—the benevolent creature" (Shepard 2013: 51). Indeed, we witness Byron in *Ages of the Moon* reflect on this selfless love, but in Shepard's world, men are almost always incapable of such love, for men are easily swayed by lust. Sally still holds onto the concept of love for Roscoe, but Roscoe's lust is drawn toward the ghostly Elizabeth.

Just as *Ages of the Moon* considers the relations between women as perceived by men, *Heartless* interrogates those same relations from a woman's perspective. The subject of men and women is addressed in dialogue between Roscoe and Mable. Mable holds up mothers as practitioners of unconditional love, yet "not fathers so much—fathers are a whole different bag of worms. . . . Fathers make impossible demands. Expectations, then disappointments. One's the product of the other. A snake biting its own tail" (Shepard 2013: 52). For Mable, fathers (and by extension men) are "full of judgement and condemnation" (Shepard 2013: 53) and susceptible to the power of lust. In addition, as with other fathers in Shepard's work, they can be cruel. Whitmore's abuse of his wife is discussed, as is his penchant for wantonly shooting squirrels from the porch. But, for Mable it is lust that drives men and fathers from their families. Indeed, it is what drew Roscoe away from his family, and what led Shepard away from his wife O-lan to Jessica Lange. In *Heartless*, Roscoe is entranced by Elizabeth and succeeds in seducing her (or her seducing him), Mabel recognizes the transformation, commenting, "Oh, now he's turning against us. He was full of gratitude before. Full of humility" (Shepard 2013: 103).

Mabel does concede that not all mothers are examplars of matriarchal greatness, locating examples in folklore and sensational headlines. She explains that there are mothers "who've gone bad" by "devouring their children. Stuffing them in Dumpsters. Drowning them in muddy pools under the full moon. . . . What do you suppose it could've been? Revenge? Infidelity? Betrayal of one kind or another. Maybe just plain old madness" (Shepard 2013: 59).

Connections between women seem to biologically based, be it mother and daughter or between a woman and the ghost of another woman who donated her heart. As with *Ages of the Moon*, it seems as if men and women are caught in perpetual tension and men will never be able to understand women. Yet, in contrast, women seem to easily recognize the primordial urges of the men, but also fall victim to their charms, only to be predictably abandoned by them.

As with *Far North*, women are able to only locate fulfilling relationships within the homosocial realm, while men's fruitless attempts at communion with women end with abuse, abandonment, neglect—and even in a most idyllic form such as with Byron in *Ages of the Moon*, death. The late Shepard finds that the division between men and women is irreparable and that satisfaction and meaning can be located for women only with one another. With men, perhaps satisfaction and meaning is never achievable with women, and attempts to locate such qualities through relationships with women are doomed not only to fail, but also to create a trail of wreckage in its wake. Indeed, Shepard's men—even in their attempts to locate communion with a woman through a relationship—are destined to wreak havoc and destruction on all those connected to the relationship. Essentially, men attempting to enter relationships with women will produce collateral damage—both mental and perhaps physical—on a scale that will be irreparable.

Roscoe's abandonment of his family is given a narrative. Like the Woman's narration from "Evanescence, or Shakespeare in the Alley," it seems to be a sudden moment which is juxtaposed with the quotidian chores of family life. Roscoe explains, "I didn't see it coming. In a moment everything comes unraveled. Years and years—kids—schools—peanut butter sandwiches—then—your whole life turns upside down. Just like that. It's devastating. Suddenly you're on the road—by yourself—driving—looking for a place to take a shower" (Shepard 2013: 75). As with other father figures in Shepard's work, Roscoe flees from his marriage and then later flees from Sally and her family, earning the condemnation of the women of the family. As Lucy comments, "Running away is a cowardly act. There's nothing else to be said about it" (Shepard 2013: 109). Like many of Shepard's other male figures, Roscoe is unable and unwilling to commit to the responsibility demanded by a relationship and a family. When confronted, Roscoe—like the equally guilty Ames in *Ages of the Moon*—claims innocence, asking, "What have I done? WHAT HAVE I DONE!! Why me? What have I done to you people? I'm just a visitor here. I haven't done anything. I'm totally innocent" (Shepard 2013: 108). Of course, this is not true as his sexual escapade with Elizabeth is viewed as an act of betrayal not just against Sally, but also against the entire house of women.

The story "The Door to Women" explores male homosociality, yet the two men at the center of the piece are separated in age by decades. In the piece, the reader encounters a young man (referred to only as "the boy") who feels stifled by his grandfather's scorn of women. The homosocial, intergenerational space is in a home, from which the women have been exiled. In fact, "every last woman had been driven from the house—some by betrayal, most by neglect. There was only the boy and his grandfather left. They liked it that way. It was peaceful" (Shepard 2002: 43). It has been roughly a year or more since the boy's mother and sisters fled the house. The boy's father abandoned the family, an intertextual trait that appears in much of Shepard's work. Prior to the events of the story, the house was flooded during a storm and all of the belongings of the boy's father were covered in mud and sludge. The boy's mother gathered up the slimy signifiers of masculinity, such as "fishing gear, old leather jackets, Indian saddle blankets" (Shepard 2002: 48) and "old photographs of cattle, train magazines, busted guitars, quarter horse trophies" (Shepard 2002: 49) and shipped the materials to the father, still covered in the water, dirt, and mud of the flood. The wife/mother has exorcised the space of the man's masculine belongings, yet she too would eventually be exiled from the house.

In the story, the boy assists his grandfather, even clipping the yellow toenails on his gnarled feet. The grandfather, like many other patriarchs in the Shepard canon, spends the day alone, smoking Pall Malls and reading the daily horse racing periodical. But unlike other Shepardian patriarchs, the grandfather is neither physically nor verbally abusive, but rather expresses his anger and disappointment with his grandson through long periods of silence. The boy assumes that the grandfather holds all women in contempt and possesses the traits of the archetypal misogynist. During one of these primitive pedicure sessions, the grandfather reminds the boy of an earlier evening when the two went out to eat. The waitress at the restaurant apparently knew the boy. The grandfather interrogates the boy about the waitress, but the boy is at once aloof, then evasive.

The grandfather reminds the young man of her "'Black hair. Magnificent eyes!'" (Shepard 2002: 44), yet the boy pretends to not have noticed her. The young man finally concedes that he knows her from the feed store. Instead of berating his grandson or insulting the young woman, the grandfather confesses, "'She seemed to like you very much. . . . It's important to notice things like that. Don't let that type a thing slip through the cracks. Something like that could change your whole entire life. A moment like that'" (Shepard 2002: 45). To the boy, this comment is most unexpected and seems to contradict what he previously believed about his grandfather.

The boy continues to deny that there is an attraction between himself and the waitress, but the boy does reveal that her name is Mina. At the conclusion of the tale, the reader learns that the young man does indeed know Mina and the two are in love. But, why does the boy not confess his love for Mina to the grandfather? Why does he not acknowledge that Mina even attempts to gain his attention at the restaurant? Does the boy view this as a test of loyalty by his grandfather—between a homosocial existence and crossing the gender line to love a young woman? All the boy can say, in response to the grandfather's observation, is that "she kept coming around" to their table is "'I didn't notice'" tinged "with a note finality, hoping to turn the subject" (45).

When the boy speaks of Mina, the grandfather is appalled that a girl of such beauty tends to goats. The boy pointedly responds, "'What's wrong with that?'" (Shepard 2002: 45). The boy "doesn't understand this feeling that surges up in him of wanting to defend the girl" (Shepard 2002: 45). This is the first hint of conflict with his grandfather, yet it indicates how women—within this homosocial domesticity—hold the potentiality to split the bonds between males, a bond ruled by psychic and corporeal codes of masculinity. The grandfather continues, saying "'She's very lovely, that one. Never seen eyes quite like that. Beyond her age, I'd say. . . . Closer to being a woman'" (Shepard 2002: 46).

The grandfather prizes his grandson and "admires the structure of the skull, the perfect arch of the cranium, and inwardly congratulates himself on the boy's very masculine genealogy" (Shepard 2002: 47). The grandfather even states "'It's been quite some time since we've had any women around the place'" (Shepard 2002: 47). Perhaps attempting to gain favor with the boy and give permission, the grandfather even confesses that "'I kinda miss a woman's touch around the place'" (Shepard 2002: 50). The grandfather even suggests hiring Mina to clean the house, a recommendation that the boy flatly rejects. Perhaps the grandfather suggests it because she is Mexican, and as revealed earlier in the piece, the grandfather regularly hires Mexicans to tend to the almond harvesting. The grandfather may also be indicating that a woman would be welcome in the house. The boy knows the past behavior of his grandfather regarding women and fears a similar result if Mina were invited to their home.

As the boy continues to tend to the old man's feet, the grandfather feels the

> nausea of the past losses; past aloneness. Women leaving him. Him leaving women. A parade of beauties. All gone. Thank God he was over that. He would like more than anything to protect his grandson

from that kind of desolation. He is too young to fall in there. (Shepard 2002: 49–50)

The grandfather, instead of enacting a code of masculinity that simply banishes women, is actually attempting to guard his grandson against the pitfalls of love. Indeed, the boy is hesitant to reveal his relationship with Mina for fear that his grandfather will condemn it. Yet, the grandfather only wishes to protect his grandson from the pain involved with love.

The grandfather proclaims that he will ask Mina that night if she would like to work in their home. As the boy walks to work "he thinks of Mina. He knows her name quite well. He says her name to himself and smiles. The sound of it makes him laugh. The sound of her name pushes him into a little trot. . . . He can't believe how just the thought of her transforms his breath" and he recalls how he can "feel Mina's long waist . . . the way her back always breaks out in hot bands of sweat when he touches her breasts" and how "he can taste her neck and feel the deep tremble in her chest as she pulls him tight to her and wraps her leg high up around him whispering Spanish in his ear" (Shepard 2002: 52).

The reader is not given a resolution to the tale, but it is revealed that the grandfather, who seemingly drove the women from the house, is concerned about his grandson's well-being. The boy is hesitant to reveal his love for Mina because it seemingly violates their homosocial realm. In addition, Mina is the "Other" not only because of her gender, but also because of her ethnicity (Latina) and class (working). This homosocial space, seemingly ideal for honest discussions between males, also serves as a location for gauging each other's opinions on women. The boy's assumptions about his grandfather are incorrect. The grandfather does not hate women, rather he has experienced the pain accompanied by love and wishes to protect the boy. The grandfather does not disapprove of the relationship, rather in a reversal of the boy's expectations, the grandfather encourages it.

The grandfather displays an internal, emotional comprehension of what the boy is experiencing and offers a method by which women can be introduced back into their home. Though it appears that the grandfather distrusts and dislikes women on the whole, as the story progresses, the reader realizes that the grandfather is simply attempting to guard the boy from the fallout of love. The grandfather does not embody the unyielding code of masculinity and gynophobia as exhibited by Bertrum, nor does he demonstrate the unbending fundamentalism of some homosocial relationships as exhibited in "Great Dream of Heaven." The grandfather, unlike Ames in *Ages of the Moon*, still believes in the (small) promise of love and has not cynically surrendered to his libido. No, quite the opposite, instead of pursuing women, the grandfather has assumed a solemn life without women. Just as Ames learns to regret his actions, the grandfather too meditates on his regret; however, he is offered an opportunity to transform his regret into hope for his grandson. Byron's life was given meaning and purpose through the relationship with his wife, and the grandfather still recognizes that same promise of fulfillment in the blossoming love he has identified between Mina and the boy. Superficially, the grandfather embodies some of the traditional and archetypal traits associated with a Shepardian father figure, yet through conversation, he is revealed to be a man of great emotional depth who does not loathe women, but is acutely aware of the precarious emotional lives that men—and boys— lead and how those lives can be altered and impacted by love.

As the concept of age and aging has consistently crept into Shepard's later writings, the story "Great Dream of Heaven" demonstrates the delicacy of a homosocial relationship between two elderly men. Having grown up as friends in South Dakota, Sherman and Dean now spend their autumnal years in a cinderblock bungalow in Twentynine Palms. Their wives are dead and their children have dispersed across the country. Everyday, the men compete to see who can rise the earliest. Of all their activities (which are few), "the one great daily pleasure they both looked forward to was their walk down to Denny's by the highway for coffees and patty melts. This was truly like heaven for them" (Shepard 2002: 130). Every day at noon "they would shower and shave, put on clean shirts, bolo ties, and their pressed khaki paints and don their 'Open Road' Stetsons, then hike down the long dusty frontage road to the highway" (Shepard 2002: 130). Part of the reason the two men enjoyed traveling to Denny's was their mutual attraction to a waitress named Faye. For Sherman, in particular, the actions of rising, dressing, and walking down to Denny's have become ritualized and have given his life meaning. All of these actions are performed by Sherman and Dean almost in unison. This ritual is shattered when Sherman wakes one morning and Dean is nowhere to be found. Sherman is forced to journey to Denny's alone and "there was an awful sense of betrayal about it. . . . He'd gone through all the waiting for Dean and looking all around the place" (Shepard 2002: 133). Sherman realizes that Faye is not working either. Sherman rightly concludes that Dean and Faye are together. Sherman returns to the bungalow and finds Dean, who attempts to explain his "betrayal." Sherman packs his army rucksack and without a word heads out the door, ignoring Dean's explanations and apologies.

Sedgwick's notions of homosocial desire are present as a dynamic within "Great Dream of Heaven." Both Sherman and Dean have lost their wives to death and have lived together for eleven years. Dean is first identified as Sherman's "longtime partner" (Shepard 2002: 128). Later, when Sherman searches for Dean, he refers to him as "my partner" (Shepard 2002: 136). Though these identifications can be tied to antiquated, "Old West" concepts of partners on the cattle trail or even popular culture notions of cowboys (Sherman and Dean do indeed wear Stetsons), these terms in contemporary context indicate a certain queer desire present between the men. With the exclusion of women in their lives, Sherman has grown to trust and love Dean. When Dean breaks their ritual, Sherman takes the action as one would in an incident of romantic infidelity. The love Sherman has for Dean is also embodied by their daily actions. The two have a daily competition to see who can rise the earliest each morning, yet neither has ever spoken of this competition. In fact, the reader is told that many of the thoughts of the men are never shared. Under the concept of competition, Sherman rises early most often, and the pains he takes to not disturb his companion demonstrates a love in the most seemingly mundane of actions. Sherman would rise at 4.30 a.m. and "shuffle barefoot across the red linoleum . . . careful not to pick his heels up and cause any snapping sticky sounds. He would wrap a wash rag around the little chain switch . . . to muffle the hum as the light heated up and cast its flickering greenish gleam across the dreaming face off his partner Dean" (Shepard 2002: 128).

When Sherman settles in for the morning and watches Dean dream, he contemplates what images haunt the other man's dreamscape. Sherman thinks, "Not women anymore—surely not that. Dean hoped it wasn't a dream about women. For Sherman's sake" (Shepard 2002: 128). Sherman believes that they are "too old for that. Too painful. Why torture yourself when there were the simple pleasures of desert life to keep you company?" (Shepard 2002: 128) Yet, the reader is aware that if Dean is dreaming of women, that could be tantamount to infidelity and would in turn threaten Sherman and Dean's homosocial existence. As we are told, Sherman is grateful "to have an enduring friendship, a true partnership. At their age and not be condemned to some horrible blithering sentence of aloneness in one of those glassed-in 'homes' they'd pass now and then out by Palm Springs" (Shepard 2002: 132).

Sherman's emotional connection to Dean is conveyed in a passage that centers on a "Great Dream of Heaven" from which the story and the volume takes its title. Sherman remembers his own personal vision of heaven that occurred when he was ten years old. Sherman's dream was a sartorial moment that gave him a sense of place and purpose, and this experience has only been experienced a second time by Sherman, and that is when he is with Dean. The reader is told that the dream involved "being connected to some force as strong as the sun itself. For days, as a boy, he walked around with the memory of that dream in his head, but the light never appeared again until this business with Dean developed" (Shepard 2002: 129). For Sherman, the loving relationship with Dean—even if unconsummated and unspoken—has given these final years of his life meaning and purpose.

Sedgwick's homosocial desire is predicated on a "love triangle" that implicitly reveals amorous longings between the two men involved.

When Sherman learns of Dean's "betrayal" of their homosocial relationship, he does what many other men have done in Shepard works: Sherman simply walks away. This reaction certainly plays like that of a lover scorned. Like the grandfather in "The Door to Women," Sherman harbors a delicate, sensitive interior life that is only visible at certain moments. Of the two, Sherman emerges as the most emotionally fragile. When Dean kills some quail on their back porch and actually serves the bird over eggs for breakfast, Sherman openly weeps and cannot understand Dean's cruelty.

Unlike his elderly counterpart who attempts to protect his grandson, Sherman's hostility toward Dean is a manifestation of the bitter resentment associated with betrayal. When Sherman learns that Dean had been in Denny's the night before—alone, and during Faye's shift— "Sherman felt something hit him between the shoulders like an electric jolt. At first he thought it might be his old bolt of light that he'd taken to be heaven-sent, but this was a sharper, more wounding kind of jolt like jealousy. That's exactly what it was" (Shepard 2002: 137). Is Sherman jealous of Dean, or is Sherman jealous of Faye? The betrayal injures Sherman to such a degree that during his walk back from Denny's, following his realization of Dean and Faye's whereabouts, he "had trouble remembering exactly where he was. . . . He hadn't had this panic of aloneness for a long, long time" (Shepard 2002: 137).

The waitress Faye serves as the schism between Sherman and Dean. As the reader is told, Faye was one of their "new and more exciting concerns" (Shepard 2002: 130). The men are interested not in "cute or sexy waitresses but waitresses with heart" (Shepard 2002: 130). The two are "well aware of Faye's work hours and always arrived intentionally at the height of lunch hour so they could watch Faye in action" (Shepard 2002: 131). Their daily ritual recognized that the "days of the 'gentleman' were long dead but they made their appearance at Denny's each day at noon to remind Faye that her sort of beauty was a great blessing in the midst of all this sad madness" (Shepard 2002: 131). Both Sherman and Dean are attracted to Faye, but only one is given the opportunity to develop the relationship outside of the restaurant. When Sherman cannot locate Dean and Faye is not at the Denny's, he becomes upset and frightens the waitress and the patrons. As Sherman adds up the clues and evidence, he feels that his luck has run dry again and fears that "he would be plunged back into all the lost dark days before his peaceful life out here with Dean. . . . Back when he'd find himself waking up in ditches with broken ribs and his pockets ripped out. It could happen that fast. He knew it could. He'd see it happen" (Shepard 2002: 135). Instead of confronting Dean, Sherman quietly ignores his partner when he returns home, packs his belongings and leaves the abode, with Dean screaming out, "It wasn't my idea, it was hers!!" (Shepard 2002: 139). Like Ames' unnamed wife, Sherman feels jilted and as a result, separates himself from his partner. Unlike the women of *Far North*—but similar to Byron in *Ages of the Moon*—Sherman must have a partner to give his life definition. Once his own personal "Dream of Heaven" is shattered, Sherman retreats and is destined to become like Ames—cynical and alone.

In the Late Style, Shepard extensively explores issues of gender through homosociality. Shepard uses the homosocial space as a region to contest patriarchal assumptions and hegemony, establish viable alternative visions of a non-patriarchal community, confront the failure of masculine expectations, and examine same-sex desire. Though Shepard may have not determined a conclusive method to cease gender conflict, he recognizes the homosocial space as a unique location for exploring gender dynamics.

Notes

1   It is intriguing that Shepard's first excursion into the extensive exploration of female characters occurs in a medium dominated by men, utilizing a mode of production that parallels heteronormative constructs (director as father, actors as children, etc.) and works as a contested location of female representation. It is fitting that film helped to "birth" extensive studies of the male gaze in connection to female representation.

2 A similar image is utilized in Shepard's other directorial effort *Silent Tongue* when a warrior woman is envisioned on horseback.

3 Jilly's method of alcohol consumption is in direct opposition to the accepted "norms" regarding women and drinking which are delightfully lampooned in Paula Vogel's *How I Learned to Drive* (1997).

4 Ames is also a name of the philandering horse race official in Shepard's play *Simpatico*. In addition, *Ages of the Moon* features multiple references to the Kentucky Derby, the celebrated horse racing event that figures prominently in *Simpatico*.

5 In the documentary *Shepard and Dark*, the playwright muses that "there must be an art to aging and dying just like there is to growing up and living."

6 A number of Shepard's plays involve women as ghosts, spirits, or other supernatural entities that exist outside the realm of explainable phenomena.

7 Smith starred alongside James Dean in 1955's *East of Eden*. As Mabel and her family live in the house that once belonged to Dean, this creates an interesting meta-theatrical connection.

Conclusion

From inhabiting the role of dramatist *du jour* of the early 1960s New York alternative theater scene to earning the Pulitzer Prize and gracing the pages of the *New Yorker*, Sam Shepard has continued to transform throughout his career. In this late stage of his corpus, Shepard has become a multi-hyphenate: a writer-actor-director in both theater and film. Far from relying on the heavily trafficked terrain of his family cycle, Shepard's Late Style exists as a unique *mélange* and panoply of subject matter, aesthetics, and media. Indeed, this is a celebrated playwright working and experimenting (not always with the most successful of results) in many forms (theater, film, stories) and resolving issues posed by earlier works, even though his cultural moment is long past. Beginning with *Far North*, Shepard signaled a distinct break with his most popular cycle of plays, typified by works such as *Buried Child* and *A Lie of the Mind*. In this Late Style, Shepard thoughtfully explores his own persona through a continual performance of self.

Shepard in this late period has progressed from his earlier incarnations and has eased into the position that has long been a subject of both vehemence and fascination—that of a father. Shepard conveys this persona not only through his presentations of self, but also through his extensive acting resume. In this, the public is witness to the transformation of a persona that straddles the saddle, with literature on one flank and popular culture on the other. This renegotiation with his own persona has led to a renewed interest in the concept of authenticity and its interplay with artistry. For Shepard in this late period, authenticity is eternally elusive. Hobart Strother faces certain doom because of his desire for authenticity, yet Howard Spence locates authenticity in a most surprising location—a family.

Memory in Shepard's work of this period turns less to the cultural mythology of American West and more to the personal, traumatic memory associated with the modern condition. The characters of *Simpatico*, *The Late Henry Moss*, and *When the World was Green* are haunted by the specters of the past. These traumas are inflicted on a personal level and resonate to the present day. Beyond simply meditating on these traumas and memories, Shepard demonstrates a method through which characters may confront and reconcile these traumas. Through the reenactment and re-performance of elements associated with the traumatic condition, the victim is able to begin life anew in the present.

Previous to this Late Style, Shepard was often accused of being politically unengaged. In his late career, Shepard makes a political turn and casts a scorching retort to the conservative narratives that arose during the terms of President George H. W. Bush and his son George W. Bush. By interrogating the narratives that conservatives utilize to frame events, Shepard reveals himself to be a writer with a keen sense of political satire. Beyond the overtly political, Shepard also explores territories colonized by Hollywood and NAFTA. In *Silent Tongue* and *Eyes for Consuela*, Shepard looks toward American history as well as the late twentieth century to ruminate on the tensions between the cultural and economic forces of the United States and indigenous peoples. This is found most potently in Shepard's analysis of hybridity, identity, and borders.

Finally, in the most dramatic move of this period, Shepard reengages with issues of gender. Often the subject of criticism for his depiction of women, Shepard, in his late career, begins to further consider the relations between genders. Through the work of this period (*Far North*) to his most recent plays (*Ages of the Moon* and *Heartless*), gender can be viewed as the beginning and ending of this cycle. To reconcile the clash between genders, Shepard purports a utopian leaning that revels in the possibilities and promises of homosocial existence. In all, Shepard's Late Style, from its explorations of new aesthetics, media, and subjects to its resolutions to dilemmas posed in earlier works, stands as a vital component not only in understanding Shepard's entire corpus, but also when considering writers who continue to work in the years following their cultural, commercial, and critical apex.

References

Allen, C. (2003), "Indigenous Literatures and Postcolonial Theories", in
D. Madsen (ed.), *Beyond the Borders: American Literature and Post-colonial
Theory*. London: Pluto Press, 15–27.

Allen, J. (1988), "The Man on the High Horse: On the Trail of Sam Shepard",
Esquire 110 (September 1988): 141–51.

Als, H., "Fantasy Suite", *The New Yorker*, July 28, 2008, http://www.newyorker.
com/magazine/2008/07/28/fantasy-suite (accessed August 1, 2012).

Als, H., "Mother Knows Best", *The New Yorker*, September 10, 2012, http://
www.newyorker.com/magazine/2012/09/10/mother-knows-best-4
(accessed September 13, 2012).

The Assassination of Jesse James by the Coward Robert Ford (2007), Directed by
Andrew Dominik [DVD]. Los Angeles: Warner Brothers.

Atkinson, M., "Nolte and Bridges Flog a Dread Horse", *Village Voice*, February
8, 2000, http://www.villagevoice.com/2000-02-01/film/nolte-and-bridges-
flog-a-dread-horse/ (accessed August 1, 2011).

Atkinson, M., "Barroom Sprawl", *Village Voice*, March 15–21, 2006, http://
www.villagevoice.com/2006 03 07/film/barroom-sprawl/ (accessed
January 1, 2011).

Auslander, P. (2008), *Liveness: Performance in a Mediatized Culture*. London:
Routledge.

Barker, H. and Yuval, T. (2007), *Faking It: The Quest for Authenticity in
Popular Music*. New York: Norton.

Bennett, S. (1993), "When a Woman Looks: The 'Other' Audience of Shepard's
Plays", in Leonard Wilcox (ed.), *Rereading Shepard*. New York: St. Martin's
Press, 168–79.

Bigsby, C., "Ballad of a Sad Society of Two", *The Times Literary Supplement*,
April 28, 1995, http://www.the-tls.co.uk/tls/reviews/arts_and_
commentary/article727049.ece (accessed August 1, 2011).

Bigsby, C. (2002), "Born Injured: The Theatre of Sam Shepard", in Matthew
Roudane (ed.), *The Cambridge Companion to Sam Shepard*. Cambridge:
Cambridge University Press, 7–33.

Black Hawk Down (2001), Directed by Ridley Scott [DVD]. Los Angeles: Columbia.

Blackthorn (2011), Directed by Mateo Gil [DVD]. Los Angeles: Magnolia.

Bottoms, S. (1998), *The Theatre of Sam Shepard: States of Crisis*. Cambridge: Cambridge University Press.

Brantley, B., "Sam Shepard, Storyteller", *The New York Times*, November 13, 1994, http://www.nytimes.com/1994/11/13/theater/sam-shepard-storyteller.html (accessed August 1, 2010).

Brantley, B., "Sam Shepard of Today, And of Many Days Ago", *The New York Times*, November 8, 1996, http://www.nytimes.com/1996/11/08/theater/sam-shepard-of-today-and-of-many-days-ago.html (accessed January 1, 2011).

Brantley, B., "When Love is Blinding as Well as Blind", *The New York Times*, February 11, 1998, http://www.nytimes.com/1998/02/11/theater/theater-review-when-love-is-blinding-as-well-as-blind.html (accessed July 15, 2011).

Brantley, B., "No-Good Dad Whose Tale Is Told Repeatedly", *The New York Times*, September 25, 2001, http://www.nytimes.com/2001/09/25/arts/25MOSS.html (accessed January 1, 2011).

Brantley, B., "That's No Girl Scout Selling Those Cookies", *The New York Times*, November 7, 2004, http://www.nytimes.com/2004/11/17/theater/reviews/17hell.html (accessed July 15, 2011).

Brantley, B., "My 3 Sons: Cloning's Unexpected Results", *The New York Times*, December 8, 2004, http://www.nytimes.com/2004/12/08/theater/reviews/08numb.html (accessed December 1, 2011).

Brantley, B., "It's Old Timers' Day at Shepard's Arena", *The New York Times*, January 28, 2010, http://www.nytimes.com/2010/01/28/theater/reviews/28ages.html (accessed June 15, 2012).

Brantley, B., "All the Discomforts of Home", *The New York Times*, August 27, 2012, http://www.nytimes.com/2012/08/28/theater/reviews/sam-shepards-heartless-with-lois-smith.html?_r=0 (accessed August 28, 2012).

Brantley, B., "'*A Particle of Dread*,' Sam Shepard's Take on Oedipus", *The New York Times*, November 23, 2014, http://www.nytimes.com/2014/11/24/theater/a-particle-of-dread-sam-shepards-take-on-oedipus.html (accessed December 1, 2014).

Brothers (2009), Directed by Jim Sheridan [DVD]. Los Angeles: Lionsgate.

Brustein, R., "Plays for the Parch", *The New Republic*, January 2, 1995, http://connection.ebscohost.com/c/entertainment-reviews/9501037777/plays-parch (accessed August 1, 2010).

Brustein, R., "The New Relevance", *The New Republic*, December 11, 2001, http://connection.ebscohost.com/c/entertainment-reviews/5478995/new-relevance (accessed August 1, 2010).

Brustein, R., "Theatre After 9/11 . . . *The God of Hell*", *The New Republic*, November 3, 2005, http://www.newrepublic.com/article/theater-after-911 (accessed August 1, 2010).

Brustein, R. (2006), *Millennial Stages: Essays and Reviews, 2001-2005*. New Haven: Yale University Press.

Brustein, R. (2008), "Theatre After 9/11", in A. Keniston and J. F. Quinn (eds), *Literature After 9/11*, New York: Routledge, 242–45.

Butler, J. (1990), *Gender Trouble: Feminism and the Subversion of Identity*. London: Routledge.

Callens, J. (1998), "Introduction", *Contemporary Theatre Review* 8(3): 1–17.

Callens, J. (2000a), "Diverting the Integrated Spectacle of War: Sam Shepard's *States of Shock*", *Text and Performance Quarterly* 20(3): 290–306.

Callens, J. (2000b), "Introduction", *Contemporary Theatre Review* 8(3): 1–17.

Canby, V., "Sam Shepard Goes to the Races and Wins", *The New York Times*, November 20, 1994, http://www.nytimes.com/1994/11/20/theater/sunday-view-sam-shepard-goes-to-the-races-and-wins.html (accessed August 1, 2010).

Canby, V., "A 'Three Sisters' With a Poignant Russian Forecast", *The New York Times*, February 15, 1998. http://www.nytimes.com/1998/02/15/theater/sunday-view-a-three-sisters-with-a-poignant-russian-forecast.html (accessed January 1, 2011).

Caruth, C. (1991), "Unclaimed Experience: Trauma and the Possibility of History", *Yale French Studies* 79: 181–92.

Case, S. E. (1989), "Towards a Butch-Femme Aesthetics", in L. Hart (ed.), *Making a Spectacle: Feminist Essays on Contemporary Women's Theatre*. Ann Arbor: University of Michigan Press, 290–9.

Cold in July (2014), Directed by Jim Mickle [DVD]. New York: IFC Films.

Cott, J., "The Rolling Stone Interview: Sam Shepard", *Rolling Stone*, December 18, 1986: 166.

Crum, Jane Ann (1993), "'I Smash the Tools of My Captivity': The Feminine in Sam Shepard's A Lie of the Mind," in Leonard Wilcox (ed.), *Rereading Shepard*. New York: St. Martin's Press, 196–214.

Csicsery-Ronay, I. (2003), "Marxist Theory and Science Fiction", in E. James and F. Mendlesohn (eds), *The Cambridge Companion to Science Fiction*. Cambridge: Cambridge University Press, 113–24.

Culler, J. (2011), *Literary Theory: A Very Short Introduction*. Oxford: Oxford University Press.

"Cycle", *Oxford English Dictionary On-Line*, http://www.oed.com.er.lib.k-state. edu/view/Entry/46505?rskey=Cdi7FD&result=1#eid (accessed February 1, 2009).

Demastes, W. (1987), "Understanding Shepard's Realism", *Comparative Drama* 21(3): 229–48.

Demastes, W. (1988), *Beyond Naturalism: A New Realism in American Theatre*, Contributions in Drama and Theatre Studies, Number 27. New York: Greenwood Press.

Demastes, W. (1990), "The Future of the Avant-Garde Theatre and Criticism: The Case of Sam Shepard", *The Journal of Dramatic Theory and Criticism* 4(2): 5–18.

Demastes, W. (1996), *Theatre of Chaos: Beyond Absurdism, Into Orderly Disorder*. Cambridge: Cambridge University Press.

DeRose, D. (1992), *Sam Shepard*. New York: Twayne Publishers.

DeRose. D. (1993), "A Kind of Cavorting: Superpresence and Shepard's Family Dramas", in L. Wilcox (ed.), *Rereading Shepard: Contemporary Critical Essays on the Plays of Sam Shepard*. New York: St. Martin's, 131–49.

DeRose, D. (1998), "Indian Country: Sam Shepard and the Cultural Other", *Contemporary Theatre Review: An International Journal* 8(4): 55–73.

Dieckmann, K., "All My Women", *Village Voice*, November 15, 1988: 64.

Dolan, J. (1985), "Seeing and Being Seen: The Avant-Garde and Other Egotists", *The Hudson Review* 39(1): 113–17.

Dunne, M. (1992), *Metapop: Self-Referentiality in Contemporary American Popular Culture*. Jackson: University Press of Mississippi.

Dunne, M. (2001), *Intertextual Encounters in American Fiction, Film and Popular Culture*. Bowling Green: Bowling Green State University Press.

Dyer, R. (2007a), "Heavenly Bodies", in S. Redmond and S. Holmes (eds), *Stardom and Celebrity: A Reader*. Los Angeles: Sage Publications, 86–89.

Dyer, R. (2007b), "Stars", in S. Redmond and S. Holmes (eds), *Stardom and Celebrity: A Reader*. Los Angeles: Sage Publications, 78–84.

Falcon, R. (2006), "*Don't Come Knocking*", *Sight and Sound* 16(6): 46.

Falk, F. (1981a), "Men Without Women: The Shepard Landscape", in Bonnie Marranca (ed.), *American Dreams: The Imagination of Sam Shepard*. New York: PAJ Publications, 90–103.

Falk, F. (1981b), "The Role of Performance in Sam Shepard's Plays", *Theatre Journal* 33(2): 182–98.

Favorini, A. (2008), *Memory in Play: From Aeshylus to Sam Shepard*, Palgrave Studies in Theatre and Performance History. New York: Palgrave Macmillan.

Earnest, S. (1999), "*States of Shock*", *Theatre Journal* 51(4): 458–9.

Feingold, M., "Loner Stars", *Village Voice*, November 22, 1994: 77.

Feingold, M., "A Banquet of Sam", *Village Voice*, September 17, 1996: 37.

Feingold, M., "Pure Joe", *Village Voice*, November 18, 1996: 79.

Feingold, M., "Spanishing Acts", *Village Voice*, February 24, 1998: 147.

Feingold, M., "Sightlines: *The God of Hell*", *Village Voice*, November 24–30, 2004, http://www.villagevoice.com/2004-11-16/theater/theater/full/ (accessed August 15, 2010).

Feingold, M., "Deathville, USA", *Village Voice*, July 23–29, 2008: 34.

Feingold, M., "Heartless: The Shepard's Tale: The Playwright Returns to Form at the Signature", *Village Voice*, August 29, 2012, http://www.villagevoice. com/2012-08-29/theater/sam-shepard-heartless-review/ (accessed December 1, 2012).

Felman, S. (1991), "Education and Crisis, or the Vicissitudes of Teaching", *American Imago* 48: 13–73.

Felton-Dansky, M., "*Kicking a Dead Horse*", *Theatre Journal*, 107–8, http:// muse.jhu.edu/journals/tj/summary/v061/61.1.felton-dansky.html (accessed June 1, 2010).

Fish, S. (1982), *Is There a Text in This Class? The Authority of Interpretive Communities*. Cambridge: Harvard University Press.

Gelb, H., "Long Playwright's Journey", *The Nation*, December 25, 2000, http:// www.thenation.com/article/long-playwrights-journey# (accessed August 1, 2011).

Gelber, J. (1976), "The Playwright as Shaman", in S. Shepard (ed.), *Angel City & Other Plays*. New York: Applause Books, 1–4.

Geraghty, C. (2007), "Re-examining Stardom: Questions of Texts, Bodies and Performance", in S. Redmond and S. Holmes (eds), *Stardom and Celebrity: A Reader*. Los Angeles: Sage Publications, 98–110.

Glore, J. (1981), "The Canonization of Mojo Rootforce: Sam Shepard Live at the Pantheon", *Theatre* 12(3): 53–65.

Golub, S. (1994), *The Recurrence of Fate: Theatre and Memory in Twentieth-Century Russia*. Iowa City: The University of Iowa Press.

Gritten, D., "Sam Shepard on *Blackthorn*: the Man who Puts the Butch into Cassidy", *The Telegraph,* April 13, 2012, http://www.telegraph.co.uk/culture/film/starsandstories/9189139/Sam-Shepard-on-Blackthorn-the-man-who-puts-the-butch-into-Cassidy.html (accessed May 15, 2012).

Hall, A. (1993a), *"A Kind of Alaska": Women in the Plays of O'Neill, Pinter, and Shepard*. Carbondale: Southern Illinois University Press.

Hall, A. (1993b), "Speaking Without Words: The Myth of Masculine Autonomy in Sam Shepard's *Fool for Love*," in L. Wilcox (ed.), *Rereading Shepard*. New York: St. Martin's Press, 150–66.

Hall, A. (2002), "Sam Shepard's Nondramatic Works", in M. Roudane (ed.), *The Cambridge Companion to Sam Shepard*. Cambridge: Cambridge University Press, 247–56.

Hamill, P., "The New American Hero", *New York*, December 5, 1983: 75–102.

Hamlet (2000), Directed by Michael Almereyda [DVD]. Los Angeles: Miramax.

Hart, L. (1987), *Sam Shepard's Metaphorical Stages*, Contributions in Drama and Theatre Studies Series 22. New York: Greenwood Press.

Hart, L. (1988), "Sam Shepard's Pornographic Visions", *Studies in the Literary Imagination* 21(2): 69–82.

Hart, L. (1989), "Sam Shepard's Spectacle of Impossible Heterosexuality", in J. Schlueter (ed.), *Feminist Rereadings of Modern American Drama*. Rutherford: Fairleigh Dickinson University Press, 1989, 213–26.

Hogg, C., "Sam Shepard: The Good Guy and Bad Guy Stuff Just Doesn't Interest Me", *The Guardian*, November 30, 2013, http://www.theguardian.com/stage/2013/dec/01/sam-shepard-interview-oedipus-derry (accessed January 15, 2014).

Holden, S., "Another True West Tale of Phantom Family Ties", *The New York Times*, March 17, 2006, http://www.nytimes.com/2006/03/17/movies/17knoc.html (accessed November 1, 2012).

"Inter", *Oxford English Dictionary On-Line*, http://www.oed.com.er.lib.k-state. edu/view/Entry/97516?rskey=7q3xb6&result=5#eid (accessed February 1, 2009).

James, C., "Sam Shepard's Spiritual, Imagistic Vision of the Old West", *The New York Times*, February 25, 1994, http://go.galegroup.com/ps/i.do?id=G ALE%7CA174359846&v=2.1&u=ksu&it=r&p=AONE&sw=w&asid=82a8 034ba17592c063b0acd5ffcbed98 (accessed December 1, 2012).

James, C., "*Great Dream of Heaven*: Cast Adrift", *The New York Times*, November 3, 2002, http://www.nytimes.com/2002/11/03/books/ review/03JAMEST.html (accessed August 1, 2012).

Jenkins, H., "Transmedia", Henry Jenkins Website, http://henryjenkins.org/ 2007/03/transmedia_storytelling_101.html (accessed September 14, 2010).

Kachka, B., "How the West Was Lost: Sam Shepard Takes on Cowboy Poseurs – and His Own Iconhood", *New York*, June 22, 2008, http://nymag.com/ arts/theater/profiles/47966/ (accessed August 1, 2012).

Kane, L. (2002), "Reflections of the Past in True West and A Lie of the Mind", in M. Roudane (ed.), *The Cambridge Companion to Sam Shepard*. Cambridge: Cambridge University Press, 139–53.

Kavanagh, P., "One More For the Old Rogue", *The Times Literary Supplement*, February 3, 2006, http://www.thetls.co.uk/tls/ (accessed November 2011).

King, K. (2002), "Sam Shepard and the Cinema", in M. Roudane (ed.), *The Cambridge Companion to Sam Shepard*. Cambridge: Cambridge University Press, 210–26.

Kirn, W., "The Highwaymen", *The New York Times Book Review*, January 17, 2010: 1, 7.

Kolin, P. (2002), *The Undiscovered Country: The Later Plays of Tennessee Williams*. New York: Peter Lang.

Kroll, J., "Shepard the Thoroughbred", *Newsweek*, November 28, 1994, http://www.newsweek.com/shepard-thoroughbred-186462 (accessed July 1, 2010).

Kroll, J., Guthrie, C. and Huck, J., "Who's That Tall Dark Stranger?", *Newsweek*, November 11, 1985: 68–74.

Kuharski, A. J. (2002), "*The Late Henry Moss*", *Theatre Journal* 54(3): 500–2.

Lahr, J., "The Theatre: *Simpatico*", *The New Yorker*, December 5, 1994, http:// archives.newyorker.com/?iid=18554&startpage=page0000008#folio=128 (accessed August 15, 2010).

Lahr, J., "Giving Up the Ghost", *The New Yorker*, December 4, 2000, http://www.newyorker.com/magazine/2000/12/04/giving-up-the-ghost (accessed August 1, 2011).

Lahr, J., "Shadowboxing: Rage Takes the Stage", *The New Yorker*, November 29, 2004, http://archives.newyorker.com/?iid=15269&startpage=page0000175 #folio=160b (accessed August 15, 2010).

Lahr, J., "The Pathfinder: Sam Shepard and the Struggles of American Manhood", *The New Yorker*, February 8, 2010, http://www.newyorker.com/magazine/2010/02/08/the-pathfinder (accessed December 1, 2013).

Londre, F. (1987), "Sam Shepard Works Out: The Masculinization of America", *Studies in American Drama, 1945-Present* 2: 19–27.

Madsen, D. (ed.) (2003), *Beyond the Borders: American Literature and Post-colonial Theory*. London: Pluto Press.

Malkin, J. (1999), *Memory-Theater and Postmodern Drama*, THEATER: Theory/Text/Performance Series. Ann Arbor: The University of Michigan.

Marowitz, C., "Sophisticate Abroad," *Village Voice*, September 7, 1972, https://news.google.com/newspapers?nid=1299&dat=19720907&id=FeNLAAAA IBAJ&sjid=NIwDAAAAIBAJ&pg=6281,2110281&hl=en (accessed March 1, 2015).

Marranca, B. (1981), "Alphabetical Shepard", in B. Marranca, *American Dreams: The Imagination of Sam Shepard*. New York: PAJ Books, 13–34.

Marranca, B. (1981), *American Dreams: The Imagination of Sam Shepard*, New York: Performing Arts Journal Publications.

Maslin, J., "*Far North*: Sam Shepard Ventures Into Directing", *The New York Times*, November 9, 1988, http://www.nytimes.com/1988/11/09/movies/review-film-far-north-sam-shepard-ventures-into-directing.html (accessed November 1, 2012).

McDonough, C. (1997), "Sam Shepard: The Eternal Patriarchal Return", in C. McDonough, *Staging Masculinity: Male Identity in Contemporary American Drama*. London: McFarland & Company, 35–69.

McDonough, C. (1997), *Staging Masculinity: Male Identity in Contemporary American Drama*, Jefferson, NC: McFarland & Company.

McKinley, J., "Pointed New Play to Arrive Just Before Election", *The New York Times*, October 4, 2004, http://www.nytimes.com/2004/10/04/theater/04shep.html (accessed December 1, 2011).

McNulty, C., "The Naked and the Dad", *Village Voice*, October 2, 2001: 67.

McPherson, C. (2012), "Introduction", in S. Shepard (ed.), *Fifteen One Act Plays*. New York: Vintage, xii–xv.

Moore, A. (2002), "Authenticity as Authentication", *Popular Music* 21/22: 209–22.

Mud (2012), Directed by Jeff Nichols [DVD]. Santa Monica: Lionsgate.

Noh, D., "*This So-Called Disaster*", *Film Journal International*, May 2004: 41.

Out of the Furnace (2013), Directed by Scott Cooper [DVD]. Beverly Hills: Relativity.

Painter, K. (2006), "On Creativity and Lateness", in K. Painter and T. Crew (eds), *Late Thoughts: Reflections on Artists and Composers at Work*. Los Angeles: Getty Research Institute, 1–11.

The Pelican Brief (1993), Directed by Alan J. Pakula [Film]. Los Angeles: Warner Brothers.

Poirier, R. (2003), "The Performing Self", in P. Auslander (ed.), *Performance: Critical Concepts in Literary and Cultural Studies*, Vol. 4. New York: Routledge, 3–21.

"Post-Traumatic Stress Disorder", DSM-IV, Trauma Theory/Trauma Narratives Website, European Society for Traumatic Stress Studies, https://www.estss. org/learn-about-trauma/dsm-iv-definition/ (accessed March 1, 2015).

Powers, A., "Reel to Reel: *Silent Tongue*", *Village Voice*, March 1, 1994: 57.

Putzel, S. (1987), "Expectation, Confutation, Revelation: Audience Complicity in the Plays of Sam Shepard", *Modern Drama* 30(2): 147–60.

Ramadanovic, P., "Introduction: Trauma and Crisis", Trauma Theory/ Trauma Narratives Website, http://pmc.iath.virginia.edu/text-only/ issue.101/11.2introduction.txt (accessed November 1, 2012).

Rea, S. (2008), "Forward", in S. Shepard (ed.), *Kicking a Dead Horse*. New York: Vintage Books.

Redmond, S. and Holmes, S. (eds) (2007), *Stardom and Celebrity: A Reader*. London: Sage Publications.

Regev, M. (1994), "Producing Artistic Value: The Case of Rock Music", *The Sociological Quarterly* 35(1): 85–102.

Rich, F., "Sam Shepard Returns, On War and Machismo", *The New York Times*, May 17, 1991, http://www.nytimes.com/1991/05/17/theater/review-theater-sam-shepard-returns-on-war-and-machismo.html (accessed July 15, 2011).

Richards, D., "American Nightmare in a Family Restaurant", *The New York Times*, May 26, 1991, http://www.nytimes.com/1991/05/26/theater/sunday-view-american-nightmare-in-a-family-restaurant.html (accessed July 15, 2011).

Riemer, J. (1986), "Integrating the Psyche of the American Male: Conflicting Ideals of Manhood in Sam Shepard's *True West*", *University of Dayton Review* 18(2): 41–7.

Roach, J. (1992), "Mardi Gras and Others: Genealogies of American Performance", *Theatre Journal* 44(4): 461–83.

Roach, J. (1996), *Cities of the Dead: Circum-Atlantic Performance*. New York: Columbia University Press.

Roach, J. (2007), *It*. Ann Arbor: The University of Michigan Press.

Rosen, C. (1993), "'Emotional Territory': An Interview with Sam Shepard", *Modern Drama* 36(1): 1–11.

Rosen, C., "Sharp Corners", *Village Voice*, May 7, 1996: 76.

Rosen, C. (1998), "Sam Shepard, Feminist Playwright: The Destination of *A Lie of the Mind*", *Contemporary Theatre Review* 8(4): 29–40.

Rosen, C. (2004), *Sam Shepard: A "Poetic Rodeo"*, Palgrave Modern Dramatists. London: Palgrave Macmillan.

Ross, L., "The Talk of the Town: The Boards: Resonating", *The New Yorker*, November 22, 2004, http://www.newyorker.com/magazine/2004/11/22/resonating (accessed August 15, 2010).

Roudane, M. (ed.) (2002a), *The Cambridge Companion to Sam Shepard*. Cambridge: Cambridge University Press.

Roudane, M. (2002b), "Sam Shepard's *The Late Henry Moss*", in M. Roudane, *The Cambridge Companion to Sam Shepard*. Cambridge: Cambridge University Press, 279–92.

Roudane, M. (2002c), "Shepard on Shepard: An Interview", in M. Roudane, *The Cambridge Companion to Sam Shepard*. Cambridge: Cambridge University Press, 64–80.

Said, E. (2007), *On Late Style: Music and Literature Against the Grain*. New York: Vintage Books.

Sam Shepard: Stalking Himself (1998), Directed by Oren Jacoby [VHS]. New York: Great Performances/PBS.

"Santa Fe Institute", Santa Fe Institute Website, http://santafe.edu/ (accessed October 15, 2012).

Savran, D. (1984), "Sam Shepard's Conceptual Prison: *Action* and *The Unseen Hand*", *Theatre Journal* 36(1): 57–74.

Savran, D. (1992), *Communists, Cowboys, and Queers: The Politics of Masculinity in the Work of Arthur Miller and Tennessee Williams*. Minneapolis: University of Minnesota Press.

Schroeder, P. (1989), *The Presence of the Past in Modern American Drama*. Rutherford: Farleigh Dickinson University Press.

Sedgwick, E. (1985), *Between Men: English Literature and Male Homosocial Desire*. New York: Columbia University Press.

Sellar, T., "Approach Sam Shepard's *Particle of Dread* with a Particle of Dread", *Village Voice*, November 26, 2014, http://www.villagevoice.com/2014-11-26/theater/a-particle-of-dread-review-sam-shepard/ (accessed December 1, 2014).

Shepard and Dark (2012), Directed by Trina Wurmfeld [DVD]. Chicago: Music Box Films.

Shepard, S. (nd), *Don't Come Knocking*, Browne Popular Culture Library Manuscript, Bowling Green State University, Bowling Green.

Shepard, S. (1972), *The Unseen Hand and Other Plays*. New York: Bobbs-Merrill.

Shepard, S. (1981a), *Chicago and Other Plays*. New York: Urizen.

Shepard, S. (1981b), "Language, Visualization, and the Inner Library", in B. Marranca (ed.), *American Dreams: The Imagination of Sam Shepard*. New York: PAJ Publications, 212–13.

Shepard, S. (1986), *Sam Shepard: Seven Plays*. New York: Bantam.

Shepard, S. (1987), "True Dylan", *Esquire*, July 1987: 57–68.

Shepard, S. (1993a), "Far North", *States of Shock, Far North, Silent Tongue*. New York: Vintage Books.

Shepard, S. (1993b), "Silent Tongue", *States of Shock, Far North, Silent Tongue*. New York: Vintage Books.

Shepard, S. (1993c), "States of Shock: A Vaudeville Nightmare", *States of Shock, Far North, Silent Tongue*. New York: Vintage Books.

Shepard, S. (1995), *Simpatico*. New York: Vintage Books.

Shepard, S. (1996), *Cruising Paradise*. New York: Vintage Books.

Shepard, S. (2002a), "Eyes for Consuela", *The Late Henry Moss, Eyes for Consuela, When the World was Green: Three Plays*. New York: Vintage Books.

Shepard, S. (2002b), *Great Dream of Heaven*. New York: Vintage Books.

Shepard, S. (2002c), "The Late Henry Moss", *The Late Henry Moss, Eyes for Consuela, When the World was Green: Three Plays*. New York: Vintage Books.

Shepard, S. (2002d), "When the World was Green", *The Late Henry Moss, Eyes for Consuela, When the World was Green: Three Plays*. New York: Vintage Books.

Shepard, S. (2005), *The God of Hell*. New York: Vintage Books.

Shepard, S. (2008), *Kicking a Dead Horse*. New York: Vintage Books.

Shepard, S. (2011a), *Ages of the Moon*, Shepherdstown. West Virginia: Contemporary American Theater Festival, Shepherd University Manuscript.

Shepard, S. (2011b), *Day Out of Days*. New York: Vintage.

Shepard, S. (2012), "Evansescence, or Shakespeare in the Alley", *Fifteen One-Act Plays*. New York: Vintage Books.

Shepard, S. (2013a), *Heartless*. New York: Vintage Books.

Shepard, S. (2013b), *A Particle of Dread (Oedipus Variations)*. New York: ICM Partners.

Shewey, D., "Fools for Sam", *Village Voice*, September 14, 1993: 103.

Shewey, D., "CIVIL-ization: Shepard, Chaikin, and Uhry at the Olympics", *Village Voice*, August 13, 1996: 71.

Shewey, D. (1997), *Sam Shepard*. New York: Da Capo.

Shewey, D., "Sam Shepard's Identity Dance", *American Theatre*, July/August 1997: 12–17, 61.

Shewey, D. (1998), "Hidden in Plain Sight: 25 Notes on Shepard's Stage Silence and Screen Presence, 1984-1993", *Contemporary Theatre Review: An International Journal* 8(4): 75–89.

Shewey, D., "Patriot Acts", *Village Voice*, November 17–23, 2004: 36.

Shewey, D. (2004), "Rock-and-Roll Jesus with a Cowboy Mouth (Revisited)", *American Theatre*, April 2004, http://www.donshewey.com/theater_articles/sam_shepard_2004.html (accessed August 15, 2010).

Smith, S. (1997), *American Drama: The Bastard Art*. Cambridge: Cambridge University Press.

Smith, S. (1998), "Trying to Like Sam Shepard: Or, the Emperor's New Dungarees", *Contemporary Theatre Review: An International Journal* 8(3): 31–40.

Smith, P. (2010), *Just Kids*. New York: Ecco.

This So-Called Disaster: Sam Shepard Directs "The Late Henry Moss" (2004), Directed by Michael Almereyda [DVD]. Los Angeles: IFC Films/MGM.

Soloski, A. (2008), "True East: American Icon Sam Shepard Returns to New York for his First Public Theater Play in 28 Years", *Village Voice*, June 24, 2008, http://www.villagevoice.com/2008-06-24/news/true-east/ (accessed August 1, 2010).

Steven, A., "Confronting the Sins of the Father in a Posthumous Reunion", *The New York Times* January 26, 2005, http://query.nytimes.com/gst/fullpage.html?res=9C05E4DC163BF935A15752C0A9639C8B63 (accessed January 1, 2012).

Stokes, J., "Apocalypse Cow", *The Times Literary Supplement*, November 4, 2005. http://www.the-tls.co.uk/tls/reviews/arts_and_commentary/article755605.ece (accessed June 15, 2010).

Suvin, D. (1978), *Metamorphoses of Science Fiction: On the Poetics and History of a Literary Genre*. New Haven: Yale University Press.

"Trans", *Oxford English Dictionary On-Line*, http://www.oed.com.er.lib.k-state.edu/view/Entry/204575?rskey=TKO1V7&result=3#eid (accessed February 1, 2009).

Vanden Heuvel, M. (1991), *Performing Drama/Dramatizing Performance: Alternative Theater and the Dramatic Text*. Ann Arbor: The University of Michigan Press.

Wade, L. (1997), *Sam Shepard and the American Theatre*, Contributions in Drama and Theatre Studies, Number 76: Lives of the Theatre. Westport, Connecticut: Greenwood Press.

Wade, L. (2002), "*States of Shock, Simpatico,* and *Eyes for Consuela*: Sam Shepard's Plays of the 1990s", in M. Roudane (ed.), *The Cambridge Companion to Sam Shepard*. Cambridge: Cambridge University Press, 257–78.

Wade, L., "Question Regarding Roach and Shepard", e-mail to the author, February 20, 2009.

Watkins, G., "Sam Shepard Gives a Rare Interview, Thinks *Safe House* Could've Been Better", *GQ*, June 2012, http://www.gq.com/entertainment/tv/blogs/the-stream/2012/06/sam-shepard-interview-safe-house.html (accessed August 1, 2012).

Weiss, K., "Cultural Memory and War Trauma in Sam Shepard's *A Lie of the Mind, States of Shock,* and *The Late Henry Moss*", *Xchanges* 4(2) (2005), http://www.xchanges.org/xchanges_archive/xchanges/4.2/weiss.html (accessed February 15, 2009).

Wilcox, L. (ed.) (1993), *Rereading Shepard: Contemporary Critical Essays on the Plays of Sam Shepard.* New York: St. Martin's Press.

Index